P9-CFY-153

Wedding Chimes, Assorted Crimes

Wedding Chimes, Assorted Crimes

Christine Arness

Five Star
Unity, Maine

Five Star Romance.
Published in conjunction with Lori J. Ness.

December 1999

Standard Print Hardcover Edition.

Five Star Standard Print Romance Series.

First Edition

The text of this edition is unabridged.

Set in 11 pt. Plantin by Al Chase.

Printed in the United States on permanent paper.

Library of Congress Cataloging-in-Publication Data
Arness, Christine, 1957–
    Wedding chimes, assorted crimes / Christine Arness.
        p.   cm. — (Five Star standard print first edition romance series)
    ISBN 0-7862-2316-2 (hc : alk. paper)
    I. Title.   II. Series.
PS3551.R4865 W43 1999
813'.54—dc21   99-050008

Dedication

This book is dedicated to all the members of my supportive family, especially my sisters, Linda & Karla, for making sure I'm not a starving writer.

I also want to thank my friends for giving me joy in life, my writing cohorts, Denise, Kay & Mary, for their assistance and all of the wonderful folks at Landmark for just being wonderful.

A grateful thanks to Steve Carlson for his introduction to the world of wedding photography.

Chapter 1

"A Yippee Ki Yi Yai to you, too, sir," Keely murmured, dodging a man in a bola tie who was en route to the bar. The brim of a hat deep enough to hold ten gallons of Panhandle Punch shaded Alderman Gilbert's well-known craggy features.

He lurched to a stop, tipped back his hat. "Reba, honey! You gonna sing us a song? Saw you on TV in one of your videos the other night and you were wonnerful."

Reba? Gilbert had mistaken her for the famous country western singer. Looking into his sodden eyes, she decided not to take it as a compliment. He was in no state to recognize his own mother.

"I'll sing for you later, darling." Keely gently disengaged his hand which had somehow managed to hone in on her waist.

" 'Kay. I'll jush grab another lil' drink." Judging by the unsteadiness of the councilman's gait as he wandered off, he'd already guzzled enough potent punch to make a steer stagger.

A pix of him in this condition would make a great campaign poster for the opposition. Keely grinned, mentally captioning the picture "Your Local Government on the Go," a grab shot worthy of any flash-popping member of the paparazzi.

Although going against the migratory flow to the bar, she managed to reach the hallway unscathed just as the band struck up "Got My Heart Set on You." She wondered what Flo Netherton, Lake Hope's social arbitrator through her gossip-style newspaper column, would write about today's affair. The straw bales stacked in the corners of the dance floor merited a caustic sentence or two, even if the bride was the mayor's daughter.

Pausing to flex toes pinched by her borrowed boots, Keely addressed the marble Cupid squatting in a nearby niche. "This is my first—and, hopefully, last—western gig, so you can wipe that smirk off your face!"

She had a hunch, however, this was only the first of the marital round-ups; a decent fitting pair of boots might be a wise investment. Theme weddings were the current rage in Lake Hope and, as high society's shutterbug of choice, Keely was expected to preserve the precious moments of each motif, no matter how kitsch.

So far this year she'd photographed a Winter Wonderland with the attendants dressed as snowflakes, a Valentine's Day ceremony predictably awash in satin hearts and crimson roses, and Deb Ralston's flower-strewn extravaganza, "Springtime Ecstasy." According to her calendar, she had "Georgia on my Mind," "Swiss Bliss," and "Love under the Sea" to look forward to.

Eyeing the bandanna knotted around Cupid's chubby throat, Keely decided Tricia had outclassed everyone in promoting her beloved western theme. A turquoise vase overflowing with Tropicanna roses, a spectacular version of the centerpieces, stood beside the marble god of love.

Adjusting the strap of the power pack, Keely resumed her trek. The gift salon was dramatically secluded at the end of a corridor featuring plush carpeting and subdued lighting. In her private opinion, it resembled the viewing room at an expensive funeral home, but the rest of the building was spectacular.

The Pavilion, built on prime lake frontage, had been designed especially to host receptions. Due to demand, the

Greek Revival style structure had to be reserved two years in advance. The affluent suburb of Lake Hope and its upscale, exclusive service providers drew eager custom from both nearby suburbs and the City of Chicago. In Lake Hope, the "haves" heavily outnumbered and outspent the "just getting by on a paycheck" segment of the population.

Back on the hardwood dance floor, Keely's assistant videotaped the hilarity as an upper crust more familiar with ballroom dancing tried their hand at country line dancing.

Keely's feet shuffled to the distant melody and her hips swayed. Triple step. Military turn. Recalling her protests at her mother's choice of country tunes on the car radio, Keely chuckled. Moira would be speechless at the sight of her daughter, that steadfast booster of rock and roll, prancing through the steps of the Tush Push.

Keely paused with one boot in the air. She'd actually thought about her mother without experiencing a surge of resentment. I'm getting better, she reflected. Making progress!

Even her equipment seemed lighter as she pranced down the hall. The Pavilion was honeycombed with similar corridors designed to give service providers quick access to the entire structure. The architect had even added a short passage near the gift salon which opened directly into a loading area. Gifts could be transferred to vehicles without having to be carried the length of the building. The kitchen featured a similar entrance to expedite food deliveries. Everyone agreed the Pavilion was a dream of a reception hall. The dance floor boasted both baby and colored spots, and tonight's bridal couple had chosen to do their spotlight slow dance to "Love in the First Degree."

Tricia looked darling in her white satin cowgirl hat complete with a pouf veil. The guests had arrived attired in western wear in response to an invitation which spoke of "roping the right lifemate." Amid the ruffled skirts and silver belt buckles, Flo Netherton's mauve lace gown appeared as exotic as a lily in a flock of tumbleweeds. Keely, hoping to blend in, had borrowed boots and a hat from a neighbor who was a country line dance fanatic.

Aided by generous cups of Panhandle Punch, the crowd at the reception quickly got into the spirit, whistling and stamping until the bride whipped off her skirt and cathedral train to reveal a white leather mini and matching boots. Each guest would be toting home a miniature version of the groom's cake, a chocolate cowboy boot frosted in mocha mousse.

After taking a few shots of the bride admiring the gift tables, Keely planned to return to the ballroom, where the festivities were winding down. She had come ahead to double-check the lighting while Tricia touched up her make-up.

The honeymooners were booked for two weeks at a working dude ranch and Keely wouldn't be surprised if Tricia, in the interests of authenticity, scorned the standard limousine for the ride to the airport. Grinning at the mental image of a pair of sturdy cow ponies pawing at the curb, Keely opened the salon door.

The smile froze on her lips. For a split second, she thought she'd entered the wrong room. A cyclone had stripped the tables of their displays of silver, crystal, and china. Table skirts of torn silver netting served as a backdrop for forlorn turquoise and peach bows hanging askew. A crystal swan, the focal point of the display, lay shattered, only the graceful arch of its neck intact.

Keely gazed at the devastation, comparing the room to its orderly appearance during her earlier visit. Belatedly, she realized the husky security guard, ill-at-ease in his rented tuxedo, no longer stood at his post.

Taking a tentative step forward, Keely stumbled over a brass candlestick lying just inside the doorway. Functioning on automatic, she picked it up before moving to gaze down at the shattered swan.

Hearing a groan, Keely whirled. A woman lay huddled beside one of the ransacked tables. She recognized the rucked-up gray satin dress as the one worn by the bride's grandmother, a strong minded woman with the mild appearance of a dove and the voice of a crow. Keely's first thought was that Mrs. Westhaven must have walked in, seen the wreckage, and collapsed.

"Help!" Shock had diminished the elderly lady's raucous caw to a feeble cheep.

Keely hurried to the fallen woman, whose eyes were closed, and knelt beside her. Raddled cheeks appeared pale under a heavy application of rouge. A purplish swelling marked her forehead. Keely's stomach lurched—this was no victim of a maidenly swoon!

Robbery. An elderly woman assaulted. With the mayor and half the City Council doing the Boot Scootin' Boogie down the hall.

Keely swallowed the lump of incredulity rising in her throat and shouted for help.

"What happened?"

Startled at the instant response to her cry, Keely pivoted on one knee to find a man crouching on jean clad haunches beside her. Her photographer's eye instantly registered the details of his appearance, including the red kerchief which added a southwestern flair to his blue silk shirt.

"Gifts gone—guard missing—she's hurt!"

The newcomer seemed unperturbed by the disjointed phrases tumbling from Keely's lips. "That's quite a goose egg, but at least she's breathing regularly." He leaned forward, his fingers encircling the victim's bony wrist. "Pulse is fairly strong."

"We need an ambulance—and the police!" Keely nodded at the tissue-wrapped box the man held in his left hand. "Someone's stolen the other gifts and attacked Mrs. Westhaven!"

In response to her name, the woman moaned and opened dazed eyes, slowly focusing on Keely and the man at her side.

"Grandma!"

The horrified cry wrenched Keely's gaze away from the injured woman's face to the doorway as the bride and her entourage spilled into the room.

Her cowgirl hat tilted rakishly over one eye, Tricia demanded, "What happened to my grandmother? Is she ill?"

Mrs. Westhaven struggled to raise her head. "Man . . . taking gifts. Tried . . . stop him . . . hit me with candlestick—" Amid a ragged chorus of shocked gasps, she slumped back to the floor and Keely became the focus of attention. Perplexed, she glanced down to discover that she held the weapon.

She dropped it as if the brass burned her flesh.

Chapter 2

Keely's temples throbbed with each stride down the station corridor. She placed each foot carefully to avoid unnecessary jarring to her head. Her skin, stretched too tightly across the bones of her face, prickled under the wash of cool air from an overhead vent.

She felt as if she'd been confined in this inhospitable environment for days. The recycled air tasted stale. Even the stark furnishings had a hostile look, as though this island of bureaucracy hadn't been designed to support civilian life forms.

Her uniformed escort stopped. "Wait here. Someone'll come get you when your statement's ready to sign."

"How long will I have to wait?"

"Shouldn't be more than an hour or so."

An hour! Too drained to utter the protest forming on her lips, Keely studied her surroundings. "Here" was the dingy foyer serving the public entrance of the police station, its atmosphere redolent with stale tobacco and silent despair. The sole amenities were several battered vending machines and a bench occupied by two small girls. One child clutched a rag doll, the other sucked her thumb. Keely smiled encouragement, but they shrank together as if she'd made a threatening gesture.

She wanted to put her arms around them and escape to the fresh air outside. Instead, she leaned against the wall and watched a woman—presumably the children's mother—argue with a granite-faced officer secure behind a counter. A sign on the Plexiglas barricade read "Public Information and Complaints."

"But he wouldn't rob a liquor store! I know some of his friends are pretty wild, but my David's a good boy!"

Keely looked away. The lines of pain carved into the woman's face were freshly inflicted gashes over old scars, her frantic pleas a reminder of the steep price exacted by family. No matter how heinous or repeated the offense, you were supposed to piece the fragments of their life back together while your own dreams faded—

"Howdy, ma'am."

Keely turned. The speaker was the man who'd answered her cry for help at the Pavilion. Still propping up the wall, she studied him with open curiosity—manners seemed absurd baggage in a place where emotions ran unchecked.

He stood with thumbs hooked in the front pockets of his jeans. "Waiting for your statement to be typed?" At her nod, he drawled, "These lawmen are the slowest typists in the West."

He had such an open and pleasant face that, despite her exhaustion, Keely smiled back. "I hate to break a stranger's heart, but that's the worst imitation of Gary Cooper I've ever heard."

He was ten times better looking. Dark hair, bronzed skin, and classic features betrayed an Italian heritage, his eyes the translucent blue of the Mediterranean. Gazing at the well-shaped shoulders which topped the man's muscular frame, Keely realized her own had a definite sag. She suddenly lacked the energy to sustain even this idle conversation.

The stranger clapped his hands to his chest and staggered back. "Straight through the heart! I'm a goner! My last request is that you bury me six feet deep with my boots on."

Keely smiled. "You'll survive—I heard tell that only the good die young."

Her companion made a miraculous recovery. "In that case, I guess I'll be around for a few more years."

He sent a playful grin in the direction of the two little girls who stared in awe at the adults clowning like children. They offered shy smiles in return. Apparently Keely wasn't the only female present who found this counterfeit cowboy engaging.

The man ruffled his hair. "Since we seem to be stuck here for a spell, how 'bout a cup of java?"

She hesitated. He flashed that disarming smile again. "My treat. Shall we mosey over to the vending machines?"

Suspecting capitulation would be less tiring than resistance, Keely yielded.

Her companion examined the dimpled dents in the machine's side. "Looks like folks have been venting their frustrations. Maybe the cops should consider installing punching bags."

His vibrancy stimulated Keely's own lethargic cells; she no longer felt in danger of slipping into a coma. "Not a bad idea. I'm in the mood to go a few rounds myself."

Coins jingled as the newcomer delved into his pocket. "Go ahead, choose your poison. Sky's the limit."

They both selected coffee that steamed furiously in Styrofoam cups as they retraced their steps. The desk officer shuffled papers. The little girls and the distraught woman had vanished.

Keely's companion indicated the vacant bench. "Those poor tykes looked petrified. Some people don't realize kids need security more than clothes or a bed." He held out his free hand. "By the way, I'm Max Summers."

"Keely O'Brien."

By unspoken agreement, they sank down on the bench.

Keely sighed as the pressure eased on her aching arches.

Max inspected the murky looking liquid in his cup with a rueful frown. He looked much as she remembered, aside from having discarded his red neckerchief. She judged him to be in his mid-thirties. Summers had an air of self-assurance and an incandescent smile that would melt a harder heart than Keely possessed.

Sipping his coffee, Max stretched his legs and crossed his ankles. The legs ending in supple leather boots looked capable of dancing the Tush Push into the wee hours of the morning. Keely longed to shuck her own boots, but was afraid she'd never get them back on her swollen feet.

"Keely." Her name lingered on his tongue. "An unusual name."

"Irish Gaelic, meaning 'beautiful.' " Keely dug her thumbnail into the yielding, pebbled surface of her cup. "My mother told me I was a beautiful baby."

Rising a notch in Keely's estimation, Max didn't jump in with a compliment. Gazing straight ahead, he murmured, "According to my maternal parent, God makes all babies beautiful. 'So your poor mama would get attached before you turned into such a brat!' "

From this angle, Keely could see the bump on the bridge of Max's nose marring an otherwise clean profile. She was relieved to have found a flaw. Her companion was charming and possessed a healthy sense of humor; Keely instinctively distrusted someone who presented a perfect appearance.

Max caught the direction of her gaze. "Broke my nose punching cows. Rascally critters started punchin' back." Unperturbed, he continued in a normal voice, "I knew today would be a total loss when my alarm clock shattered a perfect souffle dream."

Keely found herself entering into the pretense that this

was an ordinary encounter. "What's a perfect souffle dream? I'm familiar with dreams of falling and of being naked in church, but I've never heard of a perfect souffle dream."

Although the bench had been designed to provide maximum discomfort, Max managed to achieve a comfortable slouch. "The perfect souffle dream can be discussed only by those fortunate few initiated into the mystic culinary circle. A psychiatrist would probably theorize that the dream has something to do with male fantasies concerning the ideal woman."

"In other words, you won't tell me."

"Correct." An impudent grin. "But I'm open to other questions of a personal nature, such as age and marital status."

Keely let that pass. Memories of tonight's reception had blurred into endless clicks of a camera shutter in her mind, but she couldn't shake the impression that Max looked familiar. "Are you a friend of the Westhaven family?"

"My reason for mingling with the other extras at this evening's spaghetti western was business. I'm temporarily managing Feast of Italy." Max shook his head in disbelief. "I should be loading a mammoth dishwasher, not wishing I'd baked a cake with a file in it."

"You're running Feast of Italy? What happened to Anna Marie?"

"Broke an ankle playing hopscotch with her overly active granddaughters."

Keely winced. "Ouch!"

"Ah, but the pain fades beside the agony of handing over the reins of her beloved enterprise to a lumpish nephew who, to put it in Anna Marie's own inimitable way, 'couldn't prepare a decent sorrel sauce if his life depended on it.' "

"Double ouch!"

Max grinned. Each time he smiled, Keely had the oddest sensation that the harsh glare of lighting in the foyer softened.

"Poor lady had no other option. I'm the only family member with any experience in the food biz—I served an unforgettable apprenticeship with Anna Marie before escaping to college.

"Tonight was my first solo effort. That's why I don't care how long it takes for them to type my statement. My aunt's waiting for a report and I still have to come up with a story that won't launch her out of bed like a heat-seeking missile aimed at my heart."

Max's doleful expression elicited a sympathetic pat on the hand from Keely. In her role as pre-wedding chronicler, she'd attended many consultations with the matriarch of Feast of Italy.

Anna Marie, wooed by the socially conscious, was shaped like a bushel basket with legs and had a bark like a drill sergeant. Her elite catering service ran as a dictatorship, not a democracy. In Lake Hope, the name Feast of Italy stood for superb food imaginatively served. Like Keely's Key Shot Studio, it maintained an unblemished reputation for providing satisfaction.

Until tonight's disaster. Keely's shoulders sagged.

Max grunted, apparently sharing her gloomy thoughts. They sat without speaking as members of the public trickled through the front doors. Some cursed, others cried—a few looked as if they had no more tears left. Keely sipped the bitter tasting coffee, hoping to melt the block of ice in her chest.

"Ready to talk about what happened tonight?"

Meeting Max's sympathetic gaze, Keely sighed. "I'd rather go home. This place has all the ambiance of a dark alley."

"Scary, isn't it? I can't shake the feeling that I'm in danger of being dragged off to some dank dungeon."

Keely liked Max all the more for not putting on a macho act for her benefit. "Are we in trouble?"

"Depends on how you define trouble." Max tasted his coffee and grimaced. "They've thrown in a worn-out tire along with the beans, but at least the brew meets the two most important criteria for coffee: hot and black."

Keely tipped her aching head against the cool tiles of the wall. Ask for reassurance, get a commentary on coffee.

With an inward tremble, she recalled feeling powerless as her inked fingertips were rolled on a card. Keely peered at her hand, searching for traces of ink in the whirls of her fingertips.

"All the perfumes of Arabia will not sweeten this little hand," she declaimed dramatically.

"Relax, Lady Macbeth. You haven't killed anyone." Max turned to regard her with a bemused frown. "Or have you?"

"Please, don't joke! I wish I'd never picked up that candlestick. They claimed they just want to eliminate my fingerprints. What if mine were the *only* prints?"

Max studied her face. "We need to talk about this or you'll never be able to sleep. Let's pretend this bench is a psychiatrist's couch."

"Nothing I like better than a rousing game of 'let's pretend.' While we're at it, let's pretend tonight never happened."

Max ignored her flippancy. Placing his cup on the floor, he poised an imaginary pen over an invisible notebook. "Okay, start gut spilling. I've got another patient due in twenty minutes."

Stalling, Keely shifted position and winced. A stiff neck from hauling around the flash power pack was an ongoing professional liability; twinges from today's exertion were manifesting themselves early.

Max waited with an exaggerated air of concentration. Clearing his throat, he raised his brows interrogatively.

Keely surrendered. "Okay, I'll play. I'm a photographer— I own Key Shot Studio. When I walked in to shoot the gift tables, I found Mrs. Westhaven. Then you showed up, followed by a cast of thousands. End of story."

She fidgeted with her cup. "That moment'll leave a psychic scar: everyone gaping as though I'd just confessed to being Elvis Presley's love child."

"Shoot. Scar. Elvis. Love. Patient uses words with violent or passionate connotations and quotes from the ultimate dramatization of guilt, *Macbeth*." Max rubbed his hands together greedily. "You will need many sessions. Many costly sessions."

Although his use of psychiatric jargon set Keely's teeth on edge, she kept her voice light. "What's your diagnosis of the root of my problem, Dr. Summers?"

"The root? Could be something as simple as—Ah hah!" Max waggled one hand under her nose and asked in a rasping Viennese accent, "Do you dream of blue-eyed men whose fingertips smell like garlic?"

"Never." Keely sniffed, wrinkling her nose. "Is that the feminine version of the perfect souffle dream or a hazard of the catering profession?"

Max blinked, then roared. The boisterous sound seemed to bounce off the ceiling and dingy floor until it echoed inside Keely's head. This is crazy! she thought giddily. We should be exchanging the names of criminal attorneys and theories about the robbery, not quips!

Sobering, she said, "Your turn."

"Where's your pen?"

"I'm a modern shrink. I use a tape recorder." Keely punched an invisible button. "Okay, let's begin with you being close enough to hear me yell for help instead of in the kitchen where all good little caterers belong."

Max bent over to pick up his cup. "I suppose you know about my aunt's goofy tradition of presenting a bride's gift with enough pomp to crown a queen—"

"Goofy?" Keely skewered him with an outraged glare. "Anna Marie bustles out in a beaded jet gown and kisses the bride before presenting a marzipan love token. A wonderful, theatrical touch! This winter, she made the most exquisite snowflake—"

Max shuddered eloquently and Keely tossed him a wicked grin. "So which part bothers you most? The beaded gown or the kissing?"

"I'd rather flip omelets for two hundred hungry Shriners than stage such a silly charade," he muttered sourly.

"I think the presentation is romantic, not silly." An image of Max crouching beside her and holding a box wrapped with a satin bow flashed before Keely's eyes. "Wait—you chickened out! You were going to sneak the token in with the other gifts!"

"If it hadn't been for the goons who cleaned out the room, I would have succeeded."

Toying with the idea of asking her companion to employ his garlic scented fingers as a masseuse, Keely eased her tight shoulders back against the wall. "Did the police accept your story?"

"After a stiff grilling and a warning not to even think about leaving town. Cops apparently view possession of a box of candy to be as incriminating as clutching the assault weapon."

Keely flinched from the memory of the brass candlestick

in her hand. Her own interrogation had been thorough and curt. All film had been confiscated as "evidence," but she had no doubts about eventually getting every roll back. Tricia was, after all, the mayor's daughter. Keely decided to put together a spectacular photograph album. The poor girl wouldn't be deprived of a pictorial record of her wedding along with her gifts.

The sight of the uniformed man behind the counter reminded Keely that their ordeal might not be over. "Those interviews were just a formality. We couldn't actually be under suspicion, could we?"

Max looked as though someone had ordered him to disillusion a child concerning the existence of Santa Claus. "We'd be in a better position if Mrs. Westhaven hadn't woke up and accused us of clouting her."

"She was disoriented." Keely massaged the toe of her right boot. "As anyone would be after being slugged with a candlestick."

"A candlestick covered with your fingerprints," Max pointed out with glum relish. "We were caught looming over the victim with the traditional blunt instrument and one of the few gifts that wasn't stolen. The cop taking my statement seemed dubious about my tale of skulking in passageways to deliver a box of candy."

"They're grasping at straws."

"Unfortunately, Keely, we're the straws they happen to be grasping. Disoriented Mrs. Westhaven may be, but she's still the mayor's mother and I imagine His Honor's howling for blood."

Keely unclenched her jaw. "Guard or no guard, the gift room is an open invitation to thieves! Isolated, quiet—anyone could back up a truck and haul everything out in twenty minutes. They can't blame us for an architect's design that made the salon vulnerable—"

"Or that the security guard was apparently in on the robbery." Max patted her knee in an avuncular fashion. "We're innocent until proven guilty, Keely. Remember that."

"I've never found myself at the mercy of the criminal justice system before, Max. Even though I know I'm innocent, I can't help worrying."

"Speaking of mercy, I need to use that pay phone and call Anna Marie. I left my cell phone in my car so as to avoid her demands for a minute by minute update during the evening."

Max rolled his eyes dramatically. "After dialing my number four thousand times without success, she's probably got bloodhounds tracking me down. That's the price you pay for working for family. My aunt's adopted Tallulah Bankhead's motto: 'I'd rather be strongly wrong than weakly right.'"

"Family! We might as well have millstones tied around our necks." Remembering the face of the woman pleading for her son, Keely couldn't prevent an edge from underscoring her words, a harshness which lingered like the bitter aftertaste of the coffee.

Max's hand jerked at Keely's response and his own drink slopped on the knee of his jeans. Muttering under his breath, he yanked a red bandanna out of his back pocket for mop-up operations. Watching him, Keely wished she could blot out her angry words. To Italians, the family unit is the core of life; her companion was probably reassessing her in light of her last remark.

Max stood up, his jeans molding muscular thighs while the silk shirt softened the outline of his torso. Keely's toes curled in their cramped space. At least her body wasn't too numb to appreciate the finer things in life . . .

Stuffing the damp bandanna back into his hip pocket,

Max started to speak, but Keely forestalled him. "What was the love token for the wedding?"

With a raised eyebrow, Max accepted her diversionary tactic. "Crossed branding irons with heart brands, but I lack my aunt's skill with marzipan. Now what's this about millstones?" He frowned. "I don't want you to misunderstand me. I don't consider my family a—"

"Then what was in that beautifully wrapped box?" Keely concentrated on pinching a chunk from the lip of her cup.

"A horse, but the front legs crumbled. After reshaping, as near as I could tell, I'd created a kangaroo."

"A kangaroo? Max! For the mayor's daughter? No wonder you didn't dare make a formal presentation!"

Keely chortled at the sudden vision of Tricia Westhaven unwrapping a stale marzipan kangaroo in front of her in-laws, but the hysterical laughter died on her lips. Following the direction of Max's gaze, she saw a uniformed man approaching.

He wasted no time on pleasantries. "Keely O'Brien? Maxwell Summers? Your statements are ready to sign."

Keely followed him to a separate room and affixed her signature to the brief statement. Hoping to finish their conversation, she waited for Max near the bench.

He still hadn't emerged from the warren of offices and corridors when a woman came through the front doors and approached the information counter. Her hesitant gait marked her as one on unfamiliar, treacherous ground. Clothing and hair were impeccably stylish—only a crooked smear of hastily applied lipstick betrayed distress.

"I'm Barbara DuShay. I heard there was an accident on Barrington Road, a young woman." She spoke rapidly, her polite smile a ghastly counterpoint to the fear in her eyes. "My daughter isn't home yet—she always calls when she's late—I'm rather worried."

"Your daughter's name, ma'am?"

"Maddy DuShay. She's only sixteen."

The policeman's expression didn't change, but the impersonal tone softened. "Have a seat, I'll find someone to talk to you."

"I spent the evening at my bridge club. I'm afraid I panicked when I arrived home and she wasn't there. Her curfew is ten-thirty." The woman paused to wring the strap of an expensive leather handbag. "Maddy was at a party at a friend's house. I called, but they said she'd already left. I suppose I'm just being silly, but Maddy probably would have driven home by way of Barrington—"

A uniformed woman appeared and the policeman said gruffly, "This is Mrs. DuShay. She's here to inquire about her daughter."

"Ma'am, would you please come this way?"

"I'd like for you to tell me it wasn't her." She clung to the edge of the counter, voice shrilling. "Tell me I'm being ridiculous and overprotective. Tell me that the girl who was killed wasn't my daughter."

The desk officer said quietly, "Mrs. DuShay, if you'll follow Officer Walters, she'll answer all of your questions."

The woman cast a frantic look at her proposed escort. "For mercy's sake, don't leave me to imagine the worst—tell me now!"

Keely's headache was back; blood roared in her temples. Forgetting Max, she turned and fled out the front doors, but the scream of a woman for whom a mother's worst nightmare has just become reality pursued her into the night.

Chapter 3

The insistent ringing of the telephone woke Keely. Grumbling, she rolled over and fumbled twice before bringing the receiver to her ear. " 'Lo?"

"Keely, it's Margo."

"Have you no respect for the dead?" Keely groaned, pushing a curtain of tangled hair out of her eyes.

The events of last night slammed into her sleep-softened body like bricks. The police station. Max. The porcelain face of Maddy DuShay's mother shattering into a thousand pieces—

"Oh, Keely, yesterday was such a nightmare! I was shaking, literally shaking, when they took my statement. The police confiscated the videotapes I made yesterday!"

"I'm sorry you were traumatized, but we'll get them back." Keely smothered a yawn, irritated by the whine in Margo's voice. No one would ever consider her assistant a solid rock in the shifting sands of a crisis. "They'll probably turn them over when they finish sniggering at the sight of Alderwoman Wallace doing the Electric Slide with His Honor."

Keely squinted at the clock on her bedside table until the blurred numbers came into focus. Ten-thirty, Maddy's curfew. Too late to go to church and beg for a miracle, to pray that God would rewind the clock of life twenty-four hours and bring back Maddy DuShay, only sixteen . . .

"Greg's upset, Keely." Margo's voice dropped to a dramatic whisper. "He's talking about lawsuits."

Margo and her theatrics. "You weren't hurt, were you? No bruises from police brutality?"

"Greg's always been against me having this job, Keely, especially with the weekend work. Now he's putting his foot down."

"Please assure Greg there's nothing to worry about." Keely stretched, her neck muscles protesting the movement. The silence at the other end of the line was deafening. "You were never in danger, Margo. Your husband will calm down—"

"I'm sorry, Keely. I'm going to have to quit."

"Margo, please—"

"Good-bye, Keely. I enjoyed working with you. You can mail me a check for last week."

Click. Buzz. Keely slammed the phone down. Jumping out of bed, she drop-kicked her pillow across the room, then retrieved it with a shamed-face smile.

Have a care, Missy! You've got your father's Irish temper and one day, it'll land you in big trouble! Keely had often tried to ignore her mother's criticism but the irritating, often painful burr-words stuck in her mind.

Thinking of her mother, Keely's gaze drifted to the water-color hung on the wall over her bed. It was often the first thing she saw every morning, an overblown rose in an opalescent bud vase. Moira had painted the flower's heavy head drooping over the lip of the vase, crimson petals strewn across the cloth underneath. The rose was just past its glory, the few petals that had fallen signalled the beginning of the end.

Yanking on her robe, Keely remembered how Margo had avoided her during the uproar following the shocking discovery in the gift salon. Her assistant had simply gotten cold feet. Greg probably didn't give two hoots whether Margo continued to work for Keely.

She knew from past experience that rather than risk a confrontation, Margo raised her husband's edicts as a shield whenever she had something unpleasant to impart. "Greg doesn't want me to work this weekend" or "Greg thinks I need a salary increase."

Minus one trained and fairly reliable assistant, Keely stalked downstairs and made herself a cup of tea. Sipping the hot liquid, she tried to relax, but the image of a woman standing in the ruins of a building kept intruding. The woman had Keely's face; the wreckage was a once prosperous business.

Word of mouth and referrals were responsible for a large percent of her clientele and Lake Hope was a town with a sharply defined upper echelon where money, new or old, was the ticket of admission to the rarified air at the top. In the lace and tulle world of society weddings, whispers that so-and-so hadn't performed up to satisfaction were enough to torpedo even an established concern.

Key Shot Studio. A bold name for a woman plagued by insecurities to hide behind. Through hustle, ingenuity, and sheer grit, Keely had clawed her way to the top of the "A" list of portrait and wedding photographers in Lake Hope and neighboring communities. A stack of discreet ivory toned brochures in her reception area proclaimed Key Shot specialized in "preserving a record of your fantasy wedding, from the selection of the perfect gown, flowers, and cake to the final romantic limousine ride."

Keely accompanied brides-to-be to consultations with wedding planners, florists, and caterers. Up to thirty hours of videotape and still shots were then edited into a documentary style presentation, complete with music and special effects, the only touches not done "in-house." Keely handled the camera work, with Margo responsible for rough editing, detail work, and photo retouching. Margo also assumed the role of videographer at receptions.

Until yesterday, Keely had felt secure in her reputation for promising the spectacular and always delivering. Her prices, which included a traditional wedding album, were steep, but an unbelievable number of clients wrote out the checks without flinching. Weddings possessed a singular mystique, that "once in a lifetime" aura which hypnotised otherwise sensible women into unlimited spending.

Shredding a piece of toast into ragged pieces, Keely dropped them into her empty cup. Whenever she learned of a former client's divorce, she wondered whether either spouse retained custody of the tape showing the exchange of vows of commitment, that first kiss as husband and wife . . .

Placing her cup in the sink, Keely gazed through a window which needed washing at a lawn that needed mowing. The bridal wreath hedge enclosing the back yard was beginning to flower, displaying delicate white blossoms.

Could her business survive if she was reduced to taking portraits of chubby cheeked babies and smiling anniversary couples? How would she pay the mounting bills from the clinic?

The sun shone as if it had never seen a dark cloud. Fat robins stalked hapless worms in the spring grass and Keely felt an empathetic pang for those poor, dumb creatures crawling beneath the surface. Innocent, unaware, content with a lowly lot in life. Then, wham! Suddenly, you're somebody's lunch.

Bleak winter was a fading memory. A few more weeks and June, the traditional bride's month, would arrive on a magic carpet woven of baby's breath, illusion lace, and pearls. June, when Keely worked twelve to fifteen hour days and savored every minute of her hectic schedule.

Again she visualized a figure of a woman surrounded by the rubble of a once magnificent edifice. Yesterday's disaster would probably receive full media coverage, with Keely's name prominent as first on the scene.

She shook her head vigorously, denying the mental headlines. She was the proprietor of Key Shot Studio. Enough of huddling in her robe and drinking tea like a friendless old woman!

She needed a shower and a pedicure. Needed to gloat over her appointment book with its lines filled solid for the next three months. Today called for some serious post-wedding pampering.

You'll survive, Keely assured herself. You've lived through worse things than a little bad publicity and losing Margo. Perhaps after the mud dries up and blows away, you might even meet Max Summers for a cup of decent coffee and finish that conversation—

The phone clamored for attention. Half-expecting a reporter's insistent questions, Keely answered cautiously.

She immediately identified the familiar background sounds: loud talking, shrill laughter, and—overriding the babble—a woman's convulsive sobs.

"Please, Mom, don't cry," Keely whispered. "Everything's going to be okay."

"MAX! THIS IS A DISASTER!"

When upset, Anna Marie Cinonni spoke in capital letters. Holding the receiver away from his ear, Max rolled over and punched the speaker button on the bedside phone.

Shaking his head to clear away the cobwebs, he replied sweetly, "And good morning to you, my favorite aunt."

"GOOD MORNING—MY MARBLE CAKE! HAVE YOU SEEN TODAY'S PAPER? YOU'RE MENTIONED

AS BEING QUESTIONED IN CONNECTION WITH THE ASSAULT ON THAT POOR WOMAN. FEAST OF ITALY DOESN'T NEED THAT TYPE OF PUBLICITY!"

Max locked his hands behind his head and gazed up at the ceiling, which was rather ordinary as ceilings go. He considered painting a mural on its pristine whiteness. Perhaps a panorama of gorgeous women holding perfect souffles. Other men could make pilgrimages to view his art work—he could call it the "Pristine Chapel." Grinning, Max abruptly realized the rumbles from Anna Marie's last verbal thunderclap had subsided.

"MAX, ARE YOU THERE?"

He started violently, nearly slipping off the black silk sheets that were the only tangible mementos remaining from his marriage. If Uncle Tony were a drinking man, he'd have murdered his wife years ago and no all-male jury could ever convict him. Imagine the inhumanity of forcing a guy with a hangover to endure the torture of Anna Marie in full voice.

"Yes, I'm here. And no, I haven't seen the paper."

"THAT'S BECAUSE YOU'RE STILL IN BED, NO DOUBT. HOW CAN A MAN MUTATE FROM WORKA- HOLIC TO BUM IN LESS THAN SIX MONTHS?"

Good question. Max scratched his chest thoughtfully. Just have the workaholic's trusted partner steal his wife and business and see if the poor sap ever bestirred himself again. The only reason Max agreed to manage Feast of Italy was his mother's threat to permanently take to her bed if he didn't help out her dear sister in her hour of need.

Despite the family perception that Max was as discerning as a pan of lasagna, he'd immediately recognized emotional blackmail. His mother was quite capable of tripping Anna Marie, deliberately disabling her sister to ensure Max's recovery. So her son paid, but grudgingly. As soon as his aunt

31

was capable of turning on an oven, he'd turn in his apron.

Heavy breathing over the speaker warned Max that his relative awaited an answer.

"No one will pay attention to the half truths, innuendos, and misinformation disseminated by the Lake Hope newspaper. The forest fire of gossip will die down within a few days from a lack of oxygen—er, interest." Max knew he was puffing hot air, but maybe in her invalid state she'd buy it—

"IN LAKE HOPE? NOT A CHOCOLATE COVERED CHANCE. REMOVE THE FOUNDATION OF GOSSIP AND THIS TOWN CRUMBLES LIKE STALE POUND CAKE."

Max thanked the gods of surgery that they'd immobilized his fractious relative with a pin in her ankle. If she'd been ambulatory, no doubt he'd have been jarred into wakefulness this morning by a loaf of crusty Italian bread vigorously belaboring his ears.

"We went all through this last night, Anna Marie. I told you everything—"

"NEVER MENTIONING THIS IRISH WOMAN WITH WHOM YOU SHARED A CELL. I HAVE TO READ ABOUT IT IN THE NEWSPAPER. KEELY? WHAT KIND OF NAME IS KEELY?"

"Keely's a lovely name for a lovely woman." Deciding to sacrifice his morning coffee for a trip to obtain a newspaper, Max rolled out of bed and groped for a pair of pants. "You must know her. I'm told that she photographs all the important weddings."

Silence. Anna Marie, a lioness still alert for a threat to her cub, didn't take the flattery bait.

Max cleared his throat. "To set the record straight, we shared coffee—not a cell. The guardias never got that far. And pull down your skirt—your ethnic prejudice is showing."

An indignant gasp, amplified by the speaker. "OF COURSE I KNOW THE GIRL—SHE'S CHARMING IF YOU LIKE A RED-HEAD WITH CAMERAS HUNG ROUND HER NECK. IF I HEAR THAT YOU'RE FLIRTING WHILE MY BUSINESS FLATTENS LIKE A BUMPED SOUFFLE, I'LL ENSURE YOU NEVER BROWN ANOTHER BLINI. MAX, EVEN A COOK OF YOUR LIMITED ABILITY KNOWS THAT IRISH AND ITALIAN MIX LIKE OIL AND WATER. TRY IT SOME TIME!"

Crash. Max flinched. Oil and water. At least bad mouthing Keely had distracted his hot tempered aunt from cross-examining him again on the presentation of the bride's gift.

As he buttoned up his shirt, Max pictured Keely as he'd seen her last night—weary, but still able to laugh with him. Cinnamon brown hair. Eyes the rich color of creme caramel. White chocolate mousse skin with a sprinkling of nutmeg across her nose.

Max couldn't help smiling at the imagery. Lisa used to complain that he looked at a serving of Oeufs a la Neige with more appreciation than he did his own wife's legs.

He sighed. He could still hear that incredulous lilt in Keely's voice: "A kangaroo? Max!"

Come to think of it, all the women he'd mentally sketched on the ceiling this morning possessed Keely's generous mouth and shapely legs.

Max, self-avowed cynic and temporary caterer, found Keely O'Brien charming. An old-fashioned word for a modern woman. He rubbed his bristly chin, remembering the bitter note when she spoke of family. A mystery to be probed and solved, a tempting challenge for a man searching for an anchor in life.

Wait, he was forgetting that he was through with women. Since the divorce, his mother accused him of dispensing charm like penny candy. "You don't give anything worthwhile, Max. Smiles are a dime a dozen unless you put yourself into them." Too bad—he wasn't giving away anything. The conflict marked by Lisa's treachery and his own blockhead stubbornness left barely healed wounds, a painful lesson only a fool would refuse to heed.

As Max left the apartment in search of a newspaper, the challenge of mixing oil and water stayed on his mind.

Chapter 4

"Say cheese!"

"Cheese!" The flash bathed Max and the marbled foyer of the Postwaite mansion in bright light.

Keely lowered her camera as the caterer positioned a bowl of pate between a wheel of Brie and a round of red coated Edam. "Never was that hackneyed phrase more appropriate."

"My grandma had us shout 'Pizza Pie!' before blinding us with the flash," Max remarked. "I grew up in a family of photo fiends."

Was it Keely's imagination or was he watching to see her reaction to the word "family"? She chuckled and Max's answering smile approved both her reaction and her appearance. The black lace bodice of Keely's dress was accented with fringe at the waist and sleeves while skirt and bodice dropped to a handkerchief hem. Both the gown and low heeled pumps fit Keely's criteria for working clothes: elegance and comfort.

Max whistled. "Isn't it considered poor etiquette for the photographer to outshine the bride?"

"Have you seen Dorothea? Next to her, I look like Cinderella before her fairy godmother's arrival."

Keely's conscience reminded her, *"Not in front of the servants!"* and she risked a look over her shoulder at her black and gray liveried shadow. Jackson stared back. A faint smile quirked his lips. Her escort's air of amusement over a private joke made Keely uncomfortable.

"New assistant?" Max studied the man behind Keely.

"This is Jackson. Jackson, Max Summers." The men exchanged curt nods. "Jackson is the chauffeur, but Mrs. Postwaite assigned him to me. My assistant quit and my back-up videographer couldn't stay for the reception. Speaking of video, may I have that camera, please?"

Jackson made a production of handing over the unit, his fingers brushing Keely's hip. Annoyed by the man's repeated efforts at physical contact, she moved out of range. After ten minutes, Keely had pegged him as a creep who'd grope a fence post if it had breasts. Although heartily sick of his visual strip searches, her only other option was to grow another arm.

Max, unaware of the edgy by-play, beckoned to a youth dressed in the white pants and sharp looking black tunic of Feast of Italy's staff. "I need Stilton and Brie de Meaux to fill in this corner."

Looking through the viewer, Keely panned the table. "More? You've already got enough cheese to feed an army of mice."

Under the camera's unblinking eye, Max's assistant deftly added two more dishes to the display.

"Thanks, Steve. A cultured horde this size can go through thirty pounds of Camembert and then devour a full course dinner," Max retorted. "Hold it—is there a mike on that thing?"

"Relax. Your disrespectful wisecracks won't be recorded for posterity. Ask your aunt sometime—Anna Marie's starred in more video productions than Madonna."

Keely increased the viewing field. "We'll dub in a few words of reverent narration: 'Caterers arrange fine cheeses and pate for the guests' delight,' etc. Keep smiling and tell me how you calculate the amount of food to prepare."

"Rule one: blue-haired ladies under five feet tall eat double their weight in hors d'oeuvres." Max turned to a man carrying a tureen heaped with Roquefort grapes. "Doug, for the last time, straighten your tie!"

As Max centered the dish containing the cheese covered fruit, Keely caught the resentful glare tossed in his direction by Doug, who retreated with one hand on his white bow tie. Apparently she wasn't the only one afflicted with personnel problems.

"Good to see you again, Keely. Perhaps later we can find time to talk." Max departed at a trot, followed by Steve.

Keely returned to work with renewed energy. The knowledge that she would soon be face to face with Max Summers had interfered with her concentration during the pre-wedding portraits. Now she could focus on the task at hand.

The week had sped by at a hectic pace, but Keely had spared a few moments to think about Max. She'd been intrigued, both by the man and by the remembrance of their immediate rapport.

On Wednesday, the police released a statement that Sara Westhaven was unable to supply a description of her assailant. The weight of the world dropped from Keely's shoulders. The press release, in repudiating the elderly woman's confused accusations, cleared her and Max of involvement in the brutal assault.

Keely had sent pale pink camellias to the hospital, but her gift hadn't been acknowledged by the family. She hated to see a professional relationship end this way. The savage attack on a woman who could have been easily overpowered angered Keely, and left her troubled.

Several times, she considered calling Max at Feast of Italy, only to decide against it. She'd been unaccountably nervous about seeing him again, apprehensive that the affinity she'd felt was an illusion. But tonight they'd slipped easily into comfortable banter and only Keely's professionalism prevented her from trailing Max into his kitchen domain.

She had her hands full from Margo's defection. Handling both the photos and the videography for tonight's reception kept her busier than a cat guarding multiple mouse holes, but the odious Jackson was a quick study.

"Jackson—" (Using only his surname made Keely feel like an imperious dowager but according to Ives, the Postwaite butler, lowly chauffeurs didn't have first names.) "Tripod, please."

Setting up in the dining room doorway, she peered through the viewfinder at tables sleekly coated in French damask and glittering with Baccarat crystal, sterling silver flatware, and Minton china. Polished woodwork gleamed like molten honey under the diffused light of massive chandeliers. Floor to ceiling arched windows overlooked the sloping lawn and terraced pool which sparkled like a sapphire in the moonlight.

Dorothea had chosen the Moody Blues song, "Nights in White Satin" as her theme. Surveying the result of months of planning, Keely felt a rush of pride for the hostess.

No one could fault the perfumed candles floating in crystal bowls or white satin sculpture centerpieces. Snowy trumpet narcissus adorned the bride's table and lacy wrought iron pedestals ringing the room supported cascades of Amazon lilies.

"Imagine wasting that cash on flowers when there's better white stuff to sniff."

Keely clicked the shutter without responding. If Jackson's sly reference to drugs was intended to elevate himself in her eyes—dream on, Bozo.

Jackson appeared trim in his tailored gray uniform. He

had regular features and well brushed blond hair. His "me he-man, you plaything" attitude, however, would irritate even the most unliberated woman. There must be a severe shortage of chauffeurs for the Postwaites to keep this unsavory specimen on staff.

When they returned to the spacious foyer, the guests converged on the buffet. Using a technique perfected by hours of practice, Keely cradled the video unit in her right hand, waist level, with the lens pointing slightly upward, and circulated. Whatever she saw would be recorded on videotape.

The camera caught the bride accepting a congratulatory kiss from a papery-skinned great aunt and the groom giving his four year old niece a bear hug. The actual ceremony had been private, family only, performed in the octagonal pavilion beside the pool and lit by the setting sun two hours before the reception.

Rose Postwaite had proudly displayed gifts that had arrived from all over the country. Shaking off a shivery feeling of deja vu, Keely had photographed the gorgeous packages flanked by calligraphic cards bearing the giver's name.

Rose's husband, a recently retired oil company executive, shook hands with everyone within reach. Keely paused to capture ruddy-faced Clarence, whose silvery hair matched his wife's gown, as he directed a newcomer to the bar.

Hovering behind Keely, Jackson muttered, "Old man thinks he's big stuff. Gets off on ordering people around."

Keely ignored Jackson, calculating how soon she could ditch him. His derisive tone reflected contempt for his employers, his respectful demeanor in their presence a disgusting sham.

Rose summoned Keely with the discreet lift of a finger. "Keely, wouldn't a picture of the packages that were brought in this evening be a wonderful addition to Dorothea's album?"

Keely gave her a reassuring smile. "I'm on my way."

She knew under the polished, mother-of-pearl exterior lurked a shy woman whose insecurities surfaced under pressure. Rose, overwhelmed by the idea of orchestrating the wedding, panicked at the prospect of society's approved planner, Tracee Dale.

"Tracee's such a supercilious creature," Rose had complained to Keely at their first conference. "She looks down her nose at my every suggestion!"

Keely privately thought the weddings Ms. Dale arranged for outrageous prices lacked true creative flair, but she offered only an encouraging smile and polite murmur.

Rose had admired the portraits hanging on the walls of Keely's studio. "You've excellent taste," she had said. "Since you'll be accompanying me to the consultations, Keely, perhaps you could just give me a nudge if I put a foot wrong."

During the months of extensive preparations, Keely had learned her primary role was to supply reassurance. Rose gradually gained confidence, but still required approval of each decision.

Trailed by Jackson, Keely entered a salon draped in white tulle. Pink crystal vases filled with waxy gardenias and starflowers dotted the room. Accepting the flash camera from her attendant, she focused on the gifts arranged on a walnut inlay table. The exquisitely patterned paper and ribbons were works of art; Keely wondered if this bride of privilege would feel compunction in destroying such masterpieces.

Dorothea Graham, nee Postwaite, seemed devoted to her mother. Keely had garnered the impression Dorothea would have preferred less elaborate arrangements if a grand wedding hadn't been so important to her mother.

Suppressing an envious twinge at the closeness of their relationship, Keely changed the F-stop for a tight shot of a silver foil package with a spray of silk lilies of the valley tucked under its ribbon.

Before returning, she inserted a fresh roll of film, thankful the medium format camera took smaller negatives than the one she used for studio portraits. Since the average wedding required a minimum of a hundred fifty exposures, thirty shots to a roll instead of twenty meant fewer enforced breaks in her shooting rhythm.

Jackson tucked the exposed film roll Keely handed him into the equipment case. "We make a great team. How about hiring me as a permanent assistant? If you teach me to use those cameras of yours, I could do some fascinating nude studies of your hot little bod, baby. We could use a wedding cake as a prop, one with plenty of gooy icing—"

Keely rejected his insinuating advance with a curt shake of her head, but Jackson continued to close in. "After the pictures, we could both get naked. I'll bet the ride you give is unforgettable—"

Twisting free, she raised the camera, triggering the flash which exploded its dazzling light in his face. Blinking furiously, Jackson recoiled with an oath.

"Any remarks more personal than 'Yes, ma'am,' will be unacceptable," Keely snapped. "Is that clear?"

The implication she would report Jackson's behavior to his employers hung in the air. A muscle in the man's jaw twitched and he stooped to pick up the equipment case.

"Yes, ma'am." He spat out the words, his features contorted with fury and humiliation.

For the next hour, Jackson hovered behind her like Banquo's ghost at the feast. He limited his responses to her requests to "Yes, ma'am," but the insolent tone turned the words into a taunt. His gaze stripped away her chic black dress, leaving her exposed and vulnerable.

Fearing he might seek revenge for her rejection, Keely took the precaution of entrusting her equipment cases to the butler's care before going in to dinner.

Seated at a table near the double doors, she discovered that Doug, his tie still askew, would be her waiter. The plump woman in taffeta on Keely's right introduced herself as Winona, a second cousin on the Postwaite side from Oklahoma.

Winona, who cheerfully announced that she was "on the shady side of forty and the sunny side of fifty" sported pink lipstick and turquoise eye shadow. In between bites, she kept up an equally colorful commentary on the decorations, music, and guests. "Mmmmm. That caterer's even tastier lookin' than his food." Watching Max direct his staff, Winona purred. "I'd like to sample his dumplings."

Keely, forking up a bite of smoked filet of beef, choked as Max glanced in her direction and smiled. Winona, who resembled an overstuffed pink mushroom in her taffeta dress, intercepted Max's salutation, waggling her fingers in a coy wave. He hastily turned, leaving Keely smothering her laughter in her napkin.

"My, he's a shy one." Winona looked pensive. "I've been winkin' at that boy all evening. I single-handedly ate enough cheese to constipate an elephant, but he just kept smilin' polite-like and sending for more. My daddy—rest his soul— always said, 'You're an unplucked rose, baby girl, but some day a man who don't mind a few thorns is going to snatch you up.' "

Struggling for control, Keely made noises of agreement.

Winona buttered a cracked wheat herb roll with a lavish hand. "That caterer can whip me into a froth just by lookin' at me. I'd tell him, "Beat me, baby. Faster, faster!"

Max was close enough to overhear the last remark. The occupants of nearby tables stared at Winona, who winked at Keely. The plump woman clearly relished being the center of attention.

Leaning closer, she gave Keely a pink lipsticked grin. "I love sayin' outrageous things! If I behave, nobody pays me no never mind. My daddy—may he enjoy his everlastin' rest—told me, 'Speak your mind. You and your stomach will stay on good terms.' "

"I'm sure you'll never have an ulcer," Keely managed to say, wondering if Max was flattered or appalled to be the object of such unabashed lust.

Since social convention dictated humble photographers be banished to the Siberia of duty guests and distant relatives, Keely usually endured these dinners. Tonight, however, entertained by Winona's lurid comments and Max's nervous peeks in their direction, she didn't regret her exile.

Her duties were nearly over. She'd photographed the couple sipping champagne as husband and wife and the ceremonial cutting of the cake draped in swags of iced honeysuckle and roses. Perhaps later, she could meet Max for that cup of coffee. At the first opportunity, Keely meant to try Winona's daddy's advice about healthy living and speak her mind—

"Excuse my rubberneckin', but this room's got more rhinestones than a country music award show." Winona twisted in her chair to study the other diners.

Keely couldn't resist the temptation to do a little rubbernecking herself. Under the muted glow of the chandeliers, diamonds glittered, brilliant fireflies hovering near pampered throats, hands, and wrists. "Rhinestones? Winona, you're going to get us banished to eat with the servants!"

"Pooh! I'm family. I can say whatever I like." Winona

peered avidly at her hostess. "Bet that necklace Rose's wearing cost Clarence a pretty penny. Those sparklers are real diamonds, bought for their anniversary. Ain't it an eye-popper?"

Keely agreed and looked at Rose with concern. Although she continued to smile, Rose appeared weary as she played the part of the gracious hostess. At the head table, Dorothea kissed her new husband with a tenderness evocative of intimacy.

Inexplicable tears blurred Keely's vision. Strange, she reflected, wiping her eyes with a corner of her napkin, weddings don't usually affect me this way—

"Okay, hon? Feelin' sentimental or got a tummy ache?"

"Just tired." Keely felt the urge to confide the story of the catastrophic ending of last week's reception to Winona who, no doubt, could put things in perspective with a pithy comment.

But Winona had gone back to ogling the other diners. "Who's the tough lookin' hen with the bleached hair and rings big enough to choke a horse?"

Keely followed the direction of Winona's gaze. Emeralds flashed as Flo Netherton, publisher of the Lake Hope daily paper and author of the popular "Flo Knows" society column, smoothed back a sleek tendril of ash blond hair. A haughty smile curved the woman's lips.

"She owns the local paper, *Lake Hope Ripples*. Except Flo makes waves—not ripples."

"I'd steer clear of that gal, if I were you. Her smile looks hard enough to scratch a diamond." Scandalized, Winona clucked her tongue. "And, Lord have mercy, she's showin' enough bosom in that green dress to shock a stripper!"

Flo's figure was up to the challenge of her decolletage neckline. Hostesses courted the columnist like royalty although Flo's needle-sharp prose often left fang marks in her subjects. Local legend held that a few brave souls had withheld invitations and suddenly found that, socially, they'd ceased to exist. Through bribery and intimidation, Flo had created a network of spies to supply scandal and gossip for her columns.

Winona gazed at the chandeliers draped with freesia, roses, variegated ivy, and baby's breath. "Calmin' and peaceful," she said reverently. "Like an airy angel garden."

Surprised at this poetic turn by her earthy companion, Keely told Winona with sincerity she regretted that their acquaintance had to end with the meal.

The string quartet played a soft accompaniment to the genteel clink of china and silver. With Winona concentrating on cleaning her plate, Keely amused herself by speculating what marzipan symbol Max had prepared. Had Anna Marie bullied him into making a formal presentation?

Her reverie was interrupted by the muted rumble of serving trolleys. The cake arrived, with the first cart pushed by Max himself.

"That boy's got a body so fine he should be poppin' outta cakes, not serving 'em." Winona eyed Max with a covetous gaze. "Wonder if he does birthday parties? Mine's coming up faster than a hog to the trough."

Laughing, Keely reached under her chair for the video camera. "It's been fun, Winona, but I've got to get back to work." If Max meant to welsh by slipping the marzipan gift to the bride along with the first slice of cake, she determined to get his performance on film.

The waiters circled the tables with the precision of a well drilled team, removing plates in anticipation of the cake's distribution. The string quartet rippled into "Nights in White Satin" and an expectant buzz arose. Dorothea's father smiled broadly, champagne glass in hand. Keely eased closer to record the toast.

The host's mouth opened—and the martial strains of John Philip Sousa's most famous march blared forth. Mouth agape, Clarence Postwaite stared stupidly at something behind Keely. She spun around to find her distorted reflection in the mirrored surface of a brass tuba.

Chapter 5

Dumfounded, Keely retreated as a marching band in scarlet regalia and gold braid invaded the dining room.

Chaos spread like a plague, devastating the tranquil scene. Tables lurched and chairs fell over as people milled helplessly, their protests drowned out by the thunderous music of "The Stars and Stripes Forever."

The band dissolved orderly ranks, marching between the tables and driving bewildered guests before them like cattle. Keely caught a glimpse of Dorothea clutching her new husband's arm, her face blank with shock.

Rose emitted a piercing scream which overrode even the cornets' brassy wail. Clarence shouted something unintelligible as his wife collapsed into her chair.

Keely stood riveted, a witness to anarchy. A wild-eyed Winona rushed toward her cousin, only to crash into a serving cart. Cake-filled plates clattered to the parquet floor.

The band switched to "Seventy-Six Trombones." One of the marble cherubs supporting garlands woven of hydrangeas, calla lilies, and French tulips crashed face down to the floor. A guest and a weedy percussionist wrestled over possession of a pair of cymbals.

Beside the overturned serving trolley, Winona struggled to her knees, hampered by the taffeta skirt and the slippery floor. Wallowing in mocha buttercream, she began heaving handfuls of cake at the intruders, showering friend and foe alike with white chocolate icing.

Keely's peripheral vision caught movement near the

47

double doors. She turned in time to glimpse the back of an emerald green dress as its wearer disappeared. Flo, taking advantage of the chaos, was taking an unescorted tour of the mansion! Hoping to protect Rose's home from prying eyes, Keely followed.

The band's blare had degenerated into squawking horns and tootling reeds. The tide was turning, but the outcome was still in doubt as bandsmen fought to retain their instruments. Ducking a wildly swinging clarinet, Keely dodged a pair of French horns and gained the safety of the doorway.

Outside the dining room, she found a small knot of twittering servants. Flo had vanished.

"Sounds like the party's really hopping," a grinning Jackson contributed.

Keely spoke to the butler. "Isn't there a way to stop this insanity before it turns into a riot?"

Ives attempted to straighten his livery. "I opened the door and they marched in," the butler said dazedly. "An entire army! I tried to stop them, but there were too many—"

"Why don't you call the police?"

"The police?" The portly man looked as though she'd suggested introducing cockroaches into the house. "I don't believe Mr. Postwaite would want the authorities summoned—"

Keely gave up and turned to Jackson. "Did you see a woman in a green dress come out of the dining room?"

"Yes, ma'am." The tone was respectful, but his sneer betrayed the deliberate parody of her earlier directive.

With difficulty, Keely kept her temper. "This is no time to play games! Where did she go?"

His smile broadened. "Thattaway."

"Thanks." Keely started in the direction he indicated.

"That's it? A lousy thank you?"

Keely ignored him, hoping Ives would quit gobbling like a startled turkey. The reception was already ruined, but someone might end up injured in the ludicrous scuffling match.

Alert for a flash of emerald silk, Keely's rapid footsteps were muffled by a crimson runner. Closed doors on both sides of the passageway and an occasional oil painting, mirror, or table marked her progress. Realizing she might not be able to locate Flo without a room to room search, Keely slowed. Perhaps Jackson had sent her on a wild goose chase.

Reaching the decision to turn back, she came upon a corridor branching off to the right and saw Flo deep in conversation with a man. Turning to look at Keely, she made a dismissive motion. Her dark haired companion pivoted and strode away.

Flo blocked the passage. "Why are you following me?"

Keely had recognized the black pants and white shirt of Flo's companion. Apparently she'd stumbled on a prearranged rendezvous. "That was Max Summers!"

"One of the catering staff. I don't know his name."

Feast of Italy's other employees wore the reverse—black tunics and white trousers. The man had to be Max, but Keely didn't argue. "Why did you leave the dining room?"

"That fat cow of a cousin started throwing cake and I didn't want my gown ruined. While looking for a powder room, I met that man and he asked me what happened."

The oddity of Keely questioning her movements belatedly struck the newspaper publisher. "What business is it of yours what I do or where I go? Who are you, anyway?"

Flo knew very well who Keely was, but the woman's ice-edged tone was meant to remind Keely she had no right to demand answers. They'd attended many of the same functions, but Keely might have been a lamp for all the attention the columnist had previously paid to her.

When Keely didn't respond, Flo said, "You're the photographer who's a suspect in the Westhaven robbery."

Keely's hackles rose at the flat statement. She remembered Winona's warning to "steer clear". "I'm not a suspect."

"I happen to know that your prints were the only ones on that candlestick." Emerald teardrop earrings glittered as Flo tilted her head. "Why were you following me?"

"I'm looking for a phone." Keely stared into Flo's eyes, daring the woman to contradict her. "The servants seemed reluctant to take the initiative and call for help."

Flo's disdainful expression indicated what she thought of Keely's honesty. "Perhaps we could look for a telephone together. But first, I'd like that videotape in your camera."

"What?" Keely realized she still held the lightweight unit at waist level, in the usual position for unobtrusive taping.

Flo's voice hardened. "The tape, if you please."

"Why?" Shocked by the woman's audacity, Keely couldn't remember if she'd turned the camera off when Clarence's toast was interrupted. Operating the unit was second nature, the action of switching it off as automatic as locking a car door.

"I have my reasons."

"You haven't answered my question. Why should I?"

"You don't want to antagonize the press." In the discreet light shed by bronze wall sconces, Flo's eyes blazed, banked fires prodded into life; her face remained smooth, eerily expressionless. The smile hard enough to "scratch diamonds" was still firmly in place and Keely moved the camera behind her. Backing away, she fumbled with the eject mechanism. With a muffled click, the tape popped into her hand.

"The bride's a selfish society princess and her mother would sell her soul for a bottle of cheap booze."

The hatred in Flo's voice jolted Keely. The next stage seemed inevitable: the two of them scuffling for possession of the tape like school girls fighting over a boy. And what if Max returned? Together he and Flo could easily wrest the tape from Keely, leaving her with nothing but her word against theirs.

Keely retreated until her heel struck something with a hollow thud. Her exploring fingers swiftly identified the lip of a huge jardiniere and a glance over her shoulder revealed that the vase behind her was filled with forsythia branches in golden bloom. "What's that?" Keely jerked her chin at the wall behind Flo, who turned. During that moment of distraction, Keely shoved the videotape into the shrubbery.

Straightening, she brought the camera out from behind her back as Flo spat out a curse and lunged. Keely hung on to the camera, buffeted by the waves of anger emanating from the woman.

"Bitch!" Flo's porcelain smooth mask cracked. "Give me that tape!"

They continued the ridiculous tug-of-war until Keely stumbled free. This had to be a bizarre nightmare. Her opponent's wild-eyed anger was out of proportion to Keely's refusal.

Flo lunged again, gouging Keely's arm with her nails. Convinced she was dealing with a maniac, Keely cried out, but the shadowy walls swallowed up the sound. They grappled until Keely managed to kick her opponent in the kneecap.

The columnist gasped and recoiled, bent double with pain. "Ladies! I'm shocked!"

Keely whipped around to see Jackson grinning broadly. "Sorry to interrupt, but I was sent to tell you the cops are here and they want everyone assembled in the dining room."

Flo recovered first. Straightening, she smoothed her hair into place. "You haven't heard the last of this, Photo Bitch."

Keely's skin stung and prickled as if she'd thrust her unprotected arm into a nettle bed. "You're nuts!"

Flo checked her earrings and straightened her neckline. "Continue to be uncooperative and you'll find out just how crazy I can be." With that melodramatic warning, she walked away, her gait—but not her dignity—marred by a slight limp.

In passing, Flo gave Jackson a look which wiped the smirk from his face.

Returning to the dining room, Keely found the police in possession of the battleground. Scarlet clad prisoners had been herded into one corner while the others checked themselves for wounds and exchanged combat tales.

Now that the troupe was no longer in motion, Keely saw that the brave red uniforms were threadbare veterans of many marches. The eye of one bandsman had swelled shut and another held a blood-soaked handkerchief to his nose. A piccolo and a trombone lay abandoned on the floor.

Keely looked for Max. He walked in minutes later and was immediately surrounded by his staff. Skirting overturned chairs, Keely hurried towards him.

Max greeted her with a wry smile. "Brass bands, clowns— I'm waiting for the rest of the parade."

"We've got to talk."

With a perplexed smile, he studied Keely's disordered hair. "What in the name of Julia Child happened to you?"

Still flushed with the heat of battle, she demanded, "What were you and Flo talking about? Why did she want the tape?"

"Flo? Tape?" Concern replaced bewilderment. "Are you all right? You didn't get run over by that tuba player, did you?"

She avoided his outstretched hand. "I'm not in the mood

for games, Max. I've been manhandled enough for one day."

His lips tightened. "I'm sorry, but I haven't the foggiest notion what you're talking about."

"Don't deny it, Max, I saw you!"

His thick, dark brows drew together. "Keely—"

"Are you a member of the catering staff?"

She turned to find a uniformed policemen at her elbow. "No, but—"

"Please take your place with the other guests. You, sir, back with your staff."

Keely protested, but she was escorted to where guests clustered around the Postwaites like bees around a queen. Some appeared to be in shock, others angry.

A bright-eyed Winona pushed her way to Keely's side. The dumpy woman's hair stuck up like straw stubble. "Did you ever see such a barn burnin' brawl in all your born days?"

Winona's dress, face, and hands were plastered with mocha buttercream, but she sounded exhilarated. "What a rumpus!"

Rose Postwaite was surrounded by a protective entourage. A guest who had apparently made a side trip to the bar offered his disheveled hostess a drink, but she shook her head. Recognizing the look in Rose's eyes, Keely recalled Flo's heartless description and looked around for the columnist.

Flo stood nearby, her implacable gaze fixed on Keely.

"That gal's been staring at you and she looks meaner than a sow shorted of her dinner slop." Winona prodded Keely in the ribs with a sticky finger. "I told you to watch out for her."

"She'd better watch out for me," Keely retorted with false confidence. She suddenly remembered the tape still concealed in the vase.

"I'll prosecute you for malicious trespass! You've ruined my daughter's wedding and you'll pay, mister, I promise!"

Clarence appeared on the verge of apoplexy as he harangued the band leader, a chubby faced man whose uniform buttons strained over an ample belly.

"It was supposed to be a joke!" Cradling a white plumed hat, the man mopped his forehead. "We were paid to play a couple numbers and blow, but things got out of hand. Hey, folks started swinging—we had to defend ourselves."

"Out of hand?" A brawny policeman surveyed the upset serving cart, frosting-smeared band uniforms, and Winona, who ruffled up like a banty rooster. "That's an understatement. Who paid you to crash the party?"

One of the men near Keely clapped his hand to his chest. "Hey, my wallet's gone!"

A patter of pocket slapping was followed by a second outraged cry. "Mine's gone, too!"

Pandemonium erupted again.

"Calm down, folks. Everyone, SETTLE DOWN!" Hands on hips, the policeman turned to resume his interrogation of the band leader, but another interruption occurred.

Ives, his black tie awry, hurried into the room. "It's a disaster, Mr. Postwaite!" the butler cried. "All the wedding gifts are gone! We've been robbed!"

Rose gasped, her hands flying to her throat.

The policeman grimaced. "It's a repeat of the Westhaven mess," he muttered to his companion. "Tell dispatch to call Gifford and Dawson. They're catching the flak on this one."

All traces of amusement vanished from his face when he swung his bulk back. "Who paid you to create a diversion?"

"He didn't say nothing about a diversion!" The fat man's face paled to match the plume on his hat. "It sounded crazy, but gigs are scarce! Dude said he was best man—the bride and groom loved this kind of horseplay. We got half the cash up front and we were gonna get the rest after he saw what kind of job we did."

"*Saw* what kind of job—" The policemen exchanged significant glances.

Keely, along with the rest of the guests, looked at the best man, a willowy blond in wire-rimmed glasses.

The groom's features were heavy with menace. "Scott, how could—"

"I didn't!" Scott raised his hands in a defensive posture. "Only a lunatic would play such a prank!"

"Not him!" The band leader shook his head. "Guy who hired me was a dark haired, husky fellow."

Keely held her breath as the man's darting gaze paused on the staff of Feast of Italy.

A stubby forefinger jabbed. "There, that's the funny man! The one in the fancy white shirt."

The finger pointed at Max.

"He's crazy!" Max looked convincingly outraged. "I've never seen this band of Loony Tunes in my life—"

"Cousin Rose!" Winona wagged a frosted finger at her hostess. "Where's your anniversary necklace?"

"My necklace?" Rose patted her bare throat.

"Lowlife scum!" Clarence's thick neck flushed purple as he glared at Max. "I'll ruin you!"

"What a shame he turned out to be light fingered," Winona mourned and licked the sweetness from her fingers. "Prison time will knock the bashfulness right out of that boy."

This couldn't be happening. Keely felt as if her head were about to split. Clutching her temples, she looked straight into the narrowed eyes of Flo Netherton.

The columnist's lips shaped the words, "Keep quiet or I'll ruin you."

There seemed to be a lot of that going around.

Chapter 6

In the commandeered command post of Clarence Postwaite's study, Gayla Gifford studied the pair of needlepoint chairs drawn up before the desk and brooded. One of those chairs probably cost more than her mortgage payments for six months.

Promotion to detective bore a hefty price tag. Gayla's assignment to a new offshoot of the division, special crimes, involved taking cases where the media crucified the police for being inept or venal, crimes guaranteed to stain one's soul.

Not to mention the weird ones. They were calling these thieves the "Sterling Ring" down at the station.

Brian "Robocop" Dawson regarded his partner with concern. "Everything all right at home? You seem preoccupied."

"Tonight was family night, Brian. Hank and me and the kids baked chocolate chip cookies after supper."

Nothing short of six points on the Richter scale ever rocked Brian. He stopped to inspect a lighted globe of the earth. "Be grateful for small favors. Hank'll get stuck with the mess."

Gayla scowled. "I'd trade this mess for that one in a heartbeat."

Since the Westhaven robbery involved crimes against both person and property, Gayla figured the larceny 'tects would get stuck with it. But on Wednesday, Kowalski had seen fit to toss the grenade to her, unconcerned if it exploded in her lap. Gayla had fielded calls from the mayor in his combined roles of indignant public official, outraged son, and irate father.

Clues from the first scene had been scarcer than a detective's day off, with the victim insisting the operator of a prestigious catering service had slugged her with a candlestick.

"Gayla, be nimble, Gayla, be quick. Solve this case or end up licked," she muttered.

Brian twirled the globe until land masses and seas blurred together. "I recommend you cut back on reading nursery rhymes to your kids."

"They favor Winnie the Pooh." Gayla regretted the lost opportunity to scrub chocolate smears off precious faces. "I feel like the bear with very little brain."

Thumping her forehead, she mumbled in her best Pooh imitation, "Think, think, think."

"Does self-abuse work for the bear?"

"Honey's the only thing that stimulates his thought processes." Gayla paged through her notebook. "How's the rest of the team doing?"

"They've finished going over the first floor. Didn't come up with squat. The perps had time to whisk half the furniture out of this palace before Jeffers secured the scene."

"Anyone get a content description on the wallets?"

"Unnecessary—we found 'em." Brian hooked a meaty thumb through his belt. His shoulders strained the seams of an off-the-rack suit, his very presence a silent deterrent to those inclined to violence. "Under a table in the dining room. Light Fingers must have ditched them when he or she heard the siren."

"That only leaves the rocks unaccounted for." Gayla nibbled the nail of her index finger. "We don't know exactly when the necklace disappeared. We've got conflicting testimony whether Mrs. Postwaite was wearing it prior to the band's arrival. That's why the third videotape's so important. I hope the O'Brien woman had the camera running—"

"Don't chew your nails." Brian nodded at her hand.

"You're always crabbing about hang nails."

"Schedule me for a manicure. I'm free all day tomorrow."

When he flashed that mischievous smile, Brian reminded Gayla of her three year old. "Only if you promise to do something about that messy hair at the same time. You look like a poodle due for a trim."

Gayla shrugged. "Hank loves me just the way I am. Stop criticizing my personal style and I'll quit ragging on your pathetic taste in shirts. Back to business. I haven't heard screams, so I assume there were no strenuous objections to being searched."

"I think a few were actually turned on by the experience." Brian kept a straight face. "The usual ominous mutters about calling attorneys, but so far everyone's cooperating. We found plenty of jewelry, but no concealed diamond necklace."

"You know you're having a bad day when lawyers top you in the ol' popularity poll." Gayla gave the bulky furniture a disdainful glance. The study, clearly a rich man's domain, was big enough to stage a one-ring circus. "We'll interview people here, starting with the leader of Alexander's Ragtime Band."

Deadpan, Brian checked his notebook. "I have here 'Benjamin's Brass Marching Band.' "

Gayla chuckled. Working with Brian was like watching a caterpillar in the pupa stage. All activity was concealed beneath an opaque surface. They were gelling into a team, with Gayla handling interviews and Brian contributing intimidation and occasional inspiration.

The monied atmosphere was beginning to oppress Gayla, who felt the advance guard of a tension headache creeping up her neck. "Let's keep our caterer friend separated from everyone else. He's got a lot of explaining to do."

Waiting for the first arrival, Gayla closed her eyes, picturing the looted gift salon. The security system had been switched off for the reception; the thieves had taken advantage of the situation to remove an entire window, frame and all. Presumably, the gifts had been packed into boxes and handed out to a van parked behind the house. The perps had probably enjoyed a good undisturbed hour during the circus in the dining room.

"We're talking inside help, Robo, no question. The tracks showed the van drove directly to the right room."

"A guest might have scoped out the scene and communicated information by cell phone."

Gayla nodded thoughtfully. The crime scene techs were currently wielding their magic powder, but if the pattern of the first one held true, the thieves had worn gloves. She wasn't holding out hope for even a partial.

Gayla realized she was chewing her nail again and wished she dared smoke. No ashtrays were visible; she didn't think Clarence Postwaite would be pleased if she and Brian took any liberties. He was already hostile, angry with the invasion of his home and blaming the police for failing to protect his family.

This case could be a career buster. Gayla's boss, Leon Kowalski, was closing in on retirement and loved nothing more than tweaking the tails of society lions. When giving Gayla the assignment, he'd informed her that he wanted results, not hand holding and ruffled feather smoothing. Few people in Lake Hope would lose any sleep over society brides being deprived of silver and china, but the rich and powerful took this personally.

Her reflections triggered a new notion. "Maybe we're dealing with a character who thinks he's a modern day Robin Hood."

Brian shook his head. "Just a plain hood. The man of Sherwood Forest would never have clobbered the mayor's momma. If it was Summers, I hope I get the chance to show that jerk how a crack on the noggin feels."

"Control yourself, Robo. A man with a concussion can't answer questions."

Gayla went over the known facts again. Folks had scattered to the four winds after the original upheaval quieted down, but according to the servants, only three actually left the dining room during the height of the melee: Flo Netherton, Keely O'Brien, and Max Summers.

"Why did they leave the room, Brian? Weak bladders? To check on the robbery? I've got a hunch one of them is the key."

Brian was learning to keep pace with Gayla, whose agile thoughts often leaped ahead of his own plodding logic. "Summers says he knew the band's arrival meant trouble. He dashes to his catering van and calls 911. The newspaper woman claims she went in search of a powder room prior to the parade. Ms. O'Brien's pretty vague about her movements. Whalen took her prelim and he thinks she's holding back."

Brian paused to give Gayla a beatific smile. "If you want my personal opinion, the photographer's pretty, period."

"Stop drooling. Keely O'Brien could be the inside contact for this 'Sterling Ring.' I want every inch of that catering van checked—including an impression of its tires to see if they match the ones outside the window."

Discounting Ms. Netherton left Max and Keely and their penchant for wanderlust at a critical time. Gayla hadn't placed much credence in Mrs. Westhaven's powers of observation. A knock on the head had left her understandably confused; her description of the man who struck her had been given little credence.

Tonight's events changed matters. Along with the speed and skillful execution, other common denominators in the thefts were Max Summers and Keely O'Brien.

"Bri, someone's got a nasty sense of humor."

He chuckled. "I watched the line dancing section of the Westhaven video. My favorite is when State's Attorney Nervous Nelson gets his boots tangled up and takes a nose dive doing the Sierra Rose—"

"O'Brien's the most likely candidate for selling information," Gayla murmured. "She's in on the planning process and has access to details that a caterer wouldn't know."

"Unless he asked the right questions." Brian scratched a massive elbow. "The service providers all know each other. Summers is one smooth operator and Benjamin insists he's the joker who hired his band."

A grandfather clock in a mahogany case chimed the hour as Gayla assumed her game face. "Time to shake a few trees and see what falls out."

She knew the interviews wouldn't be pleasant, with witnesses convinced that social position exempted them from impertinent questions by civil servants. Especially black female civil servants. Flo Netherton's paper maintained a critical attitude toward the police; Gayla didn't expect paeans of praise for her skills to appear in print either.

She flipped to a fresh page in her notebook. The hallmarks of these crimes were greed and contempt for the victims. If Summers and O'Brien were guilty of anything other than bad luck, God have mercy on them. Gayla certainly wouldn't.

Chapter 7

Along with the Postwaites, the butler, Flo Netherton, and several others, Keely was ushered into a drawing room and instructed not to discuss the robbery with anyone.

Not that anyone seemed inclined to chatter. Like anxious family members awaiting a surgeon's verdict, the room's occupants were engrossed in their private thoughts and fears.

A cluster of waiters, however, defied orders to gather in the corner, voices hushed to disgruntled whispers. Keely heard the word "overtime" and concluded that tonight would cost Feast of Italy in more ways than one. She recognized Doug's sulky scowl and wondered why he'd been detained. Where were they keeping Max? And why had he denied his meeting with Flo?

Flo sat on the edge of a damask covered chair, staring into the cold depths of the unlit fireplace. The furrow between her elegant brows suggested complex calculations. When her name was called, she didn't deign to glance in Keely's direction, but rose and sailed out of the room like a queen.

Rose, flanked protectively by her husband and daughter, slumped on a settee. Her face was ashen and old. At intervals, convulsive shudders racked her body. Clarence, on the other hand, looked like a pressure gauge about to blow into the red zone. After a few muttered comments, he surged to his feet and stalked over to browbeat the policeman stationed at the door.

"I demand to talk to someone about the despicable treatment accorded to my family and guests!"

"I'm sorry, sir, for any inconvenience—"

"Inconvenience? My house has been violated and turned upside down, my wife reduced to tears—"

"Dad!" Dorothea tugged on her father's arm. "They're just doing their job. Please, come sit down."

Rose sat alone. Unable to resist the pathos of the figure huddled in the brocade gown, Keely knelt beside her.

"I'm so sorry, Rose."

Her eyes glistened with unshed tears. "Clarence won't let me have even a small glass of brandy."

Hearing the desperate note, Keely's heart sank. During the wedding preparations, her relationship with Rose had changed to friendship, with the breakthrough to confidant coming at the art gallery where Rose had commissioned the satin table sculptures.

Rose had refused the wine offered by the obsequious staff. She'd explained, "After Clarence's promotion, the only way I functioned as a hostess was with the aid of a stiff drink. Soon I needed 'help' all day, every day—and ended up in a clinic. Haven't touched a drop in years, but I'm scared, Keely. Coping with these details makes my throat as dry as a good martini."

A throaty chuckle. "You see? I still think like a drunk!"

Remembering that valiant laughter, Keely took Rose's trembling hands in hers. "A drink won't help. You'll just want another. And another."

"A band—a brass band!—ran berserk through my dining room! Poor Dorothea. I wanted things to be so lovely—everyone will be talking about this fiasco for months—"

"Your friends will understand," Keely soothed.

"I wish Clarence and I had never left our little apartment in Oklahoma. Life was simpler. My neighbors and I played canasta every Monday and I scrubbed my own floors. Clarence and I used to go bowling with Winona and her daddy on Saturday nights.

"I've become a snob, the type of person I despise!" Rose sighed. "Keely, I'm ashamed to admit I didn't put Winona at our table tonight because I was afraid she might embarrass me."

"I think that would have been a certainty," Keely said dryly. "But at least I got the pleasure of meeting her. Rose, trust me. Drinking won't bring back those days in Oklahoma."

"My foolish pride." Rose dabbed at her eyes. "Dorothea didn't want a spectacular reception, but I insisted. I got married by a justice of the peace in my sister's best dress and I wanted my daughter to have something more."

"Don't blame yourself."

Rose wrung her hands. "I saw you carrying your video camera. I don't want anyone to see my guests chased like a flock of chickens, or Winona throwing cake—cake!—at those awful men—"

She broke off, convulsed by sobs, and Keely put her arms around the stricken woman. "Rose, it's okay. My camera wasn't on."

"It wasn't?" Keely saw the dreadful specter of thirst retreat, just a little, in the woman's eyes.

"No one will ever see what happened," Keely promised recklessly. "Just don't take that first drink—"

She broke off as she was pushed away by Dorothea. "I'll take care of her—she's my mother!"

The two women stared at each other over Rose's sagging form until Keely walked stiffly back to her chair. The group dwindled rapidly. Keely was the last person to be summoned to an audience in the study.

Her stomach shriveled to the size of a prune, she entered

with what she hoped was a confident step. Her facade of assurance was overset by the sight of Max seated facing the desk. A freckle-faced man who could crush beer kegs with his bare hands loomed like a miniature mountain against the wall.

The woman behind the desk nodded at the vacant chair. "Have a seat. I'm Detective Gayla Gifford and this is my partner, Brian Dawson. I presume you know Mr. Summers."

Keely obeyed. The detective had mocha colored skin, the cheek bones of a magazine cover model, and gently slanted eyes. Her denim skirt and blue blouse projected a no-nonsense attitude at odds with her exotic looks, while the bright yellow stars dangling from her earlobes hinted at a vibrant personality.

Beside Keely, Max assumed a relaxed posture, his right ankle resting on his left knee. The toe of his polished black shoe protruded into her peripheral vision.

She felt like an actress shoved on stage without a script. After the band leader's identification, Max had to be a prime suspect for setting up the diversion. But his meeting with Flo might have been a harmless exchange, unconnected with the theft. If only they could talk privately!

She didn't think Anna Marie's nephew would be involved in anything criminal. Judging by the treatment the Postwaites had received, however, community position didn't mean much to Detective Gifford. The shoe intruding into Keely's field of vision remained motionless; she felt an irrational twinge of vexation. For a man in the hot seat, Max seemed entirely too relaxed.

Gifford got straight to the point. "The two of you possess an unfortunate knack—or should I say 'gift'—for being at the scene of trouble."

"Knack or gift, we're here to cooperate." Max sounded

almost cheerful. "What would you like to know?"

Her look made it clear she didn't appreciate wise guys. "Benjamin Bartlett claims you paid him to 'shake up this snoozefest' with his band."

"I never saw Mr. Bartlett before in my life." Max remained unruffled. "He tried to squirm out from under by implicating someone else, namely me."

"I see." The detective's eyes were hard and bright as polished stones. "Ms. O'Brien, according to witnesses, you left during the ruckus in the dining room. Why?"

Keely hesitated. "I wanted to see what Flo Netherton was up to," probably wasn't a good idea. "I was looking for a telephone," she said finally. "To call the police."

"Curious, isn't it? You and Mr. Summers's first impulses were to rush out and call the police. I wish all citizens were as civic-minded." Gifford turned to Max. "I want to know every step you took both inside and outside this house."

The detective's see-saw method of interrogation unsettled Keely. Leaning forward, she recognized the sketched diagram lying at Gifford's elbow as the mansion's layout. As Max talked, Dawson bent over it, marking the caterer's route with a broken line.

Max stated he'd hurried out to his van to call the police. Before returning to the dining room, he'd checked on the other Feast of Italy van and his employees in the kitchen. Not a word about a side trip to meet Flo Netherton.

Keely, stung by the omission, stiffened.

Detective Gifford said quickly, "Care to add anything, Ms. O'Brien?"

"That's not true." The words slipped out before Keely could stop them.

Snapping upright, Max lost his air of insouciance and whipped around to stare at Keely. "What?"

"Are you disputing his statement, Ms. O'Brien?"

"I saw—" Keely hesitated.

Looking for support, she saw Mount Dawson had straightened, the pen reduced to the size of a toothpick in his meaty hand. Too late, Keely realized just what she'd gotten into by speaking up. If the videotape she'd hidden was blank, she'd be challenging Max's version without proof. It would look as if she'd tried to cast suspicion on an innocent man to save herself.

And what of her promise to Rose that no one would ever see the footage shot in the dining room? Tongue-tied with indecision, Keely felt the icy tendrils of panic curl around her insides.

"We'll get back to the question of Mr. Summers's veracity." Gayla's tone made it clear the subject wasn't closed. "Let's first discuss a discrepancy in your statement, Ms. O'Brien."

Keely's stomach flip-flopped.

"You turned over two videotapes. According to your preliminary statement, one was used for the ceremony and the other for the reception. Yet a witness reports seeing you insert a fresh tape before you went in to dinner."

Jackson! It took all of the self-control Keely could muster not to fidget in her chair. The snake had taken his revenge for her rebuff in the gift salon. If Keely revealed the tape's location, she'd also have to explain why she felt threatened enough to hide it. She looked helplessly at Max, who stared back.

He'd completely recovered his Agent 007 calm, too cool for a man whose truthfulness had just been challenged. Why was Max lying? A meeting with Flo didn't tie him to the robbery . . .

"As a breed, Ms. O'Brien, cops don't get much respect."

Gifford's emphasis on the last word triggered a recording of Aretha belting out her signature tune inside Keely's head. Like Alice, she'd fallen down the rabbit hole—this entire evening must be a dream. But instead of the comical Dormouse and Red Queen, her Wonderland contained Winona as a pink piglet wallowing in icing and Flo, a lady turned tigress.

Keely closed her eyes. Opened them.

Gifford hadn't dissolved into the mists of a nightmare. "Folks cherish the stereotype of the police as all brawn and no brains. We're crude, rude, and just plain D-U-M."

Keely's persecutor slapped her pen against her palm. Tick. Tick. Tick. "But even a stupid cop can count. You used three tapes, but only turned over two. Your video camera's empty—we checked. People reported seeing you with the camera in your hands during the confusion. You were also carrying it when you returned from your little excursion. Where's the third tape?"

Keely found it difficult to breathe. "I think I can clear this up, but first, may I talk privately with Rose Postwaite?"

"You left the dining room. Not to look for a telephone but to dispose of that videotape. Where is it?"

Keely's thoughts tumbled like clothes in a dryer. First Flo was frantic to get her hands on the tape and now Detective Gifford. Why was a glimpse of high society enacting slapstick comedy so important? Rose trusted Keely implicitly—betrayal might send her running for the false comfort of the bottle.

In Lake Hope, Flo Netherton had sources everywhere and more influence than a Washington lobbyist. Flo's purchase of the newspaper had brought a tabloid tone to the publication. Videotapes could be copied. Would a visual record of the Postwaites' humiliation be safe in police custody?

"Withholding evidence carries a substantial penalty, Ms.

O'Brien. Where's that tape?"

Looking into Gifford's unblinking eyes, Keely decided she could live with guilt. Guilt was mother's milk to her. She knew the taste, the scent, the texture of it. She could probably even lecture Lady MacBeth on the subject.

With her gaze fixed on the hands clenched in her lap, Keely described seeing Max and Flo, the confrontation with the columnist, and her subsequent demand for the tape. By the time she finished, Max was breathing hard.

Gayla glanced at her partner who shook his head. "We've searched the lower floor. No tape's turned up."

Max tried to interrupt, but Gifford raised her hand. "Wait your turn, sir. Ms. O'Brien, where is that tape?"

"I told you—I hid it in the jardiniere."

"Why would Flo Netherton want it?"

"I don't know. I thought her request and her behavior were bizarre, to say the least. She seemed desperate." Keely licked dry lips. "I was afraid she planned to use the dining room footage to embarrass the Postwaite family."

"Why would she do that?" This from Dawson.

"Ask her!" Keely snapped, losing control.

She regretted her response when Gifford said mildly, "Why don't you trust Ms. Netherton?"

"Flo referred to Rose, who's a recovering alcoholic, as a woman who'd sell her soul for a bottle of cheap booze. Flo's columns are composed chiefly of rumors, innuendo, and venomous slams padded in purple prose." Keely felt very tired. "I suppose that's why people can't wait to read what she has to say."

"Did Flo have the opportunity to retrieve the tape?"

Keely shook her head wearily. "I don't think she saw me hide it and she was in my sight until she was taken out of the drawing room to be interviewed."

Gifford turned to Max. "Mr. Summers, were you in that hallway and if so, why?"

Silence. Keely risked a glance at Max. No more Mr. Cool. The fingers tapping the arms of his chair betrayed his agitation.

Gifford prodded, "Do you have an explanation, Mr. Summers? Was it an accidental encounter, a lovers' tryst, or did Flo Netherton need an emergency catering consultation?"

"I can only say that Ms. O'Brien," Max spat out Keely's name, "must have been hallucinating. Check the 911 tape. That's my voice reporting a home invasion. I was not lurking in any corridor with Flo Netherton. I stand by my original statement."

Judging by the expression on Max's face, he'd prefer to be standing on Keely's throat, but he settled for glaring at her.

"You have a cellular phone, Mr. Summers," Gayla pointed out. "I'm afraid you'll have difficulty proving you were actually in your van when you made that call. You could have been anywhere. In the kitchen where you stopped to establish your presence, outside, or . . ."

She paused. The words "overseeing the robbery" hung in the air.

"The fact that your whereabouts are unaccounted for during a crucial time forces us to take a second look at you." Gayla shook her head and the yellow stars swung in orbit.

Five minutes ago Keely had found the room unbearably stuffy. Now she shivered uncontrollably.

Max sounded shaken. "What did Flo say? Did she claim to have slipped out to meet me?"

"On the contrary, Mr. Summers. Ms. Netherton claims to have spent the entire time in question in the bathroom." Gayla smiled sweetly. "Apparently, something she ate disagreed with her."

Wedding Chimes, Assorted Crimes

★ ★ ★ ★ ★

Keely emerged into night air balmy and heavy with the sweet perfume of star jasmine. The climbing shrub's dark green leaves blended into the entryway's shadowed walls, leaving only the pale clusters of the blossoms visible.

She drew a breath, savoring her release from the tension of the study. Then she froze, her heart pounding. Her car was parked only a few feet from the door.

A man leaned against the vehicle's right front fender, smoking. He looked up and the radiance cast by the flood lights illuminated Jackson's face.

"Why did you move my car?" Keely demanded.

"Haven't you heard? I've been promoted to parking valet. Keys are in the ignition." Jackson surveyed Keely insolently. "So the lady detective's letting you go. Bet her hubby's afraid to step out of line. A woman packing handcuffs and a pistol is one dangerous female."

Keely's stomach could have churned butter. Max was still detained with Gifford and Dawson, but Keely knew she remained a suspect.

No amount of questioning could make her produce what she didn't have or change her story. Innocent until proven guilty, she reminded herself and marched past the chauffeur.

Jackson's mocking voice stopped her as her hand gripped the car's door handle. "Things look bad for your friend." He flicked away his cigarette, which landed at her feet. "Being fingered for hiring the band, I mean."

As if hypnotized, Keely watched a narrow column of smoke curl up from the glowing end of the tube. Friends didn't accuse friends of lying in front of a pair of police detectives. Friends trusted each other.

But she owed Max Summers nothing. Keely hadn't been the one playing fast and loose with the truth tonight.

Chapter 8

Max rubbed burning eyes and watched as Keely stooped to pick up the newspaper outside her front door. She walked around the house to a screened-in side porch where a discreet sign marked the entrance of Key Shot Studio.

His sleepy brain prodded him into action. Jumping out of his Bronco, Max hurried up the walk. He found Keely, keys in her hand, staring blindly at the closed door.

Max's voice was rougher than he intended. "We need to talk."

The key ring dropped with an irritable jangle as Keely spun around. "What are you doing here?"

"Don't look so shocked." Max crouched to scoop the keys off the wedding bell welcome mat. "I'm still a free man. May I come in?"

Without waiting for permission, he inserted the largest key into the lock. Pushing the door open, he strode in, nearly treading on an envelope lying just inside the door.

Keely followed. Picking up the envelope, she tossed it, along with the newspaper, onto a desk. "What are you doing here?" she repeated.

Max made a deliberate survey of his surroundings. The reception/conference area, intimate in its proportions, contained a conversational grouping of a couch and chairs in muted pastels; sample wedding albums were presented on a glass coffee table. One wall held a row of portraits framed in a variety of woods.

He turned to his reluctant hostess. "I never figured you'd

be working out of your home."

"I use the outer entrance to keep my personal and professional lives separate." Keely's voice was brittle. "Coffee? I can guarantee that mine isn't flavored with tire scraps."

Max's facial muscles ached from the effort of controlling them. He hadn't slept and knew he looked it. "I didn't come for refreshments, but to ask why you lied to the police."

Keely looked infuriatingly cool in a summery green dress and a matching beaded necklace. Gold rings glinted at her ears beneath the smooth waves of shoulder-length hair. Her clear-eyed gaze met Max's in a direct challenge.

"You and Flo are the liars. I saw you talking together and if *someone* hadn't taken my videotape, I could have proved it!"

Max didn't like her emphasis on "someone." "Are you suggesting *I* took the tape?"

"You were there. You stayed out of sight during our little cat fight and then removed the tape from the jardiniere—"

Where had this woman learned to tell whoppers with such composure? "I went directly to the van and called the police. Remember I told you after the Westhaven reception that I keep the cell phone in the van to keep Anna Marie off my back—"

"Since you brought up the Westhaven reception, explain again how you just happened to be outside that gift salon. You've got a bad habit of lurking in hallways, mister."

Tamping down the desire to shake her until her eyes rattled, Max stuffed his hands into his pockets. "Whoever you videotaped with Flo wasn't me."

"Do you expect me to take your word for it?"

"You expect me to believe that the videotape exists?"

Her outraged gasp made Max feel better, mean-spirited, but better. "Come on, Keely, level with me. The cops think there's something important on that tape and my future depends on knowing what it is."

Keely hesitated. "I don't remember turning off the camera. Operating the video's second nature to me." Her brow cleared. "The camera sees what I see and I saw you and Flo together."

Max winced. Blindsided again.

Keely moved to put the desk between them. Wheeling beneath a portrait of a girl holding a vase of flowers, she challenged, "Why won't you admit the truth? I saw you!"

Reminding himself that his purpose in coming here was to talk Keely into retracting her story, Max scraped the bristles on his unshaven jaw. "I never spoke to Flo Netherton. That's the truth. I'm asking you to keep an open mind."

She shrugged, turning to fiddle with a picture frame. "If you didn't come for coffee or to tell the truth, why are you here?"

"Because I'm in trouble and you're responsible."

"I'm responsible for you meeting that dreadful woman and then lying to the police about it?"

Max snorted. "I thought—God knows why—you'd be reasonable. I did not meet Flo Netherton, nor did I remove the tape. Keely, I don't know why you persist in—"

"Get out." She pointed to the door. "I don't have to listen to your lies."

"Keely, please! Think about what you're saying. Does it matter whether I spoke with Flo or not?"

"The truth always matters." She tugged at her necklace as though the rope of beads hampered her breathing. "Get out or I'll call Detective Gifford and tell her you're harassing me."

"Go ahead." Max folded his arms across his chest. "Make an even bigger fool of yourself."

He saw her stiffen before she lunged for the phone. Max's

hand slammed down on Keely's as she lifted the receiver.

Although the bulk of the desk was between them, his face was only inches from hers. Max could see fear in Keely's eyes, but when she spoke, her voice didn't falter. "Planning to add an assault charge to your other problems, Mr. Summers?"

Max was furious, but he released her, raising both hands in a gesture of surrender. "In your heart, you know I'm innocent of any involvement in the robberies."

Doubts about the testimony of Keely's own eyes had crept in overnight. Had she actually seen Max's face in that dimly lighted corridor or had her imagination supplied his features above the familiar white shirt and dark pants?

She shook her head. Although her memory wasn't photographic, years of practice had developed her observational skills. She hadn't imagined that muscular frame or the dark hair brushing across his forehead—

"Keely, I wouldn't risk Feast of Italy for the sake of getting my hands on some china and flatware!" Max's voice softened. "I give you my word."

"Your word? We both know what that's worth—you lied last night. Just admit you talked to Flo. If you won't back me up, that woman's going to get away with lying—"

"I don't know whether she lied. I never saw her!"

Keely felt sick with disappointment. "You can't expect me to believe—"

"Whatever I expected, I was wrong, wasn't I?" Max paced the room with choppy strides. "I hoped we could synchronize our stories, come up with a hunk of raw meat to distract the police dogs. Anna Marie's dedicated her life to Feast of Italy and I won't allow some harpy to destroy thirty years of—"

"Harpy!" A flush seared its way up Keely's throat and into her cheeks.

"Cool your shutter, Ms. O'Brien, and read today's paper.

I was referring to Flo Netherton and her vitriolic pen. A harpy is a winged monster with the head of a woman and the talons of a predatory bird."

"Thanks for the mythology lesson." This discussion was accelerating down a steep grade, a bloody crash inevitable. Keely spoke to the back of his head. "You've lied to me. I can't work with someone I can't trust."

Max spun around. "What are you, woman, a parrot? You lied to me, you lied to me, you lied to me! I don't know what hallucination you had, but I didn't meet Flo in any hallway!"

"And I'm saying I saw you together! If only I had that tape!" Keely plucked at the belt of her dress. Cameras were the props she used in difficult moments, the perfect gadgets for occupying jittering fingers: advance film, check F-stop, look through viewfinder, distance herself from unpleasant emotions by the thickness of the lens—

"The conveniently missing tape? The only thing you've accomplished with that story is to cast suspicion on both of us."

Hearing the sound of Max's harsh breathing, Keely felt as if she were trapped in a room with a bomb that lacked a timer. She could hear the ticking, but had no inkling when the explosive was set to go off. She braced herself, but detonation never occurred. Instead, Max stalked over to the portrait wall and nodded at the head shot of an elderly man in horn-rimmed glasses. "I see strength in this fellow's gaze, the serenity of a long life well spent. No regrets in those eyes."

Keely watched as Max marched along the row and paused before another portrait. "Here's someone who's endured, rather than lived. Resignation in those eyes and folded hands, resentment in the set of the lips."

Keely blinked. Mary Singer's husband had been a demanding invalid. Viewers always commented that the portrait portrayed a saint—until now, Keely had been the only one to glimpse an embittered martyr behind the long-suffering facade.

"Tell me, Keely, how can a woman who exercises keen insight into character through a lens be so blind?"

"My keen insight tells me that what I see is my business, Mr. Summers. Saving your sorry tail is yours!"

Max turned, but his dramatic exit was spoiled when he bumped into the desk, jarring a Beatrix Potter music box which toppled over, releasing a trill of notes.

Keely moved swiftly to pick it up. "My receptionist would be extremely upset if you broke Jemima Puddle-Duck. Now, if you'll excuse me, I have a *business* to run."

Her rescue had put them nose to nose again and she saw Max's arrogant Roman nostrils flare. "Not for long, Ms. O'Brien."

"Is that a threat?"

Max gestured at the music box. "I don't know how you've lasted in business. You haven't got the survival sense God gave a goose."

"It's not a goose, it's a duck!"

The studio door banged. Max was gone, leaving a vapor trail of fury behind him.

"Forget him," Keely said aloud. "Liars are a dime a dozen." Smoldering, she snatched up the envelope she'd picked up from the floor, tore it open. A piece of paper fluttered out.

Stooping, she retrieved and read the printed words, "Turn over the tape or I'll turn up the heat."

The message was unsigned.

Chapter 9

Keely vented her seething passions by shredding the unsigned note. Flo was drunk with power of the press if she thought she could intimidate via an anonymous threat shoved through a mail slot, a cliched threat, at that.

Keely reached for the scheduling book. Put him out of your mind, she counseled herself. Any empathetic sparks between you and Max at that first meeting were purely imaginary. Like you told the man, you've got a business to run.

Although she had a fair idea of her appointments, Keely flipped through the pages anyway. Margo, the rat, had picked a rotten week to desert ship. Morning portrait sessions, an off-site appointment, proof book assembly, retouching work, a session with the DJ for the Turnbull reception, Cammie Miller's pre-wedding portrait session, Tuesday's evening bridal shower . . .

She picked up the telephone receiver and dialed.

"Postwaite residence."

She recognized the butler's mashed potato voice. "Ives, this is Keely from Key Shot Studio. May I speak to Rose?"

"Madam is not available to callers."

"When will she be available?"

"I am not at liberty to say."

"If I came over, Ives, would she be able to see me?"

"Madam is not taking calls or receiving visitors."

Keely pictured Rose hiding in her lavishly decorated golden French-style bedroom, consoling herself with liquor. She made a final attempt. "You still have my equipment cases. May I drop by this afternoon and pick them up?"

"I will arrange to have them delivered to you."

"Give Rose a message to call me, please."

"Of course, ma'am." A decisive click severed the connection. Judging from his tone, Ives hadn't forgiven her for criticizing his handling of the crisis. Keely suspected her message wouldn't travel any farther than the butler's ears.

The rattle of the knob interrupted her gloomy thoughts and she hurried to open the door.

Ida Burke looked like Hollywood's version of a grandmother, from her cap of white curls to her sensible footwear. But her hands revealed the unfettered spirit dwelling within the matronly body: Ida wore the colors of her soul on her fingertips, a different exotic polish on each nail. Gemstones in ever changing cuts and settings crowded her knuckles.

A devoted member of a television shopping club, Ida often showed Keely clothing, dolls, and gadgets purchased as gifts for her children and ever expanding flock of grandchildren.

Today the receptionist's arms were laden with a sheaf of flowers wrapped in waxed paper, a blue stoneware vase, two paperback romances, and a stuffed patchwork rabbit which Keely assumed was another bargain.

"What's the flower for this week?" Keely helped unload the eccentric assortment onto the desk.

"Freesia. So fresh and pure! To me, the colors fairly breathe springtime! They symbolize innocence—"

Blushing, Ida broke off. Grabbing the vase, she hurried away. Admiring the fragrant, trumpet-shaped flowers, Keely awaited her return.

Something was wrong. Ida, who prided herself on knowing the language of flowers as well as she did the dates of her grandkids' birthdays, was ordinarily unshakable.

Ida's broken sentence still hung in the air. "They symbolize innocence." Innocence! The Lake Hope Ripples. Recalling Max's acerbic reference to Flo, Keely snatched up the newspaper. "Sterling Ring Strikes Again" shrieked the headline. Underneath, "Postwaite–Graham Nuptials Latest Victim."

Keely read on, her lips growing numb. She started when a gentle hand touched her arm.

"I think you'd better sit down, dearie."

Staring dazedly at the cotton ball curls of the woman at her side, Keely felt like a liner being towed into harbor as Ida Burke guided her to the couch.

"A cup of tea with honey? I can make one in a jiff—"

Keely shook her head. "Have you read this?"

"Yes, dear. I'm sorry."

Keely massaged her temples as she bent over the story again. "This makes it sound more like a slapstick comedy than a home invasion," she muttered.

In the reporter's playful prose, Dorothea's reception had been choreographed by a comedic genuis comparable to Mack Sennett and lacked only an appearance by the Keystone Kops to add the perfect touch of buffoonery. The account also contained a devastating description of the bedraggled Winona, along with a few of the woman's more earthy pronouncements. Poor Rose!

Ida twittered. "I would have loved to see Lake Hope's society leaders being pursued by trombones and trumpets!"

As would just about everyone else in town. "Nights in White Satin" as staged by the Marx Brothers! Rose's instincts were sound—if a tape of the fiasco were made public, her family would be ridiculed. Now, thanks to Flo's interference and Keely's negligence, the tape could be anywhere.

She said carefully, "I'm in a position of trust. I can't gossip about what happened last night."

"Of course not, dear." Ida agreed, bravely struggling to mask her disappointment.

She returned to her flower arranging while Keely gazed disconsolately at the newspaper. She had to retrieve the tape before it surfaced and drove Rose back to drink. "Ida?"

Ida's shoulders quivered.

"I'm sorry, Ida. I didn't mean to be harsh."

A veritable earthquake shook the woman's frame. She was laughing! "Keely, I'm sorry, but I just can't help it. I picture Robert Preston leading that band into the dining room—"

A wheeze of helpless mirth escaped Ida's throat. The memory of the violinist from the string quartet hiking up her long skirt and legging it for the door flashed into Keely's head along with an irreverent thought: dub Harpo Marx into the scene in pursuit of the girl and you'd have a classic comedy.

The telephone interrupted. Ida removed her right earring and used the patchwork rabbit's ears to dab her streaming eyes.

"Key Shot Studio. May I help you? Oh, Mrs. Hoover. Yes, next Wednesday evening for the initial conference—"

Keely swallowed the last chortle. If weddings were the hot fudge sundaes of her profession, the Hoover nuptials would be the ultimate cherry. Only a dress from a Paris designer would grace Pamela's model thinness. Keely had already drawn up a tentative list of locations for the formal bridal portrait.

Mrs. Hoover was the bellwether of the socially conscious sheep of Lake Hope: wherever she roamed, the others would follow. Keely suspected the woman would prove to be difficult, but was determined to smilingly endure all slings and arrows.

She saw the color drain from Ida's face, leaving islands of rouge on a chalky sea. "Mrs. Hoover, you should discuss this with Ms. O'Brien—Yes, ma'am. I'll give her the message."

She fumbled to replace the receiver, knocking the stuffed rabbit to the floor.

Keely picked up the bunny. "Was her highness checking to ensure we have a red carpet to roll out for her first visit?" *Please, God, let it be something so trivial!*

"Not exactly." Ida beheaded a freesia before tossing both stem and blossom into the wastebasket.

Keely didn't need to be a meteorologist to spot the signs that a severe weather system was forming. "Not exactly?"

Another freesia met the same fate. "Remember when you said being picked for the Hoover wedding was comparable to getting a nod from the queen?"

Keely wet her lips. "Yes."

"The queen ain't nodding, she's turned thumbs down." Ida's voice became an imperious falsetto. "Pamela's changed her mind. We—the royal we—shall be hiring another photographer."

"Another photographer?" Cradling the patchwork rabbit to her chest, Keely stumbled to the couch and collapsed.

A sharp pain tunneled under her breast bone. The newspaper lay open on the coffee table.

Keely reread the editorial. "By a strange and fascinating coincidence, Key Shot Studio and Feast of Italy Catering were again service providers. Ms. O'Brien's brochure boasts of 'preserving a record of your fantasy wedding, from the selection of the perfect gown, flowers, and cake to the final limousine ride.' Feast of Italy Catering prides itself on service above and beyond the rigorous standards set by this multimillion dollar industry.

"Service providers are, of necessity, privy to confidential information. Weddings are meant to be a time of joy—not fear. We urge the police to stop the Sterling Ring before this vicious gang blights someone else's happiness."

"I'll ruin you," Flo had whispered, her eyes filled with hatred. "I'll turn up the heat," an anonymous note promised.

One editorial. Two businesses trashed. Words that could wipe out years of fluffing veils, spraying gowns to reduce static, and coaxing smiles from tearful flower girls. Evenings sacrificed to lingerie showers, floral consultations, and acting as peace maker when mother and daughter couldn't agree on tapered sleeves or flowing.

Ida had tears in her eyes and most of the freesias had lost their heads. "What are we going to do, Keely?"

"Do?" Keely straightened her shoulders and rose. "I've got a calendar crammed with appointments. I don't need Amelia Hoover's blessing to run a successful business."

"That's the spirit! What shall we do first?"

"Help me set up the studio for the Ashburn portrait session. Margo won't be coming in, so I'd like you to tackle the retouching stack. While I'm gone this afternoon, please sort the proofs that arrived Friday. Match the numbers on the negative mask to the ones on the sleeve."

Keely touched a mutilated freesia, acknowledging her attraction to Max. That was why it hurt when he persisted in his falsehoods. From first hand experience, she knew lies poisoned relationships with fatal results.

"It's only one cancellation, Ida."

As if denying Keely's confident assertion, the phone rang. Over the devastated flower arrangement, the women's eyes met. Turn up the heat . . . Turn up the heat. . . .

Chapter 10

"May I suggest Aioli Monstre?" Max kept his voice matter-of-fact.

Mrs. Dunlap drew plucked brows together. "I expected to meet with Mrs. Cinonni."

"Until she returns, I'm in charge of planning." Max poised his pen over a rose-colored legal pad. "August would be the perfect month for this traditional Provence feast."

The magic word "Provence" was enough to deflect Mrs. Dunlap from her grievance, although she didn't have a clue whether aioli was an entree or a fancy name for mashed turnips.

"Aioli, yes, the perfect dish." Stumbling over the pronunciation of the unfamiliar word, she scrambled to retrieve her dignity. "I'm afraid Mother isn't fond of foreign foods."

"Everyone loves this garlic-laced mayonnaise. Picture bowls of hard-boiled eggs dotting platters of miniature endives, scallions, and cherry tomatoes. Green beans and tiny ears of flash-cooked corn represent the goodness of the earth and sun. Dipped in aioli, they become taste sensations."

Mrs. Dunlap tugged at a cluster pearl earring. "Sounds lovely, Mr. Summers. But so foreign—"

"Trays of steamed broccoli, cauliflower, and miniature red potatoes. Nothing exotic about them! We'll serve chicken. Lamb, if you prefer. Cheese—a table covered with cheeses." Max's expansive gesture encompassed the desk top. "As a centerpiece, we'll use an earthenware bowl brimming with crisp apple slices and juicy figs. Imagine reed baskets heaped with crusty rolls."

She swallowed. Max didn't blame her, his own mouth watered at the thought of biting into a snail after its bath in a massive stone crock awash in creamy aioli. Forget the anniversary—if this overfed, overdressed, and overperfumed fusspot nixed the idea, he'd whip up a batch and throw a private party for one. Max mentally reviewed the items in his pantry. Garlic, eggs, lemon juice, cloves—

"I'm trying to picture this buffet, but it's difficult." Mrs. Dunlap, clinging to her vision of finger sandwiches and salted almonds, was reluctant to abandon France completely.

Attitude! Max reminded himself. He'd seen firsthand how people ate up Anna Marie's legendary arrogance. Women reported to their friends with pride how wonderfully rude the dictator of Feast of Italy had been to them.

But Max couldn't bring himself to squelch the dowdy little woman. He gave her the gift of his most charming smile. "Feast of Italy doesn't cater the ordinary. If you prefer the standard anniversary party fare, you'll have to go elsewhere."

Her eyes pleaded for understanding. "But what would I do for decorations? I was thinking lavender streamers and tissue paper wedding bells . . ."

Max regarded her with tender pity. "We'll have it outdoors, Mrs. Dunlap. I assume you have a patio or terrace? This could be the anniversary party of the century! We'll supply fabulous food—you supply the imagination."

In his urgency to help her share his vision, Max forgot his lethargy. He spoke knowledgeably of joyful peasants celebrating a saint's day, describing the cobblestone square, a quaint village church, and a benevolent sun blazing on contented people.

His unfeigned enthusiasm elicited a tentative smile. A creative spark glowed in Mrs. Dunlap's eyes. Soon they were deep in a discussion of seafood preferences and the proper wines.

Mrs. Dunlap, her cheeks flushed with enthusiasm, suggested rustic baskets and brown glass serving plates. In turn, Max's proposed backdrop of colorful hangings met with mutual approbation.

After escorting a satisfied client to her car, Max sprawled in his chair. The lady lived in Heatherfield and, by some miracle, didn't subscribe to the *Lake Hope Ripples*. She'd hear the bad news about last Sunday through the grapevine as Feast of Italy's other clients had, but fortunately so far only a few had demanded deposit refunds.

Anna Marie couldn't return to her throne soon enough to suit Max, but he would miss the challenge of turning monotonous lives upside down.

He snorted at his own pomposity. "Are you listening to yourself?" Who was he to sneer at Mrs. Dunlap? Life's injustices had reduced Max Summers, noted restaurateur, to a couch potato.

Yanking the booking schedule in front of him, Max scribbled "Aioli Monstre Buffet" on August 23rd. Flipping back to July, he penciled in a tentative date for the final conference and began a preliminary checklist. Brown linen napkins with a coarse weave. Earthenware serving platters. Crocks on stone pedestals?

As soon as her ankle healed, Anna Marie would go back to haunting antique stores and garage sales for the distinctive linen and table services which overflowed the huge storage cupboards of Feast of Italy. Presentation, Anna Marie drilled into her troops, is everything. Before August, she'd unearth the perfect service for the Dunlap party or break the other ankle trying.

Max was compiling a cost estimate for the buffet when a

knock at the door jarred him from his concentration. "Come in." He sat back, rolling his head to loosen the tension in his neck.

His welcoming smile faded when he recognized his visitor. "Detective Gifford! Where's your partner, the Terminator?"

"Can the sarcasm. You can't afford to antagonize me."

Max usually liked candor in a person, but Gifford wielded it like a truncheon. She paused, her gaze taking in the delicate lines of the antique cherrywood desk and the shelf which ran a complete circuit of the office. Above the dark line of wood, the richness of heart-shaped copper trays alternated with the glitter of silver ring molds and exquisite English lustre plates.

"Not bad. Cooking must pay better than I thought."

"This is my aunt's domain."

"You're the one I'm interested in." She clumped over to the client's chair and sat down, crossing her legs.

Max blinked. He hadn't seen platform shoes in years.

She noticed the direction of his gaze. "I don't chase perps any more, Mr. Summers. I've graduated to plain clothes."

Anything less plain than her yellow dress spattered with red poppies he had yet to see, but he kept his expression neutral. "How may I help you? I thought we covered everything Sunday."

"Place is quiet today. Took a wrong turn when I came in. Didn't see anyone working in that fancy kitchen of yours."

Not believing the wrong turn story, Max wondered whether Gifford had been snooping in the right kitchen. Feast of Italy's work area was simply that, a no frills room featuring huge ovens, industrial size dishwashers, and a mammoth island complete with double sinks and gleaming pasta racks. If she hoped to find hot brass candlesticks tucked in with the torte pans, she'd been rattling the wrong drawers.

"How come you're alone? Business falling off?"

"Wednesday's conference day." Max gave his visitor a gritty smile. "The day I see clients."

"Enlighten me. Hank and I eloped so I never had to deal with a caterer. What do you talk about at these conferences?"

He kept his reply brief, serving up the meat without the fat, another Anna Marie maxim. "Menus and party sizes. Presentation. Fee schedules."

"Fees." Gayla tented slim, brown fingers. "I imagine the deposits are sizeable. I've heard your food isn't cheap."

Food? Max shrugged, thankful that Anna Marie was still flat on her back and miles away from the detective's caustic comments. Denting a police detective's head with a cast iron skillet probably carried a stiff penalty.

He recited his customary spiel. "Anna Marie has built a clientele based on her reputation for surpassing the ordinary, disdaining the mundane. Feast of Italy is the best and I intend to maintain the status quo until she returns to work."

"You mentioned reputation." Gifford settled back and fingered the scarlet poppy dangling from her left ear. "A ten letter word vital to your business."

Two robberies and a brutal assault and the woman wanted to play word games. Choking back an offer to get out the Scrabble board, Max nodded.

"How does Mrs. Cinonni feel about the recent negative publicity?"

Triple word score. Max concentrated on the sparks thrown by the silver pen twirling between his fingers. Anna Marie insisted Max use her lucky pen.

Gayla flashed white teeth in a smile. "Your aunt, Mr. Summers. How does she feel?"

Max hadn't told Anna Marie about the cancellations. It wasn't that he was a coward, but he figured the poor woman had enough healing to do.

Today's cancellations left holes in the schedule, which last week had been crammed from 9:00 a.m. until 7:00 tonight. No one, Max reflected bitterly, wanted a caterer with sticky fingers, unless he'd gotten them rolling cheese straws.

"Negative publicity, Mr. Summers. Things don't look good, the paper's virtually accusing you of being the inside contact for this 'Sterling Ring.' Mind if I smoke?" Gifford was already lighting up.

Max shrugged, aware Anna Marie would have a fit if she caught a whiff of tobacco in her office. "Wood absorbs odors," she'd informed Max curtly from her hospital bed. "Though I love you like a son, I don't want you eating anchovies or garlic toast at my desk." Max rolled his chair back and raised the window.

Gayla appropriated a crystal dessert plate as an ashtray. "You and your friend O'Brien have major credibility problems."

Max remembered the contempt in Keely's eyes when she accused him of lying. He'd blown any chance of establishing communication by marching into her studio with his nerves shredded to confetti.

He didn't understand why she persisted in saying she'd seen him with Flo. Oil and water—together he and Keely were more like a stick of dynamite and a lit match . . .

"Mr. Summers?" Gifford's voice cracked like a whip. "We're talking about Flo Netherton's trashing you in print."

Max pulled himself together. "Feast of Italy will survive the innuendos made by any journalistic assassin." On that pontifical note, Max unobtrusively slid his elbow over the appointment book to cover up the crossed-out entries.

"You and Ms. O'Brien were seen together when she returned to the dining room at the Postwaite residence. What was the subject of that conversation?"

Here was the curve ball. Max opted to let the pitch go by with a shrug. "I don't remember. We were stunned by what had occurred—I suppose we commented on the unusual situation."

"Was she demanding an explanation about your meeting with Ms. Netherton?"

"Why should Keely care? We only met each other last week. Is it a crime to chat with a newspaper columnist? I deny talking to the woman, but even if I did, why is it so important? Or does Ms. O'Brien claim she saw me wandering the halls with my pockets stuffed with wedding silver?"

Gayla tugged a nondescript notebook from the pregnant purse in her lap and made a show of consulting one of the pages.

"This mysterious tape and Keely's testimony aside, let's talk about Max Summers before he came to Lake Hope. What are your qualifications for running Feast of Italy?"

"I told you on Sunday—I have my own restaurant."

"Wrong tense, Mr. Summers. Had, not have." The curt rebuttal slammed into Max's gut. "Max's Bistro transferred ownership last December to a David Wagner."

Smoke from Gifford's cigarette stung Max's nostrils. Smoke dulled the palate, spoiled the taste of food. "David was my partner, along with my wife, Lisa."

"Wrong again, Max. Ex-wife."

Max's throat closed. "Lisa and I divorced—"

"In December. The same month you lost your restaurant."

So far, she'd hit every nail square on the head. "I lost my restaurant—"

"To Mr. Wagner." Gayla consulted another page. "He married your ex-wife in February."

"On Valentine's Day." Max's face felt hot as he gripped

the edge of the desk. "They rubbed my nose in it—"

Gifford arched a derisive brow. "Care to explain how you managed to lose your restaurant? Did somebody sue you over a case of food poisoning? Do you have a drinking problem? Gambling?"

Max had the irrational urge to grab his persecutor by the scruff of her neck and chuck her out, but she'd probably give him a judo chop that would leave him permanently paralyzed.

Scrubbing his hand over his face, Max pasted on his most appealing smile. "I originally owned seventy percent of the restaurant, and David thirty. When Lisa and I married, I gave her half of my interest as a wedding gift."

"Thirty and thirty-five percent make sixty-five. Enough to force you out. You were too generous."

"I prefer the word 'imbecilic.' " Max threw down Anna Marie's lucky pen. The thing must be cursed. "I lost my wife and my restaurant to my partner and best friend. The judge refused to put a sufficient value on my ownership interest. Blinded by pride, I walked—virtually gave Max's Bistro away. Since I didn't have the capital to start a new business, I agreed to manage Feast of Italy while my aunt is recuperating. I wanted to stay in food service and this is more challenging than waiting tables or flipping burgers. Period."

"Not quite the end. Let's talk about your bruised feelings in terms of the Sterling Ring. You had a rough deal. Perhaps this elaborate scenario—"

"Is a twisted way of getting back at David and Lisa while picking up some spare change? Only if you're into revenge fantasies, Detective."

"Don't bullshit me. I've taken enough trash talk from guys like you to overload a landfill. I'm also getting plenty of heat from the mayor's office."

Gifford leaned forward, her nut brown eyes drilling into

Max, pinning him against the chair. "Those thieves didn't just waltz in off the street. They had help, and plenty of it. The role of inside contact is a toss-up between you and O'Brien. I suggest you start convincing me you aren't the leading candidate!"

After his unwelcome visitor's departure, Max slumped forward, with his head resting on crossed arms. The scent of burnt tobacco lingered, but Max was too drained to move.

"I'll empty the ashes," he muttered to pacify his conscience. "I'll scrub the plate, I'll steam clean the drapes—"

A rap on the door interrupted his mumbled litany of penance. Max smothered a groan. Gifford had probably returned, eager to finish off her bloodied prey.

"Go away. I'm through talking without a lawyer." Raising his head, he looked into the startled eyes of Keely O'Brien.

Chapter 11

Keely hesitated in the doorway. "We need to talk."

Max appraised her as though she were a fallen souffle. "I recall saying those exact words to you two days ago."

"That was before—"

"Before I was called a liar and shown the door."

"A woman could grow old waiting for an invitation to sit down." Keely headed for a chair. "You were right, we need each other's help. How about a general amnesty?"

She looked around. This was obviously Anna Marie's domain, decorated with exquisite taste around an antique cherrywood desk. Max had had recent company. The air reeked of smoke; a spill of ashes and cigarette butts marred the crystal plate sitting in front of Keely.

Moving the makeshift ashtray aside, she held up the newspaper she'd brought with her. "Have you read Flo's column?"

"Echoes of our last conversation persist." Max leafed through a calfskin appointment book. "Wednesday is the day I see clients. No time to chat or pour over the society page."

"You're alone." Keely waved a hand. "Where's your clamoring clients? Why did you just declare you were through talking without a lawyer?"

Max remained silent. Keely leaned forward and snatched the scheduling book before he could prevent it.

She turned to the current date. "Five appointments lined out. Cancellations?"

A muscle along Max's jaw twitched before he grudgingly unlocked his lips. "Did you come here to gloat?"

"Gloat? I knew you'd be free because after informing me my services were no longer required, Mrs. Whitney told me she'd canceled her appointment with Feast of Italy. Apparently she didn't want me to feel I was the only leper in the industry."

Keely tossed the book back to Max. "If we can't quash these damaging rumors, Anna Marie and I are likely to lose the businesses we've worked so hard to build."

"Quash away, but don't expect help from me. I've no desire to be run over again by the juggernaut of disaster." Max grabbed the plate and dumped its foul-smelling contents into the wastebasket. "I still have tread marks from the last time."

He spoke with such bitterness that Keely was taken aback. She said slowly, "But Monday you thought we could do something—"

"That was before I realized the futility of even trying." Max looked like a man whose beloved dog had just savaged him, but Keely didn't have the luxury of indulging male angst. "I came here to discuss 'Flo Knows' and what we can do to prevent her from printing these vicious innuendoes."

"Don't let me stop you." Propping his feet on the desk, Max started whistling, his gaze directed toward the ceiling.

Keely crumpled the paper. "I'm not buying this immature display of indifference!"

The whistling on the other side of the desk increased in volume. An Italian loafer shod foot jiggled with the beat and Keely curbed the impulse to give the foot a hard shove.

She raised her voice. "Poor, unfortunate Max. No one can tell you about hard times. Sitting behind a four thousand dollar desk and planning dinner parties—life sucks, doesn't it?"

The whistle cut off in mid-measure. He didn't move and

Keely was tempted to walk out, but she held her ground.

The rock spoke. "Per Anna Marie, nothing's more disgusting than overcooked asparagus or a man wallowing in self-pity." Max swung his feet off the desk. "The only part of my anatomy not yet nailed to the wall is my ears. I'm listening. What does dear Flo have to say?"

Keely bit her lip, wary of this sudden turn-around.

"Childish habits die hard." Max offered a crooked, apologetic grin. "I whistled whenever my sister Connie, bless her bossy heart, tried to lecture me—I often ended up getting punched in the pucker for my insolence. I beg your forgiveness."

Disarmed, Keely mumbled an acceptance, feeling as if he'd yanked the chair out from under her.

"Growing up, Connie and I used to square off at least once a day." Max smiled at a memory. "When she got married, I told her husband to watch out for her left jab. But enough about my past. Let's hear the bad news."

Oddly vulnerable, Keely smoothed the paper. She didn't need to consult the column; every spiteful word was engraved in flaming letters in her memory.

She cleared her throat. "Flo knows a certain photographer is ducking fallout from the latest matrimonial contretemps. This shutterbug's fame is spreading, but not in the way she'd hoped.

"Flo knows that lately the fantasy weddings the gal boasts of have had nightmare endings. Brides-to-be are taking note in increasing numbers. A whisper's reached Flo's ears that the biggest trout in Lake Hope recently slipped off this redhead's hook. Better fishing next time! You and your catering friend should take note of Emily Dickinson's definition of fame."

Max picked up the plate and polished the crystal with a

handkerchief. Keely caught herself wondering how it would feel to have those restless fingers caress her skin; an unexpected tingle of erotic desire spiralled through her. Max was too distracting.

"Trout? As in old trout?" Max stopped buffing. "Her prose has got the sharp edges of a junk yard. Who merits the unflattering description?"

"Amelia Hoover. Amelia also planned to utilize Feast of Italy's services." Keely studied Max's reaction as she lobbed the next question. "Did she cancel?"

A direct hit. The plate clattered to the desk. "Enough of this useless discussion. I've got work to do."

Shoving back his chair, Max rose and strode out.

"Neither one of us can afford wholesale cancellations!" Still clutching the newspaper, Keely followed. "By presenting a united front, we might pressure Flo to stop printing these vile insinuations—"

"I take it Feast of Italy is mentioned elsewhere in that libelous sewage Flo calls a column?" Max tossed the question over his shoulder without breaking stride.

"Last paragraph." Trotting to keep up, Keely quoted, "Flo knows that if there are any rats aboard the rapidly sinking ship of the area's most prominent caterer, they'd better don their wee life vests—"

Snarling, Max shoved open the swinging door at the end of the corridor and Keely was swept along in his wake into a kitchen the size of a small ballroom.

She momentarily forgot her mission in an awed study of her surroundings. Spotless tiles covered the floor, their oyster color repeated in the marble countertop of an enormous island. Stolid ranks of oak cupboards lining the walls were broken only by massive white appliances and the door frames of walk-in pantries. Keely counted at least a dozen burners and two confectionery ovens.

Max skirted the work station which paralleled the island and removed a clipboard from a wall hook. "Feast of Italy can survive a few cancellations."

"Reputation is everything in the wedding business and right now our name is *mud*," Keely informed him.

She started to drop the newspaper onto a nearby countertop and thought better of it. The marble surface looked as if someone had scoured it into sterility. "If Feast of Italy folds, you could always lease this room out as an operating theater."

She gestured at the countertops. "If cleanliness is next to godliness, caterers are half way to heaven."

"That may explain my aunt's god complex. I'm happy to say Anna Marie will soon resume the helm of the good ship Feast of Italy."

"Two days ago, you were the one who wasn't sure the ship would still be afloat." Keely kept the desperation from her voice with an effort.

Each cancellation hammered home the realization that, doubts about Max's veracity aside, Keely needed this man's help. Feast of Italy was a major player in the community and she needed to muster all available clout to battle Flo Netherton.

But she'd lost her audience. Her prospective ally was peering into a refrigerator and muttering something about nine dozen eggs. He made a note on the clipboard.

Although she resented talking to Max's back, Keely tried again. "I'm asking for your help. When we talked at the police station, you seemed—" she groped for the right word, "nice."

"Nice?" Outraged, Max replaced the lid on a glass container and swung around. "Nice?"

"I meant it as a compliment!"

"No more crushing word to the male ego has ever touched a woman's lips than the adjective 'nice.' Only a mother can get away with such an insult. Lady, you change opinions too fast for comfort. I'm nice. I'm a liar. Now I'm back to nice. It would be *nice*, if you made up your mind!"

Time to eat a little crow. "Anna Marie wouldn't have given you custody of her business if you weren't worthy of trust."

"She had no choice and, according to you, I've been fraternizing with the enemy." Max returned to his inventory. "You caught me red-handed with Flo, remember?"

"I decided after reading today's column that she wouldn't trash Feast of Italy so savagely if you were working together," Keely admitted. "I did see a man who looked just like you—"

"You saw black pants and a white shirt and jumped to the conclusion the guy was me. Could you swear to it?"

"I may have been mistaken in my identification."

"Now's a fine time to reach that conclusion." Max grunted. "After you've hung me out to dry for Gifford."

"I told Detective Gifford what I thought was the truth!"

"The truth hurts. Especially when it isn't true."

Keely thought about the note she'd found taped inside today's daily newspaper that warned, "Patience isn't my strong suit."

She said slowly, "There's another possible explanation for the mention of Feast of Italy in Flo's column."

"Which is?"

"She's trying to force you into some action."

Max uttered a sharp bark of laughter. "A man who's got nothing to lose can't be blackmailed."

"Nothing to lose? What about Anna Marie and Feast of Italy?"

His pen made a slashing mark. "I'm beginning to think

you were right when you said families were millstones. Sometimes those old ties don't just bind, they strangle."

"I don't care whether you were whispering in corners with Flo or not. My only concern is saving my business."

"Why are you wasting time talking to me?"

"Max, the robberies were well planned. Whoever's behind them knew the schedule of events, knew the security firm hired for the Westhaven wedding and substituted their own guard—"

Max jerked open a walk-in pantry to reveal rows of bulk herbs and spices. He checked containers, peering in before slapping lids back on. "Gifford's reached the same conclusion. What's your point?"

"They had an inside person with access to a timetable and other details. I want you to cash in Anna Marie's chips, call in every favor you can. Between us, we possess contacts throughout the local network. Someone, somewhere, knows about the robberies."

Max continued to check spice levels. "Allspice, cloves, black pepper—"

Keely's voice rose. "Are you going to take Flo's abuse lying down?"

"Do you expect me to dash to the newspaper office and challenge her to a duel? Salad forks at ten paces?" Max dropped the sarcastic tone. "During her recent visit, Detective Gifford suggested I'm the inside contact for the Sterling Ring. Please, just go. Allow me to wallow in solitary self-pity."

"I'm not leaving." Keely slipped between him and the open pantry, braced herself. "Not until I've got your promise to make a few telephone calls. United, we have a chance—divided, we perish. I won't let Key Shot die without a struggle!"

Max nodded at the newspaper clutched in Keely's hand.

"This fervent determination wasn't sparked by those lines in the Ripples. What happened?"

"I told you, I've got a business to save."

"Now who's dodging the issue?" Max's voice softened. "What brought you to my door bearing a dish of humble pie?"

Keely pleated the sheets of newsprint into accordion folds. Her shoulder brushed against the door. If she retreated another step, she'd be in the pantry. The scent of Max's Polo mingled with the tantalizing aroma of spices.

"You have expressive eyes, Keely." The gentle tone belonged to the Max she remembered from the police station. "Some renegade memory just bushwhacked you. Want to tell me about it?"

Keely avoided his intent gaze. Dazzling sunlight reflected off the polished faucets of the island sinks. *Be nice or be disagreeable, Max, just stop knocking me off balance!*

"Confession is good for the soul, Keely."

"Yesterday I met with the mothers of a bridal couple to get footage of selecting their dresses for the wedding. It's a good way to include the groom's family in the preparation segment of the video. I overheard a discussion in the dressing room."

"Go on." Max moved a step closer.

Keely focused on his shirt button, second from the top. "Marilyn's mother indicated concern that Marilyn had refused to hire another photographer. The groom's mother said, 'I wouldn't trust the O'Brien woman. There's never smoke without a fire, and she's been smack in the middle of two horrendous crimes. I give her a month and she'll be out of business and out of Lake Hope—' "

Keely crushed the newspaper into a ball. "Then she called for a saleswoman to remove a loose thread."

Max took the newspaper from Keely's unresisting hands.

"I opened the dressing cubicle and suggested she use her

sharp tongue to cut it." Keely smiled wryly at the memory of the ensuing uproar. "The only way for poor Marilyn to keep peace with her future mother-in-law was to fire me. I saved her the embarrassment and quit.

"It was humiliating." Keely clenched her fists. "I want to save my business, Max. I want my good name back."

"It's a sad irony that kingdoms can withstand armed invaders, but a reputation topples at a whisper." He took a step.

Although Max had trespassed past the border of Keely's personal comfort zone, she felt a tingle of excitement at his proximity.

"Flo described you as a red-head, but those waves look more like spun cinnamon." Max touched her hair with a reverent hand. "Maybe we could continue this discussion tonight over a privately catered dinner for two."

"You want something from me. I want something from you." Keely blushed at his knowing grin. "I'm talking business, Max, not pleasure. Will you make those calls?"

"You're a beautiful woman, Keely O'Brien." It was as if he hadn't heard her. His fingers sifted through the loose strands of her hair, his voice an intimate murmur. "I haven't had the perfect souffle dream since meeting you, Keely."

Keely suppressed the urge to kiss the lips whispering her name. Business, she told herself. Business only.

The clipboard clattered to the floor. Max stood with one hand hovering over Keely as if in benediction. His worshipful regard drew her gaze to his and suddenly she was drowning in a tide of sensual awareness.

Her back pressed against the wooden shelving of the pantry with Max mere inches away. She was a bird caught in a powerful updraft—soaring higher and higher. Unable, unwilling to escape.

Max's hand brushed her shoulder as he removed a container from the shelf behind her head. "I specialize in foods that provide a sensual delight to the palate. Eating becomes a spiritual experience, satisfying body and soul."

Keely stared, mesmerized by his voice which lingered honey sweet. Tracing the curve of Max's face with a fingertip, she gave him unspoken permission to take her in his arms.

Somewhere in the room, a refrigerator clicked on, a throaty hum which vibrated through the soles of Keely's feet. Dry-mouthed, she felt her muscles turning to liquefied chocolate. In another moment, she'd be reduced to a sweet, sticky puddle.

He fanned the flames by gently massaging the back of her neck. "A famous French chef told me that in cooking and lovemaking alike, the proper spice enhances the mundane and elevates the glorious to the sublime."

The scents of herbs and spices overwhelmed her overloaded senses. Brushing back her hair with tingling fingers, Keely was acutely aware of the slow slide of a bead of perspiration as it trickled between her breasts.

Keely's hands moved toward Max's chest, stroked the soft cotton of his shirt. Their lips were a scant inch apart when memory intruded, a vision of Max and Flo in a darkened corridor jarring Keely from her trance.

Echoes of shattered intimacy had reverberated in that passageway. The couple she'd glimpsed were involved on a dangerously deep level—what Keely had witnessed was no chance encounter.

She stiffened, pushing him away. "Do you treat all women like a dish to be devoured, Mr. Caterer? I'm proposing a business arrangement, nothing more."

The curt question dashed the desire from Max's eyes and he stepped back, releasing her. "No disrespect intended, Ms. O'Brien. A word of advice. If you can't stand the heat . . ."

"I won't invade your kitchen again," Keely promised. She still quivered inside. She had come so close to surrendering herself to someone she didn't know or trust.

Max watched her closely, his face intent. Attempting to maintain a distance between them, Keely shifted the conversation from the personal. "I refuse to allow that woman to intimidate me."

"Intimidate? Are you talking about Flo's column or has something else happened?"

An inner voice warned her not to disclose the existence of the notes. "I was alluding to the Dickinson reference."

Max hooked his thumb through his belt and leaned forward until his breath ruffled her hair. "How did Miss Dickinson of Amherst define fame?"

Keely sidled sideways, trying to shake off the invisible bands tying them together. *Mental note to self: avoid confined spaces containing Max in the future.*

He slammed the pantry door and leaned against it, arms crossed. "Dinner on for tonight?"

Keely inhaled, the scent of cinnamon was strong. She managed to keep her voice matter-of-fact. "I'm on my way to talk tough to Flo. Care to act as back-up?"

Max retrieved the clipboard from the floor. With a deft flick of his wrist, he returned it to its hook. "A warning, Keely. I don't play games in relationships—I'm strongly attracted to you. If we spend time together, I will act on that attraction."

"I'm not looking for complications at the moment."

"Then our relationship'll be strictly business." He grinned. "As long as that point's negotiable later."

Winona had been right, Keely decided, watching Max lock up the building. In his crisp blue shirt and charcoal gray jacket, he looked good enough to eat. Or at least nibble. Get a grip, girl. Your mission is to keep an eye on this guy, not admire him. Strictly business, remember?

Max shoved the key ring into his pocket. "You never told me Miss Emily's definition of fame."

"I looked up the quote. 'Fame is a fickle food upon a shifting plate.' The same description could be applied to men."

"Speaking as a man, I resent that." Max opened the driver's door for Keely with a flourish. "As I recall, whenever my plate shifts, it's usually a woman's hand doing the shaking."

Chapter 12

Keely's cell phone rang as she pulled out of the parking lot.

When she made no move to grab it off the dash, Max inquired politely, "Would you like me to answer that?"

"It's probably Ida with the latest cancellation update."

"It could be good news."

"Are you an optimist or a pessimist? Find a persona and stick to it, Max, you're confusing me."

"Pollyanna or Cassandra?" Max grabbed the phone and said in a piercing falsetto, "Ms. O'Brien's car, Pollyanna speaking."

"Idiot! What if it's a client?" She snatched the unit from his hand. "Keely O'Brien speaking."

"Where've you been? I called your office a dozen times!" The plaintive wail wiped the smile from Keely's face. "Sorry, Mom, I've been busy—"

"I need rescuing, baby! I can't stay in this place another minute. They treat me like a feebleminded child and the strongest drink they offer is lemonade."

"We'll talk later." Braking for a stoplight, Keely flipped on the left turn signal. While the engine idled, she shot a glance at Max, who appeared absorbed in the view. "I promise I'll call tonight."

"Tonight? When I've just told you I can't abide this hellhole another minute?"

"Please, Mom." Keely forced the words past a grapefruit-sized lump in her throat. "Things have been going so well. You've only got a few more weeks—"

"My roommate snores! Nobody can play a decent game of gin rummy and I miss all my friends." The tone turned wheedling. "Come on, darlin'. Get your sassy self over here and spring me from this stuffy ol' rat trap."

Be firm, Dr. Davis had advised Keely. The treatment period is usually rougher on the loved ones than the patient. Loved ones. The irony of that phrase had triggered a spasm of hysterical laughter which the doctor mistakenly attributed to Keely's grief over her mother's condition.

So tough love it was. "If you don't finish treatment, the judge said you'll have to do jail time for that last DUI. Which will it be?"

"Jail time?" Moira's laughter was bitter. "This place IS a prison. They won't let me drink or dance. Always asking me to strip my soul naked to a bunch of whining women, spill my guts on the griddle they call 'group.' Prison can't be worse than this clinic where you stuck me to be rid of me."

"Your choice, Mom. Think it over."

"I have thought it over. Come get me, Keely. I've got no money, no car—"

"I'll call you tonight."

"Ungrateful brat!" Moira's whiskey screech rose to fill the car. "I sacrificed my life after your noaccount father walked out. I worked two jobs so you'd have pretty dresses and food on the table. How can you abandon me like a wore out shoe? I've told people here about you, Keely. About how you pretend to be such a good person—!"

The swearing began. Vile accusations, tumbled on furious profanities, the voice rising to a howl of animal outrage.

Keely cut the connection. The car travelled two more blocks before the phone rang again. She pictured her mother standing in the corridor at a pay phone, her bitten lower lip quivering and her beautiful coppery hair disheveled.

She pressed her own lips together and took the next corner too sharply. During the conversation, she'd forgotten she wasn't alone. She felt humiliated and shamed.

If Max dared to answer that phone now, she'd shove him out of the car. If he said one word, she'd wail like a banshee. Her companion remained silent, his hands cupping his knees and his head averted.

The phone stopped demanding attention. Grateful for Max's unexpected diplomacy, Keely calmed, although her stomach felt as if someone had shredded it with a cheese grater. "Ignore her, Keely," the doctor often said. "She doesn't mean what she says. It's the addiction talking, not the heart."

But the words came out of her mother's mouth, in her mother's voice. Sometimes slurred, too often hateful. Keely would be paying off Moira's stay at this expensive detox clinic for years. Emotionally, the debt of her mother's grievances would never be canceled. Strange how every abusive utterance hurt just as much as it did when Keely was a child. She pressed harder on the accelerator.

Max stole a glance at the woman sitting rigid behind the wheel. Her breath came harshly, her cheeks reddened with emotion. Who could blame her? When Anna Marie berated Max, underneath the bluster beat a loving heart. Keely's mother sounded as flaky as coconut seviche.

The parking lot for the newspaper building was full, but on their second roaring circuit, a slot opened up when a Chevy backed out. Keely wrenched the wheel hard right and braked, slamming the vehicle into the narrow space with the violence of a round into a gun chamber.

"We're here." She switched off the engine.

Max, massaging the back of his abused neck, exhaled. Silence was the most judicious response to this curt announcement.

"My mother's an emotional pinwheel." Staring straight ahead, Keely gripped the wheel. As if, without her restraining hands, the car might lunge forward. "The slightest breeze makes her spin out of control."

Max shifted uncomfortably, at a loss for words. The women in his family wept and laughed with abandon, emotions displayed as openly as choice vegetables at a farmer's market. He was unfamiliar with a poker-faced reaction to verbal abuse.

He waited for his companion to climb out of the car, but she remained motionless. The reins of control were stretched so thin, the slightest pressure could snap them irrevocably.

"I'm sorry," Max offered.

Keely gulped. The outer layer of poise peeled back enough to reveal the wounded child huddled inside.

"It's okay to cry," he told her gently.

"Did you ever see an egg burst during the boiling process?" Keely sagged back against the seat and closed her eyes, lashes cobweb fine and dark against her fair skin. "Instead of hardening, the egg cracks open because it's too thin-skinned to withstand the heat—"

She covered her face with her hands. Listening to her choked sobs, Max wanted to stroke her hair, cradle her against his chest, and whisper comfort. However, she'd made it painfully clear that such intimacies were unwelcome. He waited patiently in silent sympathy until her muffled sobs quieted.

"I'm sorry." She dug a tissue from her purse, dabbed at her eyes and blew her nose. "I'm very sorry that you had to hear that."

"No apology necessary. Ready to beard the lioness in her den?"

Keely drew a quivering breath. "Let's go."

Max bounced on his toes, flexing his arms and expanding his chest. "You do the talking and I'll be your muscle."

Keely faced him over the roof of the car. "What exactly does that role entail?"

"I'll frown in a suitably menacing fashion and throw in an occasional Neanderthal grunt."

Keely offered him a watery smile. "Thanks, Max. Both the offer and the humor are appreciated."

As they entered the building, Max sighed. He'd agreed to come along to keep an eye on Keely, not to be drawn into the emotional turmoil hidden beneath her enticing exterior. Her analogy of the ruined egg haunted him.

Decorated in emerald accents and black lacquer furniture, the lobby possessed all the coziness of a snow bank. A vase of flowers on the reception desk attracted Keely's attention and she nudged Max.

"Nerine lilies," she whispered. "Ida says they symbolize majesty and power. I'll bet Flo chose them."

Max nodded. "This is your show. You do the talking."

The receptionist had a mop of vanilla yogurt curls and nails long enough to spear fish. Her smile bypassed Keely and stuck on Max. "May I help you, sir?"

Keely said crisply, "We're here to see Flo Netherton."

"Do you have an appointment?" Again, the question was addressed to Max.

He turned on the charm. "No. Does it matter?"

"She sees no one without an appointment." The young woman looked past Keely as though she were invisible. "Would you like to make an appointment, sir?"

"Ask Ms. Netherton if she can see Keely O'Brien and Max Summers, there's a good girl."

After further persuasion, she consented to contact Flo. "Yes, Ms. Netherton. I'll send them right in."

She pointed to the right. "You have five minutes. Corner suite, end of the hall."

Max paused before the door of a corner suite where a brass plaque the size of a bath mat read "Publisher." "Stay in the neutral corner till you hear the bell and come out fighting."

"My knees are shaking." Keely squared her shoulders. She knocked and they entered to find Flo enthroned behind a horse shoe-shaped black lacquer desk the size of a dining room table.

The publisher folded her hands on a green leather blotter and inclined her head. "I rather expected this visit."

Max glanced at Keely, expecting her to take the lead, but she remained mute, eyes enormous in her pale face.

Flo said coolly, "Is this fair? Two against one?"

Max had to admire her nerve. "We're here to discuss some of your recent columns."

"Reader interest. How flattering! One pours one's heart out on the printed page, but rarely hears from the public."

Max paused to let Keely jump in, but again she contributed only silence.

"Discussions are a waste of time." Flo's chin held the arrogant slant of a cat surveying an inferior. "My attorney assures me neither of you has grounds for a libel suit."

She swiveled to the side and crossed long, elegant legs with the whisper of silk stockings. Whatever her age, Flo was well preserved. Max decided the smartly styled black suit only proved that real class wasn't defined by the cut of one's clothing.

"Anything else? If not, you'll have to excuse me." With her sculpted features, milky skin and natural arrogance, Flo possessed a seductively dangerous quality. Max reminded himself that no matter how luscious the icing, the filling of this particular confection was pure poison.

Flo gave him a provocative smile as she toyed with the marble-sized pearls at her throat. "You should have come alone, Mr. Summers. Perhaps I might have accommodated you."

Anna Marie claimed you could catch more flies with honey than vinegar, although in actual practice, Max's aunt only used the sweetener in her cooking.

He returned her smile. "We'd like to appeal to your better nature—"

"I'm afraid you're making an unwarranted assumption, Mr. Summers." Silver-filigree Art Deco lamps framed the lovely picture she made seated behind the desk. An enormous ruby glittered on her right hand and a galaxy of diamond stars on her left.

Max reminded himself the subject of this exquisite portrait was bent on destroying Feast of Italy. "And that assumption is?"

"That I have a better nature, of course." Leaning back, Flo ran her fingers across the keys of her computer.

The languid gesture couldn't have been more evocative if the keyboard was on a baby grand and those were ivories Flo tickled. Each movement was calculated to create an effect.

"Care to guess my real nature, Mr. Summers?"

Max decided to take off the gloves. "When it comes to bad girl seductions, you don't hold a candle to Bette Davis."

Flo stiffened. He'd mocked her, the unforgivable sin. Her nails clattered on the keys and she exhaled in an angry hiss. Keely came to life and took a step toward the desk. "Why are you persecuting us?"

Removing a cigarette from an enamelled case, Flo thumbed a gold lighter. "Innuendos sell papers. Since I bought this rag, circulation has increased forty percent. I plan to double that."

"At whose expense?" Keely demanded passionately. "You don't care who you destroy, do you?"

"My source at City Hall tells me the mayor's pushing for an arrest. His Honor's pride, like his mother, took a beating. Amusing, don't you think?"

"You're disgusting." Keely lifted her hands in a baffled appeal to the heavens. "Mrs. Westhaven could have been killed!"

Flo's lips, startlingly red, pursed as she drew on the cigarette. "So?"

"So while you're selling papers, people get hurt and we lose clients. You're abusing the power of the press."

Atta girl! Max cheered silently.

Flo exhaled a stream of smoke. "In spite of his bad manners, Mr. Summers is just a sidebar to the main story. In your case, Ms. O'Brien, it's personal. When I'm through, you won't have a reputation or a business left."

Keely looked like a kitten who'd wandered into a strange backyard and found itself facing a pit bull. Max's instinct was to defend her, but she wouldn't thank him for intervening.

"What's the matter, Ms. O'Brien?" Flo's lip curled. "Run out of impertinent questions?"

Max's hand closed over Keely's. She squeezed back, as if she'd been handed a lifeline.

Despite her brave talk, from the moment they walked in, she'd been intimidated. Cowed by the decor, Flo's critical gaze, and the aura of power which even seemed to exude from the green velvet draperies.

Hearing Flo's vow to crush Key Shot had shaken Keely. "Why try to hurt me?"

"I asked for your cooperation and you refused." Flo turned her hard, bright gaze on Max. "Would you excuse us? We ladies have a private matter to discuss."

"Whatever you're going to say, you can do so in front—"

"It's okay, Max," Keely surprised herself by saying.

"Careful in the clinches," he muttered. "I've met piranhas with more appealing personalities." Max couldn't resist a parting shot. "Madam Publisher, if I found you unconscious, I would dial 911. But I'd dial it slowly, very slowly."

An ugly stain spread like an oil slick across Flo's creamy complexion. "You don't get it, Summers. Get on my hit list and in two months, no one will know Feast of Italy ever existed."

"I'm putting you on notice, lady. Try to destroy my aunt's business and I'll destroy you. I can guarantee you won't like my methods."

As the door closed behind Max, Flo strolled to the glossy wet bar which dominated one wall and poured an amber stream from a decanter into a tulip glass.

Sipping the liquor delicately, she eyed Keely over the gold rim of the glass. "We can still do business."

Keely had had enough of the woman's posturing. "Get to the point," she said through tight lips.

"I'll pay you a thousand dollars for the videotape."

The woman had a definite obsession. Or else she couldn't live without getting her own way. "A thousand dollars?"

"Sight unseen. I'll pay five thousand if you guarantee that I have the only copy of the videotape in existence." Flo tossed down the rest of her drink. "Deal?"

Keely wondered again why the tape was so important. "I don't have it to sell."

"Don't tell me you turned it over to the police because I'd know you'd be lying." Flo reached for the bottle of scotch and refilled the glass.

"I suppose you've a source at the police department." Keely decided on a new tack. "But you've got one thing wrong—there isn't any tape. I never turned on the camera."

Flo sipped the fresh drink. "I suggest you forget about ever running for public office. You can't lie convincingly. Get that tape to me by noon on Friday or suffer the consequences."

"What consequences? You'll ruin me? Turn up the heat? For a writer, your threats are rather unimaginative."

"I know some very unpleasant people." Flo's voice was matter-of-fact. "Choose to be difficult and you'll find there are more painful things than being flayed alive in the press."

Keely's skin crawled. She was looking into the face of an enemy.

"I think we understand each other." Flo blew a final cloud before stubbing out her cigarette in a jade bowl the same pale green as her eyes. "Friday. Noon."

"Compassion's an alien concept to you, isn't it? Someday, you'll be hurt the way you've hurt others." Keely's voice dripped with loathing. "I hope you're shown no mercy."

After the door closed behind her visitor, Flo clicked off the hidden recorder. She finished her drink and lit another filtertip before picking up the telephone.

She hummed until she heard a familiar voice. "Hello, lover. O'Brien and Summers just left. In my opinion, darling, you're better looking than Mr. Summers. His manners, however, are atrocious and you know how rudeness turns me on."

Wicked laughter on the line.

"I'm sure you're the best where it counts, babe," she reassured him and listened to his suggestive response.

"They want me to stop printing nasty things." Flo chuckled. "I gave O'Brien an ultimatum. She's scared stiff, lover. You'd have enjoyed watching her tremble in her cute little sandals. If she refuses to cooperate, pretend she's a toothpaste tube and squeeze the tape out of her. You'd like that, wouldn't you?"

Flo hung up, smiling. She'd unleashed her personal Hound of the Baskervilles but, unlike the fictional hound, her beast ran silent. The little bitch would never know it was on her track until it was too late.

Chapter 13

Max clutched at the arm rest as Keely's tires squealed around another corner.

"I've been replaying the scene in my mind." Keely seemed oblivious to the gouges Max's nails were inflicting in her upholstery. "Jackson could have watched me hide the tape. I concentrated on playing keep-away, not whether Flo and I had an audience."

Max tore his gaze from the surging speedometer. "You think this guy's going to admit he stole it?"

"That's why I'm taking you with me." Keely tossed him a whimsical grin. "You promised to supply the muscle, didn't you?"

"Brake lights ahead! I was speaking rhetorically. Anna Marie dictates that I save my hands for more delicate work—you don't really expect me to beat up this guy, do you?"

Max closed his eyes as Keely accelerated to pass a slower vehicle. He wondered if she got bonus points for leading each lap. Whatever the publisher had said to Keely in private had transformed his companion from a wee, cowering beastie into Boadicea, Queen of the ancient Britons, cracking a whip over her foam-flecked horses as her chariot thundered.

"Bluff him," Keely recommended crisply.

No longer sure what his question had been, Max nodded jerky agreement as a passing mailbox lunged like a striking snake. His foot was as heavy as the next guy's, he told himself. Only a sniveling, weak-kneed coward would ask a woman to slow down—

A garbage truck? Max peered through the windshield. Only Mario Andretti in his prime would dare to try to squeeze by that lumbering beast—

"Slow down!" he begged. "I, for one, want to live!"

The engine's roar moderated fractionally; he squinted through one eye at the blur of the passing landscape. "If it'll help, I'll beat Jackson to a pulp and arm wrestle the butler. Just tell me why this tape's so important to Madam Publisher."

Keely slammed her palms against the steering wheel. "If only I knew! She offered me money, Max. Five thousand dollars for an exclusive copy."

Keely slowed behind a string of cars, allowing Max to concentrate on something other than the odds of surviving the ride. "Then it's my guess she wants it for one of two reasons: either embarrass the Postwaites socially or else destroy proof of her tryst with this fellow you mistook for me."

"My money's on the former." A lock of Keely's hair blew across her mouth and she brushed it away impatiently. "Rose'll be devastated if copies of that tape get into circulation. The only thing worse than eye witness accounts would be to replay the invasion in living color. I'm sure the guests are already dining out on the story."

When Keely braked for a four-way stop sign, Max released his death grip on the arm rest. Their destination, Lakewood Estates, bordered on the rippling waters of Lake Hope, a scenic journey to the outskirts of town. Wild flowers filled the ditches. Glimpses of homes were infrequent, most of them sheltered from view by a heavy screen of trees.

"I keep remembering Flo's vindictive tone when she called Rose a drunk," Keely said reflectively. "She lives to embarrass the society mavens. If she got her muckraking hands on a videotape of those people making fools of themselves—"

"Count on my cooperation. But if you manage to retrieve the tape, Keely, you've also got a twenty-four karat dilemma."

She brushed the curl from her lips again. "What?"

"You can either turn the tape over to the police—thereby getting me off the hook as the mysterious man in the hallway if your camera work was good enough—or you exchange it for Flo's promise to quit sniping at Key Shot."

"But that would mean betraying Rose . . ." Max guessed from Keely's furrowed brow that this was the first time she'd considered the second option.

She drove without speaking for several miles. The wind rushing by cleared her head. Keely hadn't thought about the footage clearing Max and she felt unaccountably cheered by the prospect. But sacrifice Rose to save Key Shot? Never.

Assuming the role of her conscience, Max prodded, "Who are you going to get off your back, Keely? Gifford or Netherton?"

"I'll do the right thing," she retorted crisply.

"I'll be at your side to make sure you do."

Max must have a pretty low opinion of me, Keely reflected dismally, giving her companion a sidelong glance. For Rose's sake—and, unfortunately, for Key Shot's future—the videotape was a bargaining card she could never play.

But Max had planted the seed of self-doubt in fertile ground. In an effort to stop dwelling on the dilemma he'd suggested, Keely focused on discovering a way to protect Rose, cooperate with the police, and outmaneuver Flo at the same time.

A truce of meditative silence lasted until Keely stopped outside the massive security gates that protected Lakewood Estates from unauthorized intrusions. Several cars and a van were parked along the road. Men and women lounged against the vehicles.

118

Max said grimly, "Members of the esteemed fourth estate, no doubt."

Their arrival disturbed an anthill. Jean clad men emerged from the van, stirred into sluggish activity. One man shouldered a video camera; two power suited women pitched away their cigarettes and started towards Keely's car.

"Were either of you at the wedding?"

"Want to tell us what happened?"

"Did the bride get a plate of cake in her face? What tune was the band playing when it marched in?"

Ignoring the shouted questions, Keely removed a plastic card from her purse. Leaning out the window, she inserted the card into a slot in the gray metal box attached to a post. The box hummed and the gate split in half, each side pulling back into what appeared to be solid stone pillars. A man in an olive green uniform seated in the guard's box gave them a searching look as they drove through before returning to his paperback.

Keely checked the rear view mirror to ensure no one had slipped in behind them.

Max gave her an incredulous look. "A security card?"

"Clarence Postwaite didn't have a chance to demand it back." Keely tucked the card into her purse. "Rose gave this to me months ago. She thought it demeaning for me to be checked off on an approved list each time I visited the house."

"Does Detective Gifford know you've got it?"

"No." Keely bit her lip. "I didn't think to mention it since the card's never been out of my possession."

Most of the residences were invisible from the road, hidden behind barriers of trees or stately stone fences.

Max mused, "I wonder how extensively Gifford explored the question of how the thieves got in and out."

"Barring a helicopter and a boat, there's three ways to get

inside Lakewood Estates." Keely turned up the winding drive leading to the Postwaite mansion. "Security card, your name on the approved list, or by bribing the guard at the gate."

"You have a security card." Max frowned. "Did the Postwaites mention that interesting fact to Gifford?"

"Bite your tongue! The last thing I need is another nail hammered into my coffin."

As Keely waited with Max on the broad front steps, the delicate, creamy blossoms of the star jasmine flanking the entryway surrounded them with stereophonic scent. From the trees, a bird chirped a sleepy sounding greeting. Peace, luxury, and privacy that only money could buy—but for how long? Raising the brass door knocker shaped like an oak tree, Keely let it fall with a heavy thud.

The door swung open and the butler, a man clearly under siege, peered out. At the sight of the visitors, his eyebrows soared skyward. "Ms. O'Brien!"

Keely stepped forward with the confidence of a frequent guest and the butler retreated.

They faced each other on the gold flecked marble floor of the foyer where Max had served cheese and fruit less than a week earlier. The ghosts of gift-laden merrymakers seemed to hover around them.

Ives broke the awkward silence. "I feared you might be more of those horribly persistent hoodlums of the press." He mopped his brow. "They've tried sneaking in by canoe, in a furniture van—one even crawled over the wall but the guard caught him. All clamoring for 'colorful' quotes, the 'inside' story—"

Keely interrupted the litany of complaints. "I've phoned several times."

"Madam is indisposed and the Master is Not At Home."

Keely knew indisposed could either mean prostrate with

shock and humiliation or stinking drunk. An image of the press poised like a flock of vultures flashed into her mind. Poor Rose!

Ives stared at Max. "I thought by now you'd be in jail—" He broke off, flushing to the top of his balding head. Servants didn't have thoughts or opinions.

Max said calmly, "I don't believe that's any of your concern."

"No, sir. Of course not, sir." Ives was flustered and Keely wondered how he managed to hold his position. Weren't butlers supposed to present inscrutable facades and remain unperturbed during moments of crisis?

She asked, "Is Rose—Mrs. Postwaite—feeling up to a few minutes of company?"

Ives composed his face into a suitably somber expression. "I'm sorry, no."

Keely decided to go through the proper channels to interview the chauffeur. "Is Mr. Postwaite available?"

"He's Not At Home, Ma'am. I'm sorry."

"But this is very important!"

Ives shook his head, his eyes downcast. "I'm sorry, I have my orders."

Keely gave up. "Would you please bring me my equipment cases? I need my cameras."

The butler looked startled. "Your cameras?"

"My cameras! I can't work without equipment—"

"What's going on? Who are these people and what do they want? I warned you, Ives, no more talking to the press!"

Clarence Postwaite surged up the hall like a liner sailing into the harbor under full steam, his silvery mane of hair quivering in indignation. His eyes narrowed as he recognized Keely. "Ms. O'Brien! What are you doing here?"

Keely gave him her most pacifying smile. "May I have a

few moments of your time?"

"If you're here to collect the rest of your fee, you may talk to my lawyer, young woman. I'm not satisfied you're entirely blameless and, until I am, you'll not see another penny."

He switched his glare to Max. "You, sir, may take yourself off my property. This is a private residence. Members of the press aren't welcome—hold on, you're the caterer!"

"Yes." Max didn't flinch. "I'm here to collect a pan which was left behind in the confusion."

"Insolent puppy!" Clarence swelled visibly, his face turning an ominous shade of reddish purple.

His hands quivered at his sides; his mouth worked like a fish plucked from the water. Max gazed back, unintimidated by this display of truculence.

Wondering what Max was up to, Keely said hastily, "I also wanted to return my security card."

Deflected from his intended target, their reluctant host turned on Keely. "What's this? You have a security card?"

"My pan?" Max prompted.

Clarence shook his leonine head irritably, a noble beast plagued by a buzzing gnat. "Ives, take this fellow to the kitchen and give him his blasted pan. Don't let him out of your sight!"

Sending a significant wink in Keely's direction, Max fell in behind the butler. Uncertain of the meaning of the signal, she handed her card to Clarence. "Your wife gave me temporary use of this until after the wedding."

He said gruffly, "The Gifford woman asked me why your name wasn't on the list of approved visitors on Sunday."

Keely's heart sank. So much for keeping extraneous information from the police! "I've had the card for several months. Your wife entrusted me with it."

"Entrusted? Pah!"

"I had nothing to do with the invasion of your home, sir," Keely said quietly. "Be assured I will do anything in my power to protect your wife and daughter."

"Hmmph." Clarence flexed the card between his thick fingers. "Decent of you."

Encouraged, Keely asked, "How is Rose feeling? I've phoned several times, but wasn't allowed to speak to her."

Clarence's jaw tightened. "My wife's not taking calls."

Keely knew she had to step delicately. "I realize she's had many shocks, including the theft of the necklace—"

"The diamonds are unimportant!" His face sagged, a granite cliff crumbling. "She's taking this hard, very hard. Keeps saying Dorothea's special day was spoiled, that we're a laughingstock. She's not well."

Wondering if that meant Rose was drinking again, Keely said gently, "Please tell her that if she wants to call me, I have a shoulder to cry on. There are healthy ways of coping."

Their gazes met in mutual understanding. He sighed and looked down at his shoes, harsh-browed and sad. Keely had planned to ask his permission to question Jackson, but now was not the time to mention the existence of the missing videotape. With his wife's emotional well being at stake, Clarence wouldn't allow her access to the chauffeur.

Keely felt overwhelmed by the despair poisoning the atmosphere of this house. After sacrificing her own childhood to the god who dispensed oblivion in a bottle, she knew firsthand the damage alcohol did to relationships. She couldn't shake the inner vision of Rose huddled upstairs with a glass in her hand, her sweet face sodden with drink and despair.

With relief, she saw Max striding down the hallway towards her, Ives puffing along in his wake.

"Give Rose my best," Keely said brokenly and ran out the front door.

Max found his companion huddled behind the wheel of her convertible, the heels of her hands pressed to her eyes. "Bad news, Cinnamon." He swung into the passenger seat.

"I take it you couldn't find your pan?" She sniffed and gave the key, which was still in the ignition, a sharp twist.

"I didn't find it because I didn't leave one behind." Max hefted a battered sauce pan. "Fortunately, the cook wasn't in residence and I was able to 'identify' this as my favorite consommé pan by a nick in the handle."

Keely accelerated down the drive, remembering that she'd forgotten to press the matter of her equipment cases. Going back, however, would take more nerve than she possessed at the moment. That errand could wait until tomorrow.

She sighed. "I didn't have a chance to ask if I could talk to Jackson."

"I did."

Keely stepped on the brake, stopping the Mustang so abruptly that Max, who hadn't yet fastened his seat belt, nearly bumped his head on the windshield. "What did you say?"

"Why do you think I wanted to go to the kitchen? Not to lift some worthless pan which should have been retired years ago." Max tossed the maligned object into the back seat. "After Postwaite showed up, it seemed wise to isolate Ives before discussing his fellow employee. After a bit of prodding, I learned Ives instructed Jackson to deliver your equipment cases."

Keely felt sick at the thought of her lenses and cameras entrusted to the man's spiteful guardianship. "I called on both Monday and Tuesday. Ives assured me each time they'd be delivered and I didn't want to press too hard."

"There's more bad news." Max hesitated. "Jackson quit as of this morning. He left no forwarding address."

As Keely struggled to absorb this devastating blow, they neared the entrance to Lakewood Estates. The guard stood, preparing to trigger the mechanism which opened the gates.

"Hold it!" Max ordered. "I have a question for this guy."

The guard, a paunchy man in his late fifties, put down his Stephen King novel at Max's approach. "May I help you, sir?"

Keely's earlier use of the card had apparently impressed him, both as to their pedigree and their credentials. Max adopted his most supercilious tone. "After being harassed by that gaggle of reporters, I'm rather concerned about security. I understand that one of the residences was violated by the invasion of some rag-tag musical group."

"Yes, sir. There was a problem, but measures have been taken to correct it."

"You issue ID cards and maintain lists of approved visitors." Max gestured at the clipboard hanging on a hook inside the guard's box. "How did a band slip through your steel cordon," he gave the words a sarcastic inflection, "of security?"

"There was a wedding, sir. Lots of arrivals." The man's jowly face reddened. "But I only admitted those on my list, sir."

"You were on duty? Tough luck!" Max abandoned his sneer in favor of a buddy-to-buddy grin. "How many vehicles did it take to transport the band?"

The security guard eagerly seized the olive branch of interest. "Just one, sir. They arrived in this wheezing old bus painted red and gold and demanded entrance. I checked the list given to me that morning and they were on it."

Max glanced at Keely. "The band was on the list," he repeated hollowly. "The approved list—"

"Given to me by the Postwaites that morning." A vigorous

nod. "Police took my copy. Guess they didn't believe me 'til they saw it in black and white. 'Benjamin's Brass Marching Band,' that's what it said, both on the side of the bus and on the list."

"Thank you." Max walked toward the car. Another thought occurred to him. "When you said 'the Postwaites,' you didn't mean Clarence himself delivered the list of approved visitors, did you?"

"No, sir." The man sniggered as if he'd just heard a dirty joke. "Chauffeur always drops it off. A fellow—"

"By the name of Jackson," Max finished.

"Yeah. You know the guy?"

"Not yet." Max permitted himself a grim smile. "But I intend to make his acquaintance very soon."

Lying awake in the early morning hours, Keely gazed at her mother's painting of the dying rose and pondered the day's revelations. This was evolving into a bizarre game of "Who's Got the Tape?" Since Flo was still pushing to obtain the videotape, neither she nor her camera-shy friend from the hallway had it. Jackson must have seen her hide the tape and, in turn, hid it somewhere else. The burning question remained as to what he intended to do with his find.

Jackson had been in a unique position to tamper with the roll of approved visitors. Judging by his lack of loyalty to his employers, he was probably also susceptible to bribery. But the man had vanished, taking with him any leads to the thieves, leaving the Postwaites chauffeurless and Keely's equipment cases in limbo. Spread-eagled across the tangled sheets, Keely wondered what had happened to her carefully ordered existence. She had learned to catalog people, slot them into niches which could be sealed off the moment they became uncomfortable.

Only her mother had defied Keely's coping mechanism. Moira with her haggard face, loud voice, and boozy perfume managed to slop over the walls of her assigned cubicle, sloshing into the other compartments of her daughter's life with disastrous results.

Chilled, Keely shut the bedroom window. Outside, the trees tossed their heads in deference to the rising wind.

She leaned on the sill with both hands, gazing out across the moonlit yard. Although she carried insurance on her equipment, she hated the thought of buying new cameras.

Time for a reality check! Keely rebuked herself. Why bother replacing equipment? If you don't turn over the tape to Flo by Friday, you won't have any clients left to photograph.

The looming deadline reminded Keely of Max, the other loose cannon in her life. He was supposed to respect the boundaries she'd carefully staked out, remain in the section marked "business only." Instead, he boldly roamed over the borders into Keely's personal life whenever he pleased. That grin of his warmed her down to her toes. She wished he was here now, to melt the ice encasing her heart . . .

The bridal wreath hedge rippled in an endless, cyclical wave under the wind's lash. Only someone in a deep coma wouldn't be intrigued by the intense interest in Max's eyes, the body language telling her she was very important in his world at the moment.

How long had it been since Keely had surrendered control of her emotions? How many years since anyone had touched the vulnerable core deep inside?

Remembering the encounter in his kitchen, she pressed her hands against the hollow feeling in her abdomen. Max had talked of sustenance as a spiritual experience.

Keely bent her head, her shoulders rounded protectively.

Something precious had been lost in that moment of confrontation, thrown carelessly away without appreciation.

She stood beside the window, buffeted by conflicting desires and regrets. It wouldn't work. Any fool could see Max was tied to family and all her life Keely had struggled to cut the apron strings.

The phone rang. A glance at the illuminated dial of the clock told her it was nearly 2:00 a.m.

The caller had to be her mother. Wondering how Moira had managed to slip out of her room at this hour, Keely braced herself for a torrent of furious demands.

"See how easy it is?"

The blunt question caught her offguard. "Who is this?"

"A few unlucky incidents and a business goes down the toilet, Keely. But it might not be too late to salvage yours."

"What do you mean?" She felt the blood drain from her face. The muffled voice was obscene in its smugness, terrifying in its assurance of power.

"Give up the videotape. It's that simple. Don't forget that businesses die." A vile chuckle. "Just like people."

"Who is this?" Keely shouted, her fingers twisting the phone cord. "How dare you threaten me—"

She was yelling at a dial tone.

Chapter 14

Keely tossed the portable phone aside; it bounced on the seat cushion. "Cross Wedding Planners off our Christmas card list."

Ida gave Jemima Puddle-Duck's key a twist. Over the whimsical tinkle of the music, she said, "Tracee won't talk either?"

"According to her secretary, she's with a client, but I won't hold my breath waiting for a return call. It's a lonely feeling, like being sixteen and at a party where everyone's avoiding you. Today I've gotten more hang-ups than a heavy breather using speed dial."

Ida giggled. Outfitted in a scarlet pantsuit decorated with a colorful beadwork parrot, she touched the tiny red and gold parrots dangling from her ears. "I thought you and Mr. Summers were going to track down that chauffeur."

As she spoke, Ida checked proofs against a worksheet. The sight depressed Keely. Catch-up work, busy work. New appointments had dwindled to a trickle and cancellations continued.

Keely had given Ida an edited version of yesterday's unsuccessful trip to the Postwaite mansion. "Our free time didn't coincide. When I finish with the Deckers this afternoon, Max will be tied up in preparations for a private dinner. Neither of us can afford to antagonize the clientele we have left."

Ida clapped her hands together. "Excuse the change of subject, honey, but this is a fabulous shot! Wanda's veil looks like a cloud." Ida was on a first name basis with all brides.

129

Keely studied the proof held up for her inspection. "Yes, it's a lovely effect. I used the new light vignetter."

"Vignetters, diffusers, filters—I'll stick to a camera that takes instant pictures, thanks." Ida slid the proofs into an envelope-style folder. "This Jackson sounds like a slippery character. I'll bet he skipped because he's going to hold that videotape for ransom."

"Unfortunately for Rose, you may be right." Keely shuddered at the prospect of the chauffeur armed with the videotape. "But Detective Gifford and I aren't at the point where we freely exchange information. Neither are my friends. The list of people still talking to me would fit on the back of a business card."

Ida clucked her tongue. "You poor dear."

"They're scared, Ida. When they look at me, they see a gal being dragged out to sea by the undertow. They're afraid that if they get too close, I might pull them under with me."

"Spineless jellyfish!" Ida's cheeks flushed the crimson hue of the peonies she'd cut in Keely's yard this morning. Per Ida, the blooms symbolized determination and courage.

"I can't blame them. They have families to feed and bills to pay." Keely sighed. "But it hurts to look around and discover you're standing alone in front of the firing squad."

She stiffened in a dramatic pose, arms at her sides. "I'm blindfolded, I hear the guns being cocked. The debonair commander of the firing squad approaches. He says with a gruff, sexy French accent, 'You've 'ad your last meal and final cigarette. Any other requests, mademoiselle?' " Ida chuckled at Keely's theatrics. "You're muddling my head. Ocean undertows, firing squads—"

"Don't forget those rats leaving the sinking ship." Keely studied the bruise-dark shadows under her eyes in the full-length mirror hanging by the studio entrance. Not even an application of one-coat-covers-all paint could conceal these bags, she reflected. "Speaking of rats, if Margo calls and wants her job back, the answer is 'no.' "

Keely stifled a yawn. Her eyelids felt raw and scratchy and her jaw ached from grinding her teeth. She'd fallen into a troubled sleep at dawn, with muffled words echoing in her ears: "Businesses die. Just like people."

The voice had been eerily matter-of-fact. The reference to the tape had convinced Keely that both Flo's efforts to retrieve it and the robberies were somehow intertwined, their dark roots nourished by something more diabolic than simple greed.

Her dream following the call still haunted her. In it, Keely discovered all the petals had fallen off the rose in her mother's painting and scattered across the sheets of her bed. She stroked one, expecting to find velvety softness and touched the stickiness of blood. Shocked, she woke to find herself upright, gasping for breath.

"Are you going to hire a replacement for Margo?" Ida shuffled a stack of proofs.

Keely evaded the bird-like, beady gaze. "There's no hurry. I'll keep interviewing until I find someone we both like."

Ida nodded. Keely knew, however, she hadn't been fooled by Keely's assumed nonchalance. There was little sense in hiring anyone with Key Shot in mortal jeopardy.

Keely had decided to show Max the notes. Enough of flying solo—especially after finding another note taped inside the morning paper she'd retrieved before Ida's arrival. No longer relying on cliched threats, this message was frighteningly blunt: "Friday. Noon."

So far today's only bright spot was that Flo's next column wasn't due to appear until tomorrow. Keely toyed with the idea of calling Gifford, but decided in favor of maintaining the lowest possible profile. The notes were secure in plastic bags and if the tape didn't turn up by Friday morning, she'd hand everything over to the detective.

Unfortunately, Flo had been careful not to leave evidence tying her to the anonymous messages. I can accuse all I want, but it's still her word against mine, Keely thought grimly.

"Keely?" The parrots swung in disjointed rhythm as Ida leaned across the desk. "I'm worried. What are you going to do?"

"I'm going to meet Tracee and Elaine and Jean Decker at Mimi's Salon. Should be interesting. Jean, who dresses with the style sense of a cabbage, is picking out her wedding gown."

Keely pirouetted before the mirror to check the fit of her linen-weave slacks and tuxedo-style blouse. The upcoming session had her stomach in knots. How would the Deckers react? Embarrassed smiles or tense silences impossible to fill? With her equipment cases unaccounted for, Keely also had the handicap of relying on a back-up video which was bulkier and out-dated.

Poor me! Keely gave herself a mental shake. No whining or self-pity. "Ida, I've still got loyal clients and I'm going to fight to keep them."

"Honey, you've got the grit and gumption to do anything you set your mind to!" Ida's encouraging smile faded. "But getting folks to ignore that trash in the paper won't be easy."

Keely plucked a peony from the vase and tucked the stem through her belt. "If Flo keeps trying to destroy Key Shot, she'll find she's got a fight on her hands."

"Windsurfing on a turquoise sea. The glory of Athenry Gardens. Dunn's River Falls. Green Grotto. I envy you, Jean!" Mimi adjusted harlequin-style glasses encrusted with seed pearls. "Where are you staying? Port Antonio? Negril? Ocho Rios?"

"Montego Bay." Jean, dressed in upscale sloppy designer jeans and a loose pink shirt, tagged along in Mimi's wake, a plump baby swan behind its stately parent.

"Excellent choice! Don't forget to ride the Appleton Express—the view from those vintage diesel cars is breathtaking." Mimi never failed to applaud the proposed destination and always recommended something special, from a native dish of rum-soaked bananas to a craft shop which sold needlework handbags. Keely suspected that if a bride-to-be announced her upcoming trip to the moon, Mimi would suggest a visit to a certain crater.

Wading beside Keely through pearl white carpet deep enough to lose an egg was Jean's mother, a stylishly dressed woman with frosted hair and a discontented expression.

"I hope Mimi can work a miracle." Elaine Decker adopted a confidential murmur. "Jean's been mooning over the most inappropriate gowns in the bridal magazines—"

Tracee Dale had not shown up, phoning the excuse that a professional emergency had arisen. Keely suspected that either the wedding planner was avoiding her or else she'd decided to duck out on what promised to be a difficult session with the strong minded Ms. Decker.

Pausing just inside the viewing room, Jean fingered her engagement ring, an enormous pear-shaped diamond set in yellow gold. "It's going to be 'Romance in Jamaica,' Mimi. Do you have a dress to fit my theme?"

In reply, Mimi waved an imperious hand and mother and daughter took seats on fanback chairs upholstered in creamy velvet.

Keely studied her client with a critical eye, hoping the hairdresser Jean chose for the wedding would tame the young woman's curly brown hair without crushing its spirited bounce. Removing the video camera from its case, she inserted the tape marked "Decker-1" and checked the power supply.

Mimi surveyed the room, alert for a fold of silk drapery out of place or a wilted flower in the gorgeous arrangements set in alcoves. Apparently satisfied with her inspection, she rang a crystal bell. "Prepare to be dazzled!"

A model emerged from blush pink draperies, glided down a short runway and onto a heart-shaped dais. A rosy tinted baby spot flicked on, bathing the dress in an iridescent shimmer.

"The sweetheart neckline and fitted bodice of this first gown fairly breathes romance. At each shoulder, a pure white rose anchors an illusion watteau train which drops in a graceful fall. The fabric is silk-face satin, the gauntlets imported Belgium lace. I recommend this Juliette cap for a headpiece."

Mimi sounded as if she were narrating a PBS documentary. The dais slowly rotated 360 degrees, the model never losing her pensive princess expression.

Mrs. Decker smiled in relieved approval, but Jean twisted the hem of her shirt, picking at the fabric with unpolished nails. "It's too traditional!"

Mimi didn't miss a beat. The bell rang again, its high, pure note banishing the first model and summoning another.

"This portrait neckline will draw attention to your lovely shoulders, Jean. The empire waistline adds the illusion of height, the long pointed sleeves are figure flattering—"

"I was thinking of a dress more along these lines." Jean quit ragging her shirt tail to dig a folded piece of glossy paper from the hip pocket of her jeans.

Except for tightening her lips, Mimi's expression didn't

change as she studied the proffered page. "I can see why you admire this style, Jean, but we must ask ourselves whether the gown fits your theme. Jamaica is a place of beaches, bare feet, and suntans—not New York-style sophistication."

"Maybe I should wear a sarong instead." Jean giggled.

Her mother groaned under her breath.

"Let's look at this next gown," Mimi interposed smoothly. The first model reappeared, this time draped in ivory silk featuring leg-of-mutton sleeves and crystal rose beadwork. Lulled into a soporific state by Mimi's voice and the plush surroundings, Keely felt smothered, as though the four of them had been sealed inside the jewelled interior of a Faberge egg.

However, Flo's poison pen intruded even into this pastel palace. Mimi had been depressingly formal in her greeting. Keely was acutely conscious of the tension emanating from Elaine Decker, of the flash of doubt in her client's eyes.

One more incident would turn suspicion into conviction; even the most loyal clients would forfeit their deposits rather than risk association with someone capable of such betrayal. Key Shot wouldn't survive a third robbery or any more of Flo's innuendo-filled columns.

"Businesses die." The blunt phrase echoed in Keely's head, punctuating the civilized debate being conducted. Jean, too short and round for the hip-hugging sheath shown in the advertisement, refused to allow Mimi to steer her to a more becoming style. Elaine Decker, smoothing her linen lap, looked as if she were in dire need of an emergency root canal.

But who would want to destroy Key Shot? Pondering, Keely resigned herself that most of this footage would be unusable. Each model carried exquisite silk flowers—a single spray of trumpet lilies, masses of pink roses, an armful of brilliant yellow jonquils. One posed with a fan dripping with pearls and lavender ribbons while Mimi elicited details about the reception.

"—bank potted ferns around rented hibiscus trees." In her enthusiasm, Jean fairly bounced in her chair. "I'll carry a bouquet of hot pink bougainvillea. We'll serve spicy jerk chicken and rum punch and dance to the beat of a reggae band—even if I have to import one! The band, I mean. Not the chicken."

Forgetting her distrust, Mrs. Decker sent Keely an anguished look.

Jean shook her head vigorously. "Mimi, we're just not on the same wave length. I'm picturing shocking pink lilies and you're showing me baby's breath!"

Keely zoomed in on her client's eager smile. "I want a gown that simmers with the heat of the tropics. Think of me as a colorful parrot—not a cooing dove!"

For Keely, the enthusiastic spurt of words conjured up a vision of Jean bopping down the aisle with a sequinned macaw stitched across one satin shoulder. Ida's parrot earrings would add the perfect touch.

Mimi, with a shrug of despair, exchanged resigned glances with Elaine and rang the bell in sharp summons.

As the next model emerged, Jean gave a cry of delight and sprang to her feet. "I love it! Oh, Mimi, it's gorgeous!"

The gown featured a jewel neckline, bare shoulders, and lace gauntlets. Pearl-encrusted satin covered the bodice and outlined the model's non-existent hips before dropping to a froth of cascading ruffles at the knee. More ruffles rose to mid-thigh in the back and foamed outward into a chapel train.

"I'll be a mermaid rising from the sea and I'll tuck a hibiscus blossom behind my ear! Mimi, you're a genius!"

The salon owner rose, regally poised and slim in her

mauve silk pleated skirt and double breasted jacket. "We should take a closer look before we make up our minds."

Head high and shoulders back, she floated toward the dias. While the women examined the dress from all angles, Keely continued to operate the camera on automatic pilot, her mind toying with fanciful possibilities for Jean's formal portrait. Dramatic lighting, of course, and flowing composition. Props—perhaps a fisherman's net backdrop, studded with golden starfish and giant pearls. . . .

Who says you'll still be in business? an inner voice jeered. Businesses die. Just like people.

Keely gritted her teeth and moved closer, in time to record the compromise reached. Mimi agreed to sell Jean the gown provided she lost at least an inch off her hips before the first fitting.

Closing the camera case, Keely looked up to find Mimi watching her, the older woman's eyes inscrutable behind her ornate glasses. "Do you have a moment, Mimi? I need to talk to you."

Mimi hesitated. A woman wearing a dusty rose smock over a cream skirt arrived to usher Jean and Mrs. Decker from the room.

"Mimi, it's important."

"Very well. Five minutes. My office." She raised her voice. "I'll join you ladies shortly for tea." In an undertone to her assistant, she added, "Remove all iced cakes from the tea tray. Miss Jean's diet starts today."

Moments later Mimi, with a sigh of relief, sank down in the chair behind her battered walnut desk and kicked off her shoes. Removing her glasses, she rubbed her eyes and cursed high heels in both English and fluent French. Away from the flattering pink tinted bulbs, she looked every one of her sixty years.

Clients never saw this room. As usual, the closet-sized space was claustrophobically cluttered with swatches of silk, chiffon, faille, taffeta, and peau de soie in varying shades of pearl, platinum, ivory, eggshell, off-white, snow white, and cream. A headless dress form leaned drunkenly in the corner. Sketches of gown designs covered the walls from floor to ceiling; heaped up catalogs covered the only chair. Keely cleared them away and sat down while Mimi lit up a cigarette.

"Theme weddings, pah! These circuses will be the death of me if the cancer sticks don't get me first." She smoked fiercely, blowing out belligerent puffs. An air purifier hummed behind her in a vain effort to keep pace. "My next appointment's moving to Seattle after the wedding. I suppose I'll end up designing her a gown featuring a salmon outlined in brilliants!"

Tapping ash into a silver bowl filled with pearl headed pins, Mimi groused, "I'm a dinosaur. Girls don't honor tradition. They scorn gloves, proper etiquette. Formal, semi-formal—it's all the same to them."

She snorted. "Jean wants to look like a mermaid. Her mother calls me, begs me to 'hint' her precious lamb into something more suitable. But my hands are tied! You saw her, it was impossible to coax that silly girl into an appropriate dress—"

Definitely stalling. This from a woman who wouldn't hesitate to tell someone that her new rouge made her look like a fever victim. "Mimi, I'm not here to debate Jean's taste. If she wants to wear a fish tail, that's her prerogative. I'd rather discuss the robberies."

Mimi looked at her shrewdly and stubbed out the cigarette. "You're in the hot seat, aren't you?"

"I'm innocent, Mimi. A victim of circumstance."

"Anyone who says otherwise deserves to be seen in public

in those dreadful Spandex shorts." Mimi wound the narrow band of a tape measure plucked from the cluttered desktop around her wrist. "A shame I can't help you."

Keely recognized a stone wall when she ran into it. "Can't or won't?"

Mimi's gaze slid away. "I was horrified when I heard what happened to Tricia and Dorothea."

Keely leaned over to pick up a silk poppy lying near her shoe. She blew dust from its crinkled, white petals and tried for a casual note. "You supplied the wedding gowns, Mimi, and you've always got an ear to the ground. What's the gossip?"

Frowning, Mimi unwound the tape measure. "Fear's in the air. We thought our boat was too big to be rocked—and we suddenly realized the name of our ship's the *Titanic*."

"So far I'm the only one overboard," Keely pointed out. "The people responsible for the thefts have to be somehow connected to the industry. I'm trying to get a lead."

An exaggerated shrug. "I just dress the little darlings. I suggest you leave the sleuthing to the police. I hear that the Gifford woman's a regular bloodhound."

"The bloodhound's on my trail," Keely retorted. "My concern is to get her pointed in the right direction."

Mimi's answering smile was a nervous grimace. Digging a gilt compact from the middle drawer, she applied a fresh coat of lipstick in a shade that matched her suit. Her trademark pearl earrings were barely visible under the wings of her silvery hair.

She snapped the compact shut. "Keely, I suggest you wait out the storm and don't ask too many questions. I'm sorry I can't help you, but I'm too old to start over."

Keely caught the echo of fear behind the brisk dismissal. "Has someone threatened you?"

Mimi dropped the compact and lipstick into the drawer, slammed it shut, and got to her feet. "Sorry to cut this short, kiddo, but I can't keep the Deckers waiting. The joys of doing business! An hour wasted while Jean babbles about Tiki torches and I convince her she's got to lose at least three inches or she'll look like a ruffled sofa pillow in that gown."

Keely watched Mimi pop a breath mint and step into discarded shoes. "You're letting me down," she said softly. "I thought we were friends—"

"I can't help you. I have neither the time nor the inclination for fruitless speculations."

"Is it the prospect of negative publicity?" Keely's lips were stiff with frustration. Flo's malice had invaded the room and subverted Mimi's loyalty. "Are you afraid that if you help me—"

"The Deckers are waiting, Keely." Mimi sounded weary. "Your time's up."

Keely heard both finality and a chilling prophecy in the other woman's words. "If you hear anything that will help me—anything at all, please call." She reached out to touch Mimi's arm, but her friend stepped back.

The lines in Mimi's heavily made-up face were cruelly apparent as she gave Keely a bland smile of dismissal.

The ominous clouds of damaging publicity might intimidate Mimi into abandoning a colleague, but Keely sensed something even more sinister was responsible. She had the vision of roots of evil, thick and creeping, buried in darkness.

Her heart heavy, Keely left through the back door. As was her custom, she'd parked in the private lot behind the salon. Mimi's behavior convinced Keely she knew more than she was willing to tell. Perhaps Max might be able to charm something out of her—Mimi had a weakness for dark haired men who knew how to keep a relationship "cooking."

Keely checked her watch. Nearly 4:30. If she hurried, she might catch Max before he left Feast of Italy to cater his dinner.

Glancing up, she noticed a shape huddled beside her car. Keely stopped in mid-stride, her puzzled concern at the man's contorted posture changing to horror when she identified the object in his upraised hand as a meat cleaver.

Hearing her approach, he whirled, springing up from his crouched position and their eyes met. Keely recoiled, catching her heel in a crack in the pavement.

The man ran toward her. Keely screamed. Lifting the camera case, she held it before her like a shield, but instead of attacking, the man veered and ran past. Vaulting over the low redwood fence enclosing the parking lot, he disappeared into the alley, the sound of his running footsteps dying away.

One of Mimi's assistants poked her head out the back door. "I thought I heard someone yell. Are you okay?"

Too stunned to respond, Keely stumbled on unsteady legs toward her car. Both tires on the side facing her had been slashed. Spray painted words covered the vehicle's flank and she read them twice before comprehending the message.

" 'Next time—your face'?" The girl emerged from the building to hover beside Keely. "Ugh! How creepy!"

"Call the police," Keely said thickly, fighting for control. "Ask them to send Detective Gifford."

Glancing around the deserted lot, the girl shuddered. "You'd better wait inside in case whoever did this comes back."

Clutching her case, Keely followed, her mind whirling. She'd seen the man before, but he'd been dressed differently, in some type of uniform—

Keely leaned against the wall, her legs refusing to support

her. The man caught in the act of slashing her tires had four days earlier served her dinner on elegant Minton china. Doug, Max's surly waiter, moonlighted as a vandal.

Chapter 15

Keely's hands were still shaking when the law arrived. The officers responding to the call took their time inspecting the damaged car, their expressions carefully neutral.

"Do you have any enemies, lady?"

Keely's sight blurred until she seemed to be looking at her interrogator through a pane of smudged glass. This attack on her car was a follow-up to last night's phone call, a less than subtle reminder that the deadline for turning over the tape expired tomorrow. Friday. Noon.

A tape she didn't have and wasn't sure even existed.

The policeman tapped his pen on his notebook in an impatient tattoo. Keely hesitated. Things had gotten too complicated for a five minute explanation to someone unacquainted with the circumstances.

"Looks like you ticked somebody off, but good. Fight with your boyfriend?" Again, from the shorter cop. Stocky and muscular, even his ginger colored mustache seemed to bristle with aggression. His eyes were hidden behind mirrored sunglasses.

She shook her head, rejecting the question, and received a scowl of disbelief in return. "Lady, we see this kind of stuff every day and it's usually a domestic gone ballistic."

"Not this time," Keely said in a dull voice.

"Did you recognize the man wielding the cleaver?"

Tough question. If she said she knew him as Doug, surname unknown and last seen serving as a waiter for Feast of Italy Catering, Max was likely to get hauled in before he had a chance to explain. On the other hand, did he even deserve one?

Keely bit her lower lip in an agony of indecision. She'd already shoved Max into the spotlight by telling Gifford he was the man in the hallway. If Max wasn't involved in this latest incident, she suspected tossing him to the wolves a second time would put a definite strain on their relationship.

"Well, lady?"

Being called lady in a scornful tone, tempted Keely to be very unladylike. Any intention she had of cooperating died.

She spoke to the taller of the pair. "I asked for Detective Gifford. Do you know if she's available?"

The woman shrugged. Her tawny hair dragged back into a no-nonsense ponytail, she had the irritating habit of flicking her fingernails against the holster at her hip. "Special squad doesn't come out for damage to property complaints. If you want to see Detective Gifford, make an appointment or drop by the station."

Ginger Mustache planted himself in front of Keely. "You don't have a clue why anyone would slice your tires into rubber ribbons, huh, lady? Come on, who've you been fighting with?"

This was unbelievable! Keely chewed her already bitten lip. She, the victim, stood accused. A bitter ember of outrage glowed in her breast.

He moved closer, thrusting his face into Keely's until she backed up a step. "If you keep taking crap from this guy, the next time he might use that knife on your face."

"It was a meat cleaver," Keely corrected automatically. Whoever said, "Call a friend, call a cop" had never met this joker. Ginger Mustache was one policeman who could use a refresher course in sensitivity training.

"Officer—" She peered at his name badge. "Officer Jelke,

this is not the result of a domestic dispute. This is a blatant attempt at intimidation."

"Tell you what, lady. We'll fill out a report and tomorrow you can pick up a copy for your insurance company. Get some pictures, too. Insurance companies love pictures."

His sarcasm stung. Keely gestured toward the painted words. "I need to talk to Detective Gifford. This matter is rather complicated—"

"Complicated, huh? Guess you'd better talk to the special squad." Jelke put his fists on his hips. "The brass don't let us beat guys handle the *complicated* stuff."

The sneering emphasis told Keely he had taken her earlier request to go over his head as a personal rejection. Staring at her shredded tires, she felt sick to her stomach. The destruction had been confined to one side; the car tilted to rest on the rims of its passenger side wheels.

Both Jelke and his partner gazed at her, their mouths hard and unsympathetic.

Keely recognized a kindred anger to her own frustration with Mimi's unyielding silence. "All I have is a first name—Doug—and where he works. I don't know his motive, but I believe this is tied into another crime—"

"Hey, if I want to hear a good yarn, I'll head over to the library. Thursday's story time, ain't it, Andrews?" Jelke gave his partner a toothy grin.

Keely held out her hands, palm up. "I don't mean to seem uncooperative, but Detective Gifford and her partner are acquainted with the facts—"

"Okay. Until you two gals have your little chat," Jelke spat on the pavement, "we need some facts for our report. Come on, who trashed your car? Who's trying to 'intimidate' a nice girl like you? Gimme a name and I'll get off your back."

Provoked into rashness, Keely blurted, "Flo Netherton!"

Behind her, someone gasped. Jelke's gingery eyebrows shot up, but the reflective lenses shielding his eyes prevented Keely from reading his thoughts.

After a moment, he said, "Gal who owns the newspaper? I thought the vandal was a guy called Doug. Boyfriend, is he?"

"Doug slashed my tires, but he's never been a friend. I believe Flo hired him to intimidate me. It's confusing, but I suspect this is somehow tied into the Sterling Ring robberies—"

A hand closed on Keely's wrist and jerked her around. Mimi, her eyes bulging with horror, confronted her.

"Are you out of your mind?" The older woman kept her voice low. "How dare you accuse one of the most powerful women in the community of responsibility for this obscenity?"

"Mimi, listen—"

"No, you listen!" Mimi's hands shook. Keely couldn't tell if her overriding emotion was anger or fear. "I don't want to see you in Mimi's any more, do you hear? You're out of control—what's happening to you could happen to me! My salon could go up in flames and there wouldn't be even a sequin left in the ashes—"

"Who said that, Mimi? Who threatened you?" Keely grabbed the older woman's arms above the elbows. "Did you get a call in the night?"

"Let me go! I'm not supposed to talk to you!" Tears ran down Mimi's cheeks, plowing jagged furrows in the smooth make-up.

"You can't deny you're scared, Mimi. Flo's behind these threats. This time, she's gone too far. We've got to stick together!" Keely urged. "Unity's our only chance—"

Mimi jerked free. "I'm too old to take chances. Keep your cameras and your questions out of my salon!"

"Ever since that woman bought the newspaper, people

have been tiptoeing around, trying not to offend her, while she spews her poison. She's got to be stopped. If you won't help me, I'll do it alone!"

Mimi backed away. "Don't come inside. I'll call you a cab."

With a defeated sigh, Keely turned to discover that both cops had been attentive witnesses to the argument.

Jelke pointed his pen at her. "Since I didn't hear nothing 'simple' enough to fit into my report, I suggest you have that talk with Detective Gifford, lady. As soon as possible."

Keely massaged throbbing temples. Whatever had possessed her to shout Flo's name at this cop with his one-track mind? She didn't have a shred of evidence to connect Doug or the vandalism to the publisher.

But Doug worked for Max. Caterers used meat cleavers. Flo in a secretive conference with a man who looked like Max. Flo, the notes, that unidentifiable voice on the phone . . .

Max, she thought numbly. She would talk to Max, give him a chance to explain—

Suddenly, shock was swamped by a tidal wave of anger as Keely surveyed her damaged car. Explain? She wanted to see Max's face when she told him she'd caught the vandal in the act and recognized him as one of Feast of Italy's employees.

Doug's involvement was a powerful link in the up until now tenuous chain of evidence connecting the camera-shy "mystery" man in the hallway to Max Summers. Was Max a spy-in-the-camp, a Judas hand-in-glove with Flo? A traitor who pretended to be attracted to Keely while he monitored her movements?

She touched the soft petals of the peony still tucked in her belt and remembered her nightmare with a shudder. Peonies symbolized courage and determination.

Maybe she should have one tattooed on her ankle.

★ ★ ★ ★ ★

Max removed a pan of Oysters Rockefeller from the oven and smiled. Perfectly cooked, crinkling slightly around the edges. The faint whiff of garlic reminded him of that evening at the police station when he had asked Keely, "Do you dream of blue-eyed men whose fingertips smell of garlic?"

"That was, without a doubt, your corniest line," he muttered, transferring the oysters to a serving dish and heading for the dining room with his savory burden.

Returning to the kitchen, Max started water boiling in a saucepan and added succulent, new potatoes. Moving unhurriedly, he wiped mushroom caps with a damp cloth. After browning both sides of tender veal scallops dusted with flour, he lowered the heat and added lemon juice and Marsala wine. When the other skillet hissed a soft summons, he dumped in the mushrooms.

Max was in his element, his mind functioning as a timer on three different levels and the kitchen he'd seen only once before as familiar as if he'd prepared a thousand meals within its blue and white surroundings. He let his mind drift back to the happy hours spent in Bistro's overheated kitchen, the air replete with the scents of roast lamb, garlic, and tarte tatins, those delicious caramelized apple tarts cooling on wire racks around him. Max rolled up his shirt sleeves—working solo meant no dress code—and hummed a medley of Cole Porter songs.

He was vocalizing on "Where Is the Life That Late I Led" from the musical "Kiss Me, Kate" when the oil coated caps began dancing in the butter. Max tossed in a garlic clove and splashed in some Madeira. He shook the skillet, the potatoes were nearly tender enough to serve and the veal—

A sharp rap on the window. Max jerked his hand back involuntarily, yelping as a fine spray of oil coated his wrist.

When he dropped the pan on the burner, two mushrooms bounced out.

Mopping his arm with a towel, Max saw a woman peering in at him. Keely! Removing the skillet from the heat, he motioned her toward a door which led from the kitchen into a side yard.

Pulling back the bolt, he wrenched it open. "Has something else happened? What are you doing here?"

Keely stepped into the kitchen. "Max—"

"My potatoes!" Max dashed over to the stove and removed the saucepan from the heat.

"Can I help?"

"Drain the water, add a tablespoon of butter, and toss them together in the pot." Max busied himself in shaking the mushroom over the flame. "These will be done in a second and the veal is just about ready—"

Max almost forgot the pain of his injured wrist in the flurry of dishing up generous portions of potatoes and mushroom caps. After sprinkling chopped parsley over the potatoes, he dropped a sprig of thyme on each veal portion and arranged the plates on a serving salver.

"Don't go anywhere! I'll be right back."

He hurried from the room, his thoughts sizzling like the scallops. What was she doing here? Caught up in speculation, he took a wrong turn and found himself in the den. Retracing his steps, he was grateful Anna Marie wasn't here to share a few choice words on the subject of keeping one's mind on the job.

The Seetons didn't seem to notice Max as he deftly removed the oyster plates and served the main course. They only had eyes for each other. On Amy Seeton's finger, a ruby glowed blood-red in the candlelight.

"Snuggle Buns, I adore my ring," she murmured.

His face stoic, Max removed the bottle of Italian Pinot Chardonnay from the ice bucket and refilled the wine glasses before slipping from the room. If the atmosphere continued to heat up, the dessert he'd prepared would melt before they could get their spoons to their mouths.

Back in the kitchen, he found Keely gazing at the chaos littering the stove.

Reaching out, she touched a drop of spilled Madeira with her index finger. Brought the finger to her lips, tasted the sweet wine. "I had no idea your work required such split-second timing."

Max caught himself staring at her mouth. Turning away with brisk movements, he ran cold water over his stinging wrist. "Timing's one of my specialties. How did you find me?"

"I remembered the name from your scheduling book yesterday. The house was dark, but I saw the Feast of Italy van parked out front and followed the side path until I found the kitchen."

"The anniversary couple's dining by candlelight. Atmosphere's everything—a maxim picked up in the restaurant business." Shutting off the water, Max inspected the reddened area. Oil burns were one of the most painful hazards of his profession.

"You're hurt." Keely moved to his side, her hands gently cradling Max's arm as she examined the burn.

Staring down at her bent head, Max caught an elusive whiff of cinnamon. Or was it a sensory memory? Keely's hair, whisper soft, brushed his skin and the nape of Max's neck prickled. Overwhelmed with unexpected desire, he felt a flush of heat that had nothing to do with the stove or exertion. Whoa! Max cautioned himself. Business only. Remember?

He said with gruff nonchalance, "Part of the job. Now if

I'd been slicing vegetables and you startled me—"

At the word "slicing," Keely flinched and stepped back. Was it his imagination or had her face paled?

"What do you mean by that?" she demanded.

"Just some apparently ill-timed levity. No damage done—I've still got all my garlic scented fingers."

"Max, we need to talk."

Hearing an edge in her voice that hadn't been there yesterday, Max made a production of rolling down his sleeves. "Now why does that statement sound so familiar?"

Keely stroked the petals of a drooping crimson flower thrust through her belt. "This is serious, Max."

Charm wasn't working, time to switch tactics. "I've only got to finish the dessert. Although it doesn't appear the happy couple has an appetite for anything except each other."

To Max's surprise, Keely didn't follow up on her demand for a heart-to-heart. Picking up a sprig of thyme which had fallen to the floor, she twirled the greenery between her thumb and index finger. "You're doing both the cooking and the serving?"

Max couldn't help comparing the memory of Flo's studied attempts at arousal to Keely's more natural movements. "Don't tell the Seetons—who are paying a premium for my undivided attention—but I'm enjoying myself."

Max began to clear the stove top. "They didn't want a waiter, thought another person in the house might spoil the intimacy. I often performed both functions at Max's Bistro. As a chef, preparing a perfect dish of Poule au Pot or Canard au Chou Croquant wasn't enough. I enjoyed watching the patrons' faces when they tasted my specialties."

He sobered when he realized he'd lost his audience. "What's on your mind, Keely?"

She touched the flower as if it were a talisman. "Last night

I got a rather unpleasant phone call."

As Keely related the brief conversation, Max's fingers tightened on the handle of the skillet he was cleaning. When she finished, he said quietly, "Why didn't you call me?"

She wiped off the countertop with a damp cloth, face averted. "I wanted to tell you in person."

Not a satisfactory answer, but apparently it was all he was going to get. Keely seemed to expect he would grasp the subtle undertones of this conversation, but he remained clueless. This was a dance on a cliff's edge in the dark, where a misstep could send them hurtling into the void of misunderstanding.

Max stacked a second clean skillet on top of the first. "This missing tape must be worth more than we suspected. No one would go to all this trouble just to embarrass the Postwaites."

"Flo must be convinced there's something on it she can't afford to have anyone see." Keely scrubbed harder.

Max was no expert on body language, but his companion's jerky movements were eloquent of unbearable tension. "Am I to assume that the memory of last night's call preyed on your mind until you realized you had to either tell me or go mad? Is that why you tracked me down, Keely?"

"Not exactly." Her hand moved in smaller and smaller circles, her knuckles white above the blue cloth. "It wasn't the first threat. I also had a little car trouble this afternoon."

Max listened, aghast, as Keely described the notes she'd received and the incident in the parking lot, concluding, "If Flo meant the vandalism to intimidate me, she's succeeded."

She threw Max a challenging look which went right over his head. He understood that the vandalism was upsetting, but Keely seemed to expect more than sympathy from him.

Stalling for time, Max removed two tart shells and a bowl

of chocolate mousse from the refrigerator. He said over his shoulder, "If Flo's responsible for hiring the muscle, she's definitely missing a few sections from a full Sunday edition."

"Should I tell Detective Gifford everything?"

Keely sounded surprised. And very close. Max turned to find his companion at his elbow, her face flushed except for a colorless area around her compressed lips.

Max's fingers felt sausage thick as he fumbled to remove the lid from the bowl. "We're strictly amateur hour. Gifford's got leverage—perhaps she can pry some answers out of the Poison Pen Publisher. It's time for the professionals to take over."

Food scents affected Max's mood and the kitchen's atmosphere was redolent with garlic, wine, and succulent meat juices. Keely raised his inner temperature by her very proximity. Being in such close quarters gave Max some very unbusinesslike urges.

Concentrating on the image of a roll in a snow bank and not in the hay, Max spooned chilled mousse into tart shells in irregular dollops. Chocolate's a well known aphrodisiac, he recalled. Add rich liqueur, heavy cream . . .

Keely continued to knead the dish cloth between her fingers. Looking into her haunted eyes, he glimpsed fear and pain.

"Mimi was terrified, Max. She told me not to come back. No one else I called had time to talk to me, either. I thought some of these people were my friends—"

Keely broke off and Max slam-dunked another spoonful of mousse. Creamy, sensuously rich—he hoped Amy and Snuggle Buns choked on the blasted stuff. Dropping the spoon into the sink, he stalked to the refrigerator and yanked out another container.

Keely had made her position in their temporary alliance

unarguably clear but the vibrato of distress in her voice made Max want to break something, starting with the nose of the guy who'd carved up her tires. Some partner he'd turned out to be! Shaving chocolate into delicate scrolls while Keely was being terrorized.

"Flo will deny everything," he said brusquely. His fingers felt oddly detached from his body as they continued to arrange dark chocolate curls on the pale surface of the filled tarts. Black on white. Evil despoiling good.

Studying the abstract pattern he'd created, Max had a revelation. "That's why Flo wanted me out of her office when she made her offer for the tape—it'll be her word against yours!"

Keely began to pace, the low heels of her sandals clicking on the blue and white painted tiles. "We've got to get our hands on the tape before she does."

"Then we have to find Jackson," Max countered. "Gifford and her resources can accomplish that easier than we can." He stored the garnished desserts in the refrigerator as Keely made another restless circuit of the room. "There's something else bothering you, Keely. Talk to me, partner."

Outside, darkness had fallen. As Keely turned to face Max, the window behind her reflected a blurred image of the untidy kitchen, an uncanny, visual echo of his chaotic thoughts.

"I'd like you to explain something, Max, before I talk to Detective Gifford."

Here it came, the other shoe was about to drop. Keely's tone forewarned of bad news. Before Max's eyes, she changed into the doctor informing him that his dad had inoperable lung cancer, the banker refusing his loan application for a new restaurant, Lisa telling him that she'd filed for divorce—

He blinked and the phantoms from his past vanished.

Keely's hand clenched over the flower at her belt. "I recognized the man who slashed my tires, Max."

"I've been here since 5:30 and before that I was at Feast of Italy assembling supplies for tonight's meal. It wasn't me."

"I thought it only fair to warn you before I told Gifford."

Max didn't like the direction this conversation was taking. "Told Gifford what?"

Keely opened her hand; petals drifted down from the denuded stem in a noiseless, crimson rain. "At the Postwaite reception, you reprimanded one of your staff for a crooked tie."

Crooked tie. Max visualized Keely, graceful and chic in her black dress. They'd exchanged a few sentences, Max skillfully laying the groundwork for a late supper invitation. He'd asked Steve to fill in the rest of the cheese table. Crooked tie—

"Doug? He's fairly new and if he keeps up the sloppy work, he won't be around. But what does Doug have to do with—"

"He was the man with the cleaver."

"*Doug* slashed your tires? You tell Gifford that, she's going to tie me to this mess so tight I'll never get loose!"

Max clenched his fists, struggling with the impulse to slam them into the refrigerator. When Lisa and David stripped him of Max's Bistro, he'd fought briefly before surrendering. Folded like a gambler who'd lost his nerve.

Never again. He wasn't going to toss his cards on the table and slink away like a whipped dog. Max strode out of the kitchen.

The happy couple still held hands, the untouched food cooling on their plates. They looked up, startled, at Max's unceremonious entrance. "Dessert's in the refrigerator. I'll be back later to pack up. Happy anniversary."

When Max returned, he found Keely standing by the

window. Her apprehensive gaze flew toward his face.

"If your car's out of commission, how did you get here?"

She flinched at his harsh tone. "By cab. I've just called another one—"

"Cancel it. You're coming with me."

Keely retreated toward the stove, her gaze flickering over the skillets as if assessing their potential value as defensive weapons. "I'll scream if you come any closer."

"I'm not going to hurt you."

"Why should I go anywhere with you?"

Max folded his arms across his chest. "I don't have the leisure to supply character witnesses, so I'm asking you to trust me, at least for a few hours. I smell a frame-up, but this time I'm not going to wait meekly until I'm nailed to the wall."

Her anxious gaze raked his face. "Are you saying you had nothing to do with the phone call or the vandalism—"

"I'll swear to it. Keely, give me a chance to clear myself. Come with me to talk to Doug. I'll get answers from that slimy bastard if I have to use a garlic press on a sensitive part of his anatomy."

Flo Netherton studied her companion's broad shoulders as he walked ahead and tried to wipe the anger from her face. He couldn't help being an utter Philistine, an absolute brute. It was the nature of the beast and, she acknowledged ruefully, the essence of his appeal. She froze in mid-step, shocked by this revelation. All these years and she was still punishing Daddy for interfering—He turned to look at her. "Let me get this straight. You don't mind embarrassing these folks—robbing them, humiliating them, maybe knocking them 'round a bit, but I went too far?"

"Striking Mrs. Westhaven wasn't part of the plan!" Still shaken by her flash of insight, Flo lowered her voice. Mustn't let the neighbors hear. "She's old, frail, she could have died!"

"She walked in on me." His voice was little-boy sulky. "Shook her bony finger in my face. 'What do you think you're doing, young man?' I didn't hit her 'til she tried to grab my arm and then it was only a tap with that candlestick. Crushing her skull would have been as easy as cracking a walnut—"

"Never mind. You explained that," Flo cut in hastily.

She watched him force the door. He wasn't only an animal in bed, he was an animal, period. Complete with cunning, inexhaustible sex drive, and a complete lack of morals. Just the way she liked her men. Her nerve and intelligence matched up beautifully with brute strength and ruthlessness—

Erasing erotic memories of gymnastics performed on crimson silk sheets, Flo surveyed the room. "The videotape's got to be here. I want the notes back, too. I'm sure she saved them."

"What if the video isn't here? How far do you want me to go in squeezing it out of the O'Brien woman?"

Keely O'Brien's piquant face flashed into Flo's mind. The woman kowtowed to the rich, recorded on film the tasteless spectacles of their ceremonies. Daughters married off with the blessing of the church, sold like cattle according to bank balances, breeding lines, and social registers. The process nauseated Flo, bringing back devastating memories. She had been a similar sacrifice on a golden altar.

"Can I have fun with her if she won't cooperate?"

Flo said coldly, "I'll leave that to your discretion."

His gravelly chuckle caused her spine to tingle and she asked herself again, "What am I doing?" It was a far cry from tweaking pompous egos in print and despoiling a few pampered brides of their gifts to condoning the infliction of physical pain.

Time to crack the whip over her unruly beast man. "Babe,

I want you to stop collecting dirty money."

"What?" He looked incredulous, then angry. "You're telling me to forfeit the cash? Let 'em off the hook?"

"I won't be a part of a sordid criminal endeavor. This operation started out as a unique social protest—"

"Yeah." He stared at her, eyes narrowed. A chill tickled the nape of her neck, feathered down her spine. "You think I'm a dumb wind-up toy—point me in one direction and I'll keep trotting till I run down. No, Florrie, I've got ideas of my own. When you came up with this scheme, I saw a way to make easy money. A way to make the old man proud."

Sensing her control over him had slipped, she allowed a scornful smile to caress her lips. "Ideas? You delicious gutter-boy, any ideas in your head are ones I put there. You need me, Hard Body. Without me, you're nothing."

"Nothing?" Reaching out to stroke her cheek, her companion smiled at her involuntary recoil. "You forget I'm a quick learner. And what a good teacher you are."

Chapter 16

Long before they reached the address where Feast of Italy's records showed Doug lived, Max had changed his mind about letting Keely accompany him. The building's rundown condition provided the perfect excuse. Switching off the engine, he shifted to face her seated in the passenger seat.

"I don't think it's a good idea for both of us to confront Doug. Keep the doors locked while I'm gone."

Keely glanced at the trash littering the sidewalk. "I'm coming in with you."

"Keely—"

She faced him, her eyes dark and unreadable in the dimness of the interior. "You were so hot to prove your innocence, Max. What changed your mind?"

She lifted her hand to forestall his reply. "Do you want to talk to Doug alone to get your stories straight?"

"You have nothing to fear from me," Max began, but she shook her head.

"The other possibility is you've made an arbitrary decision that it's too dangerous for me. After six hours on my feet, I can outlast any bride on the dance floor with the handicap of a camera in my hands. I'm fully aware saving Key Shot may involve some physical risk."

"When we looked up the address, I had no way of knowing this place was a hatching ground for drug dealers." Max gestured toward the decaying building. "If Doug carved up your tires, he was probably high on something and I don't want you caught in the line of fire—"

"Doug had a chance to hurt me in the parking lot and he ran. I'm not afraid of Doug."

Max had no trouble recognizing mule-headedness. He'd grown up surrounded by stubborn women. Knowing his cause was hopeless, he made a final effort. "Doug may be a weasel and a coward, but even weasels bite when they're cornered."

"I'm coming in with you."

Shrugging, he opened the driver's side door and climbed out. Keely met him in front of the van, her hands thrust into the pockets of her slacks and her mouth set in a determined line.

Max held out the van keys and his cell phone. "Suit yourself. But if things get rough, I want you to make a run for it and call the police."

Their gazes locked. A breeze had sprung up; Keely's hair rippled like wind-stirred water. Brushing it back, she smiled again, this time without the edge, and accepted the keys and phone. "Sounds like a plan."

After a glance at the lobby, Max chose the stairs over the ancient elevator whose old-fashioned grill looked like a prison cell. According to the information on Doug's application, he lived on the third floor of this pleasure palace. The stairway stank of urine, alcohol, and mildew, its treads littered with cigarette butts that had had the life stomped out of them.

Keely didn't belong here. She appeared composed and elegant in her apricot blouse and coffee colored slacks. Only the disorder of reddish hair tumbled across her brow and the pinched look around her mouth betrayed her inner tension.

Outside the door of 303, Max paused. "Last chance," he said softly. "Say the word and I'll take you home."

Keely tucked her hair behind her ears in a nervous gesture;

tiny gold bell earrings gleamed in the dim light illuminating the narrow hallway.

She pitched her voice low, to match his. "Max, for the past week I've been pushed around. Pushed to my limit. I hate feeling helpless and scared. If confronting Doug is what it takes to get my courage back—to get my life back—"

She broke off and rapped on the door.

It was yanked open almost immediately and a scowling face appeared. "Beat it! I ain't in the mood to cruise tonight!"

Stepping back involuntarily, Keely realized by the look on Doug's face that his employer was the last person he expected to see. "What are you doing here?"

Without answering, Max shouldered his way inside. "Where's the cleaver?"

"What are you talking about?" Doug's gaze slid away from Max, only to meet Keely's stare. He swore, a trace of a drawl creeping in. "Treed like a lame possum! You recognized me."

"I'm looking for the cleaver that's missing from the racks at Feast of Italy, Doug. Where is it?"

"The one you used to slash my tires." Keely followed Max inside and closed the door. An unexpected wave of nausea rose in her throat; she choked it down. "Who hired you to trash my car?"

She could almost see the wheels turn in Doug's head as he divided his wary gaze between his uninvited guests. In his right hand, the waiter carried a gym bag. He was clad in the same dingy sweatshirt and faded jeans he'd worn earlier.

Keely's head throbbed. She braced her feet as her head spun and her limbs trembled.

It was the smell, she realized, that was making her feel ill. Familiar sour odors of unwashed laundry mingled with over-ripe garbage, stale beer, and long dead dreams. Cigarette smoke layered over musty, peeling wallpaper. Scents of a joyless life endured.

"Going somewhere?" Max demanded.

Doug shook his head, cast a betraying glance at the bag in his hand. The tension increased with each breath Keely drew and she pressed a hand against her stomach. The apartment's interior intensified the queasiness begun during her ascent up the fetid staircase.

"Alone, Doug?" Max's gaze flickered around the squalid room. "No roommates?"

"You kiddin'? Place ain't big enough to keep a goldfish." Doug decided to go with a placating grin. "Hey, I think there's been some kind of misunderstanding, buddy. A mistake."

"Yeah." Max wasn't smiling. "And you made it, buddy, when you got close enough for Keely to recognize you."

Doug retreated a step, his smile collapsing into sullenness. "You're crazy, bustin' in here, accusing me like I'm some kind of criminal—"

"A meat cleaver's missing from Feast of Italy. You were seen by Keely's car with one in your hand. How much is Flo paying you?"

Doug shook his head, his glance darting around the room as if searching for an escape avenue. "Don't know any broad by that name. Now, get outta of my apartment before I call the cops!"

"Call them, Doug. Ask for Detective Gayla Gifford." Max's voice was smooth, but the menace was there, under the quiet tone. "She wants to ask you a few questions."

Doug's prominent Adam's apple bobbed. "I don't have to talk to nobody if I don't want to. Now, get out of my place!"

"Not until I'm convinced you're not hiding a cleaver with the name 'Feast of Italy' engraved in the handle. Police need search warrants, caterers don't."

Doug was about the same height as Max, but Max had the advantage of a muscular build and grim determination. The two faced off until the waiter backed away, rubbing his hand over his mouth to smooth away the nervous twitch of his lip.

Without taking his eyes from Doug, Max gestured toward a wooden baseball bat propped in the corner. "Like to hit, do you, Doug? Nothing like smashing a few balls, is there?"

Clutching the gym bag, Doug made a guttural noise of protest when Max grabbed the bat and sauntered over to study an old poster which held a place of honor over the television set. Madonna, posed in black lingerie, smiled down at him. Casually, Max hefted the bat and took a practice swing.

"Hey, man, cool down. We can talk—"

Max cocked the bat over his shoulder. "Got something to tell me, Doug? If not, I've thought of a great way to relieve tension. I feel really stressed out. What with a valuable piece of my kitchen equipment missing—"

Doug cursed again, but in resignation rather than anger, confirming Keely's opinion of him as a coward. His aggression seeped away like air from a leaky balloon. "I'm begging you, man, don't bust up the place. I only did what I was told."

"Now we're getting somewhere." Max's voice remained deceptively soft, his body tensed like a batter awaiting a delivery from a fastballer. "Who told you? I need a name. Now!"

Doug rubbed his left palm down the thigh of his jeans. "I dunno. He was just a voice on the telephone."

"And what did this 'voice' command you to do?" Max stalked closer, backing Doug up against a sagging arm chair. "How did you locate Keely at Mimi's?"

"I followed her from her studio. That lot was fenced off, private—a good place to do the job. The guy told me to slash her tires and leave that message."

Doug hadn't taken his eyes off the bat in Max's hands. His grin was a mirthless reflex in a lifetime of fruitless placation. "The spray paintin' was easy, but didja ever try to slice up a steel-belted radial? I kept hacking away, sweatin' bullets in case some ladies walked out of that fancy store . . ."

Keely was in no mood to sympathize with the hardships of a vandal. "How much did he pay you? You didn't agree to harass me for the fun of it."

Max lowered the bat, allowing Doug to recover some of his equilibrium and his surly look.

He smirked at Keely. "Butt out, pretty lady. You oughtta be grateful I didn't—"

Before he finished the sentence, Max was on him. Dropping the bat, he grabbed Doug by the shirt front and slammed him against the wall. The gym bag slipped from the waiter's grasp and thudded to the floor.

"Watch it!" Max gritted through clenched teeth. "Tell the pretty lady what she wants to know. Or I'll do something about that bad attitude of yours, starting with your mouth."

Doug let out a sound mid-way between a yelp and an oath, his hands tugging fruitlessly at Max's wrists. His expression changed from fear to anger. He spat in Max's face, triggering an explosion of the latent violence that had been building since they'd entered the room.

The two men lurched away from the wall in a primitive, savage dance, the only sounds harsh breathing, grunts, and thudding feet as they grappled. Max brought his knee up with brutal intent. Doug yelped and bent double, clutching at himself, before falling to the floor.

Keely cried out in unison with Doug. She'd felt oddly detached, distracted by her own weakness, but Max's merciless blow had forced her to face the harsh reality of their combat.

Max's face was implacable. He kicked the bat out of

Doug's flailing reach and it rolled to Keely's feet. While the other man moaned and twitched, Max made a quick tour of the apartment, glancing into other rooms.

"Place's a regular sty." Max looked down at Doug who, mewling softly, struggled to a sitting position. "Convinced I mean business? I've taken exception to the threat you painted on Ms. O'Brien's car. I assaulted you in front of a witness. Care to swear out a complaint against me?"

Doug shook his head, a hank of hair straggling across his eyes. In a voice rusty with pain, he muttered, "No cops."

Max had the same ruthless, dangerous air as Mel Gibson's Mad Max. Evidently, Doug thought so, too. He pulled his knees to his chest and ducked his head.

"Come on, jerk face! Answer me." Max grabbed his shirt front and hoisted him to his feet. "Who paid you? How much?"

Breathing hard, Doug blurted, "Two hundred bucks."

"You value yourself cheap. Method of payment?"

"Cash. Half in an envelope shoved under my door, the other half after the job. But I didn't do it for the money. He had something on me, man. I had to cooperate!"

"What did he have on you?"

Doug shook his head and was promptly thumped back against the wall. Dust and bits of plaster rained down from the ceiling to whiten his bony shoulders.

"Wrong answer!"

"Nothing important, man. Nothing, I swear—"

Max twisted Doug's shirtfront until he made a choking sound. Keely impulsively started forward with the half formed intention of intervening, but Max turned his head and gave her a look that stopped her in her tracks.

He turned back to Doug. "I'm losing patience. I don't want to beat the truth out of you, but believe me, I will!"

Doug's lips twisted into a feeble sneer. "Go ahead. I've been black and blue more times than I can remember. You ain't got the guts to kill me, but the dude on the phone does. His voice was deader than a graveyard—gave me a creeping chill."

Keely's heartbeat quickened. Doug wasn't the imaginative type given to dramatics. His caller had to be the same person who'd phoned her last night. She shared his instinctive terror of betraying the man with the cold, deadly voice.

"Businesses die. Just like people."

Like Doug, Keely had been helpless to fight back, powerless to escape. The words smeared on her car in blood red letters, "Next time—your face" danced before her eyes.

Keely was fed up with being a victim, of being an onlooker while others fought her battles. Almost in a trance, she felt a smooth, wooden shaft in her hands and realized she'd picked up the baseball bat.

Doug noticed the object in her hands and managed a mocking laugh bordering on hysteria. "Go ahead, lady. Take your best shot at me! This just ain't my day."

It was as though someone else had taken control of Keely's body. Her feet moved across the shabby rug until she found herself standing in front of the television set. Madonna looked down with a pouting smile, her mouth ripe with promises.

Keely wanted to run, to escape the smells of cigarette smoke and rotting food, of stale sweat and spilled beer. Pungent odors pricked her soul. The air was thick with the residue of violence, the familiar stench of poverty and wretchedness, of terror and despair.

From a distance, she heard Max's voice. "Keely?" She hated Doug for living in squalor, hated Max for bringing her here. The bat felt solid in her hands. Powerful. The fire kindled by Flo's taunts and fed by threats, vandalism, and

Keely's bitter sense of helplessness erupted. A pulsing band encircled her temples; black spots danced before her eyes.

Her muscles tensed. Again, Max's voice—the words fading to an indistinct buzz in her ears. Called from its grave by sensory stimulation, a buried memory rose to possess her.

A man's hand, thick knuckles covered with curly, black hair, reached toward Keely. She whimpered. No retreat. Her back's against the wall. Her heart's jumping into her throat, her hands clutch the neckline of her nightie in a futile, protective gesture.

A distant female voice, sweet and slurred by liquor, crooned the chorus of "My Wild Irish Rose".

"Mama!"

Keely trembled like a leaf in the wind, her knees knocking together below the ragged hem of her nightie. Her favorite. The one with pink kittens prancing around the hemline.

The man whispered, his breath thick with whiskey and onions. "I didn't know Moira was hiding such a little sweetheart! Don't be scared. You'll like it when I touch you, baby. You're gonna be just like your momma some day."

Keely loathed the rasp of his sweaty hands over her skin, the stench of his foul breath washing her face. But, most of all, she hated his terrible prophecy of her future.

Keely wanted to scream, to smash his lumpy potato nose with her fists, but she stood paralyzed. She called to her mother, but the warble from the bathroom continued unabated and the cheeping cry stuck in her throat—

The shattering sound of broken glass jolted her back to the present. Keely gaped in shock at the broken television screen before her.

She pivoted, the bat dangling loosely between her tingling palms. Shaken, she opened her mouth to apologize, but Doug spoke first.

"You broke my TV!" Rivers of sweat poured down his fearful face. He appealed to Max. "Did ya see that? She's nuts!"

Max looked equally stunned. Keeping a wary eye on Doug, he approached Keely with caution. His gaze traveled from the busted television to her face in disbelief.

Keely's mouth trembled, she felt tears pressing like a migraine behind her eyes.

"Keely." That was all Max said, just her name, but shared pain reverberated in each syllable. He held out his hand.

God, what was wrong with her? It was an appeal to the heavens. She'd been punished for priding herself on her mental toughness by losing control.

She crumbled. Tears poured down her face. Clutching the bat, she bent her head and wept.

Max whirled and jabbed his fist into Doug's rib cage. The man yipped in startled protest.

"Go ahead and holler, Doug." Max felt no pity, only cold rage. "Women and kids get beat up in rat holes like this and no one ever answers their screams. Keely's in danger and you know who's responsible. How did the voice on the phone force you to cooperate? What did he have on you? Drugs?"

"Back off! Don't hit me again!" Doug panted like an overexcited puppy. "I ain't a pill freak or a peddler—and I don't got the habit. Cocaine's for losers."

He stopped, his gaze sweeping over the room. "Losers with a sight more bucks than I've got. You gotta understand, the dude knew about the wallets I took at the wedding—even though I dropped 'em when the calvary—I mean, cops— came. He threatened to flip on me, tell them I did the liftin'."

So Doug had been the pickpocket at the Postwaite wedding! Max heard Keely gasp as the import of Doug's confession sank in.

The waiter was still babbling. "I'll tell you everything if you let me get a head start on the dude who hired me. I'll blow town tonight, I promise. Just don't let your old lady near me with that bat. She's freakin' crazy!"

"What happened?"

"I lifted a couple leathers when the band marched in. When I heard sirens, I unloaded 'em. Since I was wearing them stupid white gloves, I didn't leave no prints, but the man says he's got a witness who'll swear to the cops I was the thief. Markin' her car wasn't personal—I'm not an enforcer."

Max released him. "Why did you take the cleaver from Feast of Italy?"

A shrug. "He suggested I use somethin' from your place."

Realizing Doug was telling the truth, Max swallowed his frustration. They were no closer to uncovering the identity of the man who was terrorizing Keely. If Flo was involved in this ugliness, she'd covered her back trail well.

"Can you remember anything that would help me identify the man who ordered the vandalism?"

Doug shrugged and massaged his ribs, his mouth pouting. "Naw. He was a voice. I ain't got the second installment but I figured she," he gave Keely a bitter look, "recognized me in the parking lot. I was on my way out the door—in case she fingered me to the cops, when you two showed up."

"Where's the cleaver?"

Doug wiped his brow with the sleeve of his sweat shirt. "In a trash barrel along with the can of spray paint."

"Let's take a little trip, Doug."

"A trip?" Doug looked blank and then his eyes widened. "You mean a ride, don't you? No, thanks. No, thanks, man."

"This ride isn't going to end with you in cement overshoes." Max jerked his chin toward the front door. "Show us which trash barrel. Then we'll stop at the police station for a chat with Detectives Gifford and Dawson."

"I've got priors, man! That black woman's a barracuda and her partner eats guys like me for breakfast. I talked to them, remember?" Doug touched his throat as if to reassure himself his flesh was clear of teeth marks. "Hey, you agreed to let me go!"

"How did you get Anna Marie to hire you?" Max was genuinely curious. His aunt's screening standards were more stringent than those of the FBI.

"Told her I worked in my family's restaurant in Alabama. Got my mom to front for me when your aunt checked my references. I didn't plan on rippin' anyone off. But I couldn't resist the opportunity of lifting a few fat wallets."

He looked wistfully at the door, gauging his chances for escape, before lifting his hands in surrender. "Okay, you've got me. I wanna get this behind me. Let me grab my smokes and I'll be right with you."

Doug bent over the gym bag. Max, fearing his prisoner might be going for a concealed weapon, lunged. But instead of unzipping the bag, Doug simply swung it up from the floor, catching Max square in the forehead. His skull seemed to explode and he went down like a felled tree.

Fireworks pinwheeled before his eyes; his head rang like a church bell. Determined fingers pried open his right eyelid. Groaning, Max winced from the intrusion of light. Although the fingers persisted, he squeezed his eye shut again.

"If you don't wake up, I'm calling an ambulance!"

The voice pierced the fog in Max's brain. He opened his eyes and squinted into Keely's blurred face.

"Get the license number of that truck?" he muttered.

"Were you completely out?"

"You mean did I hear tweeting birds and see stars? I— wait! Where's that creep, Doug?" Max pushed himself to a sitting position and promptly toppled forward, his face mashed between Keely's breasts.

She neither squealed nor wriggled, simply shifted the position of his throbbing head until he could breathe. Her hands cradled him with the soothing expertise of a mother comforting an injured child. "A bit dizzy, are we?"

Max gritted his teeth. "Where's Doug?" he rasped into the fabric of her blouse. "Scumbucket blind-sided me with an anvil—"

"I wish I knew more about concussions." Keely maneuvered Max until he was propped in a sitting position against the overstuffed arm chair. "After you dropped like a lead balloon, Doug went out through the bedroom window and down the fire escape."

Max was swamped by another wave of nausea. Both the chair he was leaning against and the carpet beneath him stank of dust and mildew. When he was certain he wasn't going to upchuck, he muttered, "You could have tried to stop him. Mark McGuire couldn't have handled that bat better than you did earlier."

"Doug's opinion aside, I'm not freakin' crazy. My destructive outbursts are limited to objects that can't fight back." Keely leaned over to peer intently into Max's eyes.

Her hair swung forward, brushing his cheek. He suppressed the crazy desire to bury his face in the silken strands. "If you're looking for answers, I'm fresh out."

"There are no answers."

Keely's voice and eyes were so bleak that Max reached out instinctively to touch her. She caught his hand in both of hers, held on to him like a drowning woman. Their faces were so close Max fantasized that if Keely shut her eyes, he would feel the feathery whisper of her lashes across his skin.

Max wanted to reassure her, but he remained tongue-tied.

Then Keely's mantle of vulnerability slipped from her shoulders as suddenly as it had appeared.

When she spoke, it was in the detached voice of a nurse explaining a procedure to a patient. "You've got a lump the size of a golf ball on your forehead. Fortunately, your pupils are the same size. I'm not sure what I'm supposed to do if they're not."

Utterly drained, Max raised a heavy hand to touch the side of his throbbing head. By some miracle, his skull didn't explode. "How could socks and underwear feel like a ton of bricks?" he asked weakly, gesturing at the gym bag.

Max winced as the sound of a zipper assaulted his battered brain, but Keely, investigating the bag's contents, ignored his groan of protest.

Max's stomach started hip-hopping to some internal rap music. This was the worst headache he'd had since Paris. As he recalled, he and Paul had talked about life that night. Life and food and love as black-garbed waitresses served up generous portions of salt pork with lentils and tangy Tarte au Citron. Surrounded by students, professors from the Sorbonne, artists, models, and young lovers, they ended up toasting with champagne the plans for the soon-to-be started Max's Bistro and Max's upcoming marriage to Lisa.

Closing his eyes, Max escaped the painful present by sinking into the cotton batting of memories until cool fingers touched his cheek. Dazed, he opened his eyes. The battered wainscoting and spiral staircase of the Polidor melted into the grayish walls of a shabby room, but one of the beautiful girls remained. Unlike the starved-looking models with their hungry eyes and pointed chins, this softly rounded woman was within touching distance.

Max lifted a shaking hand to finger the satin smooth hair framing the woman's face and sighed in contentment. She was real, she was flesh and blood.

"You blanked out on me again," Keely accused him.

"Just resting my eyes," Max said thickly. He was filled with an overwhelming desire to drift back to the Polidor and its dreams of an enchanted future. But this time, instead of Paul, Keely would be at the table, her knees pressed against his, their fingers entwined—

"Doug lied about ditching the cleaver in a trash can."

So much for romantic dreams. Max painstakingly gathered the scattered pieces of his fantasy and tucked them away for later re-assembly. He forced himself to straighten up.

Aware that Keely awaited a coherent response, he broke down her statement. Doug. Cleaver. Trash can. Was there a correlation between those unrelated words?

A sensible question occurred to him and he asked it. "How do you know?"

Keely waved at a scattered assortment of socks and tee-shirts. "Because it was in the gym bag. That's what knocked you into La La Land."

At least, Max reflected gratefully, he'd been spared the indignity of being cold-cocked by a pair of socks. "As soon as this room stops whirling, I'll see what else that rat's hiding."

If anything, the bedroom was worse than the living room. Overflowing ash trays and beer cans littered the floor, shabby night stand and unmade bed. Faded posters of heavy metal rock bands and a nude pin-up provided the only color on the drab walls.

Poking gingerly through the contents of the bureau drawers, Keely grimaced. "I'd pay any price for a pair of gloves!"

Max leaned against the door post for support. The floor seemed to have developed a definite slope. "I don't think we'll find much. Doug's no rocket scientist, but he's too street smart to leave anything incriminating lying around."

They finished searching the apartment, but found only evidence that the former inhabitant was a three pack a day man and lived primarily on a diet of beer and frozen pizza.

"Guy could have starved to death on what he ate." With a scowl of distaste, Max dropped a cheese-smeared box back into the trash. "No wonder the scrawny weasel was always snitching food while he was supposed to be working."

Using a plastic bag retrieved from the garbage, they sealed up the cleaver to preserve possible fingerprints and gave a final look around the disordered kitchen.

"I think we've pumped this particular well dry." Max staggered, regained his balance. "I vote we give Gifford those notes you received and tell her about the phone call. If we put all our cards on the table, maybe we can talk her into putting an APB out for Doug and Jackson."

"Or perhaps I'll be crowned Miss America. Vegas would give me the same odds."

Max grunted. "Don't be such a pessimist. Look at it this way: things are bound to get better."

"Meaning they can't get much worse?" Keely studied her companion. The bruise on his forehead stuck out like a hydrant in the middle of a parking lot and his face was as gray as his shirt. Keely followed Max's wavering progress out of the apartment, closing the door behind them. She didn't worry about locking up, there was nothing inside worth stealing. Max lurched down the hallway with Keely's support. In deference to his condition, they took the elevator down, arriving at the ground floor with a lurch that jarred a groan from Max.

Outside, the street was a sullen gray river of asphalt. Even the buildings flanking the pavement possessed a hostile air and Keely experienced an unexpected flash of empathy for Doug. If she were in his shoes, maybe she'd do whatever it took—including the odd spot of tire slashing—to get out of this hellhole.

After helping Max crawl into the passenger seat, Keely settled behind the wheel of the van. Glancing over the unfamiliar instrument panel in search of the switch for the headlights, she heard the ghost of a chuckle.

"I'd appreciate being let in on the joke," she said, buckling her seat belt.

"I just happened to think—Doug's vanished, his apartment looks like a tornado touched down inside, and our fingerprints are all over the place. All we need now is for his dear mother from Alabama to pop up and accuse us of kidnapping the little weasel."

Keely shuddered. "Don't forget about the smashed television screen."

"Sign of a struggle." Max hummed a few bars of "Take Me Out to the Ballgame." "Doug practically wet his pants when you swung for the fences."

Keely jammed the key into the ignition. She didn't want to dwell on her loss of control. Sooner or later, she'd have to confront the truth. Okay, definitely later.

"You scared me, Keely. That wasn't a picture tube you were smashing. Who was your real target?"

The empathy in Max's voice sneaked under Keely's guard. She said softly, "I think it was a drunken pervert named Harry. One of Mama's one-night stands."

"Want to tell me about it?"

Enough of sharing time. "I want to get out of this neighborhood." Keely shifted gears and pulled away from the curb with a jerk that had Max grabbing for his head.

He huddled against the van's door, his forehead resting on his right hand. "Are you sure you haven't got something you want to get off your chest?"

Remembering their proximity in the apartment, Keely smiled wryly. "You mean like this blouse? I suspect you weren't as dizzy as you pretended during your dramatic swoon."

Max chuckled again. "You'll never know, will you?"

But his voice caught on the last word and he slumped against the door.

Keely gave him a concerned glance. "I'm not convinced I shouldn't drop you at the hospital and see Gifford alone."

She could only guess at the effort it cost Max to straighten. "You're not leaving me out of this. I've got a score to settle with Doug 'the Weasel' Welch."

"From what I know of your family, I'm not surprised," The van accelerated. "Wasn't the main character in 'The Godfather' based on Anna Marie?"

"As a loyal nephew, I should resent that, but I don't. My aunt could face down Don Corleone any day."

They rode in silence, Keely planning what she was going to say to Gayla Gifford. She had the sinking feeling the detective wouldn't be falling on their necks with cries of joy. "We didn't get much out of Doug, did we?"

Max grunted. His posture had reverted to the hunch of a sick man. "Mystery voice on the phone, payment shoved under Doug's door—Gifford's going to love what we have to tell her."

The score was lopsided in favor of the bad guys. Even more disheartening was the realization that she was no closer to clearing Max of suspicion than she had been this afternoon.

Unless Doug was an actor of Academy Award caliber, Max wasn't the faceless man who had ordered the vandalism. Doug hadn't linked his boss to an anonymous voice over the telephone.

Are you being straight with me, Max? Keely wondered, keeping her companion under a covert watch. Apart from learning Doug was responsible for stealing the wallets, she was no farther ahead.

Instead, she found herself lumbered with more questions. Who was the reception guest who witnessed Doug's foray into pickpocketing? What was on the missing videotape? Was Max Summers playing a deep double game?

She had the answer to the last question within arm's reach. Keely gave the man beside her another probing glance, wishing she could see below the surface and into his soul.

Nothing ventured, nothing gained. "Tell me about your restaurant, Max."

"What?" He uncurled enough to raise his head. The glow from the dashboard painted his complexion with a ghastly pallor.

"Talk to me," she said patiently. "I don't want you slipping into a coma. You used to have a restaurant—what did you call it?"

"Max's Bistro."

"I've never been in a bistro," Keely prodded.

Max shuddered. "Just don't ask for a description of the meals served—my stomach's in the spin cycle. A bistro's not a restaurant in the usual sense of the word."

His tone softened, became pleasurably reminiscent. "A perceptive Parisian lady once told me a bistro isn't in business to make a lot of money, but to celebrate food and life. In Paris, a true bistro becomes a kind of surrogate home. A refuge, a haven from the stress of the outside world. One lingers over food and wine, talks for hours. Bistro means family."

That word again. He spoke with such nostalgic relish that Keely felt ill. Or maybe it was the smells of the apartment which still permeated her clothing. With each breath, she was forced to inhale the stench of horrific memories. "I think your definition of family and mine are a little different."

Max reached over and covered her right hand with his. "I'm sorry, Keely, that you had a terrible childhood."

She wrenched the steering wheel until his hand slipped away, pretending to wrestle the van around a corner. The pans in the back clattered a protest at the abrupt maneuver.

"I heard your mother on the phone, remember?"

She remembered all right. Humiliation has a way of hanging around longer than a saved message on voice mail. "I can't help resenting the way you talk about family. Maybe you grew up in a bed of roses, but those of us who didn't would prefer not to hear raves about the gorgeous colors and the heavenly scents."

Keely knew she sounded like a petulant child, but she no longer cared. Max had seen her in her worst moments: cowed by Flo Netherton, smashing a TV picture tube, and weeping like a baby. He'd heard her mother berate her, saw her chew her nails, knew she drove too fast when upset. She had no secrets left.

"Even in a bed of roses, there's always thorns, Keely." Max's voice was hoarse with discomfort. "No matter what I say or do, I can't change your past or influence your future. Only you can come to terms with whatever happened to you and move on."

She was almost home, Keely realized with relief. With all her heart, she regretted starting this conversation.

Max gingerly shifted position. "Keely, I'm having trouble keeping our relationship on a business-only basis. You're distractingly attractive, disturbingly sexy, and it takes all of my self-control just to refrain from kissing you senseless."

She turned to stare at him in disbelief. "You are

concussed! Next stop, the hospital."

He chuckled. "Actually, I think the blow knocked some sense into me. I've been lost without a family. I want a wife and kids and the loving and sharing that are missing from my life."

Keely couldn't tell whether the hum in her ears came from the van's engine or her rising blood pressure. She'd been tempted to kiss Max when they sat on the floor. He'd looked at her with a tenderness that was as alien as it was thrilling. Despite their wretched surroundings, she'd felt comforted and tantalized by a sense of closeness that was lacking in her life.

She guided the vehicle over to the curb in front of her house. "Max, please don't."

"Don't what? Say what I feel?" He was mocking her, his eyes inscrutable below the welt marking his forehead. "Don't worry, your heart's tied up in knots a sailor couldn't undo. Only a fool would try to free you."

Keely directed her miserable gaze through the windshield, fumbling to switch off the ignition. She was conscious of Max leaning closer, his hand coming up to stroke her hair in the loving gesture he'd used in the apartment. "Guess I'm just a fool."

Max wasn't groggy now. There wasn't a chance he'd confused her with some other dream woman. The trembling spread throughout Keely's body until her feet jittered like frightened animals on the floor mat. She heard a click as he unfastened his seat belt and murmured his name in protest. "Max—"

"A fool in love."

His fingers brushed the skin of her neck, his face only a breath away. She turned toward him, her unvoiced protest swallowed up by his lips as they closed over her mouth. The kiss deepened, became a quenching of an unbearable thirst as they drank of each other's essence.

Max rubbed his palms across Keely's shoulders. He was dizzy with unsated desire, his body and soul throbbed for contact with hers. He kissed her soft cheek, tasted the salty residue of her tears.

"Keely," Max whispered. "Keely."

Her lips sought his, her body arching toward him, responding like a flower to the sun. He must be delirious. She was nuzzling his throat, his name poetry on her lips.

The dream shattered as Keely stiffened. Her hands pushed against his chest. "Max, the lights are on in my studio!"

Bemused, still adrift in a turbulent sea of hormones, he reached for her again. "Maybe your associate's working late."

She bit her lip, fairly vibrating with apprehension. "Ida wouldn't be here, unless something terrible's happened—"

Keely's lithe body twisted free. She was out of the van and running towards the studio entrance before Max could react. Muttering, he took his time, following at a slower pace. His forehead throbbed like a balloon about to pop and his ego was equally bruised.

Keely had responded—briefly—but his kisses hadn't worked their magic if she was capable of noticing lights when she should be seeing stars . . .

Something glittered at the foot of the steps. Curious, Max bent to pick it up and almost toppled over. Regaining his equilibrium, he realized his discovery was a piece of glass. Curved like a half moon, smooth on both sides. Then he saw the other pieces, glittering like grounded stars in the grass. Max crouched with careful deliberation to pick them up, the lump on his forehead pulsating as he stooped.

His questing hand brushed something hard and hollow

hidden in the shadows of the bushes flanking the steps. Straightening, he studied his find in the faint light spilling through the outer door which Keely had left ajar. The shell casing of a gutted camera. Nausea roiled in his gut. What had Keely walked into?

Max dashed up the steps two at a time. Bursting into the reception area, he saw Keely near the entrance to the studio, her posture unnaturally rigid. She was alive, apparently unhurt.

"Keely?" His blood thundering like a waterfall in his ears, he hurried towards her. "Everything okay?"

She didn't respond but remained motionless, her head tilted as she stared at something beyond the doorway.

Holding his swimming head to keep it from falling off his neck, Max stumbled to her side. Keely gripped a tripod like a flag staff in her hands.

Following the direction of her unblinking gaze, Max saw Flo Netherton sprawled beside a wicker chair. Blood covered one side of her face, which seemed to float like a pale flower on the floor of the studio.

"She's dead, Max." Keely used the tripod as a dreadful pointer. "She's dead."

Chapter 17

Gayla Gifford rubbed the gnawing ache in her back. "Why don't more crimes take place in daylight?"

"You're not the only one looking like a newspaper left out in the rain." Dawson jabbed his thumb in the direction of the reception area. "Our friends aren't having what you'd call a good night."

"This isn't some hooker who got herself wasted, Robo, but a newspaper publisher. A woman with enough clout to make the mayor and the city council dance to the tune of her choosing."

"You got pink spots on your neck." Brian squinted critically at his partner. "A few flecks across your nose, too."

"We're redoing Samantha's room. She chose paint the shade of flamingo feathers—I can guarantee she didn't get her color sense from me." Gayla watched two men wheel a gurney into the studio. "Tell the stretcher jockeys to leave her a few more minutes. I want our friends to watch them haul her out."

Raising her voice, she addressed a man carrying a camera. "Vince! When I question O'Brien, I want to see a regular lightning storm of flashes in that studio."

Vince gave her the thumbs up signal and Brian said in an admiring tone, "You're good, Gayla. Real good. Even those pink freckles look cool on you."

"Give me your take, Oliver Stone. What scene was shot here tonight? How many actors?"

"At least two and they were looking for something." Brian

nodded at the file strewn floor. "Flo and a companion. They quarreled, she got clocked by the handiest weapon, the tripod."

Gayla snapped her fingers. "Let's hear take two."

Her partner scrubbed his cap of sandy blond hair with a ham-sized hand. "Flo walks in on the person tossing the studio. Tosser doesn't like it and lowers the boom—er, tripod."

"In both scenarios, Robo, you're letting Miss Shutterbug off the hook. Stop visualizing her legs and concentrate on facts. What if Flo was doing the tossing and O'Brien catches her in the act? Maybe our sweet-faced photog lured Flo here on a pretense, crushed her skull, and then tossed her own place?"

"In every one of your versions, you've got a problem. What's the MacGuffin they're searching for?"

"You're not catching me out." Gayla pointed a speckled finger at Brian. "MacGuffin: object of vital importance to the story's characters, but ultimately meaningless. It's a distraction, anything that takes your eye off the real action. I've told you before, you rent too many Hitchcock movies, Robo."

"Alfred H. was the master," he retorted. "Keely reminds me of the character played by Cary Grant in 'North by Northwest.' Nobody believes she's been framed, her life's in danger . . ."

Gayla shook her head vehemently. Her head throbbed and she'd never liked Hitchcock. "Framed? Life doesn't imitate art, Robo. Nobody's gaslighting our heroine. I don't subscribe to the philosophy that everything can be reduced to the dark and light sides of human nature—life ain't that simple. Get your head out of the cinematic clouds. Think. What's our MacGuffin?"

"The videotape." Brian never lost his temper, a valuable

asset in their partnership. "The one O'Brien claims will show Flo talking to Summers in the hallway. So maybe we go with scenario number one. Cast Summers in the role of the victim's companion."

"If the tripod proves to be the weapon, the killer could easily have been a woman." Gayla peeled paint from her wrist and rolled it between her thumb and forefinger. "Leverage increases velocity and force. I wonder whether Ms. O'Brien plays softball."

"I wouldn't mind having her swing for my fences." Brian gave an impish smile. "Her initials spell K.O., as in knockout."

They watched Billings, the department's best SOC man, dust the desk for prints. The stocky, balding man held up a music box. Gayla recognized the figurine topping it as Jemima Puddle-Duck.

"Ghoulishly appropriate, huh?" Del waggled the music maker. "I mean, what with that lady's goose being cooked."

"That's a duck, Del, not a goose. You need to study the section of your manual covering barnyard fowl." Gayla consulted her notes. "Robo, did you find out whether the security cards for Lakewood Estates can be copied?"

"Yeah." Brian paged through his own notebook. "According to Sentra Guard, the company that supplies them to the residents, the cards can't be duplicated."

"So either the guard let the bad guys in or else the perps used a borrowed security card."

"They could have stolen one."

Gayla idly slapped the notebook on her knee. "How many replacement cards have been issued within the past six months?"

"The guy I talked to gave me a line of bull about special safeguards in place to keep cards from floating all over the landscape, but I'd bet the farm that anybody with an ounce of determination could get their hands on one."

Gayla ran her fingers through her close-cropped curls. "So our shutterbug's still the prime candidate for the inside contact. She had possession of a card, knowledge of the reception timetable, familiarity with the Postwaite mansion lay-out, and her whereabouts were unaccounted for at the crucial time."

Noticing a paint smear on her ankle, Gayla made a mental note to supply a sample to Billings in case she'd shed any flecks near the body. "Now she discovers Flo—who's been crucifying her in print—lying dead in her studio. Looks bad for our gal, doesn't it?"

"Looks like a set-up to me," Brian protested. "The body was still warm when we got here, the blood wasn't even tacky. Summers and O'Brien claim they were together all evening."

"Doing what? Playing tackle football? Mattress tag?" Gayla pushed herself to her feet and stretched. "Mr. Max took at least one hard shot to the forehead and O'Brien's knees look like she's been crawling on the floor."

Hands on hips, Gayla surveyed the reception area, her eyes narrowed. "I can picture them in here—talking, arguing, tempers flaring. Perhaps all three were in on the robberies and what we have is the result of a falling out of thieves. Let's see if spreading a little dissension in the ranks will take care of the mutual alibi and split up our cozy twosome. Divide and conquer, Robo. That's our plan of attack."

He tossed her a snappy salute. "Lights, camera, action!"

Keely huddled on the couch beside Max. A relentless chill crept up from her fingers and toes, spread into her torso. Her head felt balloon light; her brain had temporarily shut down. How did you recover from your first glimpse of violent death?

Flo was dead. Her graceful poses permanently altered into an awkward sprawl, her ethereal beauty forever marred. Keely recalled her dream of rose petals turning into drops of blood and drew a shuddering breath.

Detective Dawson loomed like a dormant volcano behind his diminutive partner. Gifford had taken up residence in a reception room chair. The woman talked and Max answered, but bursts of static inside Keely's head distorted their words into gibberish.

She tried again to force her brain to process the rejected information. There was a dead body in her studio. Her haven had been transformed into a horror.

"Ms. O'Brien?"

Keely's brain finally locked onto the correct wave length and Gifford's voice came through loud and clear. "Are you all right, Ms. O'Brien?"

Keely nodded. All right? She had to be. Survival instinct told her this wasn't the time to admit to weakness.

"Dave Jelke sent me a copy of his report. Someone spray painted a nasty message on your car and julienned your tires."

Keely wondered how much she'd missed while drifting in the fog of shock. She was acutely conscious of Max's presence, less than an arm's length away. The discovery of Flo's body had shattered the fragile rapport between them.

At least Max couldn't be blamed for Flo's death. He'd never been out of Keely's sight. Someone else had entered the studio and killed the publisher.

"—we checked Summers's van and found a meat cleaver wrapped in plastic stored under the front seat."

Max started to say something, but Dawson held up a beefy hand. "Speak only when you're spoken to, mister."

Keely was grateful this interrogation wasn't being conducted within view of Flo's crumpled, pathetic body. "We believe that cleaver was the one used to slash my tires." Keely described the vandalism and their visit to Doug's apartment.

"You intimidated him into confessing he stole the wallets and he, in turn, gave Summers that goose egg."

Keely nodded. Her lips remained stubbornly dry, no matter how many times she moistened them.

Gifford jotted something in a notebook. An irregularly shaped pink splotch marked the back of her slim, brown hand.

Maybe it's their version of a Rorschach test, Keely thought giddily. She focused on the spot until it turned into a woman's pale, contorted face and a spreading red stain—

"We found a shattered camera and broken lenses outside." Gifford tossed the statement into Keely's lap and sat back, her sleek features vulpine as she waited for a response.

"I'm assuming they're mine. The Postwaites' chauffeur was supposed to deliver my equipment cases." Keely moved to the next level of shock, and voiced the suspicion that Jackson had taken the videotape.

Gifford continued to ask questions and Keely answered them with robotic calm. At irregular intervals, flash bulbs exploded in searing white flashes in the adjacent studio. Those walls had seen countless similar flashes, the same careful attention to detail. Only tonight no time was wasted in coaxing a smile, or in directing the subject into a more flattering pose.

Out of the blue, Keely remembered a quote from a book on daguerreotypes: *The dead made the best subjects for practitioners of this fledgling science of photography. For obvious reasons, death portraits were never blurry.*

A technician had asked Keely's permission to use her key and fill lights, flooding the studio with harsh light and transforming Flo's limp body from flesh and blood into a cardboard cut-out. She bit back an hysterical giggle. No need for fast speed film when your subject could hold a pose like that . . .

Keely described her visit to Flo's office, the notes, and the telephone call.

Gayla prompted, "Give us your exact movements after you arrived at the studio."

Keely dredged up the words, wrestled them like stones buried in mud. "I ran inside, calling Ida's name. The lights were on in the reception area, the studio dark. I noticed the tripod lying in the doorway. I knelt to pick it up and saw her shoe." Keely bit her lip. "Her face looked lopsided," she blurted. "Blood like a shadow. The shadow of death . . ."

Max leaned forward. "What was the weapon?"

Gifford's clever fox face was intent. "You've an unfortunate habit of picking up items used for assault, Ms. O'Brien."

As the significance of the statement sank in, Keely's knees and elbows liquefied. A thousand bees invaded her head. "It was the tripod—?"

"We found blood and hair on its head. Apparently she was struck by someone using a baseball-style swing."

Bile fountained up in Keely's throat and she almost vomited on the rug at her feet. The relentless lights continued to flash, imprinting her retinas with bursts of unbearable brightness even through closed eyelids.

The lights couldn't blot out the inner vision of a bat arcing through the air, a picture tube shattering into innumerable pieces.

"I think Keely's had enough."

Keely threw Max a grateful look for his intervention. His face had a bluish cast and his eyes were half closed against the intrusion of light, but his voice was firm. "Keely and I alibi each other. We were together all evening."

"A woman's been murdered, Mr. Summers." Gayla might have been chatting with a friend over coffee. "I want Ms. O'Brien's assurance that she didn't walk in on Flo searching for the videotape. I want to hear from her own lips that they didn't quarrel. That she didn't pick up a tripod and lash out at the victim for threatening to destroy her livelihood."

"I didn't." Keely nervously smoothed back her hair, aware of the dampness along her hairline. No wonder they called this "sweating the truth" out of a suspect. "I was with Max—Flo was lying on the floor when I walked in."

"Were you with her every minute, Mr. Summers? Did she have time to strike a blow before you followed her inside?"

Max started to shake his head, thought better of it. "No."

"Are you sure?" Dawson leaned forward, the volcano rumbling to life. "Doesn't take long to kill somebody. She was hit only once, but once was enough."

"She was lying on the floor when I walked in," Keely repeated doggedly.

Keely knew Max couldn't have killed Flo. He'd been with her the entire time. How ironic—the tables had turned and now she was the one under suspicion.

"Why aren't you looking for Jackson?" she demanded. "He was here tonight—the broken lenses and camera prove that! Perhaps he killed her—"

"Mr. Summers, according to your account, Ms. O'Brien found the meat cleaver in Welch's gym bag. Did you actually witness the discovery?" Gifford segued back to her see-saw method of interrogation.

Keely glanced at Max. The composure under fire that she'd envied was nowhere in evidence tonight. He looked like a man suffering from the mother of all headaches.

Sweating profusely, his face shiny and slick in the bursts of white-hot light from the adjacent room, Max touched his temple gingerly. "I wasn't noticing much at that point, but Keely told me she found it there."

"Ms. O'Brien!" Keely couldn't help flinching. "Did it occur to you that Summers and Welch were acting a charade for your benefit? That Welch defaced your car on Summers's orders?"

"No—"

"You don't believe he had anything to do with the vandalism. He doesn't believe you struck the fatal blow to Ms. Netherton. The two of you are very trusting for a couple who met a few weeks ago. At the scene of another violent crime."

Keely shifted uneasily. She couldn't shake the feeling of unreality. The sitting area of the reception room seemed claustrophobically cluttered with people and furniture. On the walls, Keely's portrait gallery watched the unfolding tableau with blank unconcern.

"Let me sum this up for you, Ms. O'Brien." Gayla leaned forward, her brown face incongruously marked by pink freckles. "You report receiving threatening notes, but they're missing from the desk where you hid them. I've only got your word that the victim tried to buy the tape from you. You claim to have received an intimidating phone call. You were the only witness to the vandalism of your car. No proof exists that anything you claim actually happened."

Keely understood why prisoners under prolonged interrogation caved in and confessed to crimes they hadn't committed. She was ready to say anything to hush that relentless voice and end this ordeal.

"Your story's full of holes, Ms. O'Brien. Remember, a woman's dead."

Keely stared at the gurney trundling past Ida's desk, mesmerized by the sight of the body bag. It was an obscenity, a plastic cocoon for the dead.

"What about Jackson? Doug Welch?" Max's voice cut into Keely's morbid reflections. "Are you going to look for those two goons or have you decided to pin everything on Keely?"

Gayla's silver spiral earrings glittered. "Let's suppose Flo's death was the result of a joint effort."

"Don't say anything else without a lawyer, Keely." Max's voice was harsh. "I don't intend to."

"I didn't kill Flo. I don't even know what she was doing here!" Keely repeated wretchedly.

"Let's assume that part of your story is true. Flo tried to buy the tape. Despite threats, you wouldn't sell. Maybe she concluded you weren't going to hand over the tape and decided to help herself." Gayla stood up. "Come with me, please."

Keely needed Dawson's assistance to get to her feet. She thanked him automatically, wondering if Marie Antoinette had been polite to the guards helping her onto the guillotine platform. Gifford led the way to the room where Keely stored negatives and videotapes. The light was already on inside and Keely gasped. The narrow space had been trashed, the contents of file cabinets and shelves strewn across the floor. Proof shots mingled with contact sheets and negatives; correspondence and bills were crumpled and torn, videotapes scattered.

Keely picked up one in each hand, stared blindly at the labels. Her business reputation torn to shreds, a dead woman had just been removed from her studio, and now months of work lay at her feet in hopeless confusion.

With a despairing cry, she flung the tapes away from her. The cases crashed into the wall and clattered to the floor. The impact echoed in the confined space and Keely was belatedly aware of the silent observer in the room.

She'd picked the worst possible time to demonstrate a lack

of self-control. I'm having a nervous breakdown, Keely thought in despair. It started in Doug's vile apartment—

"Do you have a grip now, Ms. O'Brien?"

"I'm sorry. I don't usually lose control. Seeing this mess on top of everything else . . ."

"Tell me about the videotapes."

"They cover the period of a year." Keely nudged a stack of tapes with her toe. They toppled with a clatter. "Each is labelled with the date the footage was taken."

"You can't tell if any are missing?"

"Not until they've been put in date order and cross-checked against this year's work schedule."

Gifford slipped her notebook into the pocket of her dark red blazer. "That's a job I suggest you start as soon as I give you the go-ahead. Make a list of what's missing, if anything."

Keely's self-protective instincts belatedly surfaced. "Am I being charged? I've told you everything. Before I answer any more questions, I want to speak to a lawyer."

"That's your privilege, Ms. O'Brien." Gayla gestured toward the door. "After you, please."

Keely ended up back on the couch beside Max. His head lolled against the cushions, but he mustered the energy to squeeze her hand in reassurance. She tried to smile, but a terrible lassitude dragged at the corners of her mouth.

Dawson and Gifford stood in the doorway, conferring quietly. Keely surveyed the room, wondering if it was the last place she'd see before the inside of a jail cell. The peonies still glowed in a crimson halo above the crystal vase on Ida's desk, their beauty undisturbed by the intruder. Brave red symbols of courage and determination.

Max murmured, "You shouldn't be alone tonight."

"I don't think that's a possibility." Keely's voice was brittle. "Unless they have private rooms at the county jail. I think I'm going to be charged with murder."

"Do you have an attorney? Someone you could call?"

To her despairing ears, it sounded as if Max had decided to wash his hands of her. Keely's pulse throbbed in her temples and she pulled away from the comfort of his touch. Did he believe she'd murdered Flo prior to meeting him at the Seetons' house?

She could think of no one to call. The only attorney she knew had drawn up her business agreements several years ago and he was a specialist in contract law.

Staring dully at the linked hands in her lap, she felt a pang at the thought of being abandoned by Max. Why should she condemn him for a lack of faith when at every chance she'd demonstrated her readiness to believe the worst of him?

Everything would have turned out differently if she'd taken refuge with Ida after the disastrous session at Mimi's.

"We can make popcorn and watch my shopping club," Ida had urged in issuing her invitation. "Tonight's Jewelry Jamboree."

Now Keely would welcome an evening spent watching an endless parade of glittering gemstones. Blood-red rubies like the one Flo wore on her right hand—

"Her rings!" Keely exclaimed. "She wasn't wearing her rings!"

Gifford looked up, her attention caught. "Rings?"

"Flo's rings! Diamonds in white gold on the left hand. An enormous emerald cut ruby on the right."

The detective's brow furrowed. "I noticed them when I interviewed her at the Postwaites. She always wear them?"

"I never saw her without them. They were her style trademark."

"That makes robbery a possible motive," Dawson said.

Keely held her breath. Instead of exploring the scenario

further, however, Gifford turned to Max. "Have you ever seen Ms. O'Brien lose control? Lash out at someone or something?"

Keely's startled gaze met Max's and, in that instant, she glimpsed a flicker of doubt. He'd witnessed the destructive result of her flashback—could she be capable, under provocation, of breaking a woman's head?

"Shall I take your silence as a positive response?" Gifford's voice was creamy with satisfaction.

Keely could almost hear the clang of a cell door slamming shut. "Thanks for your support," she hissed under her breath.

"I don't believe Keely would hurt anyone." Max's face set into a rigid mask. "Am I free to go?"

"Don't leave town." Gayla studied him for a long moment. "I'll probably want to see you both tomorrow—after I've interviewed other people and corroborated your statements."

"I'll bring my lawyer." Without looking in Keely's direction, Max pushed himself to his feet. He staggered, but regained his balance and left the studio without looking back. Dawson followed him out.

Keely groaned under her breath. Her tongue had just delivered the coupe de grace to any chance of a relationship with Max, working or personal. Then the import of Gifford's warning sunk in. The detective would talk to Ida. She'd question Officer Jelke and Mimi. Each would confirm that Keely hated Flo Netherton. Those comments, added to Keely's earlier loss of control—which she had no doubt Max would divulge when flanked by his attorney—and the damning window of opportunity created by Max's dallying outside the studio . . .

"I'll be honest with you, Ms. O'Brien. Things don't look

good. Broken equipment, vandalized car, a dead body. You've had more trouble today than most soap stars have in a lifetime."

"I didn't kill her." Keely pressed icy fingers against her lips, knowing her denial sounded mechanical. "She was dead when I found her."

Gayla had the last word. "To a cop, forfeiting credibility is like losing your virginity. No amount of talking or wishing can get it back."

Chapter 18

Ida Burke surveyed the sea of videotapes. "Hopeless!"

"I told you to go home, Ida."

The phone shrilled in the reception area. "Don't answer it!" Keely softened her voice. "We're not taking calls today."

"What about appointments?" The receptionist's plump fingers tugged on the golden teddy bear hanging from a chain around her neck. Today's ensemble featured a hot pink suede jacket, complete with a row of tassels across the chest, and bell-bottoms.

"No one will be making or keeping appointments. I've been isolated by society's quarantine. The only people venturing near will be inoculated by vulgar curiosity or press badges."

Seated cross-legged in the filing room, Keely picked up a tape. According to the open engagement book on her lap, Margo had taped a sweet sixteen birthday party on March 3rd. She marked the entry with a red felt tip pen and placed the tape in a box.

Ida hovered in the doorway. "My conscience won't let me leave you with this mess!"

"Just go, before you're contaminated by my disease."

Ida squared her shoulders. "I'm staying. Now that you mention it, I feel a bit of a temperature coming on."

"Ida, you're a doll and I appreciate your loyalty. Please go. Honestly, I'll be okay."

"You look exhausted." Ida scowled. "How late did those flatfoots keep you up last night?"

"Late enough." Ida had missed the opportunity to see Detective Gifford's delicately arched feet in the red strappy sandals that matched her smart blazer.

She wondered whether her watchdog/guardian still sat in an unmarked car at the curb. Gifford had informed her someone would keep an eye on the place overnight, but that hadn't kept Keely from waking up at intervals, bathed in a cold sweat.

"Why don't I sort bills and correspondence at my desk?" Ida suggested. "My bones are too old to sit in that fashion. If I tried it, you'd have to rent a crane to lift me off the floor."

Keely jumped up and embraced Ida. "Thanks. You're the only ray of sunshine in a bleak world."

They carried armloads of jumbled papers to the reception area which Ida had restored to near normalcy, but neither woman had yet summoned up the nerve to venture into the studio. Keely feared seeing bloodstains, of glimpsing again those sprawled limbs, the black velvet band holding back a spill of ash blond hair.

"What the well dressed housebreaker is wearing," one of the crime scene technicians had cracked. Last evening had blurred into a nightmarish swirl of voices, impressions, and the paralyzing feeling of dread. One moment Max was telling her in his seductive baritone how much he was attracted to her and the next, her world had been flattened by a killer quake.

Keely left Ida to her task of shuffling papers and returned to the storage room. Mindless work, better than thinking. She tried in vain to recall the happy atmosphere of the events as she checked them off in the engagement book.

When Keely heard voices in the outer room, she froze. Ida must have let in a reporter.

Well, Ida could just get rid of the intruder. Hoping the enterprising person wasn't armed with a camera, Keely got up on her knees and stretched out her hand for another tape.

"Well, Stan, this is another fine mess you've gotten me into."

Keely's head snapped up. Max leaned against the door frame, muscular arms folded across his chest. In the early morning hours, she'd alternated between self-castigation and anger at Max for walking out on her, but now, Keely felt only inordinate relief.

She couldn't tell him that. Remembering their first meeting at the police station—it seemed like months ago— she snapped, "You do a rotten Gary Cooper, a pathetic Oliver Hardy—is there any impression you can do successfully?"

"Laurel and Hardy's sight gags were terrific, but like Chaplin's, they often contained an undertone of pathos or tragedy. To me, that's the essence of true comedy."

"Tragedy is the essence of comedy? In that case, I should be laughing my head off after last night." Avoiding his gaze, Keely dropped another tape into the box.

Max crossed the room, crouched down to face her. He held a folder in his right hand. "Keely, we're in trouble."

Keely picked up another tape, stared at the label. It might have been written in hieroglyphs for all the sense she could make of the letters. "Thanks for the news flash."

Max grabbed her wrist. She tried to pull away, but his grip remained firm. "Don't shut me out. Someone's raised the stakes to murder—a lot more serious than losing a business."

Keely gazed at the fingers which held her prisoner. Sturdy and powerful, natural extensions of the strong hand of the man kneeling before her. She felt sick to her stomach.

"Why didn't Gifford believe me?" she whispered.

"It was too much of a coincidence, Flo ripping us in print

and then being killed in your studio. Gifford's frustrated, we're her only suspects. We alibi each other—"

"I'm the one squirming on the hook." Keely raised her chin, looked at Max through a blur of tears. His face suddenly dear, precious, his familiar masculine features a rock to cling to on a heaving landscape. "You think I did it, don't you?"

"No. You poor kid."

The tenderness of his smile reflected in his eyes. Keely blinked rapidly. Sympathy always devastated her self-control.

"I am the most likely suspect," she murmured. "I went in alone, I was angry at Flo—"

"I don't believe you killed her, Keely."

"After what happened in Doug's apartment last night, I wouldn't blame you if you did," she said dully. "Sometimes it seems like I could have done it. Gifford made the scenario sound so plausible . . ."

Max still held Keely's wrist. He released her, but his face with its arrogant Roman nose loomed distractingly near. "I've already talked to Detective Gifford this morning."

She swallowed. "What did you tell her?"

"You couldn't have done it. Flo was killed long after we met at the Seetons. We were only separated at the studio for a few minutes. Gifford's calling this a crime of impulse, passion. I didn't hear voices raised in anger—there wasn't time for you to have a confrontation with Flo."

Keely felt an immense weight drop from her shoulders. "Why did you walk out last night?"

"I apologize." Max touched the knot on his forehead and winced. "My head had been beat on like a rocker's bass and when you jumped on me for not coming to your defense, I faded."

"I'm the one who owes you an apology." This time Keely

initiated physical contact, running her fingers lightly across the back of his hand. "I have no right to expect loyalty after the suspicions I've entertained about you. I'm sorry, Max."

He smiled and the store room brightened. "Apology accepted. Now we have to convince Gifford and her pet gorilla that we aren't in collusion. To that end, I've been doing a little investigating of my own." Max indicated the folder. "The key to everything seems to be Flo. A woman who skewered the rich in print, yet continually sought out their company."

Keely's temperature had risen a few degrees. A symptom of the plague or a more pleasurable condition? "You believe me?"

"It's not a question of belief," Max said quietly. "But of faith."

Faith, one of the loveliest words in the English language! "Gifford's not going to award us good conduct medals and cross us off her suspect list without sufficient reason."

"Exactly." Max opened the folder. "As soon as I realized Flo had Feast of Italy in her gunsights, I called my Uncle Tony. His firm does background investigations for corporate headhunters. I hoped he'd come up with ammunition that would enable me to fight back. I received his report this morning."

Keely gazed at the folder as if it were the Holy Grail. "Let's hear it."

Max eased down into a sitting position beside her. "I'll give you the edited version. Flo's father owned the controlling interest in a chain of drug stores. Until she went away to college, her life as a rich kid was fairly uneventful, but Berkeley was a hotbed of activity in the sixties and she dove right in. She wrote inflammatory articles for an underground student newspaper and took as her lover the leader of 'Strike

Back,' a radical protest group notorious for the violence of its methods."

Keely envisionsed a younger Flo in the arms of a hard-eyed, hard-muscled rebel under a painted peace sign on the filthy wall of a commune.

"He was killed by police during a confrontation and Flo's daddy managed to extricate his little girl by tossing around money and influence in equally lavish portions. Flo, still in shock, was hustled back to respectability and a hastily arranged marriage to a shoe magnate.

"Ten years later, Hubby was killed in a car accident. Daddy died and Flo found herself in control of two fortunes. She occupied herself with charity work until she came to Lake Hope and bought the newspaper."

Keely stared at the pile of unsorted tapes—snatches of lives recorded for posterity. She thought of a woman losing the person for whom she'd abandoned every standard and felt again the searing heat of the rage which had consumed Flo Netherton.

"That explains the needles in her social column," Keely murmured, "the malice she felt toward the wealthy."

Frowning, Max tapped the folder. "It's still not clear to me. She was one of the rich herself."

"But she'd been on the other side! The police, the symbol of the system she'd tried to overthrow, killed her lover and she survived only by compromising with that same system. How she must have hated herself, hated everything and everyone who reminded her of what she'd lost."

"Such insight into a woman you met only a few times! Why did she have a grudge against you, Keely? You're not one of the rich. You're a working woman, trying to make a living."

"I'm not a victim," Keely said slowly. "I didn't fit into the categories Flo created in her mind. She spoke bitterly of spoiled society princesses and I think she saw me as a willing handmaiden to upper class excesses. She was especially scornful of the money wasted on theme weddings."

"If she meant to punish society's mavens, she certainly succeeded with that poison pen of hers." Max shook his head. "Having to invite her to an affair must have been like luring a tigress in to share your dinner, never knowing when the beast will turn and sink its fangs into you."

Keely touched Max's arm, let her hand rest there, enjoying the warmth of his skin beneath her finger tips. "We're suspects in her murder."

Max's gaze travelled up to her face, settled on her mouth. "We're innocent."

"Innocent," she whispered, achingly conscious of him.

Max leaned forward until his breath warmed her cheek. She looked into blue, blue eyes, found herself mesmerized by the intensity of his gaze. She didn't remember moving toward him but their mouths met, their bodies surging together eagerly. Tapes clattered as the pile was knocked to the four winds again, but Keely was only conscious of the solid warmth of Max's body, the shoulders broad enough to bear any burden, his mouth demanding, yet tender.

She wanted to rip away the black rimmed buttons of his shirt and peel back the cotton. Her fingers ached to explore the tautness of his belly and below. Her body became a Fourth of July sparkler, fizzing, hissing, throwing off brilliant sparks of light as Max's hands caressed her.

Keely exulted in her supple surrender to his embrace. His mouth tasted of the thousands of different flavor combinations he'd sampled and she could go on kissing him until she died and not exhaust the possibilities to savor—

"KEELY!"

Max took his time in removing the enticing banquet of his mouth from Keely's. Dazed, she turned her head. Ida's plump hands gripped the teddy bear dangling around her neck in a stranglehold. "For a horrifying moment, I thought Anna Marie had gotten out of her bed and tracked me down."

"Talk, you said. I just want to talk to her." Ida directed the words to Max but her fascinated gaze was fixed on Keely's flushed face. "I heard noises and thought you might need me."

Conscious of Ida's amusement, Keely brushed her lips with the back of her hand. She felt as if her mouth was outlined in neon bright lipstick. "Everything's under control."

"I can see that." The receptionist had recovered her customary aplomb. "You two were doing just fine on your own."

Keely got to her feet, scorning Max's proffered hand, and brushed at the dust marking her butterscotch slacks. "We were planning strategy," she said primly.

Max, comfortably seated on the floor, uttered a loud guffaw and Keely blushed again. "Go away, Ida."

"All right, I'm going." Ida grinned. "I've got to get out more. The most exciting part of my life are the show specials on my shopping club—and those Collectable Collection nights are looking pretty dull right now."

"Mimi had good reason to be terrified." Keely frowned, seeing the salon owner's frightened face instead of the traffic. "She let slip that someone threatened to burn down her salon."

"Apparently you and Doug weren't the only recipients of mysterious phone calls." Max braked, allowing the engine to idle. Today he'd abandoned the catering van in favor of a black Ford Bronco. "If our theory is correct—and God help us if it isn't—someone's targeting the wedding service providers. We find out who and why and we just might wriggle off Gifford's top ten list."

He'd stopped in front of "Jessica's Garden." Jumping out, Max hurried around to hold the passenger door open for Keely.

Gazing at the flower-filled windows of the shop, Keely felt an unexpected need for support. "While I'm talking to Jessica, what will you be doing?"

"Questioning the gnome who made cakes for both weddings."

"Gunter?" Keely smiled involuntarily. "I doubt if you'll get anything out of him. He prefers making sugar bells to conversation."

"He'll talk to me," Max said grimly.

Her partner possessed enough confidence for the two of them, Keely thought as she entered the humid atmosphere of the florist's shop. A bell tinkled merrily, signalling her arrival.

"Be right with you!" a voice caroled.

Keely moved aimlessly. On previous visits, she'd feasted her soul on the breathtaking colors and perfumed air, but last night had changed her outlook. She was a murder suspect and Jessica no longer a friend, but a source.

Refrigerated cases lining the wall held cut flowers in milky white vases. Poppies jostled in the coolness with roses and open-throated snapdragons. Buttercups and pink campion flanked an arrangement of saucy parrot tulips. Geraniums and African violets bloomed on cedar tiers and ferns stretched out feathery tendrils to brush Keely's shoulders as she passed. Ficus trees competed with crape myrtle for floor space.

Keely was studying a hanging spiral of grapevine entwined with ivy when the curtain at the back twitched and a frail woman in a cranberry shaded smock emerged, wiping her hands on a towel. "Sorry for the delay," she said gaily. "How may I help—"

She stopped in mid-sentence, color draining from her round face as she recognized her visitor.

"Hi, Jess." Keely pretended to admire a potted jonquil. "Got a minute and a cup of coffee?"

Jess pushed back feathered black bangs and shot a nervous glance toward the plate glass windows. "Of course, Keely. You know me, always ready for a chat."

Keely found herself hustled behind the curtain into the work room where her hostess dropped her arm as if she'd just learned that Keely had leprosy. "You know where I keep the cups. I have to finish these delphs before I can take a break."

In the cupboard above the sink, Keely selected a chunky pink mug that proclaimed "For Florists, Life is a Bed of Roses" and poured coffee from the pot kept perpetually simmering. She walked over to the plastic-covered table where Jessica conditioned flowers and composed spectacular arrangements.

Keely watched as Jessica skillfully wielded a minute watering can to fill the hollow stem of a delphinium and plugged the end with a piece of cotton wool.

Standing the stalk of blue flowers in a narrow vase, Jessica selected another. "Blake Caswell and her mother were in to see me yesterday." She deftly filled and plugged the stem. "Blake's theme is going to be 'I'm in the Mood For Love.' I was surprised you couldn't make it."

Keely's stomach clenched. Blake's session was one of this week's cancellations.

"We selected flowers that sound as romantic as they look." Jessica paused, resting her hands, palms down on the table. Her knuckles were reddened, the nails blunt and close trimmed.

Uncomfortable under Keely's scrutiny, Jessica flexed her fingers and picked up another flower, avoiding her visitor's gaze. "Wonderful names—bachelor's-button, Cupid's dart, blue passion flower, love-in-a-mist. Since the groom's name is Bill, we decided to use Sweet William in the table arrangements. Blake wanted orange blossoms but she'll have to make do with stephanotis like everyone else—"

"I had nothing to do with the robberies and I didn't kill Flo Netherton."

Jessica started. Water splashed and puddled on the plastic. "What are you talking about, Keely?"

"I know this town, Jess, and I'm aware of the speed of the grapevine in the wedding industry. Flo was murdered in my studio last night and I'm the prime suspect. I didn't do it, and I want to clear myself. Please, help me."

"Help you? How?" Jess tore off a piece of cotton wool and rolled it into a minuscule snowball.

"You can tell me why you're afraid to be seen talking to me. Why Mimi's scared of her shadow. Who's threatening you."

"Threatening me? Wherever did you get such nonsense?" Jess jammed a delphinium into the vase without plugging the stem and seized another stalk.

"Mimi said her store could go up in flames and there wouldn't even be a sequin left in the ashes."

"Mimi's high strung." Jessica twisted the stem. "She's paranoid, seeing threats in ordinary conversation. She was probably talking about a meeting with her insurance agent."

The flat explanation wouldn't have convinced a deaf person. Keely put down her coffee mug. "I don't blame you for being afraid, Jess. I'm scared, too. But we've got to stop whatever's going on. We can't live in fear."

The bell rang, jarring Jessica from the paralysis caused by

Keely's last assertion. The stalk snapped between her work roughened fingers. "I've got a customer." She gestured helplessly with the broken flower. "I'm afraid you'll have to leave—"

"Keely?"

The voice behind the curtain belonged to Max. "Back here!" she called.

The curtain rippled and shuddered. Max appeared.

Keely blinked. "What happened to you?"

The crisply styled clothing which he wore with such assurance was now spattered with white dots. A dark stain the shape of Australia decorated the breast pocket of his shirt.

"Gunter took offense at being disturbed during the genius of creation. He also took a vehement dislike to my face."

"And routed you with the ammunition he had on hand?" Keely touched a dot with her index finger, transferred the creaminess to her mouth. "Gunter's buttercream tastes like ambrosia." She indicated the mark on his shirt pocket. "Did you hurt him? That looks like blood."

"I never got within wrestling range." Max tapped the stain. "Black currant liqueur. Gunter was about to pour some over a genoise sponge cake when he blew his cake top."

Keely belatedly remembered her manners. "Jess, this is Max. You probably saw each other at the Westhaven reception—"

At Max's entrance, Jess had frozen, one hand still clutching the damaged delphinium. Her eyes were glazed with fear.

She jerked into motion, moving awkwardly, yet swiftly, to snatch up a scissors with long pointed blades off the work table. "Get out! Both of you! Or I'll call the police!"

Keely stepped back, her hands raised defensively. "Jess, please! We don't want to hurt you, we want to help!"

"Help?" Jessica's voice held the fear-curled edge of hysteria. "The only way you can help me is by leaving as fast as you can! And take your rent-a-thug with you!"

Chapter 19

Jessica's ragged breathing was the only sound in the room as Keely held out her hand, palm up. "We can leave your shop, Jess, but the fear will still be here. You've got to tell me what's going on, for your sake as well as mine."

Jess's hands shook. "My girls! I can't—"

"Kids sense fear," Keely said softly. "I'm sure they're hurting, just like you."

Jessica dropped the scissors which clattered, unnoticed, to the tiles. She stared down at her hands as if she'd never seen them before. "Sense it? They can smell it," she said dully. "Megan asked me this morning why I don't wear my 'flower' perfume any more when I come home from work."

She heaved a sigh which travelled all the way up from her toes. "I'm sorry about the melodramatic gesture with the scissors. I wouldn't have hurt you. I thought your friend looked like a guy I've seen hanging around my shop."

"My first visit," Max said. "Scout's honor."

Keely looked past Jessica's sagging form to the table covered with blocks of florists' foam, funnels, green gutta-percha tape, twigs, and plant misters. All harmless tools of the trade. Then her gaze moved on to the taped razor blades, the reel of fine rose wire and the scissors lying on the floor. The skin on back of her neck tingled.

"Let's go into the conference room," she suggested.

Jessica agreed listlessly and took the cup which Keely pushed into her nerveless fingers. They took seats in the ivory and mauve room where Jessica met with clients. After Jessica had been persuaded to drink some coffee, a chilling story emerged.

Three days after the Westhaven wedding, Jessica had received a phone call in the middle of the night. The caller was a man. She described his voice as cold, emotionless.

"His opening line was, 'See how easy it is to ruin someone's business? The photographer's history. No one's going to hire her.' I hung up but he kept calling back until I answered."

Keely's arms covered in gooseflesh as she recalled the voice of her own caller. Threats made in the dark watches of the night, when his chosen victim was at her most vulnerable.

In a whispery voice, Jessica described how the man, undaunted by her hang-ups, called back every night, leaving messages on her answering machine. He claimed to possess the ability to destroy any wedding service provider. "A little negative publicity, a few ugly incidents, and you're out of business."

On Friday, he had proposed a solution: a healthy cash payment to be made once a month.

"I picked up the phone and told him I was going to call the police." Jess pushed back her bangs again. "But he laughed, said a flower shop would make a nice blaze. He could manufacture enough evidence to make the police believe I'd torched my shop for the insurance money."

After the Postwaite debacle and Flo's printed digs at Key Shot and Feast of Italy, the caller phoned again. This time, a terrorized Jessica agreed to make the payments.

"I can't afford to lose that much money, Keely. Maggie needs braces and I'm going to have to replace the roof on our house . . ." Jessica wiped her eyes and sniffed. "But I also knew you were innocent and had been made to look guilty. It could easily have been me! When I heard about Flo's death,

I'm ashamed to admit I felt enormous relief that I'd agreed to pay."

Max said harshly, "Protection money."

Keely gazed at starry sprays of pink London pride mixed into the bouquet of sweet peas on the center of the rosewood table. "If the thug's getting that kind of money out of Mimi and the other service providers, he's sitting pretty."

"He said the robberies were just a show of force. Some of the police were in his pocket—no one would believe me. He told me he could ruin anyone." Jessica, ignoring scented tissues in an ivory box, blew her nose on a paper towel plucked from the pocket of her smock. "What I am going to do, Keely?"

Her round face flushed. "How selfish of me to worry about my problems when you're in such deep trouble. Keely, are you all right? You're as white as a trumpet lily."

Keely forced a reassuring smile. "I suppose I should feel better, knowing I'm just being used as an example."

Max asked sympathetically, "Would you be willing to repeat what you've told us to a police detective?"

Jessica shivered and massaged her forearms. "I can't afford to lose my business, Max. Besides, I've already made one payment. Doesn't that make me guilty of something?"

"That makes you a victim," Keely said firmly. "You need to talk to Detective Gayla Gifford. Appeal to her womanly nature."

"Except she's as womanly as a she-wolf protecting her cubs," Max muttered.

Jessica shook her head miserably. "I can't. Keely, Max, I'm sorry, but he knows about my girls. 'Aren't you proud that Julie won an award at the science fair, that Megan's so pretty?' The other night, he said, 'Annie's the image of you.' "

Jessica ran her hands through her hair, which fell back into fluffy layers. "He's been spying on me, Keely. If I go to the police, he'll know and something terrible will happen."

"This clown's a real tough guy, harassing women and children over the telephone." Max's bruised face set in a fierce scowl. "We can't let him get away with this. Jessica, I know your kids come first, but once you knuckle under—"

She shoved her mug away, coffee slopping onto the polished wood. "I hate being a puppet! If it was only my safety at stake, I'd help you, but I've got to think of my girls."

Keely asked softly, "How did you make the payment, Jess? By mail?"

"No." Jess blew her nose again. "I was told to give the envelope with the money to the first person who asked if I carried false dragonhead in stock."

"False dragonhead?"

"Physostegia virginiana, to be exact." A bitter smile creased Jessica's pleasant face as she recited the Latin name. "Commonly know as 'Obedience.' "

"This creep's got a nasty sense of humor. What did the person who picked up the money look like?" Max leaned forward.

"A teenager. Nice clean cut kid. An errand boy. I didn't ask questions, I didn't even dare look at him too closely." Jessica picked at the rim of soil imbedded under her thumbnail. "I'm not saying another word. I'll pay any amount of money, I'll sign over my shop—I'll do anything to keep my girls safe."

"Worrying about you and Gunter kept me distracted."

"What did you say?" Max stuck his head out of his bedroom and Keely saw that her host was naked above faded jeans.

"Get dressed!" She made a shooing motion. "I wasted time fretting about what you were doing to Gunter when I should have been worrying what he was doing to you."

Max grunted and vanished. He reappeared, buttoning up a blue shirt. "Before I could get a word out, that mad German pelted me with icing and hurled liqueur bottles."

"Gunter may be a trifle volatile, but he's not mad." Keely paused by the French doors leading onto a balcony. "This place has the ambience of a fifties bowling alley."

Max dropped into a black leather chair. "I'm a cook, not a decorator." he proclaimed in a muffled voice. "At least I think I am. The moment I met you, my life turned into an episode of *The Twilight Zone*."

"You think mine's been a chair of bowlies?" Max's apartment featured a high ceiling and walls painted pristine white. A minimum of furniture and no knickknacks. Judging by the lack of personal touches, Max was a man who travelled light. Yet, last night, he'd confessed that he desperately wanted a family. . . .

"You haven't got a fire-eating relative breathing down your neck," Max muttered through his fingers. "If Feast of Italy goes into the toilet, my choices will be whittled down to joining the federal witness protection program or sticking my head in the oven and switching on the gas. I trust you've heard the expression, 'Out of the frying pan and into the fire'?"

"We have to keep digging until we come up with a bone to throw Gifford."

"Agreed, but I've a hunch that woman's going to need more than a bone to get her off our tail." Max linked his hands behind his head. "The protection racket's a potential juicy tidbit."

"Judging by Mimi and Jessica's reactions, the chances of

anyone admitting they're paying protection money are slim to none." Keely gingerly sat down in the only other chair in the room, a battered recliner that looked as if its laid-back position was a permanent state. "The caller did his homework, he mentioned Jessica's daughters by name, knew all about them . . ."

Keely's voice trailed off as she grappled with an elusive thought. "Flo did a series of profiles of area service providers last winter. Jessica was one of those interviewed. What if Flo was working with this madman and she gave him the personal information he needed to terrorize these people?"

"I think you've hit on something! Flo had access to the inside details about the weddings. She could have funneled the information to the leader of the Sterling Gang." Max leaped up and began to pace. "What nerve that woman had, pointing the finger of guilt at us while all the time she was the conduit!"

Keely frowned. "Maybe we're being too hard on Flo."

"Excuse me? We're talking about the woman who sliced us like veal cutlets and tossed us to the wolves."

Keely took a perverse pride in opposing Max that had nothing to do with defending the dead woman. "Perhaps she didn't know how this guy planned to use the information she gave him."

"Didn't know? The investigator's report and Flo's own columns show that she bore active malice towards society—"

"Depriving brides of their wedding silver is one thing, but I can't see a socially prominent woman becoming involved with a protection racket."

Max slid open the doors leading to the balcony and leaned through the opening to retrieve a jug of sun tea. "I'll bet Flo was the inside contact for the Sterling Ring. She was desperate to get her hands on the videotape. She came with someone to your studio to search for it. An argument occurred, hot words were exchanged—wham! You've got a dead woman in your studio."

"Maybe the person she was working with was Jackson." Keely followed Max into the kitchen. "Don't forget about the broken camera and lenses. He was at Key Shot last night."

"Maybe Flo herself was the leader of the Sterling Ring." Max poured tea into two glasses and sliced a lime into paper thin wedges. They sat at the breakfast bar which divided the kitchen and main room of the apartment, each continuing to argue theories about the murder.

"You have to concede that killing Flo was an impulse action." Keely took another fruit wedge from the glass bowl.

"Because the murderer used the tripod to inflict the deadly blow? Granted. But what if the killer had brought along a different weapon and decided to improvise, utilizing what was available? I've got a hunch the goon behind the protection racket is a man we've met before."

"Who?" Keely wished she had a camera to capture the earnest wrinkle of Max's brow.

He popped two aspirin into his mouth and washed them down with a swig from his glass. "Jackson. He gave the list with the band's name on it to the gatekeeper. He was in the ideal position to orchestrate the Postwaite burglary."

"But he also has the videotape Flo wanted so desperately." Keely delighted in punching a hole in Max's theory. "Why would she threaten me if her confederate had the tape?"

"She wasn't aware he had it." Max tilted the glass and stared into its amber depths. "Jackson's playing a deep game. When Flo found out he'd been holding out on her, she lost her cool. Maybe she threatened him with the police or pricked him one too many times with that needle sharp tongue. He lost control, grabbed the tripod and bashed her head in."

Max's hypothesis was as valid as anything else they'd come up with. Keely thought of another scenario. "What if he'd planned to kill her all along?"

"Using the tape as bait to lure her to your studio? He kills her and leaves you holding the bag?" Max shook his head in reluctant admiration. "No wonder he wasn't satisfied with chauffeuring the Postwaites around. The Pentagon could use a mind like his for command central."

Keely sucked juice from the lime wedge. Her lips puckered in a soundless whistle in reaction to the tart tang. She caught Max staring and heat surged in her cheeks.

"Okay," she said briskly. "Time for a strategy session. We need proof we can toss in Gifford's lap."

"Give her Jessica." Max watched Keely closely. "Your friend will probably crack after five minutes of questioning."

"No! If Jess talks to the police and something happens to her girls, I'd never forgive myself. She'd only deny talking to us." Keely reached for another lime wedge and froze, her hand out-stretched. "I just had a lightning strike of inspiration. Toss me the phone, would you?"

With a puzzled look, Max complied.

Keely dialed. "Ives? This is Keely O'Brien. Wait—I don't want to talk to Rose, I want to talk to you."

She cut ruthlessly into his stuttering reply. "Has Jackson come back to work?"

"I don't believe I can answer—"

"Cut the waffling, Ives. This is could be a matter of life and death and I don't think your boss will be too happy if it comes out you've been protecting a criminal. Just tell me if you've heard from Jackson."

The sigh of a man forced into a corner whooshed in Keely's ear. "No, Ma'am."

"Jackson stole something which could prove embarrassing to the Postwaites. I'm trying to get it back. Do you have any idea where he could have gone?"

Max signalled for attention. Keely put her hand over the mouthpiece. "What?"

"Ask him if Jackson had a favorite hang-out."

Keely repeated the question.

A long silence. "We weren't bosom companions," Ives said stiffly. "What he did during his time off was his affair."

"Ives, think! This is important! If what Jackson took is made public, the Postwaites will suffer."

"Very well." A cough. "Jackson liked to play pool. Boasted of his prowess with a stick at every opportunity."

"Where did he play? A bar, friend's house, pool hall?"

"I didn't pay attention to his bragging," the butler retorted peevishly, discarding his haughty manner and cultured tone. "The man had the class of a sewer rat and the mouth of a refuse container. He was always irate when his services were required on Saturday nights because he was involved in a standing tournament at some smoke-filled dive in town...."

"The name! I need a name!"

Silence. Then, Ives said triumphantly, "Cue & Brew! That was the name of the dive!"

She thanked him, cut the connection, and relayed the news to Max. "Shall we call it a date?"

"Saturday night, Cue & Brew." Max sighed. "I imagine the most exotic item on the menu will be a greasy cheeseburger."

"I love greasy cheeseburgers. They're one of the house specialties at my place," Keely said, giddy with relief. The lead to Jackson's possible whereabouts was the first chink in the curtain of darkness which surrounded them. "You're a food snob."

"Guilty, but I prefer the term 'gourmand'." Max put his

glass in the sink. "Tell me something, Keely. If we're keeping things on a strictly business basis, why did you kiss me?"

The question caught her off guard and she stared at him, open mouthed, her glass positioned in mid-air.

"Come on. Don't tell me that you've forgotten about that little episode in your store room." Max grinned wickedly. "Kissing is like tangoing—it takes two."

She sprang off the stool and retreated to the French doors. "That kiss was just a kiss."

"And a smile is just a smile. I know the song." Max sauntered into the living room. "I told you before, Keely, I'm attracted to you. The moment you waltzed into my life with your cinnamon hair, cameras clicking and gorgeous eyes flashing . . ."

"I think you've got my eyes mixed up with my flash unit." Keely's fingers itched and she held an imaginary camera to her eye, surveyed the room. "I'd like to do a photographic essay in here."

She pretended to zoom in on a black loafer lying mateless near the front door. "I'd call it 'Study of a Solitary Man.' "

Max's voice roughened. "This place isn't a home. I hadn't planned on staying in Lake Hope."

"Speaking of home, could you take me there? I've still got to finish cleaning up the store room—"

"I'm divorced, Keely." He studied her with a challenging glint in his eyes. "Since you seem to be uncomfortable with personal subjects, I'll save you the embarrassment of asking. When my marriage dissolved, I also forfeited ownership of my restaurant. I'm not currently involved with anyone."

"That makes two of us." Keely gave him an apologetic smile. "I'm sorry, that sounded snippy. I just want to keep things on a strictly business basis between us."

"But I don't. Your words say one thing but your eyes and

lips say another. How are you going to handle the fact that I want to put my arms around you and feel your heart beat against mine? That I want to kiss you until we're both in need of CPR?" Max moved a step closer. "I'll prepare an intimate dinner for two, Keely. We'll talk, get to know each other."

"And end up in bed. The best way to avoid becoming a hit and run victim is not to lie down in the road."

"Is that what you think I want? A romp in the sack?" Max frowned. "I'm not a guy who grabs something that feels good and then moves on. Lying awake at night, I paint imaginary murals on the ceiling of my bedroom. I often draw the woman of my dreams.

"Since I met you, Keely, that woman on the ceiling has your face, your smile. Trust me, Keely."

"I trust you, Max. It's me I don't trust."

His face split in an exultant grin and he moved toward her eagerly.

The doorbell rang. Keely felt a surge of relief, followed immediately by an unexpected sense of loss.

Max was thrown off stride. "I didn't buzz anyone in," he muttered, moving to the door. "Who's there?"

"Detectives Gifford and Dawson."

Keely and Max exchanged glances. "Tell them about the protection ring," he mouthed silently.

Keely shook her head. She couldn't live with herself if anything happened to Jess and her girls, or to Mimi.

Detective Gifford entered with the purposeful swing of her hips that marked her as a woman on a mission, her partner lumbering at her heels like a trained bear. She didn't seem surprised to see Keely in Max's apartment.

"Have either of you read today's paper?"

"No." Max exchanged puzzled glances with Keely. "Why?"

Gifford was here for answers, not to supply them. "Flo's final column makes interesting reading. I'm glad you're here, Ms. O'Brien. In going through Flo's office, we discovered that the lady had a penchant for recording private conversations."

Keely had the dizzying sensation of standing at a cliff's edge.

Gifford gestured to her companion, who flipped open his notebook. "I know some very unpleasant people. Choose to be difficult and you'll find there are more painful things than being flayed alive in the press."

Keely recognized Flo's words spoken—was it as recently as Wednesday afternoon? She remembered looking into the other woman's eyes and seeing an unrelenting enemy.

Detective Dawson continued, unperturbed by the interruption. "I think we understand each other. Friday. Noon."

"We believe that was the last tape Ms. Netherton recorded," Detective Gifford remarked in a matter-of-fact voice. "Fortunately, she marked each with the date and time before locking them in her desk drawer."

Max looked bewildered and Keely recalled he'd left the office before her final exchange with Flo.

She chose her words with care. "I don't deny she said those things to me. If you have a tape of the conversation, you know I spoke the truth about Flo trying to buy the videotape."

Gayla put brown hands on narrow hips. Her cotton dress was the color of the lime Max had sliced for the sun tea. "Do you recall what you said to her in response, Ms. O'Brien?"

Keely only remembered feeling powerless in the face of Flo's contempt.

Gayla nodded at her partner. "Refresh her memory."

The bulky detective consulted his notebook. "Compassion's an alien concept to you, isn't it? Someday, you'll be hurt the way you've hurt others. I hope you're shown no mercy."

"Someone didn't show mercy, did they, Ms. O'Brien? You should be happy. Your prophesy of doom came true last night—"

"No!" Keely's denial was vehement. "I didn't want anyone to hurt her—I, I . . ."

"Do you have a lawyer, Ms. O'Brien?"

Max intervened. "Don't say anything, Keely. Gifford, there's another angle that we uncovered this morning—"

Keely interrupted. "Am I under arrest?"

"Give me a reason why you shouldn't be."

Keely closed her eyes, visualizing Jessica's fear-ravaged face. Max was on the verge of revealing the protection racket, but she wanted to hold that disclosure until she'd thought of a way to keep Jessica's family clear of danger.

"I'll do better than give you a reason, I'll give you a suspect: Jackson. He was at my studio Thursday night—the serial number on the broken camera proves it was mine."

The two police officers exchanged glances. Dawson shrugged, his heavy features inscrutable. Gifford arched her brows and smiled brightly. "I suggest you get an attorney, Ms. O'Brien. Next time, we might want to do a little more than talk. For the record."

After their departure, Max drove Keely home. He refused to let her go in alone, insisted on checking each room of the house and studio for signs of intrusion. Keely leaned against the kitchen wall and let him search without protest.

A worried frown creasing his brow, Max re-entered the room. "I don't like the idea of you staying here alone."

"I'm not crazy about it myself, but I survived last night." Keely made an apathetic gesture toward the refrigerator.

"Perhaps you should check inside. Maybe the food's gone bad."

He didn't smile. "How about going to a hotel?"

Keely shrugged, feeling numb. "I'd rather toss and turn in my own bed, thank you." Fatigue fought a winning battle with dread.

Max gave her shoulder a comforting pat. "Call me if you need anything. You're welcome to stay at my place, but I've only got one bed."

"A gentleman would offer me the bed and take the couch." They exchanged tired smiles.

Keely remained propped against the kitchen wall until the door closed behind Max. The flashing light on the message unit caught her eye. Crossing the room on leaden feet, she punched the button and listened to shrill demands from the media for interviews. The vultures were gathering.

Then came a message which jarred her to attention. "Keely! I want you to get me out of this place and I mean today! I've got no money, no car, nothing to drink!"

Keely shuddered at her mother's strident voice. The anger driving Moira had the whip hand again.

Beep. Click. "Keely, this is Jess. I'm begging you, don't tell anyone what I told you! Please, please, promise me you won't!" Jessica ended the message with a gulping, hopeless sob that bound Keely tighter than any vow ever could.

The final straw on the camel's breaking back came in a monotone, menace lurking under each unstressed syllable. "You aren't listening, O'Brien. I want that tape by tomorrow night or else you're going to hear from me. You'll do what I want. Sooner or later, everybody does what I want."

Beep. Click. The answering machine hummed softly as the tape rewound.

Chapter 20

Keely decided that the jukebox at the Cue & Brew never stopped its wailing, even after closing time. She pictured neon lights flickering over empty tables and unracked balls in the pre-dawn hours, country tunes belting out to an invisible audience.

The atmosphere would make Smoky the Bear hyperventilate. In the gloom of inadequate lighting, cigarette tips glowed, sparks for a dozen baby forest fires.

Keely and Max occupied a booth beside the sunken floor supporting the pool tables. The seats were covered with brittle red vinyl which crackled maliciously whenever she shifted position. In the crowded pool room, the air clogged with tension as honor was upheld and lost on miniature jousting arenas of green felt. Cues were favored over lances; warriors refreshed themselves from beer cans instead of flagons.

Keely's feet ached, as did her head. So far she'd danced with three guys who'd never heard of Arthur Murray and a fellow possessing the rhthym of a fence post. She'd also fended off several who tried to get up close and personal.

Keely adjusted the spaghetti straps of the red silk blouse she'd purchased for tonight's foray into the seamy side of Lake Hope. It required an astonishing amount of money to look cheap.

She blew out a frustrated breath. "Either we're not adequately describing Jackson or Ives sent us to the wrong dive."

"I hardly think he could have mistook the name of this quaint little place." Max gingerly poked at the cheeseburger huddled in a plastic basket in front of him.

"Relax, it won't bite. It's dead." Keely searched the smoky room for Jackson among the throng.

"This sandwich has definitely given up the ghost," Max agreed, fastidiously wiping his hands on a scrawny paper napkin pried from the clamped jaws of a metal dispenser. "Keely, when I suggested an intimate dinner, I was thinking more along the lines of a succulent parslied rack of lamb and Potatoes Anna. For dessert, perhaps the richness of Coeur a la Creme Fraiche . . ."

"Stop torturing me!" Keely picked up a limp french fry. Unpalatable without ketchup, but the vivid memory of Flo's battered head had caused her to forego her usual crimson pool. "What will we do if Jackson doesn't show up tonight? The creep on the phone wasn't kidding when he said, 'Sooner or later, everyone does what I want.' I'm sure he was speaking from personal experience."

"At least the police have a recording of his threats. Gifford promised you protection when you turned over the answering machine tape, didn't she?"

Keely raised her voice to be heard over the argument breaking out at a nearby booth. "Her actual words were she'd be keeping an eye on me. More of a warning than reassurance. You still haven't answered my question. What's our next step if Jackson doesn't show?"

Max's brows were drawn in a troubled frown. "We'll have to tell Gifford about the protection racket. The police are under too much pressure to sit on their hands any longer."

Sickened, Keely dropped the french fry back on her plate. "We can't reveal what we know about the protection racket without betraying Jessica and her girls—"

"I agree. But you've got to start thinking about yourself." Max shoved away the basket containing his sandwich. "Flo's final masterpiece of spite in yesterday's paper might force Gifford into making a premature arrest. Anyone reading that column will assume Flo's vicious reference to your mother's problems gave you a motive for murder."

"I'm not going to risk the safety of Jessica's girls."

Max traced the ring of condensation left by his glass of beer. "You've got to untie that millstone that's hanging around your neck, Keely."

"Millstone?" She shuddered, the vinyl beneath her creaking in protest. "I don't know what you're talking about."

"Answer this question truthfully. Is it possible that by protecting Rose Postwaite, you're trying to atone for whatever you couldn't or didn't do for your mother?"

"Leave my mother out of this!" Keely glared at Max. In black chinos and wine dark shirt, he looked out of place among the jean clad characters who inhabited the pool hall, a polished gemstone glittering in a bowl of gravel.

"Flo didn't, Keely." Max lowered his voice until she had to strain to hear. "I know your mother's an alcoholic, and she's in rehab for the fourth time. You've been footing the bills, which is why you haven't had the capital to expand Key Shot."

"That information certainly wasn't in Flo's gossip column. How did you—" The truth struck Keely just as the opening chords of "Take It Back" blared from the juke box. "Your Uncle Tony who compiled the report on Flo—you had him do one on me, too!"

"I had to know who I was dealing with, Keely. Anna Marie's business, not to mention my neck, is on the line."

"So you hired someone to dig up dirt in my back yard!" Keely shot back. The thought infuriated her. "I should have you arrested for trespassing," she muttered.

Max's gaze was compassionate. Keely switched her gaze to her plate, but couldn't pretend an interest in the unappetizing meal. In the background, Reba sang, "You said I stole your heart away by looking in your eyes—"

Keely sang along softly with the chorus. "Take it back, Take it back."

"I did what I had to do, Keely. This town's turned into a war zone and I believe in being well armed."

"As long as there's war, there'll be spies and traitors." Despite the ache in her heart, Keely felt unnaturally calm. "You must also know I was married eight years ago but it didn't work out. Did your 'spy' tell you why?"

"Keely, you don't have to explain—"

"Eric couldn't shake the fear that I was going to end up like my mother. He regulated every sip I took, every bite of food that went into my mouth. He was my monitor, not my husband, and after three years, we called it quits."

Max's expression was now more exasperated than compassionate. "At the moment, I'm concerned that your overdeveloped sense of responsibility might land us in jail."

Keely's fingers felt greasy. She glanced down and saw that she'd strangled a french fry.

Grabbing a napkin, she wiped off her hands. "Overdeveloped sense of responsibility?"

"As witnessed by your compulsion to keep bailing out your mother despite evidence that she's not falling off the wagon, but diving off, head first."

Keely looked away from the concern in his eyes and down at the shredded pieces of napkin on the table. She unclenched her hands; more pieces drifted down like snowflakes. The sense of being crammed into a box overwhelmed her. First her mother, then Eric, demands and dependency to control her . . .

The harsh, arid atmosphere caught at Keely's throat and tears from the cigarette smoke—she wanted to believe it was the smoke—pricked her eyes, blurring her vision. On the juke box, Reba continued to sing about betrayal and dismissal.

"Keely, I'm sorry. My intention never was to pry into your personal life."

"But you did, Max. Before you kissed me, you told me your faith in me was a matter of trust. All the time you had a detailed report on my personal life in your hands. Your brand of trust is just a matter of thorough detective work."

Caught up in the exchange, Keely forgot to keep an eye peeled for Jackson. Earlier, however, she had noticed a heavy-set man seated three tables away staring at Max. Now, catching sudden movement in her peripheral vision, she turned in time to see the man lurch to his feet and stumble toward them.

Max, however, was oblivious to the approaching collision. He grabbed Keely's wrist, forcing her to look at him. "Listen to me! The first moment I saw you, I knew I needed you in my life. I wanted to spend time with you, get to know you. But you keep chopping down every effort to build an emotional bridge between us. Your mother let you down, Keely. Eric let you down. How do you know that I'll do the same?"

"Hey, Bud!" The man lurched to a stop beside their table, his head thrust forward as he surveyed Max with loathing. A meaty hand landed on Max's arm.

"Excuse me." Max removed the sausage thick fingers. "This is a private conversation."

"This your wife?" The bullet head and red-rimmed gaze swung toward Keely. "Does she know about your bad habits, mister?"

"Bad habits?"

A snaky triumph slithered over the newcomer's reddened

features. "Maybe you should tell her, mister. Tell her you were flirting with my wife. Tell her how you danced real close."

Max plucked off the hairy hand which had clamped back on his upper arm. "You just sat there while I did all that?"

"I wasn't here, was I, mister? I was pulling a late shift at the plant. My friends told me what my old lady was up to in here last night, you and her rubbing 'gainst each other like animals in heat. Did you go home with her? I'll kill you if I find out you've been in my house, in my bed—"

"I'd be a real cretin to confirm it then, wouldn't I?" With a disgusted shake of his head, Max glanced over to where two equally burly gentlemen radiated beery satisfaction at having gotten their buddy fueled up for a brawl.

Keely felt like a spectator at a dog fight, where one dog was reluctant to fight and the other craved blood, but was unsure where to begin biting.

"There's been a misunderstanding." With insulting deliberation, Max removed the paw which had snagged his arm for the third time. "Listen carefully, sir. I did not flirt with your wife. I did not dance with your wife. In fact, I couldn't identify the lady in question if she appeared in a line-up of one."

A forceful snort sent beer fumes wafting across the table. "My buddies say different."

Max raised a sardonic eyebrow. In the clipped tones of an aristocrat accosted by a peasant, he said, "Since this is my first visit to this particular establishment, I can assure you that whomever your wife danced with last night, it was not I."

"Max, please don't antagonize him!"

The man's brow creased as his sodden brain replayed Max's contemptuous speech in an attempt at comprehension. Awareness crashed over his heavy features and he growled.

Keely groaned and sat very still, keeping her expression

neutral, hoping that someone—anyone—would intervene to stop this farce. The situation was patently ridiculous, but teetered on the edge of chaos. Any unexpected movement might tip the balance. Sensing the potential for violence, a crowd gathered around the booth and their hovering presence prodded the drunken intruder into action.

"I think you've got a smart mouth, mister. One that needs stopping up like a foul drain." The hand moved again, this time fastening on Max's throat.

Keely jumped up with an outraged cry, but as she did, she spotted a familiar face in the crowd of onlookers. Jackson! The ex-chauffeur's gaze shifted until he met Keely's. He began pushing through the mob in the opposite direction.

Keely glanced back in time to see Max's fist connect with the red bull's-eye of the drunk's nose. The thickset man staggered backward with a grunt, arms windmilling, and crashed into a table which overturned, sending beer and glasses flying. A woman shrieked; the more sober bystanders ducked the shower of foam.

Since Max seemed to be holding his own, Keely started in pursuit of Jackson, but the entire room dissolved into a gigantic fist fight around her. She dodged flailing arms and stumbling bodies, trying to catch up to her quarry and escape the frenzy unscathed.

Stumbling over an overturned chair near the bar, she righted herself. Just ahead, Jackson glanced back as he neared the front door and she saw blood trickling from his lip. Some helpful soul had slowed him down with a punch to the mouth.

"Jackson!" she called. "Wait, I want to talk to you!"

He hesitated as Keely broke clear of the melee. Fists on hips, he rocked back on his heels, a crooked grin on his bruised mouth.

Keely sidled closer, keeping a cautious distance between

them. Where was Max? She didn't dare turn her back on Jackson to look for him. "I think you have something I want."

"You've got something I want." Jackson's insolent gaze traveled up her short leather skirt and halted at the neckline of the scarlet blouse. "Maybe we could make a deal."

"Maybe," she said, her heart beating so loudly she was afraid he could hear the thump above the yells and the jukebox's racket. Keely hated talking to men who never looked above her collar bone. "You stole something at the Postwaite reception."

"The videotape? Yeah, that made interesting viewing. My new address will be on Easy Street—once I cash in."

Jackson gave a sly shake of his head. "I'll call you. We can do business, but it'll have to be just you and me."

He opened the door and darted out.

Keely yelped when a hand closed on her arm.

"Relax—it's me." Max was panting. He had a reddened spot on his jaw to match the bruise on his forehead.

"Jackson was here!" Keely told him excitedly. "He admitted taking the videotape—"

"Let's make tracks." Max towed Keely forward. "I heard the bartender calling the police."

He shoved open the door, letting in the howl of approaching sirens. They fled, ducking around the corner as two police cars, lights flashing, drew up in front. With unspoken accord, Max and Keely dashed down the grimy alley corridor, putting as much distance between them and the forces of law and order as possible.

As she ran, Keely drew in gulping, shallow breaths. Her feet hurt—her scarlet pumps had been designed for looking good on the dance floor, not wind sprints. Beside her, Max loped along. He looked exhilarated, a lock of hair flopping over his eye. Bar brawls and quick getaways suited the guy.

★ ★ ★ ★ ★

Max peered into the depths of Keely's refrigerator. "You must only use the ten items or less lane at the grocery store."

"I've been too busy to go shopping." Keely sank into a chair and propped her feet on the seat of another. "I wish I'd grabbed my cheeseburger before leaving."

"I'd whip up something, but even a guy with my exceptional culinary gifts can't do much with a jar of olives, wrinkled lettuce leaves, and a container of expired yogurt." He slammed the door. "Woman, you have the palate of a garbage disposal."

Keely eyed him sourly. "You seem quite chipper for a fellow who narrowly avoided arrest tonight."

"We weren't the ones breaking pool cues over other people's heads," Max pointed out as he prowled the room, opening and closing cupboard doors.

Keely yearned to remove her shoes, but feared her feet would be revealed as bloody stumps. "As abhorrent as the subject of dance is to me after tonight's experiences, I have to ask. Were you really bumping and grinding with that man's wife last night? I can't quite picture you in the role of Patrick Swayze—"

"The lush was so loaded that if he walked out on the interstate, he would have been ticketed by the state police for exceeding the tonnage limit." Max removed a box of cereal from the pantry and checked the freshness date. "Your kitchen needs some comfort food."

Keely persisted. "So you didn't check out the Brew and Cue last night on a solo trip?"

"No." Max slammed the pantry door. "The three Sloshed-kateers mistook me for someone else."

Keely knew they were avoiding the prickly subject of the investigative report. From her seat, she could see the flashing indicator on the answering machine, but she had no intention of reviewing her messages with Max present. Not when the caller could be Moira on a tirade.

Leaning forward, Keely removed a shoe and massaged her arch. "If you hadn't scared him off, Jackson might have opened up."

"Judging by his leer, your blouse was the only thing in danger of being opened." Max was eating handfuls of Captain Crunch straight from the box. "Next time you're at the store, pick up a box of Fruit Loops."

"Fruit Loops?" Despite her exhaustion, Keely smiled. "The great gourmand, Max Summers, likes Fruit Loops?"

"That's not something I tell my clients." Max licked his fingertips with sensuous enjoyment. Remembering the taste of his lips on hers, Keely felt her inner pilot light ignite.

"What do we do next? Besides wait for Jackson to call."

"Judging by his crack about Easy Street, the slime must have seen something pretty juicy on that tape." Max drummed his fingers on the table. "Since you saw what the camera saw—"

"I saw a man turning away from a conversation with Flo!" Keely pointed the heel of the shoe she still held at Max. "A man I thought was you."

"Now you know it wasn't." Max appeared unruffled by her peevish tone. "For the sake of argument, let's assume that the guy you saw with Flo is the goon who called you last night."

Keely nodded. "No argument here. Flo's desire to buy the tape indicates she didn't want evidence of that meeting lying around. If the man who threatened me is the same guy she met in the hall, he's camera shy, too."

"Concentrate, Keely. Is it possible you interrupted some type of exchange?"

Keely kneaded her thigh and gave him a disbelieving look. "Exchange? You mean Flo handing over money, drugs—"

She broke off, eyes squeezed shut in concentration as she pictured again the scene in the hallway. The man's hands had been shielded by his body as he turned away . . .

Keely gasped and sat bolt upright.

"What?" Max beckoned with both hands. "Spill it, O'Brien. I see the glitter of inspiration in your eyes."

In her excitement, Keely sputtered the words. "Rose's diamond necklace! I'll bet Flo handed over the stolen necklace! That's why the police didn't find it on the premises."

"Bingo!" Max crowed exultantly. "That would explain why she was so desperate to get her hands on the tape!"

"The man I saw was probably Flo's connection to the Sterling Ring—and the muscle behind the extortion scheme!"

"Our prime suspect as Flo's killer," Max contributed. "No wonder he called you again yesterday."

"Tonight's the deadline he gave me." Keely couldn't suppress a shudder as she looked around the kitchen. Inside was cozy with warmth and light, but outside darkness pressed against the windows and shadows crept across the grass. "Even with a patrol car cruising the neighborhood, I'm considering checking into a hotel for the next couple nights."

Max gestured toward the answering machine. "In that case, don't you think you should check your messages?"

Keely could tell from Max's expression that if she didn't, he would. She removed her other pump before rising and limping on bare feet across the floor. Leaning against the counter, she hit the playback button.

A curt, unfamiliar voice announced, "You're scheduled to photograph my daughter's wedding next Saturday."

Keely tried to visualize her decimated schedule. Saturday.

Courtney Fairmont. With the cancellations, she'd assumed the family would have already engaged another photographer, neglecting to give her the courtesy of a telephone call. Most of her appointments this week had simply failed to show up.

"I told Courtney I wanted another photographer, but she insists on having you." Hugo Fairmont sounded baffled.

Keely retrieved a visual image of the caller. Hugo Fairmont, a grizzled man who looked more like a bear emerging from a hibernation period than the president of a Fortune 500 company, was not in the habit of mincing words.

"I got Courtney to agree you wouldn't photograph the rehearsal dinner, but you're still on for the wedding. In this household," another spark of baffled fury mixed with pride, "What Courtney wants, Courtney gets."

Bless Courtney, Keely thought fervently. Bless her and all other spoiled society princesses.

Hugo wasn't finished. "If anything goes wrong at my little girl's wedding, I'm holding you personally responsible. Ask my business competitors—I always get satisfaction."

The remainder of the messages were from importunate and frustrated members of the media. Keely and Max listened in silence until the last click on the tape.

"Those clowns have freedom of the press confused with the license to harass." Max's scowl had grown fiercer with each message. "Who's this Fairmont character?"

"A man with a daughter Flo hated. No measly silver spoons for the Fairmonts. Courtney was born with an entire set of cutlery in her mouth, including a shrimp fork." Keely hobbled back to her own seat. "Her unpretentious theme is Camelot."

Max looked bemused. "Camelot? Feast of Italy's catering that affair." He frowned. "At least it's still on the calendar.

Anna Marie ordered me to keep the Fairmonts happy."

"You can probably expect a call from Papa Bear wielding an iron paw in an iron glove." Keely shed her leather jacket and ruefully inspected a stain on her silk blouse. Someone had splashed her with a drink during the fracas at the Brew & Cue. "You look beat," Max said sympathetically. "Why don't you throw some clothes and a toothbrush in a suitcase?"

Keely left her guest finishing off the box of dry cereal while she went upstairs to change into jeans and pack an overnight bag. Returning to the kitchen, she found Max scribbling on the pad of paper she used for grocery lists.

Leaning over his shoulder, Keely read aloud the items he'd jotted down. "Swithin Cream? May Sallat? Who are Swithin and May? Suspects in Flo's murder?"

Max ripped the top sheet from the pad. "Food ignoramus! I'm just going over the menu for the Fairmont wedding."

Keely felt buoyed by a surge of excitement. If she wasn't arrested for murder and dear Courtney's reception went off without a hitch, she still might have a business to salvage.

Keely dropped the overnight bag on a chair and regarded it thoughtfully. She was being pushed around again—and she didn't like it.

Max got to his feet. "May I drop you at a hotel? Or would you rather I followed you downtown as a precaution?"

"Neither, thank you." Keely squared her shoulders. "I've decided I'm not going to let a voice on the phone drive me out of my home."

"Don't be ridiculous!" Max grabbed her overnight bag off the chair. "You're alone, vulnerable. What if this jerk carries out one of his favorite threats and sets fire to your studio?"

"Detective Gifford said the police would be keeping an eye on my house for a few nights. So far, nothing's happened—"

"Nothing except a woman's been murdered in your studio! Trust me, Keely, this is not a good idea. You're either going to a hotel or back to my place."

"Trust you?" Anger blossomed in her brain, a terrible red flower. She snatched the bag from Max, cradling it protectively against her chest. "I'm afraid I don't trust you. Not without a background clearance from a detective in my hand!"

Max rolled his eyes heavenward. "Excuse me, but the bus seems to have missed my stop. One minute we're working brilliantly as a team and the next you're telling me you don't trust me?"

The rational part of Keely's brain rebuked her for overreacting, but Max's casual assumption of control raised too many unpleasant specters from her past.

"I'm not helpless, nor am I especially vulnerable. I had deadbolt locks and an alarm system installed this morning. I have my phone speed dial set on 911."

"Keely, I admire your guts, but not your judgment. Please, reconsider. Look, let me stay. Surely you've got a vacant guest room or a spare couch—"

The phone rang. Sore feet forgotten, Keely dropped the bag and darted across the room. Max took up a position directly behind her, leaning forward as she snatched up the receiver. His shoulder touched Keely's, his hand found a natural resting place on her hip.

"Yes?"

"You know who this is."

Jackson! Keely stabbed the message record button. "Go on."

"Any lawyer'll tell you that possession is nine-tenths of the law, Sweet Cheeks."

Keely tensed. She felt Max's body respond, his fingers

pressing into the flesh above her jeans. "I want my video-tape."

"I want to get rich. Since we both want something, we should be able to work out an agreement."

Keely held the phone so Max could hear Jackson's response. She gave in to the impulse to lean against him, drawing strength from the contact.

"Give me a reasonable figure and we might make a deal."

Jackson laughed, an ugly sound. "I've got another customer and that's gonna drive up the price considerably."

Max whispered in her left ear, "Set up a meeting," and Keely said quickly, "Let's meet. Perhaps we can work something out."

"I'll call with a time and place. Or better yet, maybe I'll just show up and surprise you."

Jackson severed the connection and Keely put down the phone. She realized she was still pressed against Max's lean frame. Head averted, she pushed past him, moving to the center of the room. Drawing a deep breath, she said, "Did you hear him say he's got another customer? That means I'm off the hook."

"How do you figure that?" Max followed her, pacing with deliberate steps. He stopped less than a foot away.

"Jackson must have recognized and contacted the man on the tape." Keely gestured toward the phone. "By now, the firebug knows I don't have the video. He won't be bothering me tonight."

"What if you've guessed wrong?"

Keely retreated, although Max had made no move to touch her. She felt torn between the need to assert her independence and the desire to lean against the wall of his strength again.

Max's eyes were bleak. "I can't force you to accept my

help, Keely. If you change your mind about staying at my place or needing a lift to a hotel, call me."

Just her luck, Keely thought ruefully, to find a man who actually listened to the stupidity she babbled!

Max paused on the top step and turned to face her. Keely gave him a questioning look.

"I meant what I said at the pool hall. You're a fever in my blood. When all this is over, I'll prove it to you."

"Max—"

"Let me stay, Keely. Let me help you. Don't dissolve our partnership." His face was shadowed, his eyes hooded by darkness. Moonlight silvered his dark hair.

Although the words were quietly spoken, he'd drawn a line in the sand. Keely felt a flare of irritation skip across her nerves. Was this an ultimatum? Step over that line and join him or he'd walk out?

A relationship with Max would burn like a comet—white hot, rocketing them into ecstasy. However, the laws of physics dictated that what goes up also comes down. Keely had learned the hard way that passion not fueled by love flames out just as quickly as it ignites.

She didn't have a spare ounce of emotional energy to invest in a relationship; it wasn't fair to take with no intention of giving. Looked at objectively, there was only one decision to make.

Keely's voice was steady. "Good-bye, Max."

Although he made no discernable movement, Keely sensed his withdrawal. "Is that all you have to say?"

She lifted her shoulders in a hopeless shrug. "You ask too much. I'm sorry, Max."

He started to speak, stopped. Keely stood in the doorway, staring at her bare feet and listening to Max's heels thud down the walkway until he reached the street.

The Bronco's engine started with a muted roar. Keely wanted to retract her decision, but the shifting emotional sands had obliterated the line drawn earlier, leaving her with no choice. She closed the door slowly.

The click of the deadbolt should have also locked Max out, but images of the man paraded before her. Max in the police station, with his thumbs hooked in his pockets doing that ridiculous imitation of Gary Cooper. At the Postwaite reception, his hands deftly arranging the cheeses, his warm smile reaching through the camera lens.

The overpowering scent of cinnamon as the two of them stood inside the walk-in pantry at Feast of Italy, body heat overlapping body heat. The taste of Max's lips and the hungry response of her own heart—

Keely realized she'd been frantically drawing her own lines in the sand since they'd met but Max had stepped over each one of them.

After setting the new alarm system, she trooped wearily upstairs, fragments of broken promises floating through her head. Her mother: "I swear I'll never touch another drop, honey." Eric: "I love you, Keely. We'll be together forever."

Keely stopped in the doorway and stared at her bed. She was drained, empty of emotion. No one, especially solid-to-the-core Max, could love a hollow woman.

She sighed. "Forever isn't as long as it used to be."

Chapter 21

Max was slow dancing with Keely in the private room of Max's Bistro to "Smoke Gets in Your Eyes" when the phone rang, shattering the intimacy and putting out the fire.

"Lo?" Max mumbled, eyes glued shut by sleep.

"MAX? ARE YOU STILL IN BED?"

"Anna Marie!" Max dropped the receiver. Snapping to an upright position, he groped frantically for the instrument in the sheets as her voice floated up.

"IS SOMEONE PAYING YOU BY THE HOUR TO SLEEP? WHAT DO YOU THINK YOU ARE—A SALMON MARINATING IN DILL AND PEPPERCORNS?"

Max focused on the clock on the bedside table. "Anna Marie, it's 6:30 on a Sunday morning! My day off."

His aunt grudging lowered the volume by a decibel. "What about the Braithmore dinner? Isn't that scheduled for tonight?"

Max considered, then dismissed, lying as an option. "The dinner was canceled. Or rather, Feast of Italy's role in the festivities was canceled."

"What in the name of Julia Child are you talking about?" The only time he'd heard Anna Marie talk so softly was the day she'd caught him and her thirteen year old son smoking in the garage. Justice had been swift, giving Max unique insight into the meaning of the phrase, "touched by the hand of God." To this day, the faintest whiff of smoke and his ears rang reminiscently.

You're a grown man, Max told himself sternly. At the moment you're out of reach. The perfect time to break the news that Anna Marie might not have a business left.

"Due to the negative publicity, we've had some cancellations. It's only natural, Anna Marie. As soon as the furor dies down, the phone will be ringing off the hook again."

"I see." Her words zipped through the line like bullets. "Just exactly how many is 'some'?"

Visualizing the scheduling book with its multitude of crossed out lines, Max winced. "I can't remember offhand. Why don't I go over the book and call you with detailed information?"

Anna Marie called his bluff. "I know why my business is going to Hades in a hand basket, Max. It's because you're neglecting it for that O'Brien woman."

Max regretted not having the foresight to bribe his uncle into keeping the newspapers from his volatile spouse. "I know things look bad for Keely at the moment, but I assure you she had nothing to do with the robberies or Flo Netherton's murder."

"Did she tell you that, Max?"

"Yes, and I believe her." He remembered his dramatic exit last night and felt his ears redden. Who did he think he was, Clark Gable? Frankly, my dear, I don't give a—

Anna Marie clucked her tongue. "She's not for you, Max. You need a nice, cozy Italian girl, one who wants babies, not a career. This Keely is not the woman for you."

Fine talk, coming from the queen of the catering world. If she'd trumpeted it, he could have rejected her words, but his aunt's quiet conviction, added to Keely's dry-eyed dismissal, undermined Max's confidence.

Absentmindedly, he massaged the lump on his forehead, a painful reminder of the folly of overconfidence. Last night, he'd glimpsed the glint of humor in Keely's eyes. Rooms were weirdly empty without her presence. Keely even danced through his dreams; his arms felt empty. Loneliness was a nagging ache under his breastbone.

Anna Marie sighed heavily. Adopting a funereal tone, she commanded, "Stay away from the O'Brien woman. You'll drive your mother to an early grave."

"You've got it backwards, Anna Marie. In this family, it's always the women who drive the men to the cemetery and then afterwards feast on the funeral meats. Things will get back to normal—"

Anna Marie snorted. "YOU BET YOUR STUFFED PHEASANTS THEY WILL! I'M TAKING OVER AS OF SATURDAY NIGHT."

"What!" Max sat up again. "But your ankle—"

"I'll get around. I got a call from Hugo Fairmont last night. He doesn't want you within ten miles of his daughter's wedding, so I promised to handle the catering personally."

"Anna Marie—"

"IF YOU PERSIST IN HOBNOBBING WITH A MURDEROUS REDHEAD, DON'T EXPECT ME TO BAKE YOU A TORTE WITH A FILE IN IT!"

Keely perched on the edge of the chair. Funny how the chairs in this place looked cozy but, like the sensitive princess tossing over the mattress-covered pea, she could never get comfortable. Smoothing her border print skirt, she wondered why she had dressed with such care. Putting her best foot, clad in a bright green pump, forward for disaster.

Lillian Dart, the counselor, swept in, with Moira in tow. "Sit down, Moira. Hello, Keely! You look so fresh and pretty!"

"Thank you." Keely avoided her mother's accusing gaze.

Moira wore a denim jumper, the patient's uniform at Fair Oaks. But in what her daughter instantly recognized as a gesture of rebellion, she'd chosen to omit a blouse, allowing the pale, freckled area of her upper breasts to be exposed by the scoop neckline. Alcohol had faded the freshness of her skin tone, despoiled her once striking beauty. Moira's neck was thin rather than slender, her high cheekbones mocked by the ravages of deep scoured hollows underneath.

"We've got lots to cover in this session, so let's start." Lillian gave the older woman an encouraging smile. "Moira, last week Keely shared her feelings about your showing up drunk at all of the important events in her life. Now I want you to tell her why you felt it necessary to drink before attending her high school graduation and her wedding."

Moira took her time in responding. The fingers of her right hand pinched an invisible cigarette; the other twitched in her lap. Her posture was that of a prisoner broken by inhumane treatment. Keely realized her mother had finally accepted that no amount of wheedling would grant her the freedom of the bottle.

In a whiskey rasp, Moira mumbled, "I had a couple of drinks for courage. My daughter's always looked at me like I'm a bug on the wall." A sneer contorted her mobile mouth. "It ain't easy, growin' up with a kid who looks down her nose at her mom—"

Keely felt her stomach cramp as the complaints continued. She could chime in at any point, recite the familiar litany like a memorized prayer.

Moira's voice assumed the familiar whine of self-righteousness. "So what if I needed a bit of bottled confidence to face her snooty friends and their parents? People dressed up in expensive suits and dresses that cost more money than I've seen in my whole life. Ain't been easy, you know, raising a girl without help from her father. Bastard ran out on me. I've done my best, but it's never been enough for Keely—"

Keely closed her eyes, letting the waves of self-justification wash over her. Moira recycled the same excuses each session, pushing the blame onto Keely, Keely's friends, Keely's absent father, her own parents.

Lillian showed endless patience, asking questions, poking holes in Moira's protective bubble of self-exoneration. But Keely's mother simply wrapped the cloak of her bitterness around her even tighter and stared at her daughter with bright, angry eyes.

Keely was sick of the whole process. They'd been through this so many times, but the well of Moira's resentment never ran dry. How much did Keely owe the woman who gave her life? Especially considering that she'd probably been conceived during a moment of drunken passion and not love.

Lillian was talking again. Moira picked fretfully at the arm of the chair with her fingers, avoiding the counselor's gaze.

Keely gritted her teeth. She endured these sessions like chemotherapy treatments, voluntarily subjecting herself to poisons which left her ill and weak. Suffering this torture in the hopes of killing the cancer which was destroying an already dysfunctional relationship. But the disease seemed invincible and Keely could only sit here in this sun drenched room and wonder if personal joy was a myth, a false oasis.

Face it, she thought grimly. The only thing you've ever really taken pleasure in was your business, a business with a questionable future.

Her mother's voice sliced through Keely's moody reflections. "Maybe I drink because I'm lonely. Life's not worth living without a little fun and a lot of love."

A tingle of shock raced through Keely as she realized that

that was exactly what Max had offered her. If he were here, he'd probably say she was trying to expiate the guilt for her existence, for being the reason her mother married a man who bailed out at the first excuse.

But Max wasn't here, wouldn't be again. Keely had made sure of that. She'd dismissed him before he could spin her any fragile promises or tell her more lies.

Keely debated unburdening her soul to Lillian. She ached to tell this sympathetic woman about her frenzied reaction to the flashback in Doug's apartment, but she was afraid. In light of Flo's violent death, an admission of such a loss of control could rebound to haunt her.

Moira abandoned picking at the chair arm to tug on a thread in the hem of the denim jumper. "If Keely had been a better daughter, if she'd have loved me like she should—"

A sorrowful expression crossed Lillian's face. Keely followed the direction of the counselor's gaze down to her own hands which were pleating the cotton material of her skirt.

Like mother, like daughter. Keely desperately missed the insulating filter of a camera lens.

Lillian continued to gaze at her and Keely understood she was expected to respond to Moira's stream of self-justification.

Her first thought was to terminate the session, to get up and walk out. Moira wouldn't listen. She was a woman roaring down a road that ended abruptly at a cliff's edge, deaf to warning shouts as she careened past. Keely herself had screamed until she was hoarse and her mother had never listened.

But the question haunting Keely since the night of Flo's death burst out. "Why didn't you protect me from those drunken creeps you used to bring home from your pub crawling, Mom? I was just a little girl!"

Lillian nodded approval, switching her intent gaze to Moira's liquor smudged features. Instead of answering, however, Keely's mother burst into raucous sobs, her hands covering her face and her body rocking in distress.

"Well!" Lillian looked unaccountably cheerful. "I think you're making progress."

Keely gazed back at the counselor. It took a full minute for the realization to penetrate that the last remark had been addressed to her.

Chapter 22

Ida Burke, flamboyant in a pink pantsuit spattered with sequined roses, said firmly. "This is a business, Ma'am, not a museum of horrors. If you'd like to view the crime scene, you'll have to make an appointment to have a portrait taken."

Keely rolled her eyes and grimaced. Ida, however, kept her composure, pen hovering over the open appointment book.

Hanging up the receiver, she said with relish, "Another appointment for a sitting. Fortunately for the checking account, we've got a town full of ghouls."

The phone, stubbornly silent last week, had rung continually all morning. While people wouldn't patronize a thief, they had no qualms about paying a murder suspect to take their photograph. The only bright spot to this Monday morning was that so far no one had asked Keely for her autograph.

No-shows were a thing of the past. Several casual drop-ins, two cancellations miraculously reversed and Ida had turned away a reporter and his camera operator shadow. Keely's final session this morning had involved a freckled boy in a Cubs cap who had discovered the secret of perpetual motion.

Keely had just ushered the boy, hopping on one foot, and his pudgy mother to the door. The woman voiced her displeasure in not glimpsing any traces of the murder in the studio, even asking if she could move the rug covering the blood stains.

Ida chuckled. "Seems like folks have swallowed their fear

and are now chewing on a good mouthful of curiosity."

"I hope they choke on it, Ida. If I could scrape up the extra funds to rent a studio, I wouldn't be here now."

"Don't blame you, love. Anybody'd be jittery, working in a place where murder most foul's been committed—"

"Ida, you're not helping." Keely touched the sword-shaped leaf of a lavender bearded iris in a tall purple vase and wondered if Feast of Italy was experiencing an equal resurgence of business. "These are lovely, but I've forgotten what irises signify."

"Faith." Ida chuckled, a rich mellow sound. "I wanted to bring in a bouquet of Queen Anne's Lace, but it's too early in the season. You know, honey, there's something different about you today. I just can't put my finger on it."

Keely was startled by the other woman's perception. Despite her distaste for working where Flo had died, she felt more relaxed than she had in weeks. Perhaps the abrasion of old wounds during yesterday's therapy session had been a medical necessity, enabling the healing process to begin.

Keely checked her watch. "I've got two hours before my next appointment. I'm going to grab lunch and run some errands. Can you hold down the fort?"

"Of course, dear." Ida twisted the channel set ruby ring on her right hand. "Did you see Mr. Summers this weekend?"

Keely smoothed the collar of her embroidered polo top, refusing to commit herself.

"I bet he's a fellow who knows how to show a lady a good time." Ida sighed. "Everything would be strictly first class with that guy. Romantic dining, roses, champagne—"

The memory of greasy cheeseburgers at the Brew & Cue and Max devouring handfuls of Captain Crunch brought the first smile of the day to Keely's mouth. Fortunately, the impudent chirp of the phone saved her from answering and she left Ida coping with another potential client/sightseer.

Keely drove the loaner car to the garage where she picked up her repainted car which now rode on four brand new tires. Next, she stopped in to see attorney Daniel Mount. He'd been highly recommended and Keely felt comfortable with his avuncular manner, keen gaze, and confident demeanor. After a short conference, Daniel patted Keely's shoulder and told her to give him a call if she heard from Gifford again or even if she just wanted to talk.

The time for talk was over, Keely decided on her way out to the car. During a sleepless night, she'd worked out a plan. She wasn't going to wait for Jackson to pop up like a devilish jack-in-the-box or for Gifford to locate him. Keely was convinced the missing videotape was vital evidence in murder. Only by clearing herself, could she get back to business.

The first step in retrieving the tape was finding Jackson, and Keely had an idea where he might be. Franklin Premier Limousines was known for its corporate and specialty services, with ads boasting each limousine came equipped with a color television, CD stereo, bar, intercom, and cellular phone.

Included in the much publicized fleet was a claret colored Rolls Royce with dove gray interior, classic cars, executive motor coaches, and the standard stretch limos. Its chauffeurs dressed in crisp olive green and stiff brimmed hats. Ron Franklin had a reputation for rewarding his drivers for their rigid postures and smoothly deferential manners.

If Jackson needed a temporary job while he waited for the good ship "Blackmail" to sail into port, Keely was convinced he'd apply for one here.

The receptionist inside the limo office presented the same polished and sleek appearance of the cars pulled up to the curb outside. After attempting to press brochures for night club tours, anniversary packages complete with fresh flowers, and city sightseeing excursions on Keely, she consented to contact her boss by intercom.

"There's a Kelly O'Brien here—"

"It's Keely," Keely corrected her.

Drawing plucked black brows together in irritation, the woman repeated, "a Keely O'Brien, Mr. Franklin, who wants to talk to you. I know you're already in a meeting—"

Her smooth brow furrowed again, this time in puzzlement. "Yes, sir. Certainly. I'll send her in."

Directed down a hallway carpeted in royal blue, Keely knocked on a half opened door and entered in response to a brisk invitation. Ron Franklin sat behind a mammoth desk, incongruously perched on a leather car seat. The seat came from Franklin's first limo, the one he himself had driven when starting up his fledgling fleet and whose sleek body was immortalized in bronze paint in the front yard. Keely was familiar with the story of Ron's rise to success from a profile Flo Netherton had done on Franklin Limos.

"Ms. O'Brien!" Ron stood up and held out his hand. "You're the photographer, aren't you? A pleasure to meet you."

Keely started to reply, only to sputter into silence when she saw that Franklin already had a visitor.

Max Summers, reclining on the passenger seat from the famous limousine, patted the cushion beside him. "Glad you could join me, honey."

Keely stood frozen. Ron hurried over, chattering inanities as he escorted his guest to the wide seat and practically pushed her down beside Max. As Keely tried to acclimate herself to this new development, she became aware of an odd undercurrent of tension in the room.

"Keely, I was telling Ron about our little problem." Max

smiled. "Glad you could join me." Under his breath, he added, "Great minds must think alike."

Keely swallowed her shock and smiled a cardboard thin smile at the man behind the sleek mahogany desk. Max must have reached the same conclusion concerning Jackson's whereabouts. The men continued their discussion while Keely absorbed the fact that Max hadn't abandoned her. Her spirit buoyant, she belatedly tuned into a conversation concerning the hidden cost of running a fleet of cars.

"I can certainly sympathize, Ron." Max crossed one sharply creased khaki pant leg over the other. "People don't seem to understand that caterers have to pay for food. We don't just pluck produce out of a backyard garden and collect eggs from the hen house. Then you've got to pay waiters, clean-up crew—"

"You think you've got it rough!" Ron seemed eager to top Max's recital of woe. A compactly built man with a luxurious mustache and an unexpectedly full face with pouches under his eyes, Ron fidgeted on the limo seat. "Insurance companies charge enough to cover every car manufactured in Detroit, big engines have an unquenchable thirst for gas, then there's full-time mechanics' wages—brain surgeons work cheaper—not to mention the dry cleaning fees for fancy uniforms . . ."

When Ron paused to draw breath, Max said amiably, "Don't forget protection money."

Ron nodded automatically, then his eyes popped. "What did you just say?"

"Protection money, Ron." Max gave him a buddy to buddy grin. "We know someone's been putting the arm on you to cough up money each month."

Their host's prominent eyes hardened into blue marbles. He said in a flat voice, "I don't know what you're talking about."

"Come on, Ron. We know about the threats, the payments."

One hand raking at his mustache, Ron stood up and pointed toward the door. "Get out of here. Now!"

Max lounged back in a nonchalant pose, his fingers caressing the expensive Corinthian leather seat. "Someone's already pointed out how easy it would be to sabotage your business, haven't they, Ron? A cup of sugar poured into a gas tank, lighter fluid drenching the seats, windshields smashed, tires—those very expensive tires!—slashed, headlights punched out . . ."

"Get out before I call the police!" Ron yanked at his charcoal and red striped tie as if the knot choked him. With his reddened face and furious eyes, he looked as out of place in the opulent setting as a toad squatting on a ruffled dressing table.

If Max was trying to startle Franklin into coughing up Jackson, his tactics were failing miserably. Keely grabbed Max's arm and gave it a warning squeeze. "Perhaps we'd better not take up any more of Mr. Franklin's time—"

"Listen to the lady." Ron's putty soft features solidified into granite. "Don't stick your nose into my affairs."

"I like your first suggestion," Max drawled. "Let's call the police. Ask for Detective Gifford. She'll be very interested in a discussion of the protection racket."

Ron Franklin's lips moved but no sound emerged.

"Or perhaps we could tell her a different story. I took a gander around your service yard before I came in, Ron. You've got enough goons out there to intimidate Hulk Hogan. A muscle squad capable of enforcing any demand you chose to make—"

Ron's finger stabbed at a button on his desk. Max was interrupted in mid-sentence when a previously concealed door at the rear of the office burst open and two overall clad characters stormed in.

Speaking of goons! Keely, on her feet, flinched back, a bubble of hysterical laughter rising in her throat.

Ron pointed at Max. "Make sure this guy loses any ideas about coming back here. Or about calling the cops."

He turned his enraged glare on Keely.

Next, he'd be yelling "Off with her head!" No, that was the Red Queen in *Alice*. Keely wished frantically for a potion labeled "drink me" that would make her grow large enough to frighten these goons.

Like wind-up toys set in motion, the overmuscled specimens strode forward and yanked the still seated Max to his feet. Keely turned in desperate appeal to Franklin and found him smirking at Max who stood, unresisting, between his burly captors.

Max addressed her without turning his head, "I'm sorry, Keely. I shouldn't have confronted this crook with you here." To Franklin, he said simply, "Don't do anything you'll regret."

"That's something I pride myself on." Franklin spat out the words. "No regrets."

He jerked his head in curt dismissal. Max was yanked nearly off his feet and propelled through the door which slammed shut behind them.

Keely darted over to the desk and snatched up the phone. Franklin was equally quick. His fingers closed over her wrist, his nails biting into her flesh until, with a cry of pain, she dropped the instrument back onto its cradle.

Franklin looked at her as though she'd just spilled a strawberry milk shake on his beloved leather seat cushion. "I suggest you stay put for a few moments, Ms. O'Brien. Then you may leave."

Keely wrenched herself free. The man was a maniac. A maniac with a concealed bolt hole and hired muscle. "If you hurt Max—"

"No empty threats, please. If you plan on coming back with the police, I can't guarantee Mr. Summers will be here. No one will admit to having seen him. By the time my boys are through with your loose-lipped friend, he won't have the inclination or the ability to spout any more of his nonsense." Franklin exhaled heavily, ruffling the fringe of his mustache. "Just have a seat, Ms. O'Brien. Be reasonable."

Keely took a step toward the concealed door and the limo service owner moved on the balls of his feet to block her path. Franklin had thick wrists, a broad chest, and an air of unassailable confidence. In a contest of physical strength, she'd be a certain loser. With the push of a button, the expensively furnished room had become a plush prison cell.

Keely felt like a lamb who'd wandered into the den of a fox. She'd meant to make a few inquiries, casually bring up the subject of whether Franklin Limo had recently hired any new drivers. Max certainly had another agenda. Keely's brain reeled. Ron Franklin, respected businessman, the mastermind of the extortion scheme?

Clearly he was up to no good. Keely had to save Max, but first she had to help herself. Feeling the blood drain from her face, she glanced frantically around the spotless room.

Inspiration struck and she bent double, making a choking sound, her right hand cupping her mouth. "I think I'm going to be sick!"

Ron recoiled. "Hey, none of that! Not in here!"

Keely gagged and moaned convincingly, staggering closer to the seat behind the desk, Ron's ostentatious symbol of success. "My stomach's heaving! Ugh, I'm going to throw up!"

Ron Franklin waved his hands in a frantic shooing motion.

"Not in my office! Get away from that leather! Go! Second door down the hall."

Groaning and clutching her stomach, Keely stumbled down the corridor in the direction indicated, aware Ron watched her from the doorway of his office. She pushed open the door marked "Ladies" and reeled inside. Here, the decor was strictly utilitarian, but Keely was interested in a fast exit, not sightseeing.

She almost wept with relief at the sight of a frosted window which opened outward. The window was unlatched, pushed ajar.

Keely shoved the pane open and hoisted herself up. Tossing her purse out, she wiggled through, head first. Her hips stuck momentarily, but with a vigorous twist, she catapulted forward, landing in a diving roll.

Keely grabbed her purse and scrambled to her feet. Get to her car phone, dial 911, save Max—

Orienting herself, she turned toward the parking lot and jumped back. Max, a completely unharmed Max, barred her way.

"Thank God you're all right—"

The fervent words died in her throat. Despite a startling resemblance, this man wasn't Max. Where Max's mouth was full and generous, he had a thin lipped smile that was vaguely familiar. His nose was straight and sharp, his dark hair sleek and smooth.

"I hear you've been looking for me." His smile broadened, but the voice held no inflection.

Keely gulped. "Who are you?"

"Who am I?" The man threw his head back and laughed without humor. "I'm your worst nightmare, baby."

Keely retreated, bumping into the building behind her. Despite talking like a character in a Grade B movie, he carried a distinct air of menace, power relished for its own sake. His hand shot out and grabbed her arm just above the elbow.

"Let go of me!" Keely winced as his fingers dug into her flesh.

"Not until you explain why you just dove out of the bathroom window. Are you a thief?" He grinned when he said the last word, a nasty-private-joke-at-someone's-expense grin.

Keely's purse pressed against her left hip. Shielding her actions with her body, she fumbled inside her handbag with her free hand until she felt the smooth coolness of a cut glass perfume atomizer.

She held the man's gaze with her most earnest look. "The door stuck, I couldn't get it open. I was too embarrassed to yell for help—"

"You decided to risk a broken neck instead." His eyes were the color of clay and uncomfortably intent on Keely's face.

"By crawling out a ground floor window? No risk." Keely forced her lips into a cajoling smile. "If you'll excuse me—"

"No, Ms. O'Brien. We need to talk. Let's go inside and have a chat with my father."

At the sound of her name on his lips, she shuddered. No wonder that smile looked so familiar—Ron Franklin was this man's father!

She had a sudden image of a dark haired man turning away in a dimly lit corridor. A man who resembled Max. "How did you get into the Postwaite reception?" she blurted. "Not by invitation, I'll bet!"

Startled into releasing her, he stepped back. "So you recognize me?"

With an effort, Keely firmed her trembling chin and voice. "We've talked before, haven't we? Over the phone?"

He recovered his poise with the cat-like agility of a ski

racer striking an icy patch. "Talking isn't all I've got in mind."

From his gloating tone, Keely realized she faced a man who thrived on control. Thanks to her unguarded tongue, he now knew she could place him in Flo's company as the man in the videotape.

Then an even more horrific idea occurred to Keely. He had to be involved in the Sterling Ring. That's why Daddy Franklin had gone ballistic when Max accused him of being the head honcho of the extortion racket.

Her captor's smile disappeared and his eyes turned into chips of muddy glass. He was going to hurt her, would take pleasure in the cruelty. Unable to look away, Keely shrank back, at the same time noticing a red birthmark on his neck.

When he reached for her arm again, Keely reacted. Snatching the atomizer from her purse, she sprayed a generous cloud of White Shoulders into his face.

Coughing and choking, he recoiled and Keely darted past him, intent on reaching the haven of her car. She hadn't gone more than fifty feet when she realized she was heading in the wrong direction. Somehow, she'd gotten turned around during her exit through the bathroom window.

Her pulse pounding in her ears, Keely glanced over her shoulder. Wiping streaming eyes and cursing, Max's double pivoted blindly, oblivious to the direction taken by his erstwhile captive. Keely made a desperate survey of her surroundings. On her right was the building from which she'd just escaped, to the left the rear wall of what appeared to be a shed. She headed for the latter, hoping to circle around and get to the parking lot before Franklin Junior's vision cleared.

Yanking her keys from her purse, she threaded them between her fingers, points out, and made a fist. If she went down, it would be fighting all the way.

Drawing a deep breath, Keely poked her head around the corner of the shed. No one was in sight and she darted forward quickly. Before she had taken three steps, a hand clapped over her mouth and she was dragged, struggling frantically, inside.

"Don't scream! I won't hurt you!"

Keely found herself face to face with Jackson. Too startled to do anything but gape at the chauffeur, she stopped resisting and he removed his hand from her mouth.

He sweated profusely in jeans and a black tee shirt. "They've got your boyfriend. Why did you two have to show up here? You're going to ruin the best deal of my life!"

"Where's Max?" Keely's stomach heaved and she experienced a genuine wave of the nausea she'd faked before. "What are they going to do to him?"

"Nothing nice." Jackson grimaced. "These people play rough."

"What are you doing here?" Like Jackson, Keely kept her voice low.

"Picking up my paycheck for last week." He scowled. "Now I've got to quit the best paying job of my life because you found me. I can't afford to be connected with a murder."

Murder? Keely swallowed. Was he talking about Flo's death or did he mean they were going to kill Max? "Help me now and I promise not to tell the police I found you here."

Jackson frowned. "What about the videotape?"

"I'll pay your price, but you've got to help me escape."

Over the man's shoulder, Keely spotted a phone on the wall and lunged for it. Jackson made no move to stop her. Putting the receiver to her ear, Keely hit the buttons for "911" three times before accepting that the line was dead.

"Forget it." Jackson shook his head. "There's no outside line—Old Man Franklin got burned by too many employees making long distance calls."

Only then did Keely notice a greasy piece of paper taped to the wall. The sheet contained cryptic references to "off," "service yrd," "Mr. F.," "Mr. D.," and "paint shed" along with single digit numbers.

She hung up the useless receiver and turned to face Jackson. "Look, I don't care if you stole that tape or not. I need your help. I can't get away, but you could—"

"Call the cops? No way. The police record all their calls. If either of the Franklins ever found out I saved your cute butt, I'd be wearing cement overshoes at the bottom of Lake Hope."

Both Franklins? Keely's mind raced. "What's the name of Ron Franklin's son?"

"Damien. If you think daddy's scary, don't ever run into sonny boy after dark."

"But I just did!" Keely wrung her hands. "He's searching for me right now."

Jackson cursed under his breath. "You're nothing but trouble. Bad luck all the way!"

"Help me and I'll help you," Keely bargained, her ears straining to hear approaching footfalls. "I'll pay you anything you ask, just help us get out of here alive!"

Jackson seemed to reach a decision. "Okay, I'll stall Damien. Give me the keys to your car."

His grin disconcerted her. Keely distrusted that smile but couldn't think of any other choice.

He snatched the keys from her open palm. "I'll draw Damien away. Then I'll move your car around near the entrance of the service yard and leave the engine running. Head to the right."

"Jackson!"

But he was out the door. Surrounded by dusty shelves

containing oil filters, spark plugs, and headlights, Keely waited, perspiration trickling down her back and between her breasts.

Hearing Jackson's voice, she stiffened. The rumble of another man speaking. Keely's nails dug into the palms of both hands and she prayed. Would greed win out? If the chauffeur betrayed her, she was boxed in, with nowhere left to run. The voices gradually faded until the only sound was the buzz of a fly trapped with her inside the shed.

Reflecting that necessity makes strange allies, Keely opened the door and peered out. No one was in sight and she emerged into the sunshine. Moving at a jog trot, she remained alert for danger.

Up ahead, a burst of coarse laughter. Keely stumbled, then froze, statue still.

"Almost had a ringer, Pete! My turn."

Another boisterous gust of laughter. It sounded like a spirited game of horseshoes was in progress behind a one-story wooden structure. Keely headed in that direction, hoping to enlist the game players on her side.

Slipping past two saw horses supporting a silver fender, Keely stepped over a battery with corroded terminals. An inverted leather limousine seat stood on end, propped against the wall.

Crouching, Keely slipped underneath and peered out from her place of concealment.

A man stood directly in her line of vision, an automobile tire slung over a beefy arm. With a loud grunt, he heaved the rubber ring at a stake set in the middle of a graveled yard. Keely's gaze followed the tire's flight—she had to clap her hand over her mouth to keep from shrieking in horror.

The stake had a human face. Max's face.

Chapter 23

The tire glanced off Max's shoulder. His head snapped back with the impact.

The man who'd thrown it howled in disappointment. "No points! The bastard moved!"

Another husky goon took his place, swinging a tire as casually as if it were a gym bag. "If he moved, it's your fault—you tied him up."

Keely couldn't believe her eyes. Franklin's thugs had tied Max to a wooden stake like an early Christian martyr. His face and shirt looked as if he'd been rolling in the dirt. Lips drawn back in a grimace, he faced his tormentors, his teeth gleaming an unnatural white against the grime on his face.

From her vantage point, Keely could see three other men. Two were poking under the raised hood of a silver stretch limo. To Keely's left, a third hosed down a massive dark blue automobile with a powerful spray of water. The workers occasionally paused to watch the cruel sport taking place in the middle of the yard.

If Jackson carried out his part of the bargain, Keely's Mustang should be parked at the entrance near the car wash area. Her main problem would be crossing the yard without being spotted. Although common sense dictated that her best hope of surviving unscathed was to get to her car phone, she couldn't abandon Max.

The guy holding the hose gave the nozzle a turn and the gush of water slowed to a trickle. "Going to the can," he called to the men working on the limo. "Back in a mo with some brewskis!"

One down, four to go. Keely crouched beneath the inverted seat, her mind racing. She needed a distraction to get the other men out of the yard long enough to rescue Max.

Another tire skimmed over Max's head.

The toughs were sweating. "Had enough?" one called to Max, wiping his brow.

"You bozos have missed me every time. Maybe you should buy some video games. Get rid of that aggression harmlessly and develop a little hand-eye coordination at the same time!"

Hearing the angry energy in Max's answering shout, Keely felt a rush of relief.

The bullyboy poised to throw laughed unpleasantly. "You wanna see a demonstration of hand-eye coordination? I'll show you how a quick tap with a wrench can break a knuckle."

Because of the dirt on Max's face, Keely couldn't tell whether he'd turned pale at the suggestion, but her stomach lurched.

Keely surveyed the yard again, her frantic gaze focusing on the telephone inside the open door of the building opposite her position. Squeezing out of her hiding place, Keely retraced her path of flight and regained the safety of the parts shed.

According to the greasy sheet nailed to the wall, the service yard was extension six. Keely dialed, struggling to quiet her ragged breathing as the phone rang.

A gruff voice answered. "Nelson here."

"This is—" Keely paused to visualize the name plate on the receptionist's desk. She raised the pitch of her voice. "It's Tammy! Some crazy woman set fire to the ladies room and Mr. Franklin needs your help!" She threw in an hysterical squeal for good measure before hanging up.

Keely sprinted back. Gulping air into her burning lungs, she ducked into her hiding place just in time to see the last man lumbering out of the yard.

Max, still tied to the stake, worked frantically to free his hands.

As Keely hurried forward, he glanced up and his jaw sagged in disbelief. "What are you doing here?"

She was already yanking at the knots which bound him to the post. "Saving you."

"I don't know where Franklin's plug-uglies went, but—"

"They'll be back," Keely finished. "Stop wiggling, you're making these tighter!"

Realizing her efforts were in vain, she darted over to the garage where the two men had been working. Luck was with her: a razor sharp utility knife lay on an unopened box of air filters. Handling the knife with care, she sliced through the ropes.

Grimacing, Max massaged his wrists. "I think I've got third degree rope burn."

Keely grabbed his arm as he staggered forward. "Keep going! I haven't got time to kiss it and make it better!"

"Unlike most people, I can run and complain at the same time," Max huffed, quickening his pace.

They were abreast of the car wash area when the first man, carrying a six pack, sauntered back into the yard.

He stopped in his tracks. "Hey! How did you get loose?"

He started forward, cutting off their escape route, and Max raised his fists, taking up an aggressive stance. Unfortunately, in his present condition, he didn't look as if he could outbox a ballerina.

Keely glanced around in frantic despair. A few feet away, the hose lay on the ground with a trickle of water still issuing from its mouth.

Snatching up the line, Keely twisted the nozzle until a jet of water gushed forth, catching the approaching man square in the face. The pressure was unexpectedly strong and she found herself unable to control the hose which writhed free of her clutching hands. It continued to thrash on the ground like a wounded snake, indiscriminately drenching Max, Keely, and the mechanic who was on his knees coughing up the water he'd inhaled.

A blast of spray nearly knocked Keely down. Reeling, she felt an arm go around her waist and drag her out of range. Looking up, she saw Max's face, a little cleaner now, as he steadied her. The soaking seemed to have revived her companion.

"My car!" Keely gasped. "Thataway!"

Supporting each other, they stumbled along the asphalt, shoes squishing and the clothing plastered to their bodies weighing down every step. Keely gave a shout of pure joy when she spotted her Mustang parked just outside the fence which separated the service area from the office parking lot.

Jackson had come through! Heaping blessings on the man's unworthy head, Keely darted around to the driver's side. The keys were in the ignition. Max fell in through the passenger door as the car lurched into motion. Pulling into the street, Keely glanced into the rear view mirror and saw Damien, followed by his muscle men, spill from the office like ants from a threatened ant hill.

Keely stomped on the accelerator. The limousine headquarters was located at the end of a dead-end street and she was unable to draw a deep breath until they were safely caught up in free flowing traffic.

Two cars back, Jackson watched the Mustang accelerate and grinned. He didn't regret helping the O'Brien broad escape. Just another way of tweaking the dragon's tail. He'd done it twice now and was still without a scratch.

Quite a rush, almost as heady as a snort of nose candy. One more good yank and he would be on Easy Street. Jackson chuckled at his own cleverness. The secret is to make certain the beast's distracted while you slip in behind. So far, O'Brien was proving to be ideal dragon bait. Best of all for Jackson's future plans, she was still in one piece.

Remembering the baffled, murderous rage on Damien's face, in incongruous contrast to the overpoweringly sweet perfume wafting from the man's shirt, Jackson laughed. How could a guy fail to play his cards right when life kept dealing him one full house after another?

Chapter 24

Keely glanced over at her passenger. Sodden, covered with dirt and grease, Max grinned back at her.

She said breathlessly, "You look like road kill, but at least you're still in one piece."

"You, on the other hand, look like an angel. Imagine what those hoods would have done if they were serious about hurting me." Max massaged his shoulder. "I feel like I've just been run over by an eighteen wheeler." In an obvious bid for sympathy, he added pathetically, "Loaded with pig iron."

"Overkill, Max." Keely brushed wet hair off her face. Drops of water trickled down her back. "I've never heard of a soggy angel."

"Maybe God weatherproofs celestial beings." Max flashed her an appealing grin. "Thanks from the bottom of my heart. I'd show my appreciation in a more concrete way, but . . ." He gestured at his soiled clothing.

A blush heated Keely's face and she busied herself in checking the rear view mirror for signs of pursuit. At the same time, Max leaned over to pre-empt the mirror, tilting it to inspect a fresh bruise on his jaw. Their reflected gazes collided in the glass and Keely looked away first.

Max leaned back with a stifled groan, oblivious to the damage done to her car's cream colored upholstery. "Well, we learned Ron Franklin's quite touchy on the subject of extortion."

"Touchy? He's a madman!" Keely dug under the front seat for a packet of cleansing wipes which she handed to Max.

"Jackson told me he hired on at Prestige Limousines after he left the Postwaites. I also discovered you have an evil doppelganger named Damien who's the head of the Sterling Ring."

After hearing Keely's story of her encounter with Ron's son, Max clapped his hands. "So I've got a double? Damien must be the guy Jessica saw scoping out her shop. He was also probably the one dancing with our fat friend's wife from the Brew & Cue. Gifford will have to believe us now."

But Gayla Gifford wasn't available and no one at the police station seemed enthused over the idea of questioning a prominent businessman on the say-so of two dubious looking characters. Max finally managed to talk the sergeant on duty into sending a patrol car escort with them to Prestige Limousines.

Once there, however, they were informed by the receptionist that Ron Franklin hadn't been in all day (he was visiting his mother) and Damien was out of town looking into the purchase of a used limousine. The patrolmen were welcome to look around the service yard. Prestige Limousines had nothing to hide.

The window in the bathroom where Keely had made her escape was locked, with no evidence of her impromptu exit. Both the goons and the stake had vanished. The tires used in their vile game of intimidation were neatly stacked inside the parts shed.

The man Keely had soaked with the hose was now clad in a dry coverall and engaged in buffing the sleek sides of a stretch limo while the other mechanics changed the oil of an executive motor coach. All three men appeared absorbed in their work and strangely incurious about the law's invasion. Under direct questioning, they stared blankly at Keely and Max before mumbling that they'd never seen either of them before.

Max's Bronco no longer sat in the parking lot and his suggestion that the bruisers had driven the vehicle away in an attempt to disprove his story had the policemen exchanging significant looks behind his grimy back.

Frustrated, Max held out his hands and shook his abraded wrists under their noses. "You're as observant as a pair of love birds! Don't you recognize rope burns when you see them?"

Police patience came to an end immediately after this outburst and Max and Keely were politely, but firmly, ordered off the premises. A sullen Max sat hunched in the passenger seat of Keely's Mustang, staring gloomily through the windshield, as she negotiated the afternoon traffic.

"You've got to get Jessica to tell Gifford she's been threatened," he muttered, drumming his fingers on the dash. "Today's fiasco didn't exactly strengthen our credibility."

"I tried calling Jess last night, but she's not answering her phone. I wouldn't count too much on her cooperation." Keely gestured at Max's hands. "Please, try not to touch anything else. It looks like a greased pig's been rolling in my front seat."

"I suppose those idiotic cops would have taken me seriously if I had clean hands?"

"Max, you look like you haven't bathed in this decade and I look like I just finished running an obstacle course." Keely scowled at her disheveled reflection in the mirror. "Face it, we didn't stand a chance."

Max grunted. "Yeah. It was Franklin's word against ours and all of his employees are prepared to lie for him."

Keely toed the accelerator as the car took a corner. "We should have known he'd be prepared for our return. Ron Franklin's got a reputation as a shrewd businessman. Several competitors tried to get a toehold in Lake Hope, but they all failed."

"Failed? How did they fail?"

Surprised at the sharpness of Max's tone, Keely hesitated. "Let's see. One lost an entire fleet in a garage fire and the other, Quality Rides, had such a high accident rate due to brake failures, etcetera, people just didn't use them any longer."

"I suspect intimidation and vandalism, not better prices and service, are responsible for Franklin's success," Max asserted grimly. "If his son is the shadowy figure behind the extortion racket, he's just following in Daddy's footsteps."

"I'm positive Damien's the man I saw talking to Flo in the hallway." Keely parked in the lot of Max's apartment building. Climbing out, she tried unsuccessfully to smooth the wrinkles from her slacks. "He resembles you in a superficial fashion, but his eyes are as cold and brown as pennies."

"Pennies?" Max snorted. "That doesn't sound dangerous."

"Haven't you ever heard the phrase, 'Pennies on a dead man's eyes?' Damien's eyes were dead—there's no real person living behind that flat stare." Keely shuddered reminiscently.

"So this guy looks like me, huh? Maybe the Mayor's mother wasn't talking through her little veiled hat when she accused me of bopping her with that candlestick!" Max's blue eyes glittered. "Everyone's been mistaking me for Franklin's bad boy, including, I'll bet, that overtanked hulk at the Brew & Cue. Don't forget, the leader of the brass band was convinced I was the guy who hired him. A resemblance to Damien might explain why Gunter got excited when I showed up at his cake shop."

"Gunter doesn't need an excuse to throw a creative tantrum, but Damien might be doing some collecting for his extortion racket in person." Keely remembered something else.

"One of Franklin's thugs looked familiar and I just remembered why. He was the security guard at the Westhaven wedding—the guard who disappeared along with the gifts!"

While Max degreased and showered, Keely curled up on his couch and scribbled notes. When he emerged from the bedroom, she said triumphantly, "It all fits!"

Max glanced down at his charcoal shaded slacks and dark blue shirt. "Then you don't think the shirt's too baggy—"

His sly grin told her he was back to his ebullient self. "You know I'm not talking about your clothes! I mean the facts about Damien and Flo fit together."

Max perched on the arm of the couch. "Amplify."

"Flo profiled quite a few wedding service providers. She met Damien on a visit to Prestige Limos. They were drawn together: a man burning to make his mark and a woman filled with poisonous hate. Somehow, Damien convinced Flo to help him humiliate a few pampered society brides. My guess is she didn't know about the bigger picture, the extortion racket, until it was too late."

"Go on." Max slipped off the arm of the couch, landing next to Keely with a soft thud. "Tell me more."

As a souvenir of today's excursion, Max possessed a purplish bruise on his jaw to match the one on his forehead. His hair, still damp from the shower, curled in a dark, glossy cap. Keely was acutely conscious of her own tumble-dried appearance.

She referred to the tablet clutched in her hands. "During the confusion caused by the band's entrance, Flo somehow came into possession of Rose's necklace. Maybe the catch was loose and it fell off. Being familiar with the timetable for the robbery, Flo hurried out to turn the diamonds over to Damien. Passing the risk on to him, so to speak."

"Then you came strolling along." Max's fingers walked

down Keely's arm and drew a "x" on the back of her hand. "You caught them huddled together in the hallway."

"Uh, that's right." The tablet seemed to have developed a tremor and Keely steadied her hands with an effort. "Damien took off, but when Flo saw the light glowing on my camera, she knew that to keep from ever being linked to him, she needed to destroy the, er, videotape." Keely stumbled over the last word. The scent of Max's Polo played havoc with her powers of concentration.

"When you refused to be intimidated into turning over the tape, they decided to take it." Max rubbed his jaw gingerly as he outlined the scenario. "While in the studio, they argue, Damien picks up the tripod and pow!—he's got a corpse on his hands."

He frowned. "So far we've got nothing to tie Damien to the crimes except a tape we haven't viewed. Unless your camera work was exceptional, the police may not be able to prove the man talking to Flo is Damien and not me." He shook his head. "They thought of everything. Damien even wore clothes similar to mine."

"At a distance, he wouldn't draw a second glance. Even your employees would think he was you." Keely remembered something else. "I got an up close and personal look at Damien today. He's got a birthmark on the side of his neck."

"Then I'll have to trust that you're a good enough videographer to have captured that detail."

Trust. That word again. Keely looked down to find Max's hand covering hers. The pressure was light, testing her response. She felt the skin of her face and throat flush and freed her hand with deliberate casualness to smooth back her hair.

After her divorce, Keely had taken her physical desires and stuffed them into a padlocked inner sanctum. By his proximity, Max resurrected feelings she'd thought sealed away.

He studied her as if contemplating a luscious dessert. "May I?"

Without waiting for permission, Max kissed her forehead and then her mouth. A light brush of the lips, a sampling of delights yet to come. A shiver of anticipation tickled Keely's spine and she reached hungrily for Max, but he gently disengaged himself and stood up.

"Will you give me a ride to Feast of Italy? I've got to get some work done or Anna Marie will have me boiled in oil."

Keely stifled the impulse to grab Max and pull him down beside her again. How could he arouse her so effortlessly and then walk away with that casual stride?

Prey to some very disquieting sensations, Keely also stood. "What are we going to do about Damien? We can't let him get away with what he's done!"

Max slipped his wallet into his back pocket. "We don't have proof, Keely. No evidence that he killed Flo or has anything to do with the Sterling Ring. Today we got a rather vivid object lesson that poking around Franklin's Prestige Limousines isn't healthy. I have no desire to have my skull cracked with a tire iron."

Grabbing her purse off the breakfast bar, Keely followed Max to the door. "Don't run away from me. What about Jess and Mimi? What if that creep decides to extort money from me or your aunt? This isn't over, Max. If we can get that tape back from Jackson, we might be able to put Damien out of circulation—"

"We've done all we can. Now it's time to let the police handle things." He opened the apartment door, evading her imploring gaze. "I'll call Gifford and tell her what happened."

"She won't believe you. No one believes us! You saw how those cops treated us today. Damien's in the clear—"

Max overrode her fervent protest. "I'm sure he blew town as soon as he realized we'd escaped. I'll follow up with Gifford. I'd appreciate your giving me a ride to Feast of Italy, Keely. Guess I'm stuck driving the company van until my Bronco turns up."

Sliding behind the wheel of her Mustang, Keely slammed the door. Max was as clear as glass. He wasn't planning to bail out of the investigation, he just wanted to protect her. Which was ridiculous! He was the one who attracted trouble like a magnet did iron filings!

"I don't see why you have to be the one to call Detective Gifford," she grumbled as Max climbed into the passenger seat. "You're the one who got pelted with cake. You're the fellow who got into a brawl at the Brew & Cue and ended up as the stake in a vicious game of Ring Toss."

"Since I was the victim of today's assault, I'm the logical one to make a complaint," Max pointed out. "Keely, I want you to drop this. Franklin's not the man to mess around with. Poking around could be dangerous to the point of suicidal."

Keely slammed the car into reverse. While Damien might lay low for a time, he would soon resurface. Inevitably, he would overstep in making someone an example.

Keely had recognized Damien's voice as the one uttering the telephoned threats; today he'd told her flat out that he was her worst nightmare. The struggle between them had become personal. At some point, Keely knew she'd have to stand and fight.

She glanced over to find Max regarding her sternly. "Let Detective Gifford handle Damien Franklin, Keely. She's a professional, way out of our league."

Ida often quoted the Jewish proverb, "Truth is the safest lie." Keely gave Max a reassuring smile. "Relax, I know my limitations. I'm a photographer, not a detective. I intend to

273

concentrate my energy on the Fairmont wedding."

What Keely didn't say was that she'd just pledged herself to defeating Damien Franklin.

As Keely's car pulled away from Feast of Italy, Max bolted for the office and the phone. He called the police station and made an appointment to see Gifford and Dawson.

After terminating the call, Max absentmindedly toyed with Anna Marie's lucky silver pen. He couldn't shake the feeling that disaster loomed on the near horizon. If he wasn't successful in convincing Gifford of the urgency in stopping Damien, Anna Marie's business could go up in smoke, literally.

He smiled grimly. Keely had seemed suspiciously agreeable about letting the police handle the investigation. He'd also sensed a change in her attitude, a softening. The terrifying incident at the limo yard had created a fragile harmony between them and Max was determined not to crush it.

Enough emotional sparks had been flying to set his apartment alight, but he'd held back. After boasting that he wasn't looking for a one night stand, he could hardly seduce Keely on his couch. It had taken every ounce of will power he could summon to walk away from her, but Max was determined to play things cool until Anna Marie took up the reins of Feast of Italy. Then he would be free to convince Keely that their current partnership should be dissolved in favor of a more personal and permanent arrangement.

Chapter 25

"Extortion." Gayla pronounced the word with deliberation and looked over at her partner. Brian Dawson gazed stolidly back. "You've given us food for thought, Mr. Summers. We'll chew on this and get back to you."

"In the meantime," she gave Max's battered face a pointed glance, "I suggest you keep yourself tucked away in that cozy kitchen of yours and avoid dark alleys."

The two detectives watched Max stride away, stiff with outrage.

"I think you hurt his feelings," Brian drawled.

"I meant to." Gayla removed a bottle of carbonated water from the cooler she kept under her desk. "I don't want him or the O'Brien woman doing any free-lancing. Can't you see me trying to explain to Kowalski that I've added a chef and a photographer to the investigative team?"

Brian laughed, a gentle giant kind of 'ho ho.' "The air would be blue, along with his face. If profanity was a merit badge, Kowalski'd be an Eagle Scout. Say, what did you think of the yarn Summers told us about their visit to the limo yard?"

Gayla unscrewed the bottle cap and took a swig. "I think Ron Franklin's been doing more than just advertising to keep ahead of the competition. Who does a son look up to and try to emulate, if not his successful father?"

"Franklin's quite a wheel in this town." Brian grinned to show the pun was intentional. "If we start sniffing around Prestige, we'll have more than the mayor on our backs."

"The mayor wants the world safe for weddings. A woman with influential friends is dead. The pressure on us'll only increase until we close this case." Gayla shrugged. "If Franklin's son is running the Sterling Ring with a sideline in extortion, we'd better find out."

"Do you still think Keely O'Brien is a killer?"

"She had motive and opportunity. I think Summers is protecting her. He never adequately explained how he got the goose egg on his forehead the night of the murder."

"I can't see Keely O'Brien killing anyone," Brian muttered. "She's not the type."

"Anyone can kill. It just takes the right amount of pressure applied to a weak point and . . . snap!" Gayla demonstrated, using a pencil. "You heard the tape. 'Someday, someone's going to fight back.' That's what O'Brien said the day before the woman was murdered. I can't help wondering if she fought back."

"I've got a gut feeling we're looking at "The Wrong Man," with a woman playing Henry Fonda's role."

"You wouldn't have so many gut feelings if your gut wasn't so large." Gayla tossed the broken pencil halves into the overflowing wastebasket, triggering a paper avalanche. "Now what Hitchcock scenario are we talking about? O'Brien as the innocent trapped by a web of circumstantial evidence?"

"Could be. She had an excellent reputation in the community until the first robbery." Brian shifted his bulk and the chair squeaked in futile protest. "Why don't we talk to her again, Gayla? Try to clear her off the suspect list. With a murder in her studio, she must be suffering and if she's innocent . . ."

His partner shook her head. "We've got a dead woman, two robberies, one assault and some very powerful people will be yelling for our blood if we don't make an arrest soon.

At this point, Keely O'Brien's feelings are the least of my worries."

Max was too busy to brood over his abrupt dismissal at the police station. As if a quarantine sign had been removed from the door of Feast of Italy, bookings poured in. For the rest of the week, he worked every evening until 7:30 then headed over to the Brew & Cue. Max also hired a local security firm to keep a twenty-four hour watch on Keely's house. He intended to assume the job of protecting her himself the moment Anna Marie took charge of business.

Friday morning, Max nursed a sore head and totalled up the week's reckoning. He'd played innumerable games of pool, lost over two hundred dollars in side bets, and suffered through so many jukebox renditions of "Achy Breaky Heart" that the twang of a guitar made him twitch.

Bone weary, his head swollen enough to enter in the Macy's Thanksgiving Day parade as a balloon, Max slumped on a stool in Feast of Italy's kitchen. By tonight he had to come up with a clever design for the Fairmont wedding marzipan presentation. The almonds had already been blanched, dried, and pounded into paste and mixed with powdered sugar and rose water flavoring. Now came the creative genius part.

Each sketch Max drew, however, reminded him of Keely. A line turned into the slant of her cheekbone, a curve became her generous mouth or the arch of her brow as she regarded him quizzically. He'd felt handicapped all week, as if he only had the use of one hand.

With a vigorous slash, Max crossed out his last doodle, meant to be a trumpet but instead resembling a woman's shapely leg. Put some mind muscle into it! he urged himself. It's brainstorm time. Create something romantic associated with Camelot. . . .

For one crazy moment, Max toyed with the idea of molding a bust of JFK and then burst out laughing. He was going out of his mind and he laid the blame at Keely's door.

Like an addict, he craved the fix of her smile, the intoxicating scent of her hair, the spirited tilt of her head. He ached to hold her in his arms and caress the softness of her body. The taste of her lips had spoiled Max's appetite for other foods, leaving him a starving man.

He kept remembering Keely's expression as she listened to her mother's abusive rantings, the stricken look in her eyes when she related how her husband had failed her. What did a man who couldn't hold onto a restaurant or a wife have to offer to a woman searching so desperately for wholeness?

Max regarded his canceled sketches with disgust as the first two members of his food prep crew breezed in.

"Hi, Max." Karla grabbed a full length apron off the hook and dropped it over her head.

"Morning, boss man!" Steve slung a folded newspaper into Max's lap.

He acknowledged their greetings, envying them their youth, the clean slates they had to offer a potential mate. If the past was indeed another country, Max reflected grimly, he was one of the poor schmoes searching for a border crossing.

Steve and Karla consulted the schedule for tomorrow's wedding. Karla chose to hull strawberries while Steve shredded lettuce and spinach for May sallat, a salad of fresh greens which united the leafy vegetables with green herbs, fruits, and beans.

Steve's expert fingers tore at the lettuce. "Did the greengage plums and limes come in yet?"

"Check the other refrigerator," Max said absently. He'd

scribbled the initials "K. O." Kayoed. Keely had kayoed him with one look from those creme caramel eyes.

He gazed at the pad in front of him, aware he had several hundred tasks to accomplish prior to tomorrow's changing of the guard, but unable to prod himself into action.

"I'm so happy for you and Anna Marie," Karla remarked, her deft fingers sorting through the red berry jewels. "Knowing everything will soon be back to normal must be a relief."

"Back to normal?" He looked at her dully.

She nodded, with a puzzled smile. Steve had also stopped working to stare at him.

Max didn't have a clue to what she was talking about but he hazarded a guess. "Referring to Anna Marie's return?"

Employing the patient voice of a mother toilet training a toddler, Karla said, "No, the robberies. You're off the hook, at least according to what the O'Brien woman said in today's paper."

"I wonder what evidence the killer left behind," Steve said thoughtfully as he began cutting broccoli into florets. "I'll bet she had a hidden video camera in her studio and caught the murder on tape. Wouldn't that be awesome! Hey, those tabloid TV shows would pay a fortune for footage of an actual murder."

Max blinked. "What are you two babbling about?"

"It's in the morning paper," Steve said helpfully. "About Keely O'Brien being able to finger the killer—"

Max had already tuned him out. Unfolding the paper, he feverishly read the headline and opening paragraphs of the accompanying story. With a muffled exclamation, he sprang up and tore out of the kitchen, the paper still gripped in his hands.

Karla popped a strawberry into her mouth, chewing the

fruit with relish. "Who set his tail feathers on fire?"

Steve stooped to pick up the sketch pad Max had knocked to the floor during his hasty exit. Studying the drawings, he shook his head. "My guess'd be woman trouble."

Karla gave him a pert, berry-stained smile. "You men should thank God we're never more trouble than we're worth."

"I'm going to count to three, Honey, and then I want you to look up at me and say "Cheese pizza, please!"

Honey, age six, clutched the braided white ropes supporting the swing in a death grip. Her face dissolved into an shy smile, however, when she spoke her line.

"Perfect!" Keely crouched to smooth the girl's ruffled skirt. "Only a couple more and then your mom can take you out for some real pizza."

She continued her monologue, soothing and coaxing. Honey was not a natural subject; her narrow face froze at the sight of the camera. Keely had to fight for each shot.

The rules of portraiture—don't break the facial line with the nose, keep shadows from filling eye sockets, maintain a maximum lighting ratio of 1:3 from one side to the other—had become automatic, leaving Keely free to concentrate on the visual impact of each pose.

At last she straightened. "Oke doke, all finished!"

Honey hopped out of the swing, her dark hair bobbing to frame her face. She clapped her hands. "Yippee, pizza time!"

Keely snapped off a final shot, capturing the unfettered glee, and grinned in satisfaction. This last photograph, unposed and impromptu, would probably be the best of the session.

The front door slammed. Keely heard Ida's surprised protest. "You can't go in there! She's doing a portrait—"

The heavy curtain which Keely used to separate the studio from the reception area during sessions was yanked aside as Max Summers strode in.

"Are you out of your mind?" was his fond greeting.

Honey's alarmed squeak immediately brought him up short. "Oh, you've got company." Max grinned. "Hi, brown eyes."

He crouched to the child's level, turning on his considerable charm to coax a timid smile in response. "Look, sweetie, could you wait outside with Ida? I need to talk to Picture Lady."

"We're done." Keely grabbed the little girl's hand. "Let me turn Honey over to her mother before we discuss my sanity."

Max eyed the swing when Keely returned. "Cute set-up."

"Kids like it. They relax and I get good pictures." Keely studied his fists. "Maybe you should sit down in it."

"It'll take more than a ride in a swing to make me feel better. I read your exclusive interview in the newspaper."

She fiddled with the camera, which was set on a new tripod. She'd decided she didn't want the old one back after the police were done with it. Removing the film kept her fingers busy and furnished a good excuse to avoid Max's caustic stare.

Keely couldn't shut out his sardonic voice, however. "I wonder what Gifford's going to say about your latest appearance in the headlines."

Keely closed the camera with a sharp click. "Gifford and Dawson dropped by for a visit a couple hours ago."

"You're still free?" Max's fingers bit into the braided ropes supporting the swing. "I'm surprised she didn't slap you into protective custody."

Keely slipped the exposed roll into a film canister and

snapped the lid in place. "I told her that Damien's intimidation tactics keep people from admitting they're being squeezed for cash. The only way to nail him is by provoking him into doing something stupid."

"Like coming after you." Max snorted. "Did Gifford fall on your neck with tears of joy at your noble sacrifice?"

"She wasn't thrilled, but she finally acknowledged Damien's not the type to incriminate himself without a little encouragement. She also admitted she couldn't guarantee my safety. Or provide twenty-four hour protection for any of the people Damien's threatened."

"By giving that idiotic interview, do you think you can flush him into the open?" Max flung his hands skyward, bumping the swing into motion. "Keely, pretending to possess a vital piece of evidence is the oldest trick in the book."

She juggled the film canister from hand to hand. "It's an old trick because it works. Hunters often stake out a goat to catch a tiger."

"There's a non sequitur if I ever heard one." Max grabbed Keely's hand, trapping the film canister in her fingers, forcing her to look at him. The bruises on his face had faded to a greenish yellow; his eyes were hot enough to melt butter and Keely's spine.

Clearing her throat, she baahed softly. "I've volunteered to be the goat."

Max released her, stooped in a violent motion, and snatched up the area rug covering the bloodstained section of the floor. "A woman died here, Keely. You could be next!"

"I can't live in fear, Max. No one's safe with that maniac free to terrorize. I had to take matters into my own hands. Damien's not going to go meekly away and leave me alone—he tried to set me up for Flo's murder!"

"You're not in this by yourself." Max flung the rug at her

feet. "I promised to take care of you, remember?"

"If I relied on promises for my survival, Max, I would have been destroyed years ago." Keely closed her eyes.

Max said quietly, "If you're trying to hurt me, you've succeeded." His eyes were bleak, his mouth vulnerable. Despising herself for her weakness, Keely looked away. "I'm not trying to hurt you, I'm trying to save myself! I called a reporter and told him that on Monday I would turn over to the police some new evidence in Flo's murder."

"According to the paper, you said a lot more than that." Max paced, drawing an ever tightening circle around Keely. "You also promised to release details of the protection racket, along with a list of victims and the link to a local businessman." Max shook his head in disbelief. "You're playing with dynamite."

"Which could blow up in my face." Keely detached the portrait camera from the tripod. "Detective Gifford threatened to put me in protective custody for the weekend, but I refused. I'm aware of the risks."

Blowing out his breath in a ragged sigh, Max stopped in front of her. "While you've been granting interviews, I've spent my evenings hanging around the Brew & Cue, waiting for Jackson to show up. I played pool until my fingers developed a permanent cramp. I even acquired a nickname, 'Pockets,' because I'm always digging into mine to pay up bets."

"Why?"

"What do you mean, 'why?' " He scowled. "Isn't it obvious how I feel about you?"

She turned away. "Just why are you involved? Isn't your aunt's business booming again? No one thinks you're a murderer."

"No one thinks you're a murderer, either, Keely."

"Really?" She spun around and kicked the rug. "Why are ghouls beating a path to the studio door, asking to see the blood? Why are people afraid to let me be alone with their kids? Honey's the first session I've been able to handle solo and that's only because her grandmother is one of Ida's best friends. I'm a suspect in a murder, Max. I can't live this way any longer."

"You're not alone, Keely. Didn't we make a good team?"

His tentative smile tugged at Keely's heart. She steeled herself. "Look, Max, you just don't get it. I don't want to be a part of a team. I want to nail Damien Franklin and be left alone to run my business."

"Keely—"

"I don't want your help, Max. I'd like you to leave."

He blinked, a wash of red creeping up his neck. Keely doubted that Maxwell Summers had ever been rebuffed so thoroughly. Since the day he'd learned to walk, women had probably twittered like birds when he strolled by.

"You're not telling me everything." It was an accusation. "Keely, I'm not leaving until you come clean."

At a loss for words, she stared at him. Max was a warm-hearted charmer, an engaging and considerate companion and Keely couldn't bear the thought that he might be hurt because of her.

She'd received a call at 2:00 a.m. Tuesday from Damien. His voice uttering a string of foul oaths had shocked her into wakefulness.

Before Keely could hang up, he got down to business. "I like hurting women. Flo could testify to that. I can have your precious fry cook pounded into a lump of raw meat or mess up that lush you call a mother. She gets hold of some bad booze, she'll need more than a fancy clinic to paste her back together."

Keely had slammed the receiver down and let the answering machine record the next calls. But Damien hadn't said another word, simply remaining on the line until the message tape activated before hanging up.

On Wednesday, she'd received an unsigned telegram. "Coming Soon: Judgment Day." Since then she'd taken steps to protect both her mother and Max, asking the clinic to keep a close watch on Moira and avoiding the caterer.

To monsters like Damien Franklin, saving face was a matter of ego, of sheer survival. In escaping, she'd damaged his pride. By withholding the videotape, she'd figuratively spit in his eye. Flo's sprawled body served as a horrifying example of what Damien did to those who got in his way.

Keely had no intention of twisting helplessly in the wind until Damien picked his moment to retaliate. Seeing her interview in the paper this morning had strengthened her resolve to end this torment.

If only getting rid of Max was as easy! He'd been stung by her curt dismissal, but instead of stalking out and slamming the door, he remained before her, rock solid.

She gestured toward the curtain with the camera. "Our partnership's dissolved as of today. Good-bye, Max."

"You don't mean that."

"Yes, I do!" It took all her will power not to break down and tell him the truth. "Max, why do you believe in me? You saw me lose control and break Doug's TV with a baseball bat. I could just as easily have lost control with Flo and—" her voice faltered, "and killed her."

"But you didn't." Max held out his hand. "Keep looking into my eyes, Keely. Tell me you killed Flo. Tell me you want me to leave."

"Max—I—" Keely's voice dried up. Crossing the room, she put the camera down on a shelf. "Just go. Please."

"I'm not bailing out on you. Your fight is my fight."

She turned. Max hadn't budged from the center of her studio. "Be reasonable! Gifford didn't like me talking to that reporter, but she knows why I did it. She won't let anything happen to me this weekend."

Keely fervently hoped this was true. Max said nothing.

She walked toward him, avoiding the stained area on the wooden floor. "Max, if Damien killed Flo, he's got to keep me from talking. By giving that interview, I narrowed his window of opportunity to two days. By Monday, this will all be over."

Max's scowl told Keely she hadn't convinced him.

Chapter 26

After listening to Gifford's blistering denunciation of her plan, Keely anticipated Max's vehement disapproval. She had not, however, expected his calm announcement he would serve as her bodyguard for the weekend.

"If you expect me to leave you floating on the pond like a sitting duck, you're mistaken, Keely. Damien killed Flo. He's not going to hesitate to get rid of you."

Her protests rang hollow in her own ears and, when Ida threw her not inconsiderable weight on Max's side, Keely accepted the edict that her afternoon appointments would be canceled.

After packing an overnight bag, Keely found herself bundled into a rental car.

"The cops found my Bronco early this morning in a bank parking lot," Max explained grimly in response to her questioning look. "Of course, the goons didn't leave any fingerprints. But somebody had tap danced on the hood and it wasn't the Good Fairy."

At Feast of Italy, they found themselves in a beehive of activity. Keely was pressed into service making pastry shells for a dish called Swete Fysshe en Doucette. The shells would be filled with a mixture of cold salmon, dates, almonds, herbs, and pine nuts.

Along with other workers, Keely quartered fruit for a spicy pear sauce called chardwardon. Karla explained that the sauce would be served as an appetizer, along with hard cheese and dark bread garnished with Swithin cream. Keely paused, enviously watching the deft cuts made by her companion. "Have you ever made any of these dishes before?"

Karla's white blond curls would have danced if they hadn't been tamed by a hair net. "Are you kidding? Jusselle Date isn't exactly one of our most requested dishes. I never heard of this stuff until Max handed out the final menu. He's a genius at researching authentic dishes and figuring out proportions. A medieval banquet for three hundred of your closest friends? No problem for Max. Anna Marie's going to miss him."

"What else are you serving?"

Karla indicated a rolled up sheet of parchment paper tied with a russet ribbon. "As we say in the business, 'Feast your eyes on the menu.' "

Unrolling the paper, Keely learned the guests would be dining on peppermint rice and sweet capon, along with destiny cakes. The beverage list featured a drink called Lamb's Wool, which included a non-alcoholic version prepared with cider for those who didn't like white wine.

Max moved over to the island where the three women were working. "Pack it up, folks. We've done all we can. Be back here at 9:30 tomorrow morning."

In an amazingly short period of time, food was packed away in containers and refrigerated. The floor was swept and counter tops scrubbed while utensils and mixing bowls were loaded into the gaping maw of the dishwashers. Calling goodbyes, the workers left in a group, leaving Max and Keely alone for the first time.

Keely sank down on a stool by the island and kneaded the dull ache in the small of her back. She'd never dreamed that food preparation could be so arduous.

Max, however, still looked relatively fresh. He'd spent most of the afternoon arguing with suppliers over the portable telephone he kept clipped to his belt. Between calls, he had pitched in wherever needed, able with a few words to bring order out of the chaos for a staff working with unfamiliar recipes.

Keely stretched her arms above her head, trying to unkink her spinal column. "All ready for tomorrow night?"

Max removed a covered bowl from one of the refrigerators and faced her across the island. "We're in good shape. Everything that can be stored overnight is prepared and the fruits and vegetables have been cleaned."

Keely suddenly realized that she hadn't thought of Damien Franklin once since Max had kidnapped her.

"It's nearly 10:00 o'clock on Friday night and I'm still in one piece," she announced triumphantly.

"That's a matter of opinion." Max took Keely's hand and inspected the tiny cuts on her fingers. "Your knife seemed to be flying out of control. I hope that wasn't me you were dissecting so vigorously."

"Don't flatter yourself—I didn't think of you once," Keely informed him with perfect truth. She hadn't kept an actual count, but it had been well over a hundred.

"I'm sorry to hear that." Raising Keely's hand, Max kissed each finger tip, the pressure of his lips slow and deliberate. Releasing her, he leaned across the island. "Better now?"

She gave him a tranquil smile, camouflaging the acceleration of her heartbeat. "I'm tougher than you think. What's in the bowl?"

Amiably accepting the change of subject, Max peeled off the lid. "Marzipan. I've got to make the gift for Anna Marie to present to the bride before we can shut up shop for the night."

Keely watched as Max added confectioner's sugar to the bowl's contents. In a heavy saucepan, he heated almond paste until the dough stuck to a spatula and then dumped the mass on a sheet of waxed paper. Whistling a sprightly tune, he kneaded food coloring into the mixture to tint the paste a rich gold.

Max broke off to chuckle. "I think I've memorized every song on that jukebox at the Brew & Cue. It was a form of brainwashing—the tunes keep running through my head—so don't be startled if I start talking in country-western lyrics."

Keely heard her own inner music, the wistful melody of "I've Got You Under My Skin." Despite her hectic schedule this week, she'd missed Max. At odd moments, she found herself yearning to glimpse again his slow, intimate smile, remembering the protective curve of his body when he bent toward her, the thrust of his jaw when he argued for a point.

But her own needs must be sacrificed. She couldn't bear the thought of Max being hurt. He'd offered her everything and she'd given him nothing but trouble. The least she could do was encourage him to walk away. Find someone who didn't have the threat of Damien's revenge hanging over her head or the burden of Moira. A woman who could love him the way he deserved to be loved. Someone able to play happy families.

Keely's bedroom had become unbearably lonely. Watching Max's supple fingers stroke the dough, she fantasized them caressing her own flesh and shuddered with erotic delight.

Fortunately for his peace of mind, Max was intent on his task. Removing the net which subdued her hair, Keely felt a sense of release. "What's the symbol for Camelot?"

"Got to admit, this theme's a challenge." Poker-faced, Max deftly shaped a slender rope of dough. "Tell me what you see."

Keely leaned forward, fascinated by the movements of his

hands. "Isn't that the symbol for infinity?"

She recalled her own wedding day, those sentimental dreams of unity which had so quickly turned to ashes. "Does that mean Courtney's marriage will seem like it lasts forever?"

Max paused to admire his handiwork. "This, my unromantic lady, is a love-knot. In medieval times, this little item was considered the ultimate in love tokens, representing the perfection of an affection without beginning and without end."

"In other words, an illusion." Keely's voice was light, but inside she was hurting.

"True love is an illusion only to those on the outside looking in."

An outsider, Keely thought. *I've always been one, always will be.*

"I loved Lisa." Max stared down at the love-knot, tracing the elegant simplicity of its design with his index finger. "But through my selfishness I ended up losing her."

"Max, you don't need to explain—"

But the trickle of words quickly turned into a torrent.

". . . when Max's Bistro ended up becoming my life and Lisa was shut out. When she left me for my partner, I was crushed and angry. I didn't have the right to be angry, Keely. I'd promised to cherish Lisa and my indifference to her emotional needs was just as devastating to her as her infidelity was to me."

Max's gaze never left her face, his voice softening. "Since my divorce, I've been drifting, Keely. Until I met you."

Forgetting to breathe, she became aware of a momentous sense of anticipation, as if privileged to witness the birth of the universe. At any moment, celestial lights would blaze across the sky and the majestic music of the heavens forming would shake the ground under their feet.

"I dyed this love-knot yellow because gold never tarnishes." Max leaned across the island until his breath stirred her hair. "Gold signifies eternity. Gold symbolizes forever."

Keely fell to earth with a sickening thud. That love-knot was a Holy Grail—the ultimate illusion. Unattainable. Nonexistent. At least for her.

Failed relationships, disappointments, and betrayals formed a choking lump in Keely's throat. "I'm sorry, Max. All I see is fool's gold," she whispered in apology. "Broken promises."

She raised shamed eyes and met Max's intense, blue gaze. A gaze brimming with such empathy that she was shaken into speechlessness.

Max said quietly, "I'm a man, not a genie, Keely. I won't vanish in a puff of smoke."

She shook her head, denying his words. "I'm not sure what you're looking for in a relationship, Max, but I know I'm not the person who can give you what you need."

"Keely—"

"To me, love is a four-letter word!" She held Max at arm's length with a look. "I thought I loved my mother. I thought I loved Eric. I don't know what love is!"

Max started to speak, but she stopped him with a gentle hand upon his lips. "I'm sorry, but I don't trust my judgment, Max. I'm attracted to you—I admit it!—but all I can offer is a purely physical relationship which would satisfy neither of us."

Max gripped her extended hand. Without speaking, he kissed the soft flesh of her palm. Once, twice, three times.

"I'm not your mother, Keely. I'm not Eric. My name is Maxwell Summers and I'm in love with you."

Their gazes locked. Keely forgot to breathe as Max continued, "I made the mistake once of not fighting to hold onto love and I've regretted it ever since."

He kissed her palm again, almost reverently, before stepping back. Keely closed her hand upon the pledge his lips had seared into her flesh.

Chapter 27

Keely slept that night in Max's apartment, in Max's bed. Alone. He insisted on taking the sofa so she reclined between sheets scented and imprinted with his body.

If he'd meant to torment her, he couldn't have planned a more exquisite torture. She lay on her back and pressed her palms against the silk beneath her.

After tonight's conversation, Keely couldn't imagine Max making love to another woman: his hands were made to stroke *her* skin, his mouth to trail kisses across her own heated flesh . . .

Max had opened a door between their separate lives. That door might never open again. Haunted, Keely painted the blank canvas of the ceiling with murals of a Maxless future until she drifted into a troubled sleep.

He awakened her the next morning with a breakfast tray of creamed eggs in brioches and papaya cups brimming with fresh raspberries. Max served her courteously, but restraint existed between them. They exchanged few words, polite strangers at a uncomfortable first encounter, until he left her alone with her breakfast and her regrets.

Keely sensed Max's emotional withdrawal and, illogically, it hurt. It's what you wanted! she reminded herself savagely as she pulled a coral jersey dress over her head and stepped into sandals.

As they stacked the dishes in the dishwasher, Keely studied Max with covert, sideways glances. Judging from the shadows under his eyes, he hadn't slept well either. At least she hadn't broken down and told him of Damien's harassment tactics. He'd immediately go tearing off looking for Damien and she'd only have to rescue him again.

Separated by more than the width of the car seat, they drove to Feast of Italy, where once again an organized chaos reigned. Engaged in packing the pastry shells for the salmon and fruit salad, Karla greeted Keely cheerfully. Loaves of dark bread cooled on racks around the room.

The wedding was scheduled to begin at 5:00, which meant Keely needed to start taking pictures by 4:00 p.m. Formal portraits of the bride and groom had been completed over a month earlier. After Max finished supervising the loading of the food, he drove Keely home to pack her equipment bag.

Her first thought was one of relief that Damien and his henchmen had not paid a visit to her studio. Trying to ignore the anxiety gnawing at her concentration, Keely loaded both medium format cameras and tucked rolls of 220 VPS film, filters, lenses, and a camel's hair brush into her bag.

After running through a mental checklist, she placed her cameras, tripod, and equipment bag near the door. Max wandered restlessly around the room.

"I've got to change for the wedding, Max."

"Take your time. We're on schedule."

The polite, disinterested tone of a stranger. Keely smiled wretchedly and let herself into the house, leaving Max standing in front of the portrait wall. This is what you wanted, she reminded herself forlornly as she climbed the stairs. No ties, no obligations. After this weekend, Max will be free to walk away.

The first thing she saw when she entered her bedroom was her mother's painting. The picture had been painted as therapy during a rehab session years earlier. The remaining petals of the rose seemed to tremble in an invisible breeze.

Keely imagined plucking them one by one. He loves me. He loves me not.

Not! she told herself fiercely. Not after last night! Standing on her toes, Keely reached up and removed the painting. With an irrational feeling of relief, she leaned it on the floor, turning its face to the wall.

Despite Max's disclaimer about schedules, Keely changed into her black dress in record time. Fastening her left earring, she hurried downstairs and into the kitchen, her intention to get a glass of apple juice from the refrigerator.

She stopped and stared at the blinking red light on the answering machine. Weighed the other earring on her cupped palm, the hand Max had kissed. A romantic gesture most women would have wept over. "You don't deserve to be happy," she muttered fiercely and rewound the tape.

The third message was from Jess. "I just read the newspaper—have you gone crazy? I'm begging you, don't give my name to the police—I don't want anything to happen to my girls!"

Fear, with a tinge of hysteria. Keely felt swamped with contrition for having caused the other woman such distress. "It'll soon be over, Jess," she murmured aloud, as an unfamiliar voice from a competing newspaper berated her for having granted an interview to the *Lake Hope Ripples*.

Two messages later, Mimi: "Keely, you don't know what you're doing! You're going to end up ruining us all if you persist in this madness. Flo is dead, haven't you caused enough trouble?"

My friends, Keely thought wearily, listening to a series of sharp clicks. Damien, up to his old tricks of intimidation, evidently hadn't figured out that Keely hadn't stayed home, meekly waiting to be terrorized.

She flinched involuntarily when her tormentor's voice

296

boomed from the speaker. "You've been getting my messages, haven't you? Final warning. Talk to the police on Monday, and you'll be exchanging horror stories with Flo. Face to face."

The earring slipped through Keely's nerveless fingers and fell to the floor. Numbly, she bent to retrieve the glittering bauble, but Max's hand closed over it first.

"That was Damien." His voice and breath sounds were equally harsh.

Keely nodded, still in a crouched, defensive posture. Engrossed in listening to the tape, she hadn't heard Max's arrival.

He grabbed her arm and assisted her to her feet. Although his grip was gentle, Keely could sense the latent strength held in reluctant abeyance. "This isn't the first time he's called you this week, is it, Keely?"

Reaching out her hand for the earring, she made no answer. With an inarticulate roar, Max flung it across the room. His gaze scorched her face and she involuntarily retreated a step. "I'm sick of your childish attempts at secrecy, Keely. Do you think I'd have spent my time ordering vegetables and arranging table plans if I knew that cutthroat was still harassing you?"

The anger in his voice flicked Keely on the raw. Instead of confessing that he was the person she'd been trying to protect, she snapped, "I'm a survivor, Max. I've survived because I don't rely on other people. If you want to define childish, throwing things is pretty high on the list."

Moving with deliberation, she retrieved the earring from the floor, keeping her back to Max to conceal from him that her hands were shaking.

"Throwing things is childish? I seem to recall you busting up a TV with a baseball bat!"

"I didn't—that was an accident—"

She heard the thud of Max's fist on the kitchen table. "I've had it. I'm fed up with this lone wolf, don't-need-nobody-but-myself attitude of yours. Open your eyes, woman! I'm here. I'm here for you!"

"So easy to say." Keely spun around, skirt flaring. The words flowed from a deep wellspring of pain. "I've fallen too many times in the past because I leaned on a promise not worth the breath used to make it!"

"The key word here is the past, Keely. The past." Max visibly fought for control. "I studied your portraits again. They're good—have the potential to be great—but in each one you held back. An artist always imposes their will onto a portrait. The viewer sees the subject as they do. But you're too busy snipping off dangling emotional threads—"

"Because I can't afford to get tangled up. I've kept my life together, whole—in one piece! I consider that an achievement." Keely gave up trying to fasten the earring post and dropped it onto the countertop beside the answering machine. "Why can't you understand?"

Max shook his head, his expression one of baffled frustration. "You're defining your life in terms of your business. That's why this whole mess has been so devastating for you, Keely. You've suffered as your business bled out."

"Of course, I've suffered! My business is important—"

"But it's not your life!" Max gestured wildly. "You're smothering your soul. People, relationships, that's what's vital to survival! I've watched you interact with Ida. I've seen your compassion for Rose, Mimi, and Jessie. That part of you isn't dead yet, no matter how much you deny it even exists!"

Keely was defeated. How could she describe the hollowness inside that never went away? She'd tried desperately to fill that emptiness, reaching out first to her mother, then to Eric. She yearned to experience the exquisite intimacy of two souls intertwined for eternity.

Secure in the richness of a functional family heritage, Max knew the sustaining empowerment of love and she did not. An invisible barrier loomed between them that this man, with all his passion and empathy, could never scale.

She tried to dismiss him gently. "I'm not asking you to be here for me, Max. I'm releasing you. You're free to turn the reins of Feast of Italy over to Anna Marie and leave town tonight."

Max's outthrust jaw might have been chipped from marble. "I vowed I'd see you safely through this weekend, Keely, and I intend to keep that promise. You won't be able to add me to the trophy list of those who've failed you. I'll be in the car."

The door slammed behind him. Trophy list! Shaken, Keely leaned against the counter for support, the palms of her hands pressed against her burning face. She didn't know whether to be grateful or to weep.

She closed her eyes, but couldn't shut out the vision of Max's contemptuous expression. She heard the echo of anger mingled with hurt that she'd deliberately refrained from turning to him for help.

Keely finally managed to fix the other earring in place. She shook her head, the dangling jewelry brushing her neck. Any chance for a relationship was gone, smashed by her own hands. Drained, she started toward the door, halting when the phone rang in sharp rebuke. Now who had she failed? Ida? Jess? Moira?

She picked up the receiver simply to punish herself.

A familiar voice. "Still want the tape?"

Jackson! Keely anticipating this call, had emptied her savings account, taking the money in cash. "How much do you want?"

"I'll make it easy on you—unforeseen circumstances are

forcing me to blow town. Five thousand. Cash."

Keely felt a tingle of relief. The light signalling the end of a long, dark tunnel glimmered in the distance. "When do we make the exchange?"

"Tonight."

"But I'm booked for a wedding!"

"So am I. Who do you think will be driving the bridal couple? I'll find you."

Jackson severed the connection. Keely hurried to the back porch and retrieved an envelope taped inside a newspaper stored in the stack set aside for recycling. Counting out five thousand dollars, she tucked the fat envelope into the bottom of her camera bag and hurried out to the car where a grim-faced Max waited.

"Isn't the Maypole marvelous!" Courtney Fairmont, now Mrs. Andrew Ransom, flung her arms wide as she gazed up at the ribbons of russet, hunter green, sky blue, and deep gold which spanned the room to form a silken canopy.

Although May Day had been nearly two weeks ago, Courtney scorned the calendar, utilizing the traditional pole as the center point for decorating the medieval banquet hall.

Keely snapped another photo of the princess bride. A portrait neckline framed Courtney's white shoulders and delicate star diamond necklace, a gift from the groom. A high pointed tiara studded with brilliants nestled atop the reddish blond hair that cascaded down her back in rolling waves.

Gathering up her cathedral length train, Courtney flashed an ad perfect smile. "I've just had the most marvelous idea."

Keely advanced the film and gestured to the right. "How about moving over so I can get a shot of you by the head table?"

"You mean the high table." The bride obediently posed to admire tall white candles, silver love lanterns, and winding ribbons which matched the Maypole's silken bands. "Keely, some of the college kids who were supposed to play living medieval statues didn't show. I'd appreciate if you'd choose a costume, get into the spirit of things."

"I'd like to get one of you and Andrew holding the ends of a Maypole ribbon."

"Keely, you didn't answer my question." Courtney signalled to her husband to move into the picture. Giggling, she wrapped a hunter green silk band around both of them. "How's this?"

"Say 'honeymoon'!" Keely took two exposures, one of the couple grinning at the camera and the other as they kissed, looking deep into each other's eyes.

Hugo Fairmont strode up. "How's my little girl doing?" In defiance of the discreet "no smoking" signs posted around the Pavilion, he was puffing on a slender black cigar.

"Marvelous, Daddy," Courtney bubbled. She handed the end of the silk ribbon to one of the decorator's staff to be re-anchored to the wall and shaped her mouth into an adorable pout. "But Keely's not cooperating."

"Is that so?" Hugo swung around to stare at Keely, his heavy jaw jutting.

"Yes, Daddy. She says she won't wear a costume, but I want her to! She'll have more fun."

"I'm here to take pictures, not dress up!" Keely protested, stepping back as Hugo blew an insulting cloud of smoke in her direction.

"You've taken at least four rolls and you've got your assistant videotaping everything. We can spare you for a few minutes. Go on, Keely, put on a costume!"

Patting his daughter's satin-clad arm which was wound around his thick waist, Hugo gave Keely a stiff nod. "Humor my girl, Ms. O'Brien."

Whatever Courtney wants, Courtney gets. Keely bit back an indignant retort. She had no desire to spend the evening dressed as a scullery maid or whatever quaint costume might await her, but she needed Hugo's signature on a check.

She still hadn't received a final payment from the Postwaites and, if things went as planned, tonight would cost her five thousand dollars. A small price to pay for getting evidence against Damien, she reminded herself.

Keely paused to photograph Courtney's grandparents as they applauded a "statue" which came to life to juggle oranges and apples. Lugging her camera bag which seemed to weigh more with each passing minute, Keely headed off to the dressing rooms.

She felt anticipation mixed with frustration. Jackson was indeed chauffeuring the bridal couple, but so far the only thing they'd managed to exchange had been a significant look as he handed Courtney into the limousine at the church. As soon as the meal was underway, Keely planned to slip out to the parking lot in search of the chauffeur.

Even in a wheelchair, Anna Marie dominated the kitchen. A frown creasing her olive toned forehead, she demanded, "How much ricotta cheese is in that sauce, Max?"

"The right amount." The queen is back, Max thought resignedly. How was he supposed to keep his promise to protect Keely with his aunt intent on conducting a catechism of every dish?

Anna Marie extended her hand in an imperious gesture. "Give me a taste, Steve."

Jumping to instant obedience, Steve hurried over. Anna Marie accepted the wooden spoon as if it were a royal scepter and rolled the sauce on her tongue, her face creased in contemplation.

Max wiped his brow as he awaited the ruling. The kitchen temperature rose as the warming ovens were opened and the capons removed. Five workers had formed an assembly line to arrange the main course on warmed plates.

"Too much mustard, not enough lime juice, but not bad," was the grudging verdict.

"Thank you," Max said dryly. "Is there anything else you'd like to shred before we serve? Lettuce, broccoli, me?"

Anna Marie's hair, as defiantly black as her beaded jet gown, was razor cut in a page boy style. She glanced around, hair swinging against her cheeks, looking for something else to criticize. "Why French service? I would have thought that Russian would have been more appropriate. Max! Pay attention!"

Max started guiltily. His mind had strayed out into the banquet hall with Keely. His aunt glared at him, puffing up like a bantam rooster faced with a rival.

"Keep your mind on business, mister."

Max was heartily sick of being ordered around, but he knew Anna Marie's haughty demeanor covered a severe case of "first night" jitters. They both knew that despite the sudden influx of bookings, Feast of Italy wasn't out of the woods yet.

He gave her a soothing smile. "To be perfectly authentic, we should serve roast peacock or baste a fatted calf on a spit. For a genuine medieval feast, guests would be paired off and made to share wooden trenchers, but somehow I don't think that idea would fly in this crowd."

"Don't try to be funny, Maxie. If I want stand-up comedy, I'll go to a club or ask your uncle why he forgot our anniversary for the third year in a row." Anna Marie wheeled herself over to sample a stuffed date.

Karla sliced bread, the knife blade flashing up and down. She gave Max an encouraging smile. "Pete told me the guests are gobbling the swithin cream like it's their first food in days. The chardwardon's disappearing fast, too."

"Squash blossoms." Anna Marie sniffed from her perch. "If those people knew they were eating squash blossoms. . . ."

Max started toward the swinging doors, but his aunt stopped him with an outraged cry. "Where do you think you're going? You can't waltz out there looking like that!"

Max glanced down at his elegant white shirt and sharply creased black pants. "Why not?"

Anna Marie indicated a waiter who'd just returned with an empty tray. He was clad in a slashed tunic provided by the same costumer who had outfitted the "living" statues scattered throughout the banquet hall. "He's dressed to go out and mingle. You're not."

"Low burner it, Anna Marie. I'll be right back."

"Max, Hugo Fairmont is paying us a fortune to maintain the illusion of a medieval feast for his daughter. If you're going into the banquet hall, you have to look the part."

"If you think I'm going to put on a pair of tights—"

She pursed her lips and gave him a shrewd head-to-toe survey. "Stop squawking. You've got better legs than most women."

Karla chortled, almost slicing off a chunk of her thumb; the other kitchen workers grinned. Max directed a fierce scowl around the room and everyone bent to their tasks, gleeful smiles still in place. Anna Marie's mouth set in an implacable line. Any moment now she was going to order Max to go and sit in his room until he could be a good boy.

"I would think you wouldn't mind doing this for Feast of Italy, Max, after all the trouble of the past few weeks." Anna Marie smoothed the skirt of her gown. "But I suppose I should just be grateful that I've still got a business, tottering as it is . . ."

"All right." Max flung up his hands in exasperation. When any of his female relatives adopted that martyred tone, he knew he was licked. "I'll put on a costume. Maybe they've still got a jester's cap and bells. I've sacrificed everything else for Feast of Italy—what's a little pride?"

Max made a dramatic exit to scattered applause, but changed his mind about the absurdity of wearing costumes when he met Keely emerging from the women's changing room. Clad in the garb of a serving wench, she struggled to adjust the neckline of a busty blue gown, a task made difficult by twin burdens of camera and equipment bag.

"Need some help?" Max deftly relieved her of the bag.

"Thanks." Flashing him a nervous smile, Keely also allowed him to take the camera.

Max surveyed with appreciation the low cut gown and wreath of blue silk flowers banding Keely's hair. "I didn't expect to see you getting into the medieval spirit."

"I wore boots and a hat for Tricia Westhaven's reception," she pointed out crisply. "Besides, I've just been told that whatever Courtney wants, Courtney gets. What are you doing here?"

He lied. "Looking for you."

Surprise flickered in her eyes. "I thought you'd washed your hands of me."

Max couldn't believe how much the mere sight of her affected him. Grinning like an idiot, he shook his head. "Never."

"You're a glutton for punishment," Keely retorted, clearly uncomfortable. "Are you going to put on a costume? Do you see yourself as a juggler? A minstrel?"

"I haven't decided." Max tried in vain to wipe the blissful

smile from his face. For some reason, his heart had started doing jumping jacks in his chest. His skin felt hot and prickly, as though he'd just crawled out of a warming oven.

"You should definitely go for something in tights." Keely giggled unexpectedly, the sound sweet enough to eat. "You've got the legs for it."

Without words of intimacy spoken or physical contact, something indefinable had changed between them. Keely toyed with the lace edging the neckline of her gown. Max wanted to wave his arms and shout, "Hallelujah!" The two of them had crossed a vast emotional chasm and stepped onto solid ground.

Instead, he asked, "Tights? Have you been talking to Anna Marie? She's determined to see me humiliate myself."

Keely gazed at him with a new awareness and acceptance. "I'm sorry, Max," she said simply. "I haven't been fair to you and I apologize. Friends?"

They were alone in an isolated hallway, the distant sounds of the reception barely audible. Max decided that now was as good a time as any to settle matters between them. "I don't want just a platonic friendship, Keely."

Her smile faded. Snatching the camera from his hand, she tried to brush past him, but with an agile move, he blocked her path. Frowning, she reached for the strap of her equipment bag, tried in vain to tug it from his grasp.

"Max, please! I've got work to do."

He said firmly, "I know people you've trusted have let you down, Keely, but you can't let past betrayals spoil the present and your future. Our future."

"Our future?" Her creamy bosom, enchantingly framed by the low neckline, rose and fell with each quickened breath. "Max, this isn't going to work—"

"What isn't going to work? Our relationship? How do you

know, Keely? We haven't even tried one yet."

Max lowered the equipment bag to the floor. "Don't tell me you're a coward, Keely. You proved your mettle when you rescued me at the limo yard. All I'm asking you to do is use some of that courage to transform your own life."

Keely made only a token protest as Max took her in his arms. "We can make this work, Keely."

"I don't have anything to offer you," she whispered, so low he could barely hear. "I don't know how to share myself with another person. Or how to be part of a family."

Max tightened his grip, pulling her even closer. "I'll teach you. What I don't know, we'll learn together." She looked up at him, wide-eyed. "Those are the rules, Keely."

"Rules?" She had one hand on his chest, pushing him away. "There are no rules—"

"To love? Just one. Trust your heart. Your heart is saying, 'Give this man and this relationship a chance!' "

Keely gasped as his face swooped close to hers. The camera she clutched dug into Max's rib cage as he crushed her to him, but he ignored the pain. Their lips met, Keely's at first reluctant and then hungry. The camera slipped from her grasp and landed on Max's foot, but he didn't notice the impact.

The fervid embrace lasted until passion's dance activated the flash unit slung over Keely's shoulder. The resulting burst of bright light sent the couple reeling apart.

Blinking furiously, Max stooped to retrieve the fallen camera and handed it to her. "Were we just struck by lightning or has Cupid switched to flaming arrows?"

Keely's mouth twitched. "Max, you're incorrigible!"

He wished he could take her picture now and carry the image with him always. Cinnamon rich hair tumbling around her shoulders, eyes sparkling, skin still flushed from loving.

She evaded him with elfin grace. "Whoa, knave! I've still got a reception to shoot."

Max cupped her chin, leaned forward to kiss the tip of her nose. "All I'm asking is one uninterrupted evening without this horror hanging over our heads. Be merciful, sweet lady."

He snatched the camera from Keely's grasp. "You're always fiddling with or hiding behind one of these things!"

"It's safer, okay?" The spirit Max admired glinted in her eyes and she held out her hand. "Maybe I like looking at life through a lens!"

"Keely, no man would choose to kiss cold glass over a warm woman." That wasn't what he'd meant to say, but Max plunged on. "Things were simpler in medieval times. Faint heart never won fair lady and all that. If you wanted to win her heart, you just donned armor and knocked some other poor sap off his horse. Relationships weren't analyzed to death—you made them work because you wanted to!"

Keely gazed up at him, her eyes filled with a sorrow Max suddenly understood.

He sighed. "Big talk, huh? The truth is, I probably couldn't have cut it back then. I've never ridden anything more spirited than a wooden carousel pony and iron gives me a rash. I'm no expert on making relationships work—my own marriage failed."

Max shrugged helplessly. "You've invaded my heart, Keely, conquered the territory. What are you going to do with me?"

Her face and throat flushed. She glanced down the deserted hallway as if looking for deliverance.

"Say something!" Max found it increasingly difficult to breathe. "Are you just going to let me walk out of your life?"

He saw the answer in her eyes, a moment before she shook her head with sheepish smile. "I'd be a fool if I did."

Keely put her hand on his arm. "Max, I have a confession.

After you left my house, I received a phone call from Jackson."

She felt him stiffen as he shifted gears from amorous to business. "Jackson? What did he want?"

"Five thousand dollars in exchange for the tape."

"When?"

"Tonight. He's the chauffeur for the bridal party. I saw him at the church but we didn't have a chance to speak."

"I'll go straighten that bird out right now—"

"No!" Keely's fingers closed imploringly on his sleeve. "He told me he's leaving town. Give him a chance to come forward, Max. We can't risk scaring him off again."

"I'll put on a costume." Max clearly wished Jackson was within arm's length. "That way I might be able to get close to him."

"Max, please wait until he contacts me! I'd better get back to the festivities before Hugo Fairmont sends out the troops." On impulse, Keely extracted the envelope of cash from her equipment bag. "You hang onto the ransom money. I'll signal you if and when Jackson makes contact."

"I won't let that scoundrel rob you," Max vowed. "I'll get the tape and turn him over to the police. Trust me, Keely."

Keely believed him. She leaned forward and kissed his cheek. "Thank you, Max."

He touched the spot where her lips had brushed his skin and gave her a Groucho Marx grin. "No, thank you!"

Waving the envelope, Max ducked into the changing room. Almost immediately, he poked his head back out. "Trust me, Keely," he said exultantly. "We're in this together!"

Despite the seriousness of the present situation, Keely felt almost buoyant with anticipation of the future. They were in this together!

Cradling her camera like a newborn babe, she floated back to the feast.

Chapter 28

Baby spots bathed the glittering chalice in a golden glow. Humming, "I'm in the Mood for Love," Keely photographed the chalice from several angles before signaling for Zach, her substitute videographer, to include the sculpture on the tape. He gave her a thumbs-up signal and zoomed in on the frozen roses embedded around the lip of the ice carving.

At the head table, Courtney and Andrew took places of honor marked by the sheaf of pure white trumpet lilies which had served as the bridal bouquet. Keely no longer envied the couple. It was all she could do not to grab a microphone and announce her own happy news.

The decision to yield to Max's persistence hadn't come like a bolt of lightning from the heavens, but had been shaped by the still, small voice inside her lonely heart. She wanted to dance, she wanted to sing, she wanted to be with Max. For the first time Keely could remember, her camera was a burden, not a comfort.

Waiters circulated among the guests, pouring champagne for the opening toasts. Keely rechecked her flash synchronization by bouncing the light off the wall before moving forward.

A jester in a pointed cap blocked her way. When she attempted to go around him, the mannequin came to life, hopping up and down and shaking his rattle in her face. "Ho, wench! Come to serve the honored guests?"

At first, the concept of living statues seemed charming and highly original, but, as the evening wore on, contact with them had grown tiresome. Keely had already routed a dashing duke by slapping his face when he pinched her—"Just keeping in character," she'd informed the indignant college student—and evaded a minstrel determined to render a ballad about her wine dark eyes.

The behavior of the actor playing the jester, however, had gone from mildly irritating to downright annoying. She had first noticed him standing at the end of the hallway when she emerged from her blissful encounter with Max.

Since then, he had persisted in shadowing Keely as she photographed the reception. His annoying smoker's cough was at odds with the light-hearted image presented by his colorful costume and his tight-clad legs resembled red tree trunks. The expression visible under the red and yellow half mask was anything but merry.

A recorded trumpet call sent stragglers hurrying to their chairs. Hugo Fairmont, even more bearlike in his tuxedo, rose and bent his shaggy gray head. In a booming voice, he read from a scroll the king's proclamation announcing a recision of taxes in honor of the royal marriage. Glasses were raised; toasts couched in formal language were given and answered.

Boys and girls dressed as pages scattered among the guests to hand out net bags. Each bag contained a pair of uncirculated golden American Eagle coins, Papa Bear's way of ensuring his Goldilocks had a wedding that would be remembered.

Listening to the excited whispers as the contents of the bags were revealed, Keely wondered what Flo would have written about this reception. The columnist had been such an integral part of the social scene that her absence left an almost visible gap.

A page brushing by Keely paused to press a folded piece of

paper into her hand. While the first course was being served to appreciative murmurs, she retreated to a corner and read the note. "Lake Pavilion. 20 min. J."

A trio of musicians began to play softly on a lute, flute and harp. The lights gradually dimmed until the guests were dining by the light of votive candles floating in crystal bowls.

Keely's heart raced in anticipation as she gazed around the darkened room. Her mind was already outside, in the small pavilion built on the lake. A gorgeous setting for outdoor weddings, the structure would be an isolated and lonely rendezvous.

She had no intention of going alone. She hadn't seen Max in costume yet. He must be hiding his splendid self in the kitchen. With a final survey of the banquet hall, Keely slipped away in search of her life partner.

"Mind you be careful. It's darker than a lawyer's heart out there." Anna Marie addressed the waiters filing by to pick up trays. "I don't want guests showered with May sallat or any of you falling and getting hurt."

Beaming at the dutiful chorus of acknowledgement, she turned to Max and her smile vanished. "What are you doing?"

His face grim, her nephew placed the domed lid on an enormous silver salver.

"Max, I'm talking to you!" Anna Marie wheeled the chair over to his side.

Max had returned to the kitchen clad in a garment resembling a full-length russet velour bathrobe. Fur circled the collar and hem; gold and green braid bordered the sleeves. A gold tassel drapery cord emphasized his trim waist. The female staff, prepared to issue a chorus of wolf whistles, had instead made sounds of disappointment.

The costume emerald set in the front of Max's floppy beret glittered as he looked down at Anna Marie. After a deliberate pause, he said, "I'm taking the chauffeur some supper."

"You're up to something, Maxwell. You've got that same sneaky expression you had when you and Tony, Jr. were six and the two of you decided to paint your room peanut butter brown—using Skippy as an artistic medium. Let me see what's under that lid!"

Max muttered something unintelligible under his breath, but dutifully raised the lid.

Anna Marie blinked. "But there's nothing on the tray! Just what are you planning to serve the poor man?"

"If he doesn't cooperate, a knuckle sandwich." Max slammed the lid down and pushed past the wheelchair.

A knuckle sandwich? Anna Marie watched him disappear out the back door leading to the parking lot. She knew she'd been pushing Max hard tonight, but the boy definitely had his mind on something other than food.

Max breathed in cooler air. No sense in getting his robe in a twist. In Anna Marie's eyes, he would always be a mischievous six year old. Besides, Keely loved him. He had no intention of letting her down.

He quickened his pace when he saw the stretch limo parked at the far end of the lot, pale moonlight silvering its polished exterior. Ron Franklin might have the ethics of a gangster and a thug for a son, but his vehicles were all thoroughbreds.

Hurrying forward, Max tripped on the hem of his robe and stumbled, barely managing to save the salver from clattering to the cement. This ludicrous costume might prove to be a godsend if it allowed him to get close enough to Jackson to catch him off guard. Max grinned. He couldn't wait to see the awed look on Keely's face when he strolled in and handed her both the tape and the money. The policemen guarding the gift room could take charge of Jackson once Max had squeezed a confession out of him. Like toothpaste out of a tube, he told himself.

Drawing closer to his objective, Max saw that the vehicle's hood had been raised. A man was visible beside the front fender, the upper half of his body concealed in the shadows under the hood.

Max raised his voice. "Engine trouble?"

"Checking the fan belt." The response was muffled.

"Thought you might appreciate something to eat."

Max had planned his strategy while crossing the parking lot. Thrust the serving platter into Jackson's hands and follow up with a quick punch to the jaw while the man was off-balance. Then it was simply a matter of wringing the location of the tape from Jackson and escorting him into the waiting arms of the law.

"Thanks." Jackson began to withdraw his head and shoulders.

Max frowned. The chauffeur's build was blockier than he remembered—

The man turned and Max found himself looking into a mirror. "What—"

He only got that one word out before a fist exploded against his jaw, sending him reeling back and the silver salver clanging to the ground. Another blow caught him just behind the ear and Max's knees buckled. He pitched forward, the parking lot rushing up to smack him in the face.

Against the cloudy veil which coated his brain, an indignant thought flashed in neon letters: That creep stole my plan! His head whirling like a pinwheel, Max felt the scrape of concrete against his cheek as someone tugged at his clothing.

He felt no fear or anger, only a mild curiosity.

A distant, gruff voice. "Help me strip off the robe."

"What do we do with him?"

"Dump him in the trunk. I want both of you out of sight in five minutes. If he's here, she won't be far behind."

Cold air pricked Max's limbs. Someone rolled him over; pain crashed down on his defenseless head until it throbbed. Unable to even twitch a muscle, he felt himself roughly lifted and dropped onto a cushioned surface. Then came a slamming thud which set echoes dancing in his skull like ripples in a pond. No—he was in the pond, his body caressed by wavelets as he sank through the watery layers.

Max didn't fight the pressure, allowing his body to settle into the muddy bottom of the pond. He needed rest, sleep to heal his hurting head. Relaxed and drowsy, Max tugged the darkness over him like a cuddly quilt and heard a familiar voice, silvery as a trumpet call, which pierced his lethargy. Keely!

Anna Marie was directing her troops with a drill sergeant's bark when Keely located her.

The caterer's face darkened when she recognized the intruder in her kitchen. "Keely! So you're the reason he's been burning capon instead of browning it. The water to my Max's oil, eh?"

Keely blinked at this unexpected verbal assault. "I beg your pardon?"

"Don't apologize!" Anna Marie flapped her hand in dismissal. "A woman can't help her fascination to the opposite sex—especially when the man's a hard headed Italian lad who's made it his religion to ignore sound advice." She tossed her glossy page boy and said darkly, "As a woman, I know these things."

Keely suspected this conversation could get very interesting if she let it. Unfortunately, she lacked the time to probe for further insights into Max's character. "Anna Marie, I'm looking for Max. Is he here?"

Anna Marie pursed her lips as if debating whether to answer the question.

Keely swallowed her exasperation. "I need to talk to him. Urgently."

An eloquent sniff. "I suppose hormones can make it seem that way. Oh, to be young again!"

Keely heard stifled chuckles from the workers surrounding her. Her face flamed in response, but she kept her voice level. "I need to talk to Max right away."

Anna Marie relented. The girl had spirit, which would go a long way to make up for the taint of her Irish blood. "He claimed to be carrying supper to the chauffeur, but took an empty tray. A kind heart that boy has—no one can deny it—but business sense? I'd rather send Jack-in-the-Beanstalk than entrust a commission to Max—"

But Keely was already out the door, the flash pack bobbing against her hip. She'd asked Max to let her handle this, but instead he had to act on a scheme of his own and if he lost the tape through sheer machismo, she'd never let him forget it . . .

Never mind, she forgave him. Keely laughed out loud. Tonight she'd forgive that man anything! Their encounter in the hallway had left her with a warming sense of culmination, as if she'd been travelling for years and finally arrived at her destination.

Keely spotted the silvery limousine and hurried her steps, eager to be with Max once more. Jackson was nowhere in sight but her love, wearing a robe and floppy hat more suited to a wealthy merchant than a servant, stood beside the huge car.

Her skirt swirling, she stopped in front of him and adjusted the flower wreath which had slipped askew during her dash across the lot. "Is Jackson here, Max?"

He shook his head without speaking, the floppy beret shadowing his expression.

Keely felt an unexpected chill at his indifferent reception. She pivoted, glancing around the silent parking area, searching for an explanation. Expensive cars filled the stalls, but otherwise, the place was deserted. The graceful shape of the Pavilion loomed to their right, a glowing string of lights tracing the elegant roof line.

Seeking reassurance, Keely moved closer. The night breeze nipped at her overheated skin. "I received a note directing me to meet Jackson at the lake pavilion. We've got to hurry!"

Without speaking, Max started toward the path which wound around to the lake.

Bewildered at his silence, Keely followed. "Max, is something wrong? Have you got the money?"

Another curt nod, Max seemingly determined to conserve his breath for walking. When he reached the paving stone path, he reached back to grab Keely's hand in a hard grip and broke into a trot. She stumbled over long skirts as she hurried to keep up, regretting that she hadn't left the camera and flash pack behind in the kitchen.

Keely started to say something and Max turned and pressed his free hand against her mouth, warning her to silence. Filled with a growing sense of uneasiness, she obeyed. She much preferred the warm, wisecracking Max to this remote stranger.

The route wound through the trees; ahead, the lake sparkling like a diamond in the moonlight. Keely glimpsed the octagonal open-sided pavilion set starkly against the water, its pillars carved with doves and trailing vines whitewashed by moonlight. A pier extended from the eerily lovely structure across the lake's surface like a dead end road.

At the sight of the pavilion, Keely held back, the wariness and anxiety first felt when she glimpsed Max in his borrowed robes coalescing into fear. When she stopped, he cursed under his breath and gave her arm a vicious yank.

All of Keely's inner alarm bells went off and she braced her feet against the stones, struggling to free herself.

He turned his head sharply, the rakish beret sliding forward; an enormous stone set above his forehead winked at her. Light filtering through the leaves dappled his face. Keely, aghast, looked into eyes flat and dead as pennies.

She wrenched her arm free and started to back away. "You talk to Jackson, I'm going back."

"You're not going anywhere."

The playful moon set the emerald glittering and danced on the barrel of the gun that had appeared in her companion's right hand. He was not Max. A scream rose in Keely's throat, only to die on her tongue. She backpedaled frantically until she caught her heel and nearly fell.

Regaining her balance, Keely looked up to find Damien looming over her. "Let's join your friend in the pavilion."

No coaxing was necessary. The gun pointed at Keely's heart was the perfect persuader.

She walked ahead of her captor on rubbery legs, placing each foot with care, the rational part of her mind scoffing at the absurdity of such caution. The danger from the man behind her far outweighed the consequences of a fall. Her mind spun, questions churning. Where was Max? Had Jackson set them both up as clay pigeons for Damien?

The last question was answered when Keely saw Jackson standing inside the pavilion, one arm twisted behind his back by his companion.

As she neared the building, Keely recognized the man holding Jackson as the goon who'd masqueraded as a security guard at the Westhaven wedding. Climbing the steps, Damien close behind her, Keely saw that the chauffeur's face was distorted by fear.

He cast a pleading look in their direction, all irritating cockiness wiped away by the sponge of fear. "Damien, don't kill me. I'll give you the tape—free!"

"Where is it?"

Without taking his gaze from Jackson, Damien motioned for Keely to take a seat on the low bench circling the interior of the pavilion. Still clutching her camera, she obeyed. With horrifying suddenness, the situation had slipped out of control. Even in her worst case scenario, Keely hadn't expected Damien to show up here tonight.

Jackson licked his lips, terror filming his eyes. "Just promise you'll let me go. All I want to do is get out of town, Damien. I won't go to the cops—I'll be out of state by morning."

"Fair enough. Where's the tape?" Even when asking a question, Damien's voice was the drone of a man reading letters off an eye chart.

Keely was numb with disbelief. Why hadn't she taken the precaution of contacting Gifford and reporting Jackson's call? Because you didn't think the police would take you seriously after the fiasco at Franklin's service yard, she reminded herself.

Another thought struck her. How did Damien know about the proposed exchange? And where was Max?

Watching Damien's face as he spoke to Jackson, Keely realized that the man's true menace lay in his lack of emotion.

"Where's the tape?" he repeated.

Jackson's Adam's apple bobbed. "In the trunk of the limo,

hidden under the spare. Just take it and let me go!"

Damien jerked his head in the direction of the parking lot. Keely followed his gaze and saw that Franklin's second gorilla loomed in the doorway of the pavilion.

"Get the tape and get rid of Summers. We'll handle things here." Damien ordered his henchman before turning to Keely. "It's a lovely evening. Perfect for a stroll on the pier. Ms. O'Brien?"

Keely rose to her feet, prodded by the impatient flick of the gun muzzle. Wasn't there a joke about taking a long walk off a short pier? But no one was laughing. Damien's was a doomsday voice if ever she'd heard one.

Keely gripped the heavy fabric skirt of her borrowed finery with a white-knuckled hand. She hadn't missed the reference to Max; fear for him shouldered aside her personal terror.

"You won't kill us, Damien. You can't afford to—"

"I can afford to do anything I want. Come on, move it."

"Extortion is one thing, but murder is an entirely different matter," Keely said earnestly. "You haven't crossed that line yet—"

His voice was faintly amused. "Forgotten Flo already?"

Her heart sank like a lead weight. Concentrating on talking Damien out of murder, she'd forgotten that his hands were already bloody. "You admit you killed her?"

"Why not? Jackson saw me do it. Lucky for him, I didn't see him. But he was greedy. He told me that he was there that night, wanted payment for his silence."

Keely shuddered. The casual admission convinced her of her own impending death more than any bloodcurdling threat.

Keep him talking, she told herself. Stall for time. Inside the huge building behind them at least three hundred people and two off duty policemen talked and ate. Sooner or later, someone was bound to realize she hadn't returned . . . And where was Max? What had they done with him?

Damien grabbed her arm and started down the pier. Keely moved as slowly as she dared, the gun with its menacing black mouth hovering uncomfortably close to her side.

"Why did you kill her? Because she found out about your extortion racket?"

"She wanted to humiliate some spoiled society dames, bloody a few bitch noses. Flo had the inside info and the hate. I had the muscle and the brains."

Keely winced as Damien's fingers dug into her upper arm. "You used her."

He gave her a crooked, mirthless smile. She gulped. The smile said that while Damien didn't owe her any explanations, he had a compulsion to dominate women. Although his eyes were still flat, they were no longer dead. A spark glowed in their depths. If Jackson was a bug to be crushed underfoot, hurting Keely was an experience to be prolonged and savored, as much as this emotional cripple could enjoy any experience.

Her heart hammered against her ribs. She'd ignored Damien's threats, thwarted his monstrous ego by escaping with Max from the limo yard. The gun barrel rose until it brushed Keely's chin, traced a cold path down her throat to the neckline of her gown, stopped between her breasts.

"I used Flo? Make no mistake, it was mutual."

Keely was close enough to see a muscle twitch near Damien's mouth. She stared at him, fighting to keep the terror rampaging throughout her body from overwhelming her.

"You've got guts, babe. It's a shame to waste such a nervy broad, but it's gotta be done."

As they advanced along the pier, the weathered boards

creaked faintly under Damien's heavy tread. Behind them, Keely could hear Jackson's agonized whimper. Guts? Another minute of this tension and she'd be wailing right along with Jackson.

Her stomach roiling, she said, "You impersonated Max at the Postwaite reception."

"Flo's idea." Damien shrugged powerful shoulders. "She thought the resemblance might add confusion if I was spotted inside the house. Now, shut up."

Damien Franklin, man of few words and all of them unpleasant.

To Keely's surprise, he continued. "Flo totally lost her cool when I told her at your studio about my money-making operation so I let her have it. She was getting to be a nuisance."

Keely's already queasy stomach cramped with fear when Damien released her arm and turned to face her.

"Give me the hush-a-bye, Nix." He held out his hand and his cohort promptly handed over a bulky tube which Damien screwed over the gun muzzle. Noting the direction of Keely's petrified gaze, he said, "I want to keep this as quiet as possible."

Jackson yipped in terror, but his cry was cut short when the thug holding his arm rapped him on the side of the head. The chauffeur sagged to his knees, babbling with fear, and raised petitioning hands.

"This car jockey tried to blackmail me." Damien spat into Jackson's upturned face.

"No, Damien! Not blackmail!"

"He's greedy and stupid." Damien gestured with the gun, never raising his voice. "Made me an offer only an idiot would accept—exchange a certain videotape for cash because it placed me at the scene of the second robbery. Doesn't that sound like blackmail? After I gave him a job, rewarded him for putting me and the band on the admittance list to the reception."

The toe of Damien's boot thudded into Jackson's ribs. With a gasp, the driver collapsed, curling on his side.

"I made him a counter-offer. All he had to do was get you alone, where I could get at you. And here you are. The offer of the tape did the trick."

"I did what you wanted, Damien. You've got the girl—"

"Shut up!" Damien turned to the goon. "Set this sack of gutless jelly up at the edge of the pier."

Keely spared an agonized thought for Max, now at the mercy of Damien's other hired gun. The realization that she was about to witness a cold-blooded murder, the precursor to her own, sent her scrambling for a topic to capture Damien's interest.

"Why did Flo steal Rose's necklace?"

"It fell on the floor during the scramble after the band marched in. The Postwaite woman told her earlier that she was going to give the necklace to her daughter after the dinner."

Damien stared into space. His hired muscle gaped at him and Keely realized these revelations were unusual. Damien's relationship with Flo must have run on a deeper level than even Damien acknowledged.

Keep him talking, Keely told herself. Keep feeding that overdeveloped sense of superiority!

When Damien spoke again, his voice was reflective. "Flo wasn't what you'd call a tender hearted gal. She couldn't resist depriving mother and daughter of a Kodak moment. After grabbing the diamonds, she knew enough to unload them, so she looked for me. If you hadn't been nosy enough to follow her, you probably wouldn't be here now."

"The brass band was a nice touch." Keely cast a desperate look toward the lights of the Pavilion glimmering enticingly through the trees. The dinner, with its innumerable courses, would keep everyone inside for at least another hour. The odds that another couple would decide to take a romantic stroll out to the pavilion on a darkened path were slim to none.

"Again, Flo's idea. I'm really gonna miss the lady, but she made the fatal mistake of misjudging me. Enough chit chat. Here's the plan: You're going to kill this sniveling coward. He was your partner in the Sterling Ring and you've decided he's a risk."

Keely glanced at Jackson who was still curled in the fetal position. No use looking for help in that direction.

Damien continued. "Then you're going feel real bad. Two murders, Flo and this loser." He shook his head in mock sorrow. "You throw yourself into the lake in remorse. With that heavy gown tangling your legs . . ."

Keely understood. She would drown. Either with her head held forcibly beneath the surface or else after being made to tread water until exhaustion dragged her under.

The moon trailed glowing, luminous banners across the ruffled surface of the lake. Water lapped against the pilings. In the distance, a dog barked.

Damien stared across the lake. This time, Keely followed the direction of his gaze and saw what had postponed the moment of her death. The tiny silhouette of a canoe with two occupants glided across the water, away from them.

"Sound carries over water." Damien spoke to the goon standing over Jackson. "I didn't want either of these two yelling for help until the tourists in the canoe got out of ear-shot."

Keely groaned inwardly. While she'd been desperately

trying to keep Damien talking, he'd been running a stalling maneuver of his own.

Damien raised the gun and Keely felt the cold breath of Death on the back of her neck. The perfect night for a stroll—or a suicide.

Chapter 29

"Is Jackson here, Max?"

Keely's voice sounded breathless. Max stiffened involuntarily, bumping his knee on an unyielding object.

"I received a note directing me to meet Jackson at the lake pavilion. We've got to hurry! Max, is something wrong? Have you got the money?"

Who was Keely talking to? Max forced his heavy eyelids open as the sound of footsteps died away.

No good—blackness cocooned him. He moved his head slightly and yelped, but the pain helped orient him. He was curled on his side on a carpeted surface in the dark. Either that, or he'd gone blind. Max experimented by holding a hand in front of his face. If it wasn't as black as pitch in here, he was going to be shopping for a dog and a white cane tomorrow.

Think positive, he admonished himself. You're in the dark. He began a cautious exploration of his surroundings. The ceiling was too low to allow him to sit up, but felt smooth and cool to the touch.

His knee ached. Puzzled, Max touched the sore spot and flinched. Bare flesh. He was clad only in a pair of boxer shorts!

A vague memory returned, of rough hands fumbling at his clothing. The robe! He'd been wearing that merchant's robe as a disguise to catch Jackson off guard, but he himself had ended up being the recipient of the bombshell.

Rolling onto his back, Max concentrated on his hazy recollections until he could visualize the driver emerging from the shadows under the hood. When he turned around, he'd had Max's face. Then boom! The lights went out.

He bumped a sore spot behind his ear that he didn't know existed. The pain cleared his head like a whiff of ammonia. The man who sucker punched him must have been Damien Franklin. Max carried the revelation a step further: Jackson worked for Damien, which meant the chauffeur had probably cooperated in setting up a trap to catch—

Keely! Max lurched upright, this time banging his shoulder on the ceiling of his prison. He feverishly replayed the words he'd overheard, belatedly realizing that Keely must have thought she was talking to him.

Damien had appropriated Max's costume to trick Keely into accompanying him. Max tensed, visualizing her terror when she became aware of her companion's true identity. Recalling his vow to protect her, Max groaned.

"Trust me, Keely," he muttered. "Famous last words. As a bodyguard, I should stick to making souffles."

Adrenaline sent its warm rush of determination throughout his body; Max began a methodical search for a way out of his cell.

Keely gave her camera a squeeze. So much for the insulating qualities of the lens! Photographing the scene as Damien and his bully boy discussed where to shoot Jackson wouldn't alter the current dangerous reality.

"She's shorter than you, boss. Hold the gun lower, bring the angle up."

"I suppose I should just make it a head shot." Damien scratched his jaw. "If they're supposed to be partners, Nix, he'd let her get close enough to blow him away, right?"

Keely shuffled backwards but a board creaked, betraying

the movement, and Damien pivoted. "Try something cute, and I'll rewrite this scenario to include a bullet in your gut."

Keely obediently froze, but her mind kept churning. She had to do something, somehow leave behind proof that she wasn't guilty of killing Jackson—

The obscenely bright moonlight suddenly became her ally. Keely's fingers moved with silent deliberation to disconnect the flash unit from the camera. Thankfully, she was familiar with the technique she was about to employ, having used similar angles for unobtrusive grab shots in the past.

Holding the camera at waist level, Keely coughed to cover the click of three shots taken of Damien measuring his line of fire against the head of Jackson.

"One to the heart. Okay, come over here and hold the gun." Damien turned. "Put that camera down and get over here."

Keely retreated another step and glanced over her shoulder. No place to go but into the water. She envisioned playing hide-and-seek under the pier with Damien standing over her and promptly dismissed that idea. She was a good swimmer, but not in the class of outdistancing a bullet.

When Damien gestured impatiently for her to join him, Keely protested, "You can't force me to shoot a man!"

The goon laughed a thuggish laugh. "Sure he can. You hold the gun, he holds your hand and squeezes. Bang! We've got ourselves a dead rat."

If she was going to die, it would be without blood on her hands. Keely shook her head. "No, I'd rather you killed me first."

Damien turned the gun, which to Keely's feverish eyes had enlarged to a mortar-sized weapon, from Jackson to Keely's chest. "That can be arranged."

★ ★ ★ ★ ★

His fists bruised from beating on the trunk lid, his throat raw from hollering, Max paused to rest. He was just about to resume his assault when he heard a faint whistle. The sound grew louder as the whistler approached the car.

Max opened his mouth to shout for help, but remembered the blow from behind just in time. Although he wasn't a betting man, Max was willing to stake his life that Damien had brought along Thing One and Thing Two to keep from getting his own hands dirty.

The whistler approached, his shoes crunching on the pavement, a man on a mission. Jackson, Damien, or one of his goons.

Max crouched, gathering himself for a leap. *Come on, buddy, open the trunk. Come on, creep. You whistle like you enjoy your work and I want to change your attitude.*

A rattle of keys answered Max's unspoken plea. The trunk lid abruptly rose with a hiss, letting in fresh night air and releasing Max, who shot out like a jack-in-the-box, his clenched fists colliding with his deliverer's face.

The man fell backwards with a grunt of surprise, his hands clutching at Max's throat. They fell together in an awkward embrace.

Luckily for Max, he was on top when they hit the concrete. The other man was not so fortunate, his head connecting with the unyielding surface with the dull thonk of ripe cantaloupe.

The grasping hands went limp and Max found himself sprawled atop of one of the toughs who'd played ring toss with the tires. The man lay motionless, his harsh breathing the only indication that he still lived.

Dizzy, Max levered himself up, discovering in the process of disentangling himself that the goon carried a gun concealed in a shoulder holster.

Max gingerly drew out the weapon and hefted it. He needed the gun, for bluff purposes if nothing else. Max had fired a gun for the first and last time when he shot Cousin Carlo in the arm with the BB gun he'd gotten for his twelfth birthday.

Glancing around, Max saw the silver salver lying near one of the limo's rear tires. With the vague notion of using the platter as a shield, he snatched it up and straightened. Too abruptly.

The ground tilted, Max's stomach imitated a diving roller coaster and he nearly went to his knees. The buzzing in his ears receded, however, as the thought of Keely in peril revived him like a bucket of cold water.

Max took a stumbling step forward.

Where was he going? Oh, yeah, the lakeside pavilion. Keely had gone to meet Jackson at the pavilion. A lamb hurrying into a jackal's den. No time to summon help. He had to save her.

Naked except for his boxer shorts and shoes, Max broke into a staggering run, laden with his awkward shield and the unaccustomed weight of the gun.

Chapter 30

As Keely faced Damien, the pier seemed to shrink, isolating them on the narrow boards. Jackson had fallen silent, his head bowed in passive acceptance of his doom.

The action of water lapping against the pilings created an illusion of motion. Keely braced herself against an imaginary sway, determined not to die without a struggle.

"You won't get away with this," she said bravely.

Damien stared at her with the indifferent gaze of a man about to swat an irritating insect.

Time suspended, a thousand thoughts careened through Keely's mind before snarling into a mental traffic jam. The lake sparkled, its opaque silvery depths tantalizingly offering the illusion of shelter. Keely wondered if by diving in she could evade a bullet in a deadly game of hide and seek.

Damien stared at her, his face expressionless. Keely balanced on the balls of her feet, anticipating the bite of metal into her flesh.

Their gazes locked. For an instant, Keely experienced a curious feeling of empathy, as though it were her finger tightening on the trigger. She realized, at that moment, no stronger bond existed than that between killer and victim in the moment before one exercised the ultimate act of power.

In a desperate attempt to postpone the inevitable, she made a last try at reason. "Flo's death was a crime of passion. If you shoot me now, it'll be cold-blooded murder—"

"Hey, boss!" The man guarding Jackson gestured at something near the pavilion.

Damien's head snapped to the right. "What the—"

Keely looked, too, and her mouth fell open in disbelief at the sight of a man, his naked limbs whitewashed by the moonlight, plunging along the path. Dazzling light reflected from the shining oval he carried in one hand.

When the man staggered onto the pier, Keely recognized Max. Her heart leaped in her chest; she couldn't believe the evidence of her eyes.

He stopped and bent double, his wheezing gasps for air clearly audible.

Damien muttered an oath. "I don't believe it. What's that thing he's carrying, a shield? Who does that lunatic think he is, Don Quixote?"

"He must've got Eddie." Nix sounded equally stunned.

Keely experienced a rush of emotion; tears welled up and rolled down her cheeks. No angel could have looked more wonderful than the mostly nude, puffing figure of Max, her would-be rescuer.

He'd come! He'd surmounted unknown obstacles to dash to her rescue! Mentally stepping back from the brink of death, Keely cudgeled her brain for a way of escape.

Damien raised his voice to a shout. "You're a dead man, Summers."

Max had gotten his ragged breathing under control. "Let Keely go! The police will be here any minute!"

"So? In another minute, I'll be gone and you'll be dead." Damien waved the gun in a beckoning gesture. "Come here, Summers. You can watch your girlfriend die before I kill you."

With Damien's attention focused on Max, Keely rushed into impulsive action. With a rebel yell, she thrust forward the disconnected flash unit just as Damien turned in startled response. The flash exploded in his face and Keely launched herself toward his extended arm.

Her clawing fingers caught at the cold metal of the gun which bucked in her hands. Her body slammed into Damien's, her momentum knocking him off balance.

Then she was free-falling, cartwheeling through the air, arms flailing until she smashed into the water's unyielding embrace. The impact knocked the breath out of her lungs. Gulping a mouthful of lake water, Keely gagged and kicked until, her lungs burning, she broke the surface.

Coughing and choking, she pushed streaming hair out of her eyes. Beside her, the water suddenly erupted as a blurred form thrashed to the surface. At first Keely thought the other person in the water was Max but she recognized Damien's contorted face as he went under again.

She stroked frantically away from him, the heavy material of her dress dragging at her legs. Where was Max? Had she managed to deflect the bullet meant for him?

Behind her, Keely heard more splashing and a frantic shout. "Help! Nix, help!"

Keely looked over her shoulder, shocked to discover that the panic-stricken cries were coming from the emotionless hood. Apparently, Damien's survival skills didn't include the ability to swim. At the moment, however, he was flailing enough to keep his head above water.

When Keely had put what she thought was a safe distance between herself and Damien, she rotated in the water to face the pier again, her desperate gaze searching for Max.

Then she saw him. He had closed to within a few feet of the goon and had one arm extended in a familiar posture. Treading water, Keely swiped another streaming strand of hair out of her eyes. She blinked in disbelief. Max had a gun and the drop on Damien's muscle man.

Without turning his head, Max shouted, "Keely! Are you all right?"

"Yes!" she forced the word out between ragged gulps of air. "Be careful!"

Jackson broke free and bolted down the pier. Taking advantage of the diversion, the thug made a sudden movement and a gun appeared in his own hand, aimed at Max. But Nix's posture indicated uncertainty—should he shoot Jackson or blow this crazy man away? He wavered, his attention distracted by his boss's frantic howls and splashing.

Keely started swimming toward the pier with the unformed notion of somehow helping Max, but the gown's heavy fabric tugged at her limbs. It took all of her flagging energy just to keep her head above water. Drawing a gasping breath, she sank beneath the surface, her hands fumbling at the zipper.

Just when it seemed as if her lungs would burst, the zipper gave, skimming down, and Keely lost no time in peeling the dress from her shoulders. With a powerful kick, she shot to the surface and greedily gulped air.

Using one hand, she shoved the hair out of her eyes and looked for Max, only to find that the scene on the pier had changed. In the moments while she had been submerged, other actors had made their entrance onto the moonlit stage.

A man was in the water with her, towing the now limp and silent Damien toward the pier. Max stood with his arms raised above his head; Nix had assumed a similar posture of surrender.

Keely dashed the water from her eyes and squinted at the demented tableau again. The jester, the bells on his cap jingling and his red tights appearing black in the moonlight, had exchanged his rattle for a gun.

Chapter 31

Gayla Gifford licked a crumb from the corner of her mouth. "What did you say these little tasties are called?"

"Destiny cakes." Max squeezed Keely's hand and they exchanged weary smiles.

"Very appropriate, considering Damien Franklin nearly met his fate in the water tonight."

Gifford, Dawson, Max, and Keely were seated in the Pavilion's kitchen near an open warming oven. Keely and Max were draped in matching oversized robes selected from the leftover costumes in the changing rooms. Anna Marie, her face ashen, kept patting her nephew's free hand.

"We'll get the film you took on the pier developed," Gayla was saying. "A few snap-shots of Mr. Franklin with the gun in his hand will come in handy when it's time for his trial."

"As long as Courtney gets her pictures, I don't care what happens to the rest of the roll." Keely wondered how long it would take to bake the chill out of her bones.

Max slipped his arm around her shoulders and she cuddled close. She purred deep in her throat, feeling warmer already.

"Nothing like swallowing a little lake water to take the starch out of the most vicious criminal, right?" Gayla grinned at her partner. "Damien confessed to killing Flo and threw in a few details about his extortion scheme. Somehow he got this weird idea that Robo here might drop him back into the water if he didn't cooperate."

Dawson grunted through a mouthful of capon. Anna

Marie, convinced the two detectives had saved her nephew's life, had been pressing food on them since their arrival in the kitchen.

"I still don't understand it," Anna Marie complained. "Why did that brute want a videotape from a wedding reception?"

"Because it showed him inside the Postwaite home. No place for an ex-con without an invitation." Gayla dusted crumbs from her hands. "Jackson had already applied for a job at Prestige Limos and he told us that as soon as he viewed the tape, he recognized Damien Franklin as the man talking to Flo Netherton. When he got hired on at Prestige, he decided to use the tape to squeeze Damien."

"Big mistake." Brian Dawson grinned. "Damien didn't like getting the arm put on him. He was already ticked off at Ms. O'Brien because she wouldn't turn over the tape. Now he was getting blackmailed over the robbery and Keely was telling the newspapers she had evidence to finger Flo's murderer. When guys like Franklin are maneuvered into a corner, they come out fighting."

Keely glanced at Detective Gifford. "I should have guessed that the jester was one of your men. Every time I turned around, he was right behind me."

"That outfit kind of made an oxymoron of the phrase 'plain clothes,' didn't it?" Gayla uttered another throaty chuckle. "Rudy says he'll never forgive me for making him wear those tights. I told him his ass was in a sling for goofing up. He was supposed to keep an eye on you, but lost track when they dimmed the lights."

Max scowled. "Some protection. Keely could have been killed!"

"We did our best, buddy. It ain't easy, guarding somebody without being obvious about it. We didn't want to scare off

Franklin—not when Ms. O'Brien had obligingly offered herself as a target." Brian accepted another plateful of peppermint rice with a beatific grin. The food seemed to have loosened his tongue. "But we cut it closer than we meant to—"

Max muttered something uncomplimentary under his breath. Brian plowed on, unperturbed. "After Rudy lost contact with Ms. O'Brien in the banquet hall, he searched the corridors until he stumbled into the kitchen. Mrs. Cinonni, here, told him that the two of you had gone into the parking lot. Rudy followed and found Eddie Bartolo lying by the limo, out like a light. He called for back-up."

Gayla nibbled daintily on her third destiny cake. "We suspected Ron Franklin's tactics of keeping the limousine field free from competition, but the son was new in the mix. After our conversation on Friday, I did some checking. Damien was out of circulation in prison in Indiana for the past four years on a grievous assault charge. He hit town a few months ago and met Flo when she interviewed his father."

"Poor Flo." Safe in the shelter of Max's arm, Keely could feel sorrow for the other woman's wasted life. "She was the ultimate victim of her own malice."

"She was a snake who bit her own tail and died from the venom," Anna Marie said tartly. She leaned around Max to glare at Keely. "As for you, young woman, that was a very foolish thing you did. You almost got my Maxie killed out there."

"I'm sorry—" Keely began, but she was immediately interrupted.

"Pish, tush!" The older woman dusted her hands together. "Sorry doesn't scramble eggs! But I'm going to forgive you, Keely, and welcome you to the family. That's the kind of woman I am."

Max gave his aunt a roguish smile. "I knew you'd come

around, Anna Marie. But I haven't proposed yet."

"You'd better." Anna Marie snorted. "After all, you've both seen each other practically naked!"

Keely laughed helplessly. She and Max must have been quite a sight standing on the pier, Max wearing only boxer shorts and goose bumps and Keely in her sodden, lacy briefs and bra. She chuckled again, out of pure relief, and snuggled her cheek against Max's chest.

Anna Marie wasn't finished. "So what are you two going to do next?"

Max grinned and kissed the top of Keely's head. "Get married."

"Any fool can see that, Max. But how are you going to support a wife? You've made it abundantly clear that you can't wait to get out of my catering kitchen."

"That's the problem, Anna Marie. It's your kitchen and always will be. I'd like to open another restaurant, maybe name it after the bravest gal in the world. Keely's Place."

Gayla leaned forward, the gold stars dangling from her ears swinging rapidly. "That was a pretty gutsy plan, Ms. O'Brien. Gutsy but stupid. I admit you improvised very well out there under stress."

"If I had it to do over again, I'd probably think twice," Keely admitted. "I have a lot more empathy for the goats that hunters stake out as bait."

Brian Dawson chuckled, a low plate rattling rumble. "How does it feel to be nearly devoured by a tiger?"

Max took advantage of Keely's distraction to kiss her again. Their mouths clung together for the space of a heart-beat, parted reluctantly.

Keely, flushed and breathless, grinned at the massive police detective. "How does it feel? I'll let you know after the honeymoon."

Epilogue

The music swelled. A murmur of anticipation spread through the pews as the guests rose and turned with expectant smiles. Mimi straightened the twists of silk forming the shoulder straps of Keely's bridal gown. The pearled bodice flowed seamlessly into a delicate silk skirt which fell in folds to the carpet. "You look gorgeous, honey," Mimi whispered. The two women embraced.

Then the designer stepped back with a soft exclamation of dismay. "Now your headpiece is mussed up. With deft fingers, she rearranged the lustrous pearls threaded through Keely's upswept hair.

Keely paused in the doorway leading to the sanctuary and the photographer facing her winked. "Say cheese!" he hissed and snapped her picture when she smiled.

She began the long walk down the aisle alone. Her gown, a simple, elegant design which bared her shoulders and flowed over her hips, whispered softly as she moved. She saw her mother peering at her, Moira's drawn face and shredded lipstick a silent testimony to her need for a drink.

At the moment, at least, Moira was sober, the most wonderful gift she could give her daughter on her wedding day. Whether she remained that way was Moira's choice. Keely had finally accepted her mother.

Gliding along, Keely glimpsed familiar faces in the crowd, brides whose special day she'd captured on film. Taffy Landon and her goofy but sweet Candyland extravaganza. Hazel Detwhiler whose "hepcats" theme and dynamic swing band had kept guests dancing and jiving for nearly five hours.

Today the church was packed with Max's horde of relatives, but Keely didn't feel abandoned. No one could after being hugged and kissed continually during the seemingly endless introductions. Max's family members ranged from his very Italian grandmother, to brawny Uncle Tony who ran background checks to the angelic Baby Addonna. Their welcome had been sincere; the sight of so many loving faces caused Keely's breath to catch in her throat. Keely also felt bathed in the warmth of a sweet memory. When going over the guest list, she'd pointed out the discrepancy in the size of their respective families. Max had grinned and pulled her into his arms. "We'll share," he'd said cheerfully. "Half of them approve of you more than they do me, anyway."

Rose Postwaite sat near the aisle, her face wreathed in smiles. Anna Marie stood beside Max's mother, Angelica, in the front row. Both women dabbed at their eyes. Anna Marie blew Keely a kiss.

Keely's bouquet, courtesy of Jessica's Garden, felt heavy in her hands. Ida had dictated the selection: alstroemeria for devotion, roses to supply love and joy, and Queen Anne's Lace symbolizing trust and healing. Inhaling the fragrance of the flowers, Keely locked the sensory memory in her heart to treasure.

In the hollow of her throat nestled Max's primary gift to the bride, a golden love-knot on a chain. Keely touched the token with a gloved finger and beamed at the man who stood waiting at the altar.

Her wedding had its own special theme to fit her profession, "Exposed to Love." The bridesmaids and groomsmen were dazzling in black and white and each guest had been handed a disposable camera to capture a multitude of images for an unforgettable wedding album. With Max's support,

Keely had decided to keep Key Shot Studio open, but in the future she would concentrate on portraits, her first love. No, second love behind Max.

The ceremony progressed as rehearsed until the exchange of vows.

"Maxwell Alan Summers, do you promise to love, honor, and cherish this woman as long as you both shall live?"

Max gave Keely a soulful look and—the rascal!—winked. "I do. Trust me."

Keely forgot the crowd of hushed onlookers, the pastor's hovering, white robed presence and the solemnity of the occasion. With a smile of faith, she whispered to Max, "That's a promise, darling, I know we'll both keep."